"I find you fascinating. Don't you think you are fascinating? Am I not fascinating to you as well?" she asked, those openly curious eyes drifting over his face and chest.

Oh, he felt something about her all right, but he wasn't certain "fascination" was the word for it. Maybe vexation. Consternation.

Excitement.

At this distance he could smell her, the aroma of seawater and something sweeter . . . sultrier . . . lifting off her. She was warm and compelling, soft and sensual, beckoning and beautiful.

"Beyond fascination," he admitted, his voice rough with his overwhelming desire for her. It was so unexpected, so incongruous to the state of his life, that he couldn't hope to control his next actions. He jerked her in close against his body, feeling her weight press against his chest, deepening that strange sense of intimacy between them. Then he crushed his lips against hers, fueling the kiss with his confusion and frustrated need.

BY JACQUELYN FRANK

The Immortal Brothers
Cursed by Fire
Cursed by Ice
Bound by Sin

The World of Nightwalkers
Forbidden
Forever
Forsaken
Forged
Nightwalker (eBook)

Three Worlds
Seduce Me in Dreams
Seduce Me in Flames

Ballantine Books are available at special discounts for bulk purchases for sales promotions or corporate use. Special editions, including personalized covers, excerpts of existing books, or books with corporate logos, can be created in large quantities for special needs. For more information, contact Premium Sales at (212) 572-2232 or email specialmarkets@penguinrandomhouse.com.

BOUND
by
SIN

The IMMORTAL BROTHERS

JACQUELYN FRANK

BALLANTINE BOOKS • NEW YORK

A Ballantine Books Mass Market Original

Copyright © 2015 by Jacquelyn Frank

Excerpt from *Bound in Darkness* by Jacquelyn Frank copyright © 2015 by Jacquelyn Frank

Published in the United States by Ballantine Books, an imprint of Random House, a division of Penguin Random House LLC, New York.

BALLANTINE and the HOUSE colophon are registered trademarks of Penguin Random House LLC.

This book contains an excerpt from the forthcoming book *Bound in Darkness* by Jacquelyn Frank. This excerpt has been set for this edition only and may not reflect the final content of the forthcoming edition.

ISBN 978-0-553-39343-9
eBook ISBN 978-0-553-39344-6

Cover design: Caroline Teagle
Cover photograph: © Regina Wamba/Ninestock

Printed in the United States of America

randomhousebooks.com

9 8 7 6 5 4 3 2 1

Ballantine Books mass market edition: October 2015

For Las and Christopher

No mother has loved her son more.
No son has loved his mother so well.

GLOSSARY
AND
PRONUNCIATIONS

CASIRIA (KAS-EAR-ee-uh)
CREASUS (CREE-ASS-us)
DETHAN (DEE-thun)
FALIN (FAY-lin)
HORGON (HOR-gone)
JALAYA (JUH-LAY-uh)
JAYKUN (JAY-kun)
JILEANA (JIL-ee-AN-uh)
SARIELLE (SAH-ree-el)
SILAN (SEE-LAHN)
TONKIN (TONG-kin)

The Gods

DIATHUS (DIE-AH-thus): Goddess of the land and oceans. Married to Lothas.

FRAMUN (FRAH-moon): God of peace and tranquility.

GRIMU (GRIM-OO): God of the eight heavens.

HELLA (HEL-uh): Goddess of fate, fortune, and wisdom. Married to Mordu.

JIKARO (JI-KAR-oh): God of anger and deception.

KITARI (KI-TAR-ee): Queen of the gods. Goddess of life and death.

LOTHAS (LOH-thas): God of day and night. Married to Diathus.

MERU (MER-ROO): Goddess of hearth, home, and harvest.

MORDU (MOR-DOO): God of hope, love, and dreams. Married to Hella.

SABO (SAH-boh): God of pain and suffering.

WEYSA (WAY-suh): Goddess of conflict and war.

XAXIS (ZAK-sis): God of the eight hells.

Places

KRIZA (KREETZ-uh)

MOROUN (MOH-roon)

SERENMITAZAHMIKTUBARINATY (SER-EN-MEE-TAH-ZAH-MICK-TOO-BAR-EHN-NAH-TEE)

CHAPTER
ONE

Jaykun felt the sword puncture the hard leather of his armored vest, the power of its wielder outstanding. The sword went through his vest and entered his heart, cleaving it nearly in two. The shock of it drove him to his knees.

His enemy leaned in with snarling laughter and spit in Jaykun's face.

Jaykun lost his temper.

He surged back up to his feet, startling the man looming over him. He reached for the abandoned hilt of the sword driven into his chest, and with a mighty heave, he yanked it out of his body. He knew he had only minutes before the trauma caught up to him, so he used those minutes wisely.

Finding himself armed with a sword in each hand, he hurled himself at his enemy, who was now weaponless. With an ear-splitting battle cry, he plunged both swords under his enemy's armor—one through the man's neck, the other under his arm and, reciprocating the honor, through his heart.

When this man fell, he did not get up again.

Jaykun's enemy was facedown in the mud and blood

only seconds later, having drawn his last breath in this world.

Jaykun threw down the inferior sword the man had used in an attempt to slay him and turned to look back toward the encampment. He began to walk toward it, the seconds ticking by with every pump of his damaged heart. He staggered, but he forced himself to remain on his feet. If he went down into the mud, he would be left there for hours, until the battle was over and one or both of his brothers came to retrieve his body.

Instead he walked off the battlefield, managing somehow to avoid engaging another enemy combatant. He stumbled up the embankment—the high ground from where they had launched their offensive—and lurched toward the command tent. He reached it by sheer force of will, but only just. He stumbled inside, startling his elder brother Dethan, who had been poring over a map of the field and its outlying areas—as well as the prize that lay beyond the battle: the city of Kriza.

"Jaykun!" Dethan cried out, dropping what was in his hands and hurrying to catch Jaykun before his face hit the ground full force. Dethan eased him down to the ground. "Tonkin! Where is my brother Garreth?" he demanded of his page.

"I will fetch him from the battlefield!"

"Have a care. I don't want you injured as well!" Dethan said. He rolled Jaykun onto his back and watched as he gasped for breath and grew pale and cold.

But he would not die. Only a god-made weapon that took off his head, or the gods themselves, could kill him. It had been an ordinary weapon that had pierced Jaykun's chest; that much was obvious. But it had hurt just the same and would continue to do so until Jaykun began to heal.

"It was four on one. I had them all . . . then a fifth

came out of nowhere and plunged the bloody thing in!" Jaykun panted.

"I will get the mem presently," Dethan said, looking around for a priestess within sight of the tent, who could use her healing gift and hasten Jaykun's healing processes. It would help alleviate the pain more quickly.

But oddly enough, Jaykun wasn't feeling any pain. Just cold. A bone-deep chill that had him shaking.

"You would be better served to have Tonkin fetch a mem rather than Garreth," Jaykun wheezed.

"I was not thinking," Dethan confessed. "I will find one at once."

"No." Jaykun reached up and grabbed his brother by the armored brace on his forearm. The armor was god made, just as Dethan's sword was—the sword that presently was clutched in Jaykun's hand. He wanted to make himself release it. To force himself to relax. But he couldn't seem to accomplish it. He was going numb slowly, which he supposed was better than dealing with pain. "I will be fine."

"Eventually," Dethan bit out. "But that will take time and I will not have you suffer in the interim. Next time you are wearing my armor as well as taking my sword!"

"No. I will not have you unprotected. Besides, you know I do not like to wear full armor. It slows me down."

"By the gods, you are a stubborn man," Dethan hissed at him. "Will you not let anyone help you?"

Jaykun didn't reply to that. He loved his brothers, but he would not depend on them for anything. It was not that he didn't trust them, but he would not burden them with the trials of his life. They were his to bear and no one else's.

"You! Mem! Come and help my brother!" Dethan called out suddenly to a mem passing by the opening of the tent. She was very young and fair-haired, and since she was a priestess of Weysa, the goddess of conflict and war, she wore armor. It was hardened leather like Jaykun's was, meant to help protect but light enough to move in. Of course leather armor had its flaws, as was exhibited by Jaykun's present condition, but overall it did its job.

The young mem knelt beside Jaykun, her eyes widening when she saw the evidence of where the sword had entered. "Take off his armor," she instructed Dethan as she drew a satchel from around her neck. She set it on the ground and rummaged inside it as Dethan quickly worked the straps of Jaykun's armor. He pulled the vest away, making Jaykun grit his teeth from a fresh wash of pain, which reminded Jaykun he was indeed injured. Fresh blood pumped freely from the wound Dethan had exposed. The mem's eyes widened again.

It was not common knowledge that Jaykun was an immortal warrior. There were whispers and speculation, some soldiers having taken note of how quickly he healed from injury. Too quickly, even with the help of a mem. But no one knew for certain because the brothers had not wanted to spook their soldiers with talk of them being cursed.

Now it was possible they would have little choice but to address the matter. Or they could swear the mem to silence. Most of the men and mems were more than a little intimidated by the strong and relentlessly war-hungry brothers. Still, the mem was a full witness to Jaykun being alive while wounded in a way that would have killed any other man. Depending on the nature of the mem's personality, she was likely to tell someone eventually. People talked. They simply could not help themselves. It was just in their nature.

The mem put together a poultice and spread it over his open wound. Then she laid hands on him, closed her eyes, and began to recite her healing prayers.

About ten minutes into this healing process their youngest brother, Garreth, arrived at the tent. "What happened?" he asked breathlessly.

Garreth was covered in blood, the red of it staining his god-made armor. There was an enameled picture of the wey flower, the flower of the goddess Weysa, in the center of his breastplate and it was smeared with the congealed fluid.

Garreth was the shortest of the brothers, but he was still quite tall and not more than a hand shy of Dethan, who was by far the tallest of the three. He also had a leaner, more athletic build in comparison to his bigger brothers.

All the brothers were green eyed, although each pair was shaded a bit differently. Each brother also had curly hair, but Dethan's was a chestnut-brown, Garreth's was as black as night, and Jaykun's was a deep golden blond. Dethan was wearing his hair long these days, twisted into two thin braids at his temples with a single long braid down his back. Each braid was tipped with a flame-red feather, a gift from his fire mage wife, so that he might have something to remind him of her. Garreth's hair was shorter and unadorned, curling just around his ears and the nape of his neck. Jaykun's blond locks were of a similar length.

Garreth knelt beside his brother and seemed to check his color.

Jaykun swatted him away. "Stop fussing over me as though I were an old woman who has fallen over her own feet. I will be fine given time. Tell me, is the battle won?"

"We fare very well," Garreth told him.

"Get back out there and see it through to the end. I want this city."

Garreth hesitated, not wanting to leave his brother. Oh, he knew Jaykun could not die any more than he could, but he also knew just how painful these injuries could be, immortal or no.

"Do it!" Jaykun barked.

Garreth rose to his feet. "Let's get him into a bed. Give him a cup of wine. Maybe it will improve his disposition."

He helped Dethan lift their brother from the ground and they carried him over to one of the cots in the command tent. There were three beds in the tent, one for each brother—though they saw very little use when the army was in the thick of a battle. The men laid Jaykun out on the bed, and the mem returned to his side and began to pray again. Garreth fetched Jaykun a cup of wine, handed it to him, then moved to the open flap of the tent before Jaykun could lecture him to return to the battle once more.

After their youngest sibling had gone, Jaykun looked to his elder brother. "What is our progress?"

"That is not of your concern. You will focus on healing. Dusk comes soon and I—"

"Do not talk of it!" Jaykun snapped sharply. He wanted to push the mem and his brother away, but he was too weak. He hated this. Hated being weak and incapacitated and at the mercy of whoever wanted to force conversation on him. But his brother should know better than to speak of dusk when others not in their circle were present.

"I was not going to say anything. What do you take me for?" Dethan snapped back. "Drink your wine. Garreth is right; you need to improve your disposition."

Dethan pushed away from his brother and went back to the maps. On the maps were small figures of wood meant to represent troop locations, so he could follow where they had progressed and where they had fallen back. Kriza was a coastal city with a strong armada in its docks. An armada they wanted control of very badly.

Fortunately for the brothers, an armada did a city no good on the land, and thus Kriza, for all its tremendous size and population, did not have a well-organized standing army. The men of Kriza were used to working ships in defense of their city. They were used to raids and battles that took place amongst the riggings of a vessel. But fighting in the rocky terrain that surrounded their home was another story.

Jaykun's army was a vast one. It was a compilation of warriors from many different cities—cities that the brothers had defeated and claimed as their own over the full turnings. Normally Dethan would not be in battle with them. Instead he would be making the rounds of the cities they had previously secured, making certain that the trusted men they had left behind to rule them were still securely in place and were supported if any type of discontent grew.

After all, Dethan was not immortal any longer. He had traded away his immortality for a normal life with the woman he had claimed as his own. The woman Jaykun now called sister. Selinda was the ruler of the city of Hexis and the mother of Dethan's children. She had given him three thus far, all very young, the eldest just four full turnings old. The middle child was half that age and the youngest had been born mere weeks ago. That was partly the reason why Dethan was on the battlefield. He had gone to be by his wife's side for the birth and then come straight to his brothers' location before continuing on his progress through their other holdings.

In the past it had been Dethan who had commanded a great army and taken cities in the name of Weysa, and Jaykun had been his second in command. Now their roles had reversed and Jaykun was the leader of this army, Garreth and Dethan playing second to him in turns.

Because now it was Jaykun's lot in life to win cities in the name of the warrior goddess, and his brothers were free to live and love their beautiful families in all but the summer wanings.

Garreth had a family as well. A beautiful wife and child, and another on the way. Sarielle helped him to rule over their home city of Kith. She was also a wrena, which meant she was soulbound to a mighty wyvern, a dragon-like beast that lived in the caves of the Asdar Mountains. To be soulbound to the creature meant that she could speak into its mind, hear its thoughts, and feel its feelings. To Jaykun, a wyvern would have been an excellent tool for an invading army ... except that every time the wyvern was injured, Jaykun's new sister was injured as well. The reverse also held true. And since Garreth did not want to see his wife come to any harm, they did not use the wyvern to help them advance on their target cities.

To say Jaykun envied his brothers was something of an understatement. Oh, he did not actively seek or desire a family of his own—those days were long past him—but he did envy them their contentedness. Their peace. He had never known a life that was not surrounded by war and strife, and perhaps he would be bored in a life without it ... but still ...

"Where is Tonkin?"

"He should be back shortly."

Tonkin was Dethan's most trusted aide.

He walked into the tent at that very instant. He was very tall, nearly as tall as Dethan, so he had to duck to enter the tent. He was broad shouldered and lean, and he always gave the overall impression of being very easygoing.

"Tonkin, are the supplies stowed?" Dethan asked.

Tonkin took in the tableau inside the tent, his eyes widening only a fraction as he saw Jaykun's injuries and supine position on the cot. Other than that, he acknowledged Jaykun's injuries not at all. It was typical of Tonkin to react very little to things. It was one of the reasons the brothers kept him close. Jaykun did not need someone who grew emotional at the drop of a hat. His brothers used to be steady like that . . . before they had fallen in love. Now they could be as emotional as most women were. The juxtaposition of the situation gave him some measure of amusement.

"Yes. All the supplies are well secured. We should have another caravan coming on the morrow, according to the missive I just received." Tonkin held up the letter he was referring to.

"Good."

"Sor . . . you will sleep," the mem said.

"The hell I will," Jaykun barked at her.

"You do not have a choice. Your body, however strong and enchanted it might be, will force you to sleep so that you may heal more quickly."

"I am not enchanted," Jaykun barked.

"Of course you aren't," the mem said a bit dryly. "You are merely miraculously able to live after what should have been a death stroke."

"She's got you there," Dethan said with a laugh.

Jaykun gave him a rude hand gesture. He turned to the mem. "You'll not be speaking to anyone of miracles or anything else concerning this," he said threateningly.

"Of course," she said with a patient smile. "Have good dreams."

"I am not going to sleep!" But Jaykun found himself suddenly with the desire to do just that. An overwhelming desire. An irresistible one.

He was asleep within minutes.

CHAPTER
TWO

By the time Jaykun awoke, the battle was over.
And dusk was approaching.

He sat up sharply and pain lanced through him, taking his breath away. Still, he was much better off than he had been. And he had felt much worse before. Much worse.

Garreth and Dethan were both missing from the tent. Tonkin was sitting close by, however. No doubt keeping an eye on him.

"Where are my brothers?" he asked with a groan as he threw his legs over the side of the cot. Tonkin hastened to his feet and reached to help him, but Jaykun fended him off with a raised hand.

"They are helping bring the wounded off the field."

"And the battle?"

"Won. All that's left now is the city walls to breach. But I don't imagine it will be much of a fight since they sent most of their men into the field."

"Wise rulers would have held at least some for defending the walls. But in the face of an army as massive as ours, they would have been much better served to open their gates and let us in peacefully. Now there is death on their doorstep and women without husbands and sons. Even some daughters."

"People think fighting for their way of life is more important than their lives themselves."

Jaykun straightened to his full height, although it took some doing. His whole body ached, and his chest throbbed painfully. But his heart was beating, and the bleeding had stopped. It was all an improvement over hours earlier.

"Sor, where are you going?" Tonkin asked hesitantly. He knew that questioning Jaykun wasn't a wise idea, but the brothers had told him to keep Jaykun down as long as possible.

"It is almost dusk. I have business elsewhere."

Tonkin nodded. He had been around the brothers long enough to know what came with dusk. He stepped back and let Jaykun pass.

Jaykun walked out of the tent and into the camp. The whole of it was active, but it was a weary sort of activity—men coming back from battle, tired and bloodied and some deeply wounded. But their day would not end until darkness forced it upon them. They were good men, dedicated soldiers. Jaykun was completely committed to them, as they were committed to him.

He didn't have time to find his brothers, and there was no reason for him to. They would know where he had gone.

He walked through the camp as quickly as his abused body allowed. He had chosen a spot when they encamped four days earlier. He had gone there every dusk . . . and would go there every dusk following for as long as they would be in the area.

The spot was along a not-too-distant beach. Far enough away from the battlefield and the encampment to ensure he would not be seen. The beach was littered with seals, their large, sleek bodies sprawled out in the late-day sun, catching the last of its light on their shiny fur. Natural jetties bracketed the sheltered cove and they too were full of seals. There were even some morari to be found, their bodies just as sleek, though on a much larger and bewhiskered scale, ivory tusks long and jutting out from beneath their lips.

Jaykun had found a cove—a cave, really—not too far down this beach and he headed right for it. The floor of the shale cave was submerged and that was fine. It didn't matter. He waded to the rear of the shallow cave and slowly disrobed, placing all of his clothing on a shale outcropping. Once he was fully nude, he sat down in the water. Upon being seated, the water came up to the bottom of his ribs and lapped there quietly.

From here he watched the sinking sun in the west. When the first touch of dusk came, he began to feel it. Sometimes he thought this was the worst of it . . . when he went from feeling fully normal to . . .

It always started in his hands. It felt like a stinging sensation, and then it intensified. He put his hands under the water, as if that might somehow delay what was coming.

It did not.

In the center of his palms his skin began to blacken. Then, like the sharpest burning cinder, the centers of his hands began to glow. That was because they *were* cinders. His entire body was burning from the inside out and even the water could not douse the ferocious burn. He began to glow hotly, like a star caught on land, and agony clawed through him again and again. But he gritted his teeth and refused to shout out, even though it took everything that he was to keep from doing so.

The water around him began to steam and boil, hissing as it lapped up against his fiercely burning body. It overtook him completely, every molecule of his body on fire. The water did not help or soothe.

Nothing could help.

This was his punishment and he must see it through, every night from dusk to juquil's hour. There was nothing he could do to change it. He would never be able to change it. He must suffer it alone, far away from anyone who might be accidentally harmed by what he became.

But what he didn't know was that he wasn't alone. Curious eyes were watching him, growing wide as they watched him burn and the water around him bubble.

But Jaykun was far too overwhelmed with his pain to realize it.

At juquil's hour the burning stopped. His body still glowed like the hottest ember in a fire, but now the water was able to douse that ember. The water was still steaming hot around him, but it was better than the temperature of his body, so he lay down in the water and let it cool and soothe him.

He began to heal almost as soon as the fire was out. Healing was not an instantaneous process, but it would happen quickly. As soon as his vision had healed enough to allow for it, he got up and stumbled and waded out into the colder, deeper water. The salt of it burned even as the cold of it soothed. He could hear the hoarse barking of the seals, even though he could hardly make them out in the darkness.

Slipping into the ocean, swimming into the calm waters of the cove, he let the water cool him completely. The dead, burned skin sloughed off his body, and within an hour freshly healed muscle and pink skin could be seen in odd patches on his flesh. By the time two hours had passed, there was no more blackened skin, only the scarring of the healing burns. Given enough time, that scarring would disappear almost completely as well.

Jaykun swam back to the mouth of the cave and waded into it, looking for his clothes. He was nearly dressed when he thought he heard a splash that was somehow out of place in the rhythmic lapping of the waves. Probably a seal, he thought. But he was on his guard just the same. The last thing he needed was to be ambushed by a stray enemy contingent. Especially since he had foolishly left his weapons behind. He had not been thinking straight when he left the camp, but still, the lapse was inexcusable.

He moved to the shore, stepping around the shale outcroppings with sure footing, the darkness meaning very little to him. He had keener eyesight and senses than most, so he was able to navigate pretty easily. It also helped that the moon was newly full so it shed a fairly bright light upon the beach.

Jaykun stepped from the sand and into the low, scrubby vegetation, picking his way back toward the camp. That was when he heard a shuffle of sound—the sound of brush being disturbed, but not by him. He turned about in the darkness, his eyes narrowing. He could sense that he wasn't alone.

"Get him!"

The shout preceded the launch of dark bodies out of the vegetation. Three men in dark clothing. They had been crouched down low, indiscernible from the shale rocks and long grasses. Moonlight gleamed off a raised sword and Jaykun had to move swiftly to get out of its path. As it was, the tip of it nicked his already abused skin, leaving a thin cut on his cheek in its wake.

That was the last lucky shot they were going to get, he thought with rising temper. But even though his temper began to bubble, his movements were sure and calm, almost rote. He caught the hand wielding that sword and jerked on it, throwing the wielder onto the rapid rise of his knee. His enemy grunted as Jaykun belted the breath out of the man's body, and then Jaykun disarmed him, arming himself in that same fluid movement.

The sword he had acquired was heavy in the pommel, making it poorly balanced, but it was just right for smacking the butt of it into the nose of the second man. The third man rushed in, tackling Jaykun to the rocky sand. Jaykun rolled with the weight of the man until his enemy was beneath him. Jaykun straddled the man's chest and brought the pommel of the sword down hard on his nose, breaking it and stunning him all at once. Then Jaykun jammed the heel of his free palm up under the man's chin, pushing his head back and opening his neck to the swipe of Jaykun's blade.

Blood erupted from the man's cut throat and splashed against Jaykun's clothing. Not that he cared. He was more concerned with the two remaining men, who had since thrown off the effects of his stunning blows and were now rushing him as a single force, tackling him back onto the sand. He felt his shoulder wrench under the impact, but he literally shrugged the sensation of it off. His heavy-bottomed sword, however, went flying from his hand.

He wrestled for control of the situation, trying to throw off the weight of two heavy bodies sitting on his chest and legs. He arched his back hard, twisted every way he could think of, but the fact was, he was wrung out. After being run through the heart and then suffering his nightly torment, there was almost nothing left inside him. Oh, he was immortal, but he felt every single solitary second of that immortality in one way or another. Tonight it was in the injuries he had been forced to sustain. They weakened him, made him vulnerable. And gods help him if by some rare chance one of these men was wielding a god-made weapon. All it would take was a simple beheading by one such weapon and that would be the end of him. Although, sometimes . . . at some very low times . . . he wondered if that wouldn't be for the better. It would certainly end the torment he suffered night after night. But who was to say he would not face an entirely new torment should he end up in the eight hells? At least alive there was some reprieve.

And so he fought. Oh, how he fought. He kicked and snarled, threw the both of them off himself, but they quickly pinned him down again. Still, he did not go down easy. The two men were panting hard as they held him down, their faces battered from where he had managed to punch them, their bodies bruised likewise.

"Stay down, *trega*!" the one nearest his head snarled at him, calling him what the Krizans called foreigners to their lands. The Krizan on Jaykun's chest was built for sheer brute strength. There was no grace to him, merely muscle and ferocity. His bottom canine teeth, as with all Krizans, tusked up over his upper lip, and they were capped in a silvery metal that gleamed in the moonlight. The Krizans liked to adorn their prominent teeth in all manner of ways, but the warriors preferred to keep them sharp to make the men appear more vicious. A Krizan was not above biting his enemy.

His nose was flat, his nostrils wide. He looked a great deal like one of the morari Jaykun had seen on the jetty. He had on a sealskin hat, the floppy ends of it hanging over his ears.

"So, *trega*, you fall to Lukan! You are perhaps not so formidable after all!" he said in his guttural, heavily accented voice.

"I presume you are Lukan?" Jaykun said dryly. He had relaxed, saving his strength for an opening when it came.

"Lukan! Greatest of all the mighty Krizan warriors!"

"Your mighty warriors looked more like sleepy women out on that battlefield today," Jaykun said.

The Krizan roared in outrage, spittle flying from his lips. "The demon *trega* leaders use sorcery to win their battles! Evil trickery!"

"I hate to break it to you, but we don't have any mages with us at present. The most dangerous things we have along those lines are the mem healers. Not very dangerous at all, I'm afraid."

"You are a liar, *trega*! All *trega* are liars and demons!" He hissed past his plump lips. "Now we will disembowel you and cut you into little pieces, painting a picture with you on the beach for the other *trega* to find in the morning."

So they didn't realize he was the *trega* leader. That was perhaps a good thing, Jaykun thought. Otherwise, they would have tried to kill him immediately, using him as some sort of trophy or whatever it was the Krizans liked to do to the leaders of an enemy force.

"Why don't you all just give up already? We're going to come over your walls tomorrow, whether you like it or not. No one else has to die if you simply open the gates."

"We would rather die than let *trega* like you into our city, where you will kill our children and defile our women."

"Trust me, we don't want anything to do with your women," Jaykun said. To be blunt, Krizan women were twice as ugly as their hideous male counterparts.

"Again he lies," the second warrior said. "Who wouldn't want the beauty of a Krizan warrior woman? Kill him. His words irritate my ears."

"Yes, do get on with it," Jaykun said with a sigh.

His blasé tone enraged the Krizan warrior. He balled up his fist and punched it dead-on into Jaykun's face. And it hurt. There was no two ways about it. Krizan warriors were definitely strong, if not exactly bright. Had they been bright, they would have learned how to fight on land . . . seeing as how they lived on land and not on the ocean.

The Krizan pulled a dagger from his boot and reared back to plunge it into Jaykun's chest.

Oh no. Not that again, Jaykun vowed to himself. He wrenched a hand free somehow, surprising his over-arrogant attackers and reached to catch the downward plunge, his hand grabbing the meaty forearm of the warrior and stopping the dagger dead in the air. The warrior seemed as though he couldn't believe his eyes for a second, couldn't believe that Jaykun had the strength to counteract his strike.

The two struggled for several long moments, the warrior pushing down, Jaykun staving off.

Then the softest little sound slid through the air. Like a musical note, only gentler and more beautiful. The Krizan warriors froze, and to Jaykun's surprise, all the strength behind the dagger was gone. Instead the men were suddenly tripping over themselves to withdraw.

"Prava!" one said to the other, their eyes wide. Both men scrambled off Jaykun, turned, and ran. They were trying to run so fast that they fell more than once.

Jaykun sat up, at a complete loss to explain what had just happened.

Then he heard it again. That soft, lilting note. Like a laugh. The sweetest, most singsongy laugh he'd ever heard.

He got to his feet and peered out into the moonlit darkness. That was when he saw a figure standing there in the moonlight. A woman. She was slight of build, tall but slim. She had long hair that whipped around her body in the ocean breeze. He could not tell what color it was, only that it was dark. It fell all the way to the backs of her knees. It could cover her entire body, he found himself thinking. And a good thing too, for she was completely naked.

She was dark skinned—again, an undetermined color—but it appeared to be an even and beautiful tone in the moonlight. She had small breasts, curvy hips, and long legs. And though he couldn't make out her features perfectly, he knew she was quite beautiful. Not a Krizan woman—she was too tall, too lithe, too pretty.

She came closer, increasingly revealing her beauty as she drew to within five feet of him. She was smiling softly, her eyes running down the length of him, no doubt sizing him up just as he was assessing her. She seemed . . . fascinated. She reached out as if to touch him and he jerked back. Her hand lowered.

"I won't hurt you," she said, her voice musical and sweet.

"Who are you?" Jaykun demanded of her.

"I saw you. Saw you burn. Saw the waters boil. How did you do that? Why would you do that? Do you enjoy it? Does it not hurt? Do you do that often?"

She barely paused between questions, leaving him a moment to get over the shock of knowing he'd been watched. He supposed it had to happen sometime, but he had not seen anyone in the cave. He could have sworn he was alone.

"Did the Krizan hurt your tongue? Can you not answer? Is the moon not beautiful tonight?" She turned her face up toward it, closed her eyes, and drew in a deep breath. She opened her eyes again and looked at him, and he saw they were a pale, silvery color in the moonlight.

"Who are you?" Jaykun asked again.

"Jileana. Who are you?"

"Jaykun," he answered in turn. "Where did you come from?"

"From the beach," she said. "Can you show me how to make the water bubble? I want to learn how to do it."

"No, I can't, and trust me, you don't want to know how."

She frowned at him in consternation. "Very well. If you don't wish to share. Let's go back to the beach. It's safer there."

"I would much rather go back to my encampment." He eyed her nude state. "You shouldn't be out here . . . unprotected."

"Yes, it is not safe. Men make war."

"I am one of those men," he told her baldly.

She took a hesitant step back. "Are you going to make war with me and my family?"

"I . . . I don't know who your family is. But I don't make war on just anyone. In fact, I prefer not to make war. When I first go to a city, I see whom it is they worship, then I try to convince them to let mems of my goddess set up temples there. If they refuse, I become more . . . forceful in my request."

"But my family worships Diathus. We have always worshipped Diathus."

"The goddess of the land and oceans. That would make sense, coming from . . . Well, I assume you are from around here. But everyone should worship Weysa as well. For without conflict there can be no peace, of the mind, the body, or the soul. We must be conflicted from time to time so that we may make the best choices and judgments, making us stronger and more sure."

Jaykun couldn't believe he was in the saw grass philosophizing with a naked woman, but it didn't stop him from doing so.

"You make a very good point. I shall have you speak to my father one day. He is quite learned and enjoys such debates. My mother as well." She turned her head suddenly and looked back toward the beach. "I have to go now. Will you come back tomorrow night?" she asked.

"You can be certain of it," Jaykun said wryly.

"Very well. I will see you then! Goodbye!" She waved at him and hurried off. She was fast, moving sleekly into the darkness. All Jaykun could do was watch the line of her bare body until she disappeared into the cove he had come from. Odd—there was nothing down that stretch of beach. It was the very reason he had chosen it. Where could she possibly be going?

Jaykun didn't have time to dawdle over the matter. It was late and there was danger of another enemy patrol coming by. Although, he suspected that raggedy band were soldiers who had fled the thick of the battle, waiting for darkness to hide their presence so they could perhaps escape or, as they had done, cause trouble.

Jaykun went back to the encampment without any further molestation, which was a good thing, because he found himself completely preoccupied by the appearance of Jileana. Not just the baffling question of where she had come from but so much more. Why had she been naked? There were dangerous men from both armies encamped just a short distance away. It was madness for her to be out and about at all, never mind in such a vulnerable way.

She had been really quite beautiful. As Jaykun thought about it, he could not recall having seen any woman to compare. All the more reason for her to be more cautious. Beauty could be a curse for a woman, drawing unwanted attention. Dangerous attention. And if he had to confess it, he himself had been incredibly drawn to her. Had she actually touched him . . . there was no telling what his reaction might have been.

No. Not true. He would not have had any reaction, Jaykun told himself sternly. She was just another woman who happened to be pretty. No more, no less. And he had no place in his life for women, pretty or otherwise.

He made it back to the command tent, the encampment quiet now in comparison to the activity of earlier. When he entered the tent, he found both of his brothers pacing anxiously, still fully dressed in their armor.

"At last!" Dethan cried when he saw Jaykun. "What took you so long?"

"You know why I must go."

"Yes, of course we do," Garreth said with a manner of impatience. "But you are usually back—Have you been in a fight?" he asked abruptly.

"That is why I was delayed. I was waylaid on the way back."

"Oh. I see you made it out in one piece," Dethan said.

"Don't I always?"

"You know, it is not a given that you will make it back with all your limbs or your head attached. You can still be beheaded by a normal sword and left on the ground, unable to heal until your body parts are re-united."

"Yes," Garreth said. "It is very hard to find one's head with one's body when the body cannot see the head for lack of eyes."

"This is all a moot topic. I am fine," Jaykun said, impatient with his brothers' worrying. He did not like to be coddled. He was perfectly capable of handling himself in any situation. "If you wish to discuss something, then let us discuss how we will approach the city walls tomorrow."

"I was thinking we would send a messenger, offer the leaders one last chance to open their gates peacefully to us. Their army, such as it is, has been decimated. Our taking of the city is only a matter of time. Surely they must realize it at this point."

"They might. It does not follow that they will behave wisely. Would you risk the life of a messenger?"

"Better one life than the lives of many."

"Yes, but the Krizans are very dishonorable," Jaykun

pointed out. "It is very unlikely they will respect parlay."

"So we don't try at all?"

"I think not. If they wanted to parlay or surrender, all they had to do was open the gates. They know this. We have already sent messages telling them we will not harm the citizens of the city if they but lay down their weapons. The rest is up to them. We will take this city one way or another, and we will earn the fleet of ships in their harbor. I want those ships. If we are to move on to the Isle of Moroun, and then to Shintu, we will need those ships."

"It is said Moroun is heavily protected by the goddess Diathus," Garreth hedged. "If you plan to lay siege to an island that is protected by a god of Xaxis's faction . . . It is unwise. Especially when we are a more able land army than a seafaring one."

The gods were at war. There were twelve gods in all, and they had been split into two factions. One was led by the brothers' goddess, the goddess of conflict and war, Weysa. The other was lead by Xaxis, the god of the eight hells. Meddling in the affairs of the gods was never a wise thing for a man to do, but the brothers had sworn to Weysa to do exactly that, for the power of the gods came from the multitude of their worshippers. The more the gods were worshipped, the more powerful they became. Every temple the brothers raised in Weysa's name made her and her faction more powerful. Every city they stole from Xaxis's faction made him and his faction weaker.

The only thing that protected the brothers from the wrath of Xaxis at this point was their goddess's protection. But she would only continue to give that protection if the brothers honored the agreement she had foisted upon them. An agreement they must honor no matter what, else they enrage the goddess and find themselves . . . Well, all three brothers had learned first-hand of the vindictive nature of the gods. They would not court it again for any reason.

"One step at a time," Jaykun said. "I am not certain I will try to take Moroun. First let us take this city. Then we will worry about the next. Now, I don't know about you, but I am weary." He began to take off his clothes, revealing the scarring and damage done to him earlier. His brothers watched him with troubled eyes for a long moment but then finally began to follow suit. They were each in their cots shortly after, sleeping the troubled sleep of men at war.

CHAPTER
THREE

It was two days before they finally took the city. Two days and two nights of Jaykun's nightly punishment. And never once did he see the strange beauty again.

Not until the third night, when he left his brothers in charge of the city and went back to the cove. He was watching the setting sun with one eye and picking his way into the cove with the other, so he nearly ran into her as he moved away from the rocks and waded into the water.

She was sitting in the water, the waves lapping at her bare skin, her breasts just barely touching the water's surface. It was daylight now so he could see her clearly. Her skin was not as dark as he had thought it was initially. She was a warm cocoa color, her nipples dark and as large as a gold coin. Her eyes, now plainly visible in sunlight, proved to be an iridescent green and regarded him with open curiosity.

"May I watch you boil the waters?" she asked him.

"It is not a spectator sport," he said almost irritably. But he couldn't figure out if it was because she didn't understand that what happened to him was involuntary and painful or because his body inexplicably tightened with a curious attraction toward her.

Why did she have to be so damn beautiful? Perhaps if she were less so he would find her more aggravating, find her intrusive to a fault. Because he thought he should be reacting that way, he did so without really feeling the temper of it.

"And yet I have watched you every night. Is it as painful as it looks? You burn . . . like a star. I can feel the warmth even at a distance."

"And a distance is where you should stay," he bit out.

"But . . . it is beautiful. A star in the shape of a man." She stood up and walked toward him. She reached to touch him, but he pulled away.

"It hurts. It is pain beyond anything you can imagine. There is nothing beautiful about it."

She was undeterred. She moved forward again, her hands coming to rest on his chest. Jaykun felt the coolness of her hands through his tunic. It was compelling, the sensation of her touch somehow alluring to him.

"You are not hot now. Your skin is simply warm. Like any man's would be?"

It was a question and he found that curious. Hell, he found everything about her curious. She was curious in both being and action. She was sloe-eyed, her cheeks full at the apple. She had the gentlest nose and thin little brows that crested in the middle. Her hair was straight, sleek, and shiny. It was wet from her lower back down and overall a perfect sheen of black. There were no lights to her hair, no sign of fairness. It was simply rich and dark.

"That will change very soon. And you shouldn't be near when it does. You will get hurt."

"I will be careful," she promised him. "It happens the same every night at dusk?"

"Yes. Every night."

"Why?"

"It is a long story," he said evasively.

"Well, I believe there will be time later and you can tell me then. It won't last all night."

"Only half of it," he said, his tone scoffing.

"It could last the entire night," she pointed out. "It is lucky that it is only a short while."

He supposed she had a point. But then again, she didn't have to suffer every minute of it in excruciating, burning pain as he did. She was watching it from the outside. It still made him uncomfortable to think of her watching him as he lay vulnerable and burning. It was almost like . . . like being stripped naked in front of someone he would much rather keep hidden from.

He cast an anxious eye toward the sky again. "You must leave," he said sharply.

"I will stay," she persisted. "I will watch as I have done every night these past nights. And then, when you are done, I wish to talk to you for a little while. I have so many questions."

"What if I do not wish to talk?" he said abruptly. Inside his body he could feel it. Feel it starting. Warming his skin in an all too fleeting sensation of comfort, chasing away any coolness in the air or brought by the waters.

"You will talk," she said assuredly. "I am sure of it."

"Leave," he pressed. Then in a more gentle tone, "Please."

She smiled at him, backing away and moving to the farthest edge of the cove. Then she sat down on a flat boulder, not in the water, crossing her legs and smiling at him expectantly. And whether he wanted to or not, he was going to put on the show she was expecting. He couldn't decide if that galled him or made him feel . . . comforted. There was something comforting about knowing he wasn't going to be alone. Oh, she couldn't really be a part of it, but . . . he wasn't alone.

He slowly began to undress, his eyes never leaving

hers as he did this. He was not a shy person. He really did not care if he was naked or clothed in front of strangers. He was that confident in knowing he would never be truly vulnerable in the world, that he would always be able to take care of himself even if all he had were his bare hands. Even those men who had waylaid him the night he had met her—he was sure he would have prevailed in the end.

But there was something about undressing in front of her that felt . . . provocative. Feeling her curious eyes on him was almost like feeling her touch against his skin. He tried to shake it off, but that was hard to do when his body was filling with heat at the same time. Soon he would burn. Burn for her eyes to see and watch. Again, it felt intimate. Far too intimate. He was shocked to realize that by the time he was fully naked, he was inexplicably hard. Aroused. Aware.

She took all of this in. All of him in. Her eyes were wide and curious, and she was nibbling a little on her bottom lip. Slowly he sat down in the water, letting the coolness of it wash over his hot body. And for some reason, just before he broiled into cinder and ash, his body burning away in fierce bits and pieces, he thought of how long it had been since he had been intimate with a woman. And then he thought of who that woman had been.

His wife. Casiria. The woman he had once loved with everything he was. She had birthed his sons for him. She had meant everything. But she and his sons were long gone now. He had not had the opportunity to see them grow into men, and he had no way of finding out what kind of men they had become. They were dead. Long dead and forgotten by everyone but him.

The water boiled as though in response to his turmoil, in response to his present pain and the memory of pain. Pain no one would ever understand . . . pain he had never shared with anyone.

By the time juquil's hour arrived, he felt destroyed in more ways than one, more ways than just the physical. His body was ravaged and burned, brittle and blackened. Almost everything he was had been burned away to the bones. It took some time before his eyes healed enough for him to be able to see her, for his muscles to finally move under his command.

She was close to him, her hands reaching out gently to him, touching his burned flesh.

"I see now. I see the pain of it," she said. "I could not tell from a distance before . . . but now I see how truly painful this is for you. Can I do something to give you relief?" she asked, her eyes and tone tender and warm.

"Your kindness is enough," he said. And he meant it. There was something soothing in her nearness.

"Now we can talk until you feel better. Tell me, who are you here in the world of men?"

The question was a curious one, but he answered her. "I am a warrior. But you know this."

"You are more than a warrior, to be sure. My father is a warrior, but he is also a husband, a father, and a brother. Who are you?"

"I am a brother," he said. "One of four. Two are with me here, in the city of Kriza."

"And are they warriors too?"

"Yes. Very strong ones. They are impressive men."

"And do they burn like you do?"

"One did. It was different for him. It was the flames of hell that burned him. I . . . I burn like the sun, from the inside out."

"You say he did. You mean in the past? But no longer?"

"Yes," he said, not elaborating further.

But she did not let him get away with that, and he had not expected she would. "Why did he stop?" she asked.

"It is a long story."

"Why did it start?"

"You ask too many questions," he said irritably.

"How else am I to know you?"

"What if I don't want you to know me?" he asked of her, his tone hard.

"Nonsense," she said dismissively. "You wish to know me, and so I must know you."

"I never said I want to know you."

"Of course you do," she said with a lift of her chin. "All men find me curious and compelling. They always wish to know about me and my kind."

"Your kind?"

She brushed past the inquiry. "Tell me, have you children? A wife?"

These questions irritated him further, so he almost did not answer. But in the end, he said, "I did once. What of you?"

"Oh, I do not have a wife. Nor do I have children."

He fought the urge to smile. "And what of a husband?"

She frowned. "There is one who wishes to be my mate, but I do not wish it in return." Her frowned deepened. "He cannot understand that . . ." She trailed off, clearly not meaning to speak aloud on the matter because she looked at him as though in surprise. It was strange because he felt as though she was otherwise open to his questions . . . when in fact she had smoothly dodged some of his return inquiries.

"I need to get back to my brothers," he said, trying not to sound as full of consternation over that fact as he was.

"Your brothers depend on you a great deal? Or is it you who depends on them?" Before he could work up a reaction to the affront, she said, "My brothers do not depend on me at all, but one thinks I should depend on him. But the only one I truly depend on is my father. I am in his care until such time as I take a mate. Then I will be in my mate's care. That is the way of things with my people."

"You keep saying 'my people' but never tell me who your people are."

"You have not told me who your people are. Where do you come from?"

"Nowhere. Everywhere. I used to say I was from Barost. It was the city where . . . where my wife lived."

"With your children?"

"Yes."

"What happened to her?"

"She died. Look, I do not wish to talk about her."

"All right. Where are your children?"

"They are dead too," he snapped at her, "and an equally taboo topic!"

"I see." Her mouth drifted into a sad little frown and her exotic eyes went soft with pain. "I did not mean to make you angry. I only wished to know everything about you. I find you so fascinating. I find you different."

"I am no different from any other man," he said.

"Other men do not burn like a star."

Well, she had him there. "Is that all that fascinates you about me?" he asked. "I am not some freak show meant for your entertainment."

"Believe me," she assured him in the face of his biting tone, "I find nothing about you to be any more freakish than you might think I am."

"You do not burn every night."

"No. But we all have our trials, and we are all different and strange in our own ways. And that's what is so beautiful about most living creatures, don't you think? If everyone were the same, it would be quite boring."

"Who *are* you?" he asked intensely, reaching to take her head between his hands and boring a stare into her eyes.

"I—I am Jileana. I am daughter to the warrior Creasus. I care for my people's young when they must hunt or farm. I have a brother who is a warrior just like my father. They defend our home from our enemies and I am very proud of them for that. My mother is a great woman with compassion in her soul and a firm hand.

"I love the feel of the warm sun on my body as I lay beneath it, and the coolness of the ocean waters as I swim through them. It is a simple life, the life I lead, but it is a good one."

Jaykun had to admit it sounded like a good one. Some days he thought he might trade his soul for the joys of a simple life . . . but it only took an instant for him to quell such a notion. There was too much at stake in the life he had to lead, too many people whose fates were dependent on him staying the course.

"I don't have time for this," he muttered, releasing her and looking for his clothes. "My brothers will be looking for me, and there are . . . there are more important things than having a discussion with a strange girl in a cave."

He found his clothing and felt her eyes on him as he dressed. He stole a glance at her and found her gaze to be unabashedly curious, much like she was trying to absorb every movement he made, every inch of his body. The understanding made an unexpected frisson of arousal bleed through his sharp, intense movements. He tried to fight it back, but it was hard to do when his gaze was attracted to the long supple lines of her limbs and the lush curves of her body. She was young and nubile and everything any man would find arousing. Even a man barely healed from his trials of the night.

Angry with his unruly responses and determined not to follow up the feelings with any regrettable behavior, he didn't even bother with his shirt and, bare chested, moved to push past her.

"Can I come with you?" she asked, again with that open curiosity. It was as though she found everything to be new and adventurous. An odd thing considering the land they were in at present was war torn.

Again, unwillingly, his gaze was attracted to her dark, silky flesh.

"Not like that you can't," he said sharply. "A naked girl in a camp full of soldiers? Even I couldn't stop them if . . . if . . ." The thoughts that followed were so unpalatable they made Jaykun's stomach churn.

"But if I had clothing?" she said, moving closer to him again. He wished she would stop doing that. Every time she came close, his body tightened up, as though expecting something exciting to happen. It was completely at odds with a mind that wanted nothing to do with her.

"Then you could do whatever you wanted to. I'm not likely to stop you."

"Very well," she said, her words soft and whispery as she reached out for his hand. He could have jerked away from her, put distance between them, but he was suddenly paralyzed, curious and hungry for whatever she was going to do next. Her slender fingers touched the back of his hand, stroked over it, running up over the knuckles of his fingers until his grip went unexpectedly lax. Then she was taking his tunic out of his hand.

He was still, simply staring at her as she drew the tunic over her head, letting the size of it swallow her up before it hung in place to below her knees. Even though she was tall and strong looking, she was still quite a bit smaller than he was, especially in the shoulders.

Seeing her in his clothing had a profoundly strange effect on him. It was somehow the most intimate thing he had experienced since he had been released from his personal hell of being chained to a star. Oh, he could have had sex with any one of the women close at hand; the encampment was lousy with females looking to take coin from the soldiers in exchange for it. But he'd had no desire for that kind of intimacy, wanted no sense of making himself vulnerable to another while that person made herself vulnerable to him. Of sharing something with someone. He'd been vulnerable to women in the past and knew now that nothing good could come of it.

The idea of it made him angry and defensive. He reached out for her suddenly, grabbing her by both arms and shaking her roughly. "What do you want from me?" he demanded, shaking her again. The action made her hair slide over her cheek, and she gently brushed it back behind her delicate ear without shrugging off his hold. It communicated how unruffled she was by his rough handling of her and he could not help but feel overwhelming consternation.

"I want to know you better," she said softly as she looked up into his eyes. "I find you fascinating. Don't you think you are fascinating? Am I not fascinating to you as well?" she asked, those openly curious eyes drifting over his face and chest.

Oh, he felt something about her all right, but he wasn't certain "fascination" was the word for it. Maybe vexation. Consternation.

Excitement.

At this distance he could smell her, the aroma of seawater and something sweeter . . . sultrier . . . lifting off her. She was warm and compelling, soft and sensual, beckoning and beautiful.

"Beyond fascination," he admitted, his voice rough with his overwhelming desire for her. It was so unexpected, so incongruous to the state of his life, that he couldn't hope to control his next actions. He jerked her in close against his body, feeling her weight press against his chest, deepening that strange sense of intimacy between them. Then he crushed his lips against hers, fueling the kiss with his confusion and frustrated need.

At least she had the wherewithal to be surprised . . . for a moment. Then she became bright and eager against him, her hands lifting to frame his face, ostensibly to hold him to his task. The open invitation was far more than he could bear, certainly nothing to encourage him to break off and put a stop to his madness.

No. Instead he found her mouth full of warmth and willingness. It was a potent idea, that she was being driven to this just as he was. It made him feel a little better for it, a little less like he was being managed by a practiced, seductive hand. That wasn't to say there was nothing seductive about her. In fact, she was everything compelling and sexually stimulating he could have imagined. He pulled her in, devouring her with hungry lips, opening his mouth over hers and driving his tongue between her lush lips. At first he tasted salt, but that was to be expected since they were still standing in the sea. But the impression was faint and fleeting because the next instant he was tasting *her*. A sweet and deep flavor. An alluring and compelling taste. She was like honey against a bitter tongue, soothing and dissolving and sweet.

Then there was the feel of her nubile body against his, her whole being radiating how eager she was to be alongside him. His hands left her arms and spread across her back, pulling her in tight, his body soaking in the heat of hers and the way it made him feel. And as he kissed her wildly, for a moment, for just a moment, he forgot about who he was, forgot about the curse that hung over his head, forgot about his responsibilities to his brothers and his goddess. Forgot about Casiria and all the baggage that came with his memories of his wife. And that, above all else, was the most wondrous thing about Jileana.

The moment he realized it, though, the moment he comprehended how easily she had made him forget himself, he thrust her away, leaving them both panting and dazed, her eyes looking as stunned and delighted as he was feeling. Although, he wasn't ready to admit to the delighted part. He was too busy telling himself that it was wrong for him to forget himself like that. That he had to keep focused. So why, then, in the next moment did he seize her again and draw her back into his body, kissing her once more as if his life depended on it? A strange concept, a surreal one, considering he was immortal.

But oh, she was so sweet. So tender in form and function. He had kissed many women in his time, but none had had the combination of sultry innocence he was deriving from Jileana's kisses. She was not practiced and yet she was a natural. She was not cynical; she was wide-eyed with wonder and excitement. He read all of this from her even though she now said not a word and spoke to him only through her kisses and the flight of her body against his.

He found himself regretting that he had not kissed her before she had put on his tunic. To be holding all that bare, succulent skin beneath his hands would have been more than he could imagine.

This time when he moved away from her mouth it was only in increments, just enough to see down into those iridescent green eyes of hers, to see the flush on her dusky cheeks, the wetness of her ripe lips as her breath came in rapid pants.

"Oh my," she breathed, her hands clutching at his shoulders.

It made him smile, an expression he used very little. He smiled in spite of the clamoring of his mind and the painful arousal of his body. He was not yet fully healed and his pain had been considerable to begin with. Add to it a racing heart, perspiration, and a hardened cock, and it made for a bit of discomfort.

"I suspect you were sent to seduce me," he said softly. "Perhaps by those who wish to turn my head from my warring course."

"Well, I certainly do not wish to get in your way, and I doubt I could make you do anything you don't want to do. I do not seek that kind of power over you. Those are the ways of the sirens."

"Sirens?" he asked. But then he shook his head. It was unimportant. "So if you were not purposely sent to turn my head . . . what is it you want from me?"

"Only to learn you, to know you. I confess it had not occurred to me to kiss you in order to know you, but I find doing so has given me a great deal of information."

That made him laugh because he knew exactly how she was feeling.

"So, what do we do now?" he asked. "Do I continue to kiss you?"

"If you like," she said, her tone eager and delighted. He found himself smiling again.

"And then what? Do I bed you, sea sprite? Take you into the roughness of my camp and the coarseness of my bed?"

"You do not make it sound at all attractive," she pointed out with some measure of consternation.

"It isn't. A war camp is not a pretty thing."

"Then stay with me on the beach," she said invitingly. "It is clean. The sand is soft. It makes for the best of beds."

"Hmm. Methinks you are a siren after all. You make it sound too damn inviting."

"Oh, I'm no siren," she assured him, making a face as if he had suggested something offensive as opposed to the compliment he had intended. "And sleeping on the beach is the most wonderful thing. To sleep under the stars, hearing the sound of the ocean upon the sand. The call of the sea birds as they dive for their supper. They like to eat the kelp whistles. They are the little fish that swim around seaweeds and glow in the dark. It makes the sea light up so pretty . . . and yet it makes the fish easy prey for the sea birds. So beautiful and so sad at the same time. But that is the way of things. Everything falls prey to something else."

"This is too true," he said with a frown. Even her people, wherever she was from, could fall prey to him. They worshipped Diathus. His task was to seed the world with temples to Weysa. To lure more followers to her way so she could grow stronger through their devotion. If they would not be lured by peaceful means . . . then he would more firmly demand.

"You would be well advised to make your way clear of me," he said, his frown darkening.

"My mother says I am not very good at taking the advice of others."

And just like that, his frown was gone; his dark mood lightened again.

"So," he said, moving her to his side a little so he could lead them out of the grotto, "what am I to do with you? As much as I would like to, I cannot spend the night on the beach."

"Why not?" she asked curiously.

"My brothers will be looking for me. Also, we have a newly acquired city and an army that must be managed."

"I see. Well, I could come with you. I have never seen

the city before. I have been told it holds many fascinating things."

"I'm sure it does. But if you live here, why have you never been to the city before?"

"I've never had a reason," she said with a simple shrug. "Besides, my brothers would not approve. They are quite overprotective of me. At least they are in my opinion."

"If I were your brother, I would be protective too. Especially if you make a habit of wandering the beach naked and kissing strange men."

"Well . . . I do not have any clothes . . . and I do not usually kiss strange men. But most men don't burn like a star. Certainly not and live to tell about it after. You are unique, Jaykun."

"We are all unique in some way, Jileana," he said, shrugging the matter off. He wished she had never seen him suffer his torment, but then she might not have been fascinated enough to approach him. He found that idea unpalatable on two levels: one, that she found his curse so enthralling, and two, that he would have regretted not knowing her. Even after such a brief encounter, he knew his life would have been poorer had it never touched hers. Even in the smallest of ways.

They were walking on the sand now, his arm across her back, still holding her to his side as they traveled up the beach.

"I would see this city, if you please. All I ask is for a small place to sleep that is clean. I do not want anything else . . . except perhaps to learn more about you."

"I am not so fascinating," he said.

"Oh, but you are," she argued, her eyes light and eager. "Not just because you burn. You are tall and have a very nice shape. I can see you are quite strong. I find I like your face. It is an interesting face. Your eyes are far more somber than they ought to be, but they are a pretty green and glitter like sea glass."

"Somber, hmm?"

"Yes. Quite. But not as much when you smile like you are doing now."

"Well, it is good to know it is not entirely off-putting. Though I confess to cultivating a stern look to keep my men in line."

"My father leads a great many men and he is quite jovial. Perhaps you are going about it wrong."

"Perhaps I am," he said, smiling again in spite of himself. Truth be told, he hadn't felt this light of mood since . . . well, since he had been brought back.

"What is that?" she asked suddenly.

"What?"

"The thought that takes your smile away so quickly and so thoroughly like that. What is it?"

"It is none of your concern," he said brusquely, immediately widening the distance between their bodies. But for some inexplicable reason he did not drop his hand away from her back.

"Very well. But I am sad for you because of it. Your smile is quite handsome and should spend more time on your face." She switched topics quickly and brightly. "Do you think you will let me stay, then?"

He should tell her no. He should put an end to this strange encounter right now. He had far too much to deal with and too much riding on his actions. His daily considerations were life-or-death decisions. It was clear her choices in life were of much lighter importance. But he was glad of that, glad that she was not burdened with the weight of things that would steal the bright, childlike eagerness from her features. He was not so cynical that he would begrudge her her innocent life.

But he found he could not put her off, could not make himself push her aside so he could continue on in his life without the burden of her ... whatever that burden may end up being. He found it was a weight he would willingly carry ... for the time being. Besides, if she made a nuisance of herself, she was easily disposed of. It wasn't as though she had any power over him. He was in complete command of the situation, just as he always was.

"So tell me, Jileana. Is it my bed you wish to warm tonight?"

Perhaps he'd asked the question to shock her, to sabotage the fragile trust between them. But she seemed to consider the question very carefully.

"All things considered, you would probably make a fine lover. You certainly give very exciting kisses," she mused aloud, startling a laugh out of him. "But I think I would like to know you a little bit better first. Do you not agree?"

This was territory to be cautious of. Getting to know him better implied a level of intimacy he simply was not of a mind to give, even had the circumstances been ideal.

"Then why would I want to give you a bed?" he asked baldly.

"Because you would like to get to know me better as well," she explained to him very clearly, as if it were a plainly obvious fact. To his consternation, she was right. He did want to know her better. At the very least, he found her intriguing. He told himself that he simply wanted to learn more about her people, to perhaps contemplate bringing Weysa to their temples. But the truth was, he'd already had goals set out for himself that allowed for no room for deviation. There was no way to add another city to his conquering schedule. Still, perhaps it could be a peaceful integration, something only a few days of negotiation could bring about.

"Very well, then, a clean, safe bed for the night. What

you do after . . . I suppose that is your own affair. I will not have you underfoot. I have a great deal to accomplish and won't have time to spend with you."

"A meal."

"What?" he asked.

"You must eat, I am assuming, yes? So I ask a meal of you. Well, how else are we to know each other better? It would be silly for me to stay only to spend no time with you. Since I do not wish to get in your way, we shall spend a meal together."

He thought on it a moment. It really wasn't much to ask for. And she was right; he would have to eat at some point.

"Very well," he said.

"For three days."

"Now, wait a minute—"

"One meal a day for three days. It is very little to ask of you. And I promise not to interfere in your day otherwise. Not unless you wish me to."

He thought about it for a long minute, part of him crying out that this was a bad idea all around. The sensible part of his brain knew he did not need distractions of any kind. But another part of his brain found her to be engaging in a way he simply did not experience in his life. It was impossible to turn his back on her offer.

"One meal. Three days. Otherwise, I'm not to be bothered by you."

"I promise," she swore, her hand over her heart. Seeing her slender fingers against the beige of his tunic made him frown.

"But you have no clothing." His frown deepened. "Why is it you have no clothing? It is not safe for a naked woman to walk the beach."

"Oh, I am perfectly safe," she assured him. "And my people have little use for clothing."

"Your entire people do not wear clothes? Where is this place you come from?"

"It is not far," she said. Jaykun was well aware she was being vague on purpose, but he did not press at that moment. In truth, it mattered little. Although, from a conqueror's perspective, it would be very easy to fight a people who hadn't the sense to wear clothes. Then again, she'd said she had never been to the city before, so it was unlikely her people were worth his time if they didn't have a city of their own.

"Tomorrow, after our midday meal, I will take you to the shops for clothing," he said.

"But that is not part of our agreement," she pointed out.

"I shall make an exception this once."

"But how do you know that *I* wish to make the exception?"

That took him aback. She was right. He had not even bothered to ask if she wanted new clothes . . . or if she wanted to spend more time with him than just what a meal allowed for. For some reason the thought that she might not want to spend the time with him put him out. He couldn't explain why; it just did.

"Do not worry," she said after a moment, patting him kindly on his arm. "I will accept this time."

"Well . . . thank you," he said awkwardly. Mainly because she continually shifted the world beneath him and he couldn't seem to get traction with her. He couldn't decide if he was perturbed or delighted. It had been quite awhile since he had been entertained by something in the world.

And just like that, he was looking forward to his meals for the next three days.

CHAPTER
FOUR

Finding somewhere to install Jileana was harder than it had appeared on the surface. The brothers were newly installed in the city center, in a castle that overlooked the massive harbor. The chaos of descending on the city had died down to a dull roar, but the men of their army were not entirely organized as they settled in for the night. People had grabbed beds or floors wherever they could. The men were high from their victory and many were still up, drinking and reveling by the fires all throughout the city and in the castle.

The brothers of course had the choice of where they would stay. Jaykun had had first pick and had installed himself in the finia's rooms. The finia, the ruler of the city, had found herself relocated to the lower rooms for the time being, under guard. The finia's rooms were vast, tended to by servants. Fresh linens had been put on the bed, a fire built in the front room, the sitting room, and the bedroom itself. In a rear room was a plumbed bath, tiled in silver-and-white tiles. A room beyond the bath was where the servants, two young women, slept.

The bed was a large affair, decorated with a sheer royal-purple curtain and laid with blankets and a coverlet of rich red, and a multitude of pillows in shades of purples and reds. The fabrics alternated between velvets and silks. It was just shy of looking like it belonged in a high-end brothel. The bed was large enough for three men of Jaykun's size and build, and he wondered how the squat finia had managed to not get lost within it.

Jaykun walked throughout the castle with Jileana, searching for a place to install her, until he gave up trying to find somewhere safe and quiet, and brought her to his rooms.

"You can sleep in this bed," he said. "I will find my brothers and bunk with one of them. At least this way I will know you are safe."

"No," Jileana said with a shaking of her dark head. "I won't kick you out of your own bed."

"It's hardly mine to begin with," he argued, giving her a little push toward it.

"This bed is very big and I am not used to . . . Well, there is plenty of space, is there not?"

Jaykun hesitated. His eyes fell on her body of their own accord, sliding down over her voluptuous shape from head to toe. The sleek fall of her midnight hair curved around her equally sleek body. The idea of having her in bed beside him was far too appealing, fraught with temptation and complication. The memory of what it was like to kiss her rode him hard and he knew how dangerous it would be.

"I don't think that's the wisest idea," he said with a negating shake of his head. He moved to withdraw from her before the desire that seeped through him compelled him to draw her in once again. He was floored by how overwhelming the feeling was. It filled him with a sense of disquiet. He didn't like the idea of being unable to control his own actions. He wasn't sure he wanted to be near the source of those feelings.

"Come," she said, her iridescent green eyes soft and

beckoning as she held out an inviting hand. "Come with me. I promise I will not bite you while you sleep."

"I'm rather more concerned with me possibly nibbling on you," he answered baldly as he let her take his hand.

"Would that be so bad?" she asked, invitation oozing out of her body.

"I haven't quite decided," he said as he let himself be pulled toward the bed.

"It is such a strange thing, the way you let so much noise into your head," she observed with genuine curiosity in her voice. "You feel strongly about something, and yet you force yourself to resist those feelings. Why? What is so wrong about what you are feeling?"

"Nothing," he said with a sigh, scrubbing his hand across his weary face. "I don't know. It's been a long day."

"I'm sure it has been. Especially considering the way you like to end your days."

"I like nothing about the way I end my days. You speak as though I had a choice in the matter."

"And you don't?"

"No," he said shortly. "I don't."

She looked at him then with soft, curious eyes—an expression he was realizing was very natural to her. She seemed to view the world as one great curiosity. He wished he could see the world through her perspective. As it was, his view was far more jaded.

"I think you have had enough hardship for one day," she said then, finishing their progress toward the bed. She climbed up onto it, kneeling as she pulled him after her. Giving in to her lure, he paused a moment, withdrawing from her long enough to rid himself of his boots. As he did so, she came up close against his back, her hands shaping the contours of his shoulders and arms in long, relaxing strokes. In spite of himself, he felt his body going lax beneath her massaging hands.

Fine, he thought. If she was looking for a night of physical comfort, he would not deny her or himself. It wasn't exactly a rare occurrence for a woman to want him. However, it was a rare occurrence for him to want her in return. But who could blame him for seeking out comfort wherever he could find it? His was a cursed existence, a forced slavery and penance. He should take advantage of these opportunities much more often than he did. It was, after all, the only kindness he could find outside his brothers' love for him.

When she ran her hands down the length of his bare back, he closed his eyes and reveled in the sensation. Her hands were like magic on his skin, livening up nerves he thought deadened by his nightly torture. As she ran over unhealed patches of his skin, she seemed to think nothing of it, let it faze her not at all. In fact, it seemed as though very little fazed her. After all, she had taken the sight of him burning to cinders almost in stride. A fact he should be questioning, but he found himself unable to do so as his body reacted with a surprising amount of pleasure.

"Do you do this often?" he asked, almost with the goal of turning himself off to her. "Climb into bed with strange men?"

"Not at all. You would be the first. Earlier I thought we might take a little time to know one another, but there is so little time to be had, I now realize it would be foolish to waste it. Besides, it seems you need it more than others might."

"So this is an act of pity?" he asked harshly.

"Again, not at all. I find you very appealing. Your body has many nice shapes. Your skin is warm. Much warmer than my own. See?" She held out her arm beneath his nose and he obliged her by stroking a slow hand up along her forearm. She was right. She was much cooler than he was. But that made the feel of her no less appealing. She was soft and smooth, supple to the touch, yet clearly quite strong for a woman. He liked that. He had no stomach for weak women. His brothers' wives struck him as physically genteel—although he gave them credit for being much stronger in their personalities and backbones. He could understand what had drawn each brother respectively to each woman, knowing his brothers as he did. Still, like him, his brothers had been greatly altered by the punishments they had endured. It was a wonder he even knew them at all anymore.

Jileana moved around his body, slowly throwing a leg across his lap until she was astride his thighs. Cool she may be on her extraneous limbs, but here, where her bottom rested against him, she was hot and beckoning. Of their own accord, his hands ran down the length of her torso, under her arms, down her sides, and on until he was gripping her hips in his hands.

"Would you give me comfort, Jileana?" he asked in a whisper as he looked into those bottomless, iridescent eyes.

"That and more," she promised him. "Mmm, I like the way you feel," she said with obvious pleasure as she curved her spine and pressed her chest to his. He could feel the weight of her full breasts between them, and a searing flash of aroused awareness bolted through his body. In all of an instant, his clothes—what little there were of them—felt confining and cumbersome. He was overwhelmed with a craving to be skin-to-skin with her. To feel all that sweetly supple skin against his own . . . Yes, that was a comfort he wanted very much indeed.

With purpose, his fingers slipped beneath the hem of the tunic she wore, the bulky fabric hanging heavy on her small frame—small in comparison to the body it had been tailored for, in any event. He found himself wondering how he had gotten to that point. His only goal for the day had been to take a city and make it his own. To own the city that owned the armada he so desperately needed in order to progress onward, in order to fulfill his bargain with the warrior goddess. A bargain he must fulfill lest she become angry and turn her displeasure on him or his brothers. His brothers had, for the most part, been released from their duties to Weysa, but that could easily change. They were all fodder for the gods' mercurial moods and wishes. There was no guarantee of anything when it came to the whims of the gods.

But now he was here, finding solace in a warm, shapely body, and he couldn't make himself turn away from her. He did not even want to, he thought as his hands filled with bare flesh. When he saw her naked the first time, he had wondered what all that sleek flesh would feel like, and now he was discovering the answer. It was an answer that had his body hardening with need and craving.

He exhaled a long, slow breath, almost as though he had been holding on to his breath for hours. It was possible he had been. After all, he did not need to breathe to live. But it was a strange and unrealistic thought, clearly without basis in fact. Without breath he could not speak, and it seemed he had yet to stop talking with her. In fact, he had not exchanged so many words with someone other than his brothers or his generals in a very long time.

"I like the way you feel as well," he said, the words coming out of him like a growl.

"Then we shall spend quite a bit of time feeling each other," she promised him with confidence. It made him chuckle.

"You'll get no arguments from me," he said.

"I like that you are furry," she said with a smile as she raked gentle fingers through the hair at the center of his chest.

"I like that you are not," he replied, making her laugh. It was a light, musical sound. As musical as the rest of her voice. Yes, he thought. That was the perfect term for it. Soft and melodic. And just as compelling as the mischievous smile that spread across her lush lips. Lips that hovered barely an inch above his own.

"I think I'm going to kiss you," he said roughly as his hands closed tightly around her hips, his fingers sinking into the soft flesh of her buttocks. "And then I'm fairly certain I'm going to fuck you."

"Is that what you call it?" she asked lightly. "Fucking? Hmm. I like it. It's a fun word. Hard and to the point."

"I'll show you hard and to the point," he said hoarsely as he spun them about until her back hit the bedding and he was looming over her. He felt her legs lock around his waist and he grew harder from finding himself entrapped by those long, beautiful legs.

Unable to resist a moment longer, he covered her mouth with his own, kissing her with savagery and an intensity he had not realized he was capable of. Her mouth was lush and deep, and he explored every corner of it as fiercely as he could. His tongue tangled with hers, and the depth of the link made his head spin and buzz with need and arousal. It seemed the more he kissed her, the more ferocious that need became.

Meanwhile, her hands kept busy on his skin. Her fingertips danced, her palms stroked. She was touching him everywhere she could find bare skin. Her touch coasted down his back, burrowed beneath the waist of his pants, her fingers gripping at his backside and dragging his hips forward into the lee of her thighs.

"Mmm," she purred as his sex rubbed up hard against hers, where he was still clothed and she was decidedly not. "Is this where the fucking begins?"

"It's already begun," he assured her as he lifted away from her just long enough to strip his tunic from her body. He took a moment, his breaths coming hard, to look down on her. Yes, he decided. This was a good place for her to be. Beneath him in his bed. His lust for her was almost blinding . . . almost a little frightening. But he excused his fervor. He was long overdue for this. He gave little thought to the idea that he felt much more strongly about this than he should be feeling for a casual toss of a random wench.

But she was nothing to him, he reassured himself. Nothing more than a much-needed moment of pleasure. He gave himself over to that as he let his mouth slide along her sweet skin, her slightly salty flavor streaking across his tongue as it glided down the length of her breastbone. He shaped her right breast in his hand, kneading the flesh of it almost desperately. He needed her on such a visceral level. Escape. Yes. He needed escape and she was going to provide it.

"Yes," she encouraged him with a sibilant *s*, as though she could divine his thoughts. Her fingers crawled through his hair, her hands embracing his head as he drew his mouth to the tip of her breast. He opened his mouth against her obligingly, his tongue darting out to taste her rigid nipple. He closed his mouth over her at last and sucked her deep inside. She gasped, her back arching up off the bed. In truth, she did that frequently— curved her body up into his again and again, as if she longed to connect with him for every second possible.

As he pulled at her with his mouth, he let his touch travel below her waist and between her splayed thighs. When he touched her intimately, he found her to be incredibly wet and slick; it was so inviting that he felt like he was strangling with the need to connect with her. But he would not rid himself of his clothing and be free to just take her. He didn't want this to be over that quickly. He felt they both needed more than the quick, unfeeling coupling he kept trying to relegate the encounter to, and in spite of his body, he found himself giving in to those desires. He wanted her to feel pleasure, wanted her to get just as much out of the encounter as he hoped to get. Thankfully she seemed hot and willing and wild enough to feel anything he needed her to feel.

Then her fingers were pulling at the fastenings of his pants, freeing him to her touch as her hand delved beyond and her fingers wrapped around his thick and straining cock. He surged up into her hand, felt the glory of her fingers stroking the length and breadth of him, felt him pulsing to her touch. It was blindingly blissful, everything he could want and more. Almost too much. He surged into her touch again and again with blind thrusts of his hips, all the while seeking out her clitoris with his fingers. He wanted her to feel the same beautiful pleasure he was feeling. But it seemed as though he couldn't focus beyond the feel of her touch on him. Her stroke was erotic without feeling practiced. She was simply seeking and learning, chasing down his every sound of pleasure, repeating herself each time she elicited an uncontrolled response from him. Before he knew it, she had pushed his pants down below his hips, wrapped her legs tightly around him, and jerked their hips into a perfect connection that allowed his cock to slide through the infinite heat and moisture of her sex. He was but a single thrust away from being inside her.

"Slow," he ground out. "Great gods, you're a hot little thing. Slow down before I—"

"Hush," she breathed against his ear. "Hush and just take me."

Honestly, he couldn't have resisted the temptation even if he'd tried. It was too much and he was in too much need. He gave her what she was begging for, sliding through her wet heat one last time before looking into her eyes and entering her with a hard thrust. She gasped, long and loud, then released the breath in a lusty groan. Her nails dug into his backside, her hands helping him in his second thrust, the thrust that seated him most firmly inside her.

"There, now. Now who is burning as hot as a star, hmm?" he asked her.

"Is it me?" she asked him, making him laugh.

"Yes, it is you."

"Oh, good. For a moment I couldn't tell. You are so hot you are burning me from the inside."

Her words enflamed him. He thrust into her again and again, his mouth crashing onto hers as he devoured her every way he could think of. She overwhelmed him, rocked him to his core, clawed pleasure out of him seemingly from the bottom of his forsaken soul. The feeling was unexpected and disturbing, almost disturbing enough to make him withdraw from her. But the lock of her legs and the escalating fever of her body made that impossible. He began to drive into her in earnest, working himself up, telling himself this was no more than a selfish pleasure. Her reactions meant nothing. His reactions meant nothing. None of it had any deeper meaning than the simple physicality of the joining.

"Gods above," he swore fiercely as the need to orgasm tore through him. Yes, he thought. He was going to take his pleasure and that would be the end of it. The end of her. The end of them.

And yet he couldn't seem to make himself take that pleasure without making certain she was right there with him. Why should it matter to him? Why should he care? he asked himself. She had given herself up to this thing with no promises from him. He owed her nothing.

But there was something about hearing her pleasured cries in his ear that was too compelling by far. It would not be right unless he took her over the edge with him. It simply would not do.

He thrust into her grasping body, listening to her pleasure ramp upward in the air around them. He staved off his need to come until she threw back her head, throat arching up toward him, and shouted in exultation. He surged into her once again and let blinding pleasure sweep through him. He came hard and fast, the clutch of her body around him more than any sane man could bear.

Gasping for breath, he collapsed upon her body, too weak with release to give a care to his weight against her. She was sturdy enough, he thought dazedly. She could bear up until he got his legs under him once more.

Still, after a moment he rolled onto his back and then stared at the colorful bed curtains where they attached to the ceiling as he felt her snuggle up against his body under his right arm. He was growing cold quickly and concerned she was as well. He used the last of his energy to draw the covers up over them before he did something he never, ever did . . . He fell asleep within trusting reach of a total stranger.

CHAPTER
FIVE

Jaykun awoke to a sudden weight against his chest. His eyes flew open to see the point of a bladed weapon trembling just beyond the ends of his lashes. On the other end of the weapon was a woman. The only things keeping that blade from penetrating his eye and entering his brain were the strong hands of the other woman lying against his body.

Jileana shoved the woman back with all of her strength, her lithe body coming up off the bed in the same movement. The woman, a total stranger but clearly from Kriza, went sprawling back onto the floor. Jileana was on her like a flash, her naked body straddling the other woman, her hands never losing control of the attacker's dagger hand. With sure and amazing strength, she turned the dagger onto the Krizan woman and plunged it hard into her chest before Jaykun could even get to his feet.

"Low beast," the Krizan woman gurgled out. "Vile thing. You will die." Then she spit blood into Jileana's face before taking a last shuddering breath.

"Good gods," Jaykun gusted out, his eyes wide as he absorbed the enormity of what Jileana had just done for him. His heart was pounding in his chest as he watched her wipe the blood off her face and get to her feet. And somehow, inexplicably, he thought he'd never seen a more beautiful woman in his life. It was possible it was the adrenaline and gratitude of the moment, but he didn't think so. She was a sight to behold, standing naked over her kill.

"I . . . th-thank you," he managed to say, if somewhat shakily.

"I'm sorry it came so close," she said with a sigh. "I normally don't sleep that soundly."

"Me either," Jaykun said, his awe still present in his tone. *"Never."*

It was true. He should have heard the woman the moment she entered the room. He was in what was easily hostile territory and should have been sleeping with one eye open.

"My brothers!" The thought hit him like lightning. He jerked his pants into place as he ran from the room. It stood to reason that if Krizans were going to make an attempt on his life, they would do the same to his brothers. He burst into the common dining hall on his way to his brothers' rooms and pulled up short when he saw them both sitting there, calmly breaking their fast. Two sets of eyes that matched his own went wide at his wild entrance.

"Good morning, brother," Dethan said, looking a little bemused.

"Y-you're both . . . What are you eating?" he demanded of them. Poison. It could be poison.

"Some fruits . . . meats . . . as you see."

"There was an assassin in my chambers just now. How do you know that isn't befouled?" Jaykun demanded of them.

Alarm crossed his siblings' features.

"An assassin?" Garreth demanded. "Worry not about

the food. We aren't foolish. Our own cook provided the meal."

"Thank the gods," Jaykun said on a relieved exhalation. "Thank the gods."

"Jaykun, where is the assass—" Dethan broke off, his eyes going wide once more as Jileana entered the dining hall wearing nothing more than Jaykun's tunic. That she wasn't Krizan was immediately obvious to his brother, and but while she might look completely harmless and unarmed, Jaykun had just claimed there had been a killer in his rooms. Dethan surged to his feet as if to cut her off before she reached Jaykun's exposed back.

"No. It's all right," Jaykun said quickly once he realized to where Dethan's attention had gone. "It wasn't her. She's . . . she . . . umm . . . she stopped the attack. She killed the assassin."

Shocked once again and for the third time in as many minutes, Dethan eyed Jileana. The idea of her going up against a dangerous killer had to be ludicrous to an outsider.

"Was it a Krizan assassin?" Garreth asked, as doubtful as Dethan felt.

"A Krizan woman," Jaykun informed.

Both brothers eyed Jileana skeptically once more. She smiled at them and waved, completely baffling them.

"Hi. I'm Jileana. I'm not an assassin. I'm just having a sexual exchange with Jaykun."

Garreth choked and Dethan grinned.

"Is that so? And you are . . . ?" Dethan said leadingly.

"Hoping to repeat the process," she said brightly.

Garreth choked again and began coughing over his laughter.

"Jileana," Jaykun said, determined not to blush like a young boy caught doing something wrong . . . even though that was exactly what he felt like. "These are my brothers, Dethan," he said, indicating the larger of the two, "and Garreth."

"You are much smaller than your brothers," she observed of Garreth.

"Yes, I am," Garreth said with a grin.

"Your brother Jaykun is very large," she observed again. "He also has an excellent skill in all I have needed him for thus far. I imagine you are both equally skilled individuals. Although, I should warn you now that I am not interested in sexual congress with either of you. Not that you should be insulted. You are both fine-looking warriors. But I would prefer to remain with Jaykun as far as that is concerned. I'm hungry. May I have some fruit?"

All three brothers were gaping at her so she picked up a piece of fruit and pointed to it, repeating very carefully, "May I have this?"

Dethan snapped out of his disbelief first. "O-of course," he said.

"Thank you." She went to the table, sat down just to the side of where Garreth had been eating, crossed her legs, and began to peel her fruit. "I don't consider this our one meal, Jaykun," she said, reminding him of their bargain. "I am thinking the midday meal is the one you are required to attend. It will be easier and less rushed than the evening meal."

"Less rushed?" Garreth asked as he picked up his cup.

"Yes. Before he has to burn like a star."

Unfortunately, Garreth was drinking at the moment she said this, so he sputtered and coughed. "She knows about that?" he wheezed, looking around the room hastily to see who was there to overhear her. The room was empty of all save the four of them.

"Well, of course. I've watched him these past four nights."

"Of course," Dethan said. Clearly he was disturbed that she had this intimate information about his brother. "Midday meal?" he asked, arching a brow at Jaykun.

Jaykun had not prepared himself to answer his brothers' questions about Jileana. In fact, some part of his brain had thought he could keep them completely ignorant of her existence. Now he saw just how foolish that idea had been . . . even more so now that she was standing there in front of them.

"Jileana is visiting the city for three days. I told her I would have a meal with her once every day while she visited."

Dethan frowned at that. "Jaykun, we have a great deal to accomplish before winter sets in. Garreth and I return to our wives soon and you need to have the harbor secured for the winter."

"I know what my responsibilities are," Jaykun snapped. "But it just so happens that eating is one of those things I will be doing regardless of the constraints on my time, so I don't foresee it interfering."

Jaykun had changed his tone in such a way that the brothers knew arguing further would risk his wrath— something neither of them welcomed and both had learned to avoid. The truth of it was that Jaykun was more than capable of seeing to his responsibilities and didn't need his brothers making attempts to corral him, even if Dethan was the eldest of the three and by right of birth seemed to think he had the management of his brothers as his responsibility.

Dethan was concerned. Women, whatever their use or function, were a distraction and a potential powder keg. He should know. He was at present tightly entwined around the finger of a beautiful, good-hearted woman whom he had only intended to marry as a means of getting himself a kingdom and an army. He had given up his immortality for her, now had three children by her, and couldn't imagine living a day on this planet without her. It was hard enough being required to campaign away from her in the summer months, but he knew he could have a much worse fate.

He could have Jaykun's fate. Jaykun now carried the burden of the brothers' pact with the goddess Weysa. She had forgiven Dethan and Garreth of that duty, save for the summer months in Dethan's case. Garreth was simply there to assist them as needed as he fulfilled his own agenda for the god of love, Mordu, who required Garreth to open temples in his name and garner him followers just as Garreth's brothers were doing for Weysa. Weysa had made way for the two brothers, but it was clear she would not be so forgiving a third time. No, their only hope for rescuing Maxum—their fourth brother—from unending torment was Jaykun. If Jaykun performed well, he might earn a boon from the gods. Or if they covered enough of the planet, listening to tales of the gods, maybe they could find Maxum themselves, just as they had found the Fount of Immortality that had started all of this—the fountain from which they drank and subsequently earned the wrath of the gods for their presumption.

So the complication of another woman in their midst was most unwelcome. In fact, it was quite dangerous. They could do nothing to anger the mercurial Weysa . . . and Jaykun dividing his attentions might do exactly that.

"She is but a woman to warm my bed," Jaykun muttered. "Or would you deny me even that pleasure?" he asked of Dethan.

"No. Of course not," Dethan said, his chest growing tight in empathy. His brother suffered so much. If this woman gave Jaykun even a moment's solace, Dethan could not deny him that. Still, Dethan couldn't keep his tongue from saying, "As long as that is all it is."

"For the love of the gods!" Jaykun burst out angrily. "I'm not going to marry the girl! And so what if I did? I know my duty and where it lies. I know the responsibility that weighs on me! My back is breaking from the weight of it!"

Jaykun turned and stormed back to his bedroom, leaving Jileana alone with his brothers. Completely unfazed, she was enthusiastically eating food from the display in front of her. Dethan and Garreth could only watch with bemusement as she gathered food to her and stuffed it into her mouth. She made pleasured sounds and clearly took an almost erotic satisfaction in the food . . . if her moans of delight were anything to judge by.

"Food is so delicious, don't you think?" she asked them. "I don't get to eat these kinds of things where I'm from. I especially like the fruit."

"You don't look like you're starving," Dethan observed. Although she was eating like a starving woman, she had a full, healthy shape.

"Oh no, of course not. I get plenty to eat. I only meant the kinds of food I eat are very different. You eat such a variety of foods. It's very nice. If you're not going to eat that . . . ?" she said, pointing to the toast by Dethan's wrist.

"Oh. Help yourself," he said, handing it to her.

"It's crunchy," she noted after taking a curious nibble of it. "Is it fresh?"

"It's toast. We hold it over the fire to make it crunchy on purpose," Dethan said. He gave her a quizzical look. "Haven't you ever had toast before?"

"Never! How fascinating! You simply apply heat to it and it tastes different."

"That's true of most food," Garreth pointed out with amusement.

"We don't use fire to cook food where I am from. We

prefer our food fresh and unmolested. But I like this just fine. My brother told me about cooking and I didn't believe him, but now I see we really must start cooking where I come from . . . if it is at all possible."

"And where is it you come from that they don't cook their food?" Dethan asked.

"It's not far . . . and yet it is."

"That isn't an answer," Dethan said.

"Isn't it? You asked a question and I replied. Thusly, it is an answer."

"Yes, but that isn't a real answer!"

"Well, it isn't a fake one," Jileana countered.

"Stop it this instant!" Jaykun said sharply as he reentered the room. He was fully clothed, looking tall and strong and confident as he tugged on a pair of gloves. He was dressed in a black tunic with seams of gold, the emblem of their family crest emblazoned across his chest. It was the image of four serpents coming together from four different corners of the crest, their heads making up the four sides of a square. Each serpent was of a different color and design.

"We weren't doing anything," Dethan protested.

"You were grilling her for information. She is my guest, not a prisoner or a potential source of information." Jaykun reached out a hand toward Jileana. She took it eagerly, and after pausing to stuff another piece of toast into her mouth and grabbing up one of the fruits, she let him guide her down from the table. "My lady, I believe I promised you an outing."

"Did you?" she asked through a mouthful of food.

"For clothing," he reminded her.

"Oh! You don't have to do that. I'm fine with this—or I can go without it."

Jaykun felt the stares of his brothers as he turned his back on them. "No. That is not wise," he said to Jileana. He was still angry with his brothers, but in spite of it, her openness and innocence made him smile gently at her. She honestly saw no trouble in the idea of running around naked. If this were true of all of her people, he didn't imagine they would be hard to defeat in battle . . . not if they went into the battle stark naked and unprotected.

"I think it would be much better if you had clothing," he said with a careful smile.

"If you think so," she said, her enthusiasm for his input amusing. "I shall defer to your judgment on this."

"Very well, let's go shopping. I am told that it is a favored pastime for most women."

"Well, if it is a favored pastime for most of your women, then I most certainly have to take part in it," Jileana said eagerly.

Jaykun held out his arm and she took it. In her excitement, she squeezed him. It was like that the entire time they walked from the castle to the middle of the city, where there was a great bazaar in place. The bazaar was busy overall, but almost all the vendors were severely lacking in selections. The siege on the city had taken a massive toll on the businesses. But now that the siege was over, things should return to normal.

As it was, Jaykun did not venture out to the bazaar without an armed escort. He was of course not worried for himself, but Jileana was a stranger to these people just as much as he was and they might mistake her for a member of the invading forces, which might put her in danger. He would not have her harmed. The very idea of it turned his stomach sour. He told himself it was a concern he would feel for anyone he deemed vulnerable, but in truth, the feeling ran a bit deeper than that. He didn't know why and he didn't care to acknowledge or examine it.

So they were accompanied by guards as they walked through the bazaar. It seemed the only vendors who had not been too greatly affected by the war were the clothing and household goods vendors. They had their wares on ready display, the vendors themselves tidying up in the aftermath of the war. The booth Jaykun and Jileana approached was manned by a Krizan woman and her two small children. The children took one look at Jaykun and went darting behind the protection of their mother's skirts.

"Will you service us?" Jaykun asked directly. "This woman needs clothing."

The Krizan woman took one look at Jileana and her already large eyes went wide. "B-but sh-she's . . ." the woman stammered.

"Will you service us?" Jaykun demanded. "I have gold and I know the business in this city has suffered. Are you so rich that you can afford to be prejudiced against us?"

"No, my lord," she said at last, turning her attention on him. "I-I will give you whatever you need. Th-thank you, my lord, for choosing my shop. I-I need to feed my children and we have had so little to eat since the siege began."

"I am sorry you have gone hungry," he said sincerely. "But that is over with now. The battle is over, and you and your people will be treated as fairly as you treat us in return."

"Yes, my lord," she said with a weak smile. "That is much appreciated. Now . . . how can I help the young w-woman?"

"Whatever the latest in fashion is for a Krizan woman should be fine."

"Oh, I like this!" Jileana said suddenly, dashing over to a mannequin with a dress of orange silk crepe on it. She fondled the fabric. "Oh! It feels so nice!"

"That is silk, my lady. The finest there is," the shop-keeper said with a wan smile. She cautiously approached

Jileana, her eyes shifting back to Jaykun often as she moved. It was to be expected, this kind of fear. He was one of the conquerors, after all. They had no idea what to expect from him. The one thing in his favor was that he had not allowed his men to pillage the city, stripping it of every valuable thing they could find. He paid his men well enough in gold and gave them opportunities to fight. He saw no purpose in raping a village once he conquered it. It would take much longer to get it back on its feet if he allowed that to happen. Besides, a slaughter of women and children and other nonmilitant types did no one any good.

"I love how it feels," Jileana said. Then another brightly colored dress, this one in brilliant purple, caught her eye. Krizan women were not the prettiest women on the planet, but they seemed to like colorful finery—plumage to make up for what their looks hindered. The dresses would fall to mid calf on a Krizan woman, but on Jileana, who was much taller, they would come to about her knee. There was something about the idea of being able to see her knees, perhaps flashes of her thighs, that made Jaykun go instantly hard for her. The reaction took him completely by surprise. Jileana was ignorant, laughing and coaxing the shopkeeper into relaxing. How was it she could do this to him? Make him forget where he was? Make him lose control over his body? He was a man in command of an empowered destiny. He held the lives of thousands of people in his hands. He controlled others; others did not control him.

Jileana then pulled the tunic up over her head in full view of the entire bazaar and let it fall to the ground. The shopkeeper gasped and Jaykun lunged forward, grabbing up the tunic and crowding her body, hiding her from view as best he could. Oblivious, Jileana was wriggling into the dress, letting it fall into place, all the while with a huge, bright smile on her face.

"Are you out of your mind?" he barked down at her. "Have you no shame?"

"About what?" she asked, genuinely clueless as to the source of his agitation.

"You can't just strip in public, Jileana!"

"Of course I can. I just did it. Weren't you watching?"

"I was! As was everyone else!"

"They've all seen a naked body before, silly. They have one of their own."

She moved over to a long looking glass and viewed herself in the purple dress. Jaykun had to admit she wore it well. He had been right about it hitting just at the knees. The skirt was made of dozens of hanging kerchiefs, each falling freely from the waistband of the dress so that when Jileana moved, if she kicked her leg out far enough, they fell away completely and left her leg bared to mid thigh or a little higher. It was indecent in Jaykun's opinion.

"I'll take this one," she said of course. "I do not have money, but we can barter for it. I could perhaps clean your home for you or watch your children. Perhaps I can teach them to read or write. I am a very good teacher. Or perhaps—"

"I have gold," Jaykun said with a sigh. "I said I would buy it."

"Then I will owe you something in trade," Jileana said with a smile. "Have you small children in need of teaching? Or perhaps you do not know how to read."

"I know how to read!" Jaykun said. "Several languages!"

"Oh, that is good," she said with a smile. "But I am certain we will figure something out."

Jaykun released a pained sigh. "It's not necessary. I don't expect repayment."

"Don't be silly. I am eating your food, sleeping in your bed, and now wearing your clothing. Or course there is repayment. Perhaps I could entertain you? You seem to like me naked, so I could strip and then—"

"It is a gift!" he said in a moment of inspiration before she could finish that thought aloud. Then again, he was incredibly curious as to where that thought would've ended up.

"A gift?" she asked, one of her arched brows lifting high. "But I have no gift to trade. Gifts are always exchanged. One gift for one gift. At least this is the way of my people."

"A gift means you don't have to trade. You get a gift for no reason at all and expect nothing in return."

"How odd," she said, her eyes drifting over him from head to toe as she took in the measure of the concept. She smiled enigmatically then. "Very well, I accept your gift for no reason at all."

"But this isn't the whole of my gift," he said hastily. "The dress . . . Well, you require undergarments and perhaps a nightgown."

"What is a nightgown?" she asked curiously.

"You wear it to bed."

She laughed. "Don't be silly. I'll be in your bed. It seems ridiculous to dress up when you will only be undressing me for sex a short while later."

The shopkeeper gasped and fumbled behind her skirts as if she would cover the ears of her small children. It was a fruitless attempt since it was too late already and they had four ears between them and she had only the two hands.

Jaykun couldn't argue the point. It was the truth. He was already beginning to obsess about the next time he would be able to get the shameless wench into his bed. His lust for her was extraordinary and it only seemed to be growing. He had never experienced such an instant attraction. Usually he had to work up to the idea of taking a woman into his bed. This had come so easily for him. So heatedly. It should have burned itself out after one coupling. Something that burned this hot and fast should die an equally quick death, should it not?

Yes. It would, he thought. She would only be there for three days and nights. It was more than enough time for this to burn out. In fact, he rather doubted he would want her beyond the second night. He ought to have her out of his system good and proper by then.

It was just . . . one coupling wasn't enough. It had been such a hurried affair. Something he had not had the proper amount of time to enjoy. Nor had he properly seen to her enjoyment. He was not a selfish lover. Not as a rule. He took his pleasure by giving pleasure to his partner. And the idea of making her writhe beneath him, of hearing her cry out, was an idea worth exploring.

To his shock, he was hard once again; just the thought of having her was able to give him sufficient stimulation. It simply amazed him.

"Very well," he said, pausing to clear the roughness from his voice. "Another dress, then. Perhaps something a bit more conservative."

CHAPTER
SIX

They found a second dress, but Jaykun would've hardly called it conservative. It had a sweetheart neckline, and the laces at the back of the gown pulled the waist in and accentuated the plumpness of Jileana's breasts until he felt that was all he could see of her. Those full, ripe breasts . . .

"Good gods, I've become a lecher," he muttered under his breath. It didn't help that she eschewed any sort of undergarment, insisting that the dresses were confining enough, thank you very much. If she must be clothed, then she must, but she wasn't going to strangle herself in clothing. Or so she said.

Once he had paid for both dresses, she led the way back toward the castle. She did, however, stop every two seconds to marvel over everything she saw. Like a child, she was attracted to bright colors, things that blew in the breeze, things that made noise or entertained. She spent a good half hour in a toy booth, playing with each and every children's toy she got her hands on. He ought to have hurried her along—he was wasting crucial time with her—but he didn't have the heart to interrupt her pleasure. The truth was, she was a pleasure to watch. Her long, loose hair blew in the ocean breezes that came in off the water. The sun danced on her warm, dark skin and her shiny lips. Every time she smiled she flashed brilliant white teeth, and every time she laughed it was absolutely infectious. Every Krizan they encountered was guarded and nearly hostile at first, but by the time she left a booth, she seemed to have warmed them to her considerably.

"I should make you my ambassador," he mused a bit later as they left the bazaar and headed up toward the castle. "You have that kind of charm about you, the kind that puts all parties instantly at ease."

"Oh, I don't think that would be wise. The Krizans have no more trust for my people than they do for yours. And with good reason. The Krizans have long sought a means of getting to my people's home to destroy us."

"Really? And where is your people's home?"

She smiled and took his hand in hers. "Come. I will show you."

She pulled him after her so quickly he had to run to keep up with her. She took him into the castle and then ran all around it, taking every flight of stairs she could find. She didn't know the castle any better than he did, but she knew she wanted to go up. Eventually they burst out onto the castle's battlements. She pulled him to the ocean-facing side and pointed off toward the horizon.

"There," she said, pointing to a dark gathering of storm clouds. It was clear that a violent storm was out in that part of the ocean.

"Where the storm is?" he asked as he peered over at it. He could see nothing. But if he looked to the left, he could see the small speck that was his next target, the Isle of Moroun. His eventual goal was to cross the ocean and head to the next continent, his newly acquired armada in tow, but first he would conquer Moroun.

"Yes. It is called Serenmitazahmiktubarinaty."

"Say that again?" he said with an astounded laugh.

"You can call it Serenity if you cannot say the full of it. Serenmitazahmiktubarinaty is unique, the most beautiful island you would ever know. You'll never find its like anywhere else."

"And yet we seem to have much more here than there. I can tell by your reactions to so many things."

"What you have here is *different* . . . not more. I could show you things in my world I expect would have you just as wide with wonder as I find myself to be in your world."

"Perhaps. Perhaps I should go to your world, meet with your leaders. We could discuss erecting temples to Weysa."

"And if we do not agree you will try to conquer us?"

"Perhaps," he said honestly.

"You would fail."

"Do you have an army? An armada?"

"Serenity protects itself from outsiders like you. We have no need for anything else as far as that is concerned. However, my father is leader of our legion. The legion protects us against our other enemies. Enemies far different from you."

"Different how?"

"Let's just say you should be glad the world of men holds no appeal for them."

"World of men? Is there any other kind of world?" he asked, a bit confused.

"Of course there is. You are well traveled; surely you have learned that there are many worlds out there."

"You mean races, civilizations. Yes. There are many. But in the end, we are all human. We all have two legs, two arms. We all have males and females, and we all make children and make war upon one another. Your land and people are no different."

"True, there are many similarities. But there are just as many dissimilarities."

"If your world is so protected, so distant, how is it you come to be here?"

She gave him an enigmatic little smile. "There are ways if you know them. There are special times. And believe me when I tell you, my father would be very angry if he knew where I was right now. So too would my brothers. But I will worry about that when I return three days from now." Her smile broadened. "Perhaps by then you will want to come with me. You cannot bring your army but you can come yourself. And maybe you can go before the empress of our people and perhaps she will erect a temple to your goddess. But I do not see many of our people worshipping your goddess. We worship the goddess of the land and oceans because that is what is known to us. Diathus protects her children, keeps us healthy and safe. We know no other gods."

"You know of them."

"Of course we do. But we are Diathus's children." She gave him a bright smile. "Now come. I believe it is time for our meal. Then I must let you go to your brothers so you can carry on with your business of the day. I have already monopolized your morning."

She was right. She had. The entire morning had gone by and he had not even realized it. His brothers were probably beside themselves wondering what had become of him. Still, they were more than capable of functioning without him and he was sure they had plenty to do, taking over this city and making it their own. So too did he. But he had promised her one meal a day and he was a man of his word.

He entered the main dining hall where the brothers' personal chefs were already laying out a meal for Jaykun and his chief aides. His brothers were there as well and suddenly he had the urge to take a more private meal with her. She would find herself lost amongst all these men. Amongst all the tasks and discussions that would no doubt be overshadowing the meal. Tomorrow he would see things done differently, but for now, he had no choice but to let it happen. As it was, his brothers would be champing at the bit for him to get on with the day's considerable business.

The looks they shot him as he entered the hall revealed as much. But he didn't really care. In his mind the morning had been well spent. Actually, it had been a really good morning, an easy one. And he had not enjoyed such for a very long time. His life was one of long, hard campaigns, one after another, eyes always set on the next goal. That morning his goals had been simple, not pressing or weighty. He realized he was grateful to her for it. It would not—*could* not—last of course, but it had been nice while it had been happening. He only wished he had appreciated it more.

He sat down at the head of the table, a position given to him by his brothers in deference to his rank over them. Dethan may be the eldest, but this was Jaykun's army and they wanted everyone to know it. The next available seat at the table was several places down on the left and Jaykun frowned. He hardly thought his promise of a meal with her consisted of her being out of comfortable speaking distance.

"Would everyone be so kind as to shift down," he asked of those on the left. They all paused their conversations and actions as if they had been suddenly caught in amber. Then, slowly, everyone on the left, including his brother Garreth, stood up and shifted down one seat. Luckily, Garreth did so without verbal comment, but his discontent was obvious. What it boiled down to, however, was that Jaykun's word was law and it must be respected and obeyed . . . and his brothers must be the first to set the example or there would be discontent and chaos in the ranks.

Jaykun held Jileana's chair for her as she sat. Once she was in front of her plate, he took his own seat, and realizing how hungry he was, he began to pile food onto his plate. However, neither him nor his brothers could keep up with Jileana. She was voracious, taking one of everything and then some. She didn't overstuff her mouth but instead seemed to savor every single bite.

"Oh, this is all so good! What do you call this? And this? Oh, and what about this?"

"We call it food. Do they starve you where you are from?"

She looked at Garreth and smiled in the face of his acerbic tone. "Hardly that. As I have said, it is different. I should like to bring knowledge of some of these things back with me. Can you tell me how this is made?" She held out a piece of bread.

"It's just bread. You've no bread?"

"No. And this is so warm and fluffy. It all but melts in my mouth. And yet it is chewy. Isn't it delightful?"

"Thrilling," Garreth said with a sigh.

If he'd been closer, Jaykun would have kicked his brother under the table. But the truth was, Garreth was tired and missing his wife and child. He wanted to go home to them, and the longer it took Jaykun to get entrenched in this city, the longer Garreth and Dethan would stay by his side. Winter was coming and it would take several weeks overland at best before they got home. With ships, the time could be made considerably shorter. However, the ships in the harbor were run by Krizan crews, crews that were not to be trusted if this morning's incident was anything to go by. And most of the men who had crewed those ships had died in the battle.

As if Dethan were reading his mind, Dethan said,

"Only half the armada is in dock. The other half is in the harbor or missing. We need to fetch the escaping ships."

"They shouldn't get too far," Garreth said. "They must have nothing but the barest of crews. I say we send several ships to run them down one by one. Bring them back to the harbor."

"First we need to know how many we are talking about," Jaykun said.

"Honestly, I thought there would be more missing," Garreth mused.

"They simply didn't have the manpower to sail them after throwing all their men at us. Poor planning on the part of their ruler," Jaykun said.

"The whole battle was executed poorly. This city should have lasted indefinitely in a siege against us. They had the ocean at their backs and could constantly resupply, keep from starving, and yet the shops are all but bare, the bazaar skin and bones," Jaykun reported. "It shouldn't take too long to get it back into shape, but still, what was going on here? How had the finia thought to stand against us or save her people from us? How could such a poor leader be in such a powerful position?"

"How can you ask that? You have seen it yourselves time and again. These titles are inherited, not earned. The people follow a bloodline, not a leader. It's laughable."

Garreth chuckled. "So says the man whose wife inherited her title and city," he teased Dethan.

"Be that as it may," Dethan said, grinning good-naturedly, "when it came down to it, the stronger leader prevailed. My wife is very powerful in her own right and in her love for her people. With me at her side, our city will not fall to any invading forces."

"But you are not at her side," Garreth pointed out

quietly. "A battle could be won and lost while we are here so far away from our homes."

"Easy, brother," Jaykun soothed Garreth. "You'll be home soon enough. Within the next month. I guarantee it. With ships at our disposal, we'll cut the journey in half for Dethan and take at least a week off for you as well. I'll have you back at my sisters' sides before first frost. I vow this to you."

"Then let us get to business," Garreth said impatiently. "You're wasting time . . . allowing distraction." Garreth didn't have to look at Jileana. They both knew who and what he was talking about.

"Enough!" Jaykun barked, making his younger brother jump in his own skin. "I do not need you to remind me of my duties and responsibilities. The gods give me reminder enough every day at dusk!"

"Garreth didn't mean—" Dethan began.

"Then what did he mean?" Jaykun snapped. "That I am not to have even the smallest pleasure? A fraction of a moment where war and duty does not consume me?" Both brothers fell silent. They were being selfish and they knew it. They were not by nature selfish men, but they were missing their families and the strain of it was starting to wear on them.

"Don't worry," Jileana spoke up with a bright smile. "I shall see to it that you have a great deal of pleasure in order to balance out your duties. And I will restrict our mating to the night so it won't interfere with your daily duties."

Jaykun had been considering taking a drink of wine and was suddenly glad he had not done so. He might have choked on it. Or he might have thought he was in his cups and hearing her wrongly. But the truth of it was, she meant every word and had absolutely no compunctions about announcing those words in public. He heard chuckles rippling down the table and he actually had to will himself not to blush in front of his men. Did the woman have no shame?

That was his second thought, however. His first thought was immediately picturing her as he had seen her the night before: long, sleek limbs; bare, beautiful skin; and emitting sensual sounds of pleasure. The idea of seeing her thus once again was more than a little appealing.

Actually, the craving for it was overwhelming. She was such a passionate creature in everything she did, so direct and voracious for everything she could possibly experience. He had never known anyone like her. He appreciated her honesty, her candor. She did not play games. She said exactly what was on her mind, expressed her desires and wishes the moment she knew what they were. The idea of having a woman like that in his bed was arousing to the extreme. She did not waste time being coy or demurring; she devoured her pleasure just as she devoured her food, savoring every bite and gorging herself on each flavor to be had.

She shot him a look that practically set the air to sizzling. She craved him just as he craved her, he realized. Oh, thank the gods! The idea that she had all the power between them was more than a little disquieting. But the fact that she had desire for him meant that he had at least some kind of power too.

Jaykun jumped in his seat when he felt a hand brush up the length of his inner thigh beneath the table. It was a brief touch, one that felt more reassuring than it did seductive. Just the same, the heat that ripped through him was overwhelming and suddenly he craved things far beyond the meal in front of him.

"Jileana, I prefer we not discuss these things in public," he said tightly. He could control this, he told himself firmly. He was the master of his own fate and in command of everything around him. He could easily control his passions for a simple woman.

"Why not?" she asked with her usual openness. "I thought you would want your brothers to be reassured that our sexual meetings would not interfere with your daily responsibilities."

Dethan chuckled. "I feel reassured," he said with a great deal of mirth in his tone.

Jaykun was overwhelmed with the urge to smack him on the back of his head. Both he and Garreth were enjoying his discomfiture far too much.

"I'm not sure I do," Garreth said with a grin. "Just how often are we talking about here? Once a night? Twice? The man has to get his sleep."

"I thought perhaps—"

"Do not answer him!" Jaykun cut her off sharply even though he was damned curious as to what the answer would be. The idea of having her once was overwhelming enough, but twice? More? As often as he could gorge himself on her? The idea was beyond appealing. "Both of you stop," he warned them harshly, "or you'll find yourself battling me back in the practice ring."

"Oh! Please don't stop," Jileana said eagerly to his brothers. "I should like to see that. I watch my father and brothers practice all the time. It is a fine way of seeing the warrior in a man." She slid Jaykun a hot little look. "I would very much like to see the warrior in you. I find the idea most stimulating."

"Oh, I think that could be arranged," Dethan said with a snicker as he ignored his brother's deadly glare. "Maybe we can knock some sense into him in the process."

"Which of you will it be?" she asked eagerly. "You are much larger than Jaykun is, and you are much smaller," she said to first Dethan, then Garreth. "A smaller man is usually faster. A larger man often has more power. Perhaps I should like to see you both. Not together of course, because that would be unfair, but each individually."

"You know, I really would appreciate it if you all stopped making plans for me without consulting me."

Jileana turned a warm, beautiful smile on him and he felt his temper dissolve away instantly. It was a reaction that simply floored him.

"Oh, of course we aren't making plans without you. You are sitting right here. If you had any arguments, you would certainly bring them up, just as you are right now. So which is it you prefer? Your larger brother or your smaller one?"

"It doesn't matter because I can beat them both," Jaykun muttered.

"Ha! Not likely!" Dethan scoffed.

"Hardly," Garreth chimed in.

"I can and I will. First you, little man," he said to Garreth. "An easy fight to warm me up. Then you, you lumbering ass. Maybe if I put you both in your places you'll stop bothering me!"

"Wonderful! When shall we do it? After this meal?" Jileana asked.

"Why wait?" Jaykun said, surging to his feet.

"Easy, brother," Dethan said with a chuckle, reaching to grab Jaykun's forearm and pull him back down into his chair. "You have promised the lady a meal and so you shall give it to her. Practice can wait until later. We will arrange it for an hour before supper, two hours before dusk. This way we can get some other work done first and have time to digest our meals."

"That makes every bit of sense," Jileana agreed. "Where will it be?"

"There is a practice ring to the east of the castle. The

men have already been using it. We'll meet there at the appointed time."

"Very well," Jaykun muttered as he pulled his chair back up to his plate. His brothers were right. The meal he had promised Jileana ought to come first.

The rest of the meal seemed to pass in something of a fog for him. He was trying to figure out exactly how she had managed to get exactly what she wanted out of him every single time so far. She didn't seem to ask for anything, and yet he found himself performing to her pleasure. Sex, shopping, eating, and now fighting. All done for her pleasure. The understanding bemused him. It occupied his mind quite frequently throughout the rest of the afternoon.

After the meal, she had dutifully drifted out of his reach, going off to do who knew what, who knew where. It had concerned him a little. She seemed to have a knack for doing and saying things that might cause trouble, so he had been concerned about leaving her to her own devices. Especially in a castle full of a hostile species. She had made it clear to all and sundry that she shared a place of intimacy with him. It wasn't so farfetched an idea that someone might try to hurt her as a means of sending a message to him.

It was thoughts like this that kept him listening to his brothers with only half his attention.

CHAPTER
SEVEN

Jileana was sitting in the stands that ringed half the practice circle. They were wooden and rough, and rose up only to about six levels, but it was enough to afford each person a good view of the arena. The stands were crowded save for the seats on either side of her. It seemed no one wanted to sit too close to her. No one Krizan, that is. Which was to be expected, really. However, it was only a short length of time before a couple of Jaykun's men, two of the men who had been seated at the table for lunch earlier, filled in the places beside her.

In the practice circle, Jaykun was giving his sword several test swings. He was stripped down to his bare chest and a pair of breeches, his pants tucked into his knee-high black leather boots. The snug material of those pants clung to every thick muscle in his legs and Jileana found herself staring at them with increasing covetousness. His bare chest and arms were nothing to sneeze at either. She had never seen a man with so many well-developed muscles; her people tended to be sleeker and leaner. His skin was tanned and smooth, nearly flawless now that he'd had an entire day to heal from his trial of the night before. It seemed that his body healed to a certain point of perfection. Each night she had watched him burn away until he was nothing but a skeleton, and by the time the next night approached he looked as though it had never happened.

Magic. It was some kind of magic. He said it was the curse of the gods and she believed him. Only the touch of the gods could make this happen to a man. She found herself wondering exactly what a man had to do to cause a god to exact such a vicious sort of vengeance on him. Her father and brothers would have wanted her to put as much distance between him and herself as possible, probably for fear of attracting the attention of an angry god toward her. But they had always been overprotective. To her mind, that made no sense. Surely a god wouldn't become angry with her just for being near someone they had cursed. Would a god be so capricious?

Then again, the legends of the gods told all kinds of stories about their volatile tempers. They were more apt to take vengeance on a mortal than they were to bless or gift that mortal, if the stories attributed to them were to be believed.

And even in her distant world, she thought she'd heard the story of immortal brothers cursed by the gods. The story of four men who had found and stolen the gifts of the Fount of Immortality without truly earning the blessing from the gods. In their rage the gods had cursed each brother to a torment worse than any imaginable: one brother cast into the pits of hell; another chained to that very mountain, doomed to freeze again and again; and the third chained to a star.

A star.

Bright as a star. He burned as bright as a star. Somehow he had been released from the star and yet still suffered as though he were still chained to it.

She wondered about the fourth brother. The legend had never been specific about the fourth brother's torment, only that the god Sabo had been in charge of the reckoning and that it was an unspeakable torment just like his siblings suffered.

And yet three of the four immortal brothers must have been sitting at luncheon with her today. How amazing that she was touching such an unbelievable legend.

And how sad. How sad she was for Jaykun, that he must suffer so. Did his brothers still suffer as he did? How had they come to be free? There was a story there and she craved the hearing of it.

But it would come in its own time, she realized, trying to force patience on herself. Jaykun would reveal himself to her just as slowly, no doubt, as she would reveal herself to him. They both had their stories, both had their mysteries. Both would tell their tales as they got to know each other better.

And she truly did want to know him better. She could not say exactly why she found him so compelling, why she had immediately allowed herself to be drawn in by him and his world, only that these were the most exciting moments of her life thus far. She was tired of her sheltered existence. Running away, in her opinion, was the best thing she had ever done. Oh, she knew she would have no choice but to go back in three days' time, but at least she could say she had done this, that she had come away from her protected world and done something exciting and different and new. And who knew? Maybe she would do it again someday. But the odds were that there would be no Jaykun at that time. He no doubt would have moved on by then. Never looking back.

Well, she would look back. She would make these three days into something so wonderful that she could look back on them with awe and delight. And so far she was succeeding famously. She had eaten wonderful food, had shopped for beautiful things, and had acquired a fine lover. A lover, she realized, she had only just begun to sample. And as he entered the ring and faced off with his youngest brother, her heart pounded with excitement at the very thought. Jaykun must suffer his nightly torment at dusk, but afterward . . . afterward he would be hers to do with as she pleased.

Garreth was faster than Jaykun—it was true—but it quickly became obvious that he was outmatched. Jaykun moved with sleek grace but also a thunderous power that beat Garreth back over and over again. In the end, he simply wore the smaller man out with his unrelenting barrage of sword strokes.

Garreth yielded. Jileana cheered Jaykun loudly, clapping her hands and whooping with victorious delight as if she had been the one to personally win the battle. She saw Jaykun grin and he saluted her with his sword. Jileana heard the men beside her chuckling, but she didn't care. Jaykun had won! Couldn't they see how magnificent he was?

"He is a fine warrior," she said aloud and to no one in particular.

"He is the best there is. Closely rivaled by his eldest brother," the man seated on her right said. "But Dethan is fresh and Jaykun has just done battle. I doubt he can withstand Dethan's attack."

"You are wrong. He will win," she said with all the confidence in the world—this in spite of the fact she knew nothing of Dethan's fighting style or strengths and little of Jaykun's. All she knew was what she wanted. She wanted him to win. She wanted him to be victorious. Not that she didn't like his brothers—it was clear they were fine men, if a bit too serious. She simply wanted victory. A victory to be celebrated.

Dethan was a powerful fighter. His overhand barrages sent echoes of metal ringing hard through the air as Jaykun parried every blow. His body flexed beneath each contact, straining to shove his brother off him each time. Ever wily, he made certain half of Dethan's strikes never found a sticking point to begin with. These moves made her cheer some more, as loudly as she could. She wanted him to know she was in his corner, that she was by his side in spirit if not in body.

Her faith was rewarded. Jaykun turned swiftly, and suddenly Dethan hit the ground face-first, his sword flying from his hand. Jaykun put the point of his sword to his brother's neck and Dethan laughed. He could hardly be heard over the woman shouting wildly from the risers across the way.

"You have me, brother," Dethan said, holding up his hands in submission.

"I do indeed," Jaykun said, holding a hand out to his brother and helping him to his feet. Both men were covered in sweat and dirt, and both were breathing hard with their exertions. Dethan bent to fetch his sword and looked over at Jileana, who was fumbling her way out of the crowd of people seated around her.

"You've made someone very happy," Dethan said with a chuckle.

"How can you tell?" Jaykun asked with amusement.

"Whatever have you done to inspire such fast loyalty, I wonder," Dethan baited.

"Hush," Jaykun scolded, smacking his brother's leg with the flat of his blade.

Jileana was across the ring and launching herself into his arms in the next instant. She was a projectile of black, flying hair and loud, delighted excitement.

"You've done it!" she exclaimed. "It was wonderful!"

"I am glad you thought so. I could not tell," he teased her.

"I know I promised to do so only at night," she said

breathlessly, "but I would very much like to have sex with you right now!"

Dethan burst into laughter and Jaykun felt his neck flushing red. On the other hand, his body was instantly reacting to the suggestion. He jerked her up close and tight to his body and caught her audacious mouth with his own. He kissed her until she was breathing as hard as he was and his blood was singeing with a heat that had nothing to do with his exertions of just minutes ago.

"Well, it's all right with me," Dethan said, still laughing. "How about you, Garreth?"

"Shut up," Jaykun warned before his youngest sibling could chime in. He tossed his blade to Dethan and grabbed hold of Jileana. He swung her up off her feet, into his arms, and carried her from the practice ring into the castle. At the first shadowed hall he could find, he backed her up against a wall and pressed his body along the front of hers.

"You have to stop doing that," he growled against her ear.

"Doing what?" she asked, her soft breaths panting into his hair as he nuzzled her hotly.

"Talking about sex."

"But it was the truth. Do you not prefer when I tell the truth?"

"I do prefer it, though I take exception to you telling it in front of my brothers. At least the parts about sex. It is unseemly to speak thusly in front of other men."

"Unseemly? Oh. I do not wish to be unseemly. Do I?"

His hands shaped around her waist, feeling the sleek curves of her sides. The truth was, if she were seemly, she very likely would not be letting him touch her like this. Last night he had mistaken her for a camp follower or a woman who might sell her sexual favors for a betterment of her life . . . but he had long since come to realize that was not the case. Jileana was merely forthright and honest about her desires. She knew her mind and knew it quickly. Somehow he had been lucky enough to gain her favor and she had not wasted time with seemly behaviors. Yes, he decided, this was much better than all the courting nonsense he didn't have the time or the inclination for.

His inclination was for the full, warm flesh of a willing woman in his hands and that was exactly what he had. His hand traveled up to her breast and he heard her breath catch.

"Actually, now that I am thinking on it, I rather like you unseemly."

She sighed in exasperation. "You are confusing me. I want to do what you wish me to do. Tell me what it is you would like me to change."

He looked down into her iridescent green eyes. "Nothing," he whispered on a soft breath. "Nothing at all. You are perfect as you are. Forgive me. I am merely . . . I am not used to a woman who speaks her mind so clearly."

"Women of your people do not speak their minds?"

"No. They play games. They like to tease and make promises they don't intend to fulfill."

"Well, I like to tease," she said slyly, "but I intend to fulfill every promise I make to you. Else I will not make it."

"Good. I like that," he said heatedly. "Gods above, you smell good. And feel good. And if memory serves, you taste good as well."

"Why rely on memory? I am here now. Taste me."

He groaned softly and caught her up in his hands, pulling her up onto her toes as his mouth descended onto hers. Her lips were plush and wet, warm and oh so willing. She opened her mouth to him, inviting him in deep with her tongue. With a deeply indrawn breath, he devoured her, took her with every ounce of intensity he could muster. He kissed her until she was moaning with pleasure, reveling in the feel and taste of him. Her hands climbed his arms and neck and reached into his hair. She gripped at him, her grasp fevered and passionate. His hands came to her breasts, feeling the plumpness of them through the depth of that sweetheart neckline. But the dress was laced in back and frustrated his efforts. He fumbled at her back for the laces and she made a sound of frustration.

"Too many clothes," she panted.

He couldn't have agreed more. As soon as the laces were free he pulled away from her mouth and lowered his lips to the swells of her breasts. She smelled so good, the scent of soft femininity and sweet musk. She reminded him of a kelp flower, a particularly fragrant blossom that grew in ocean inlets, around docks and jetties and other relatively still places in the ocean.

He drew the neckline of her dress down, baring both of her breasts to the nipple. By all rights he should be taking her to the privacy of his chambers, but he couldn't seem to make himself stop. He couldn't keep himself from filling his mouth with one of the sweet, pointed tips. He sucked on her until she gasped from the pressure. Suddenly his hands were under her skirt, grabbing her thighs and hoisting her up the wall so he would not have to bend to reach her. The next he knew, a pair of strong, lithe thighs were locking around him, dragging him in tight. He could feel the heat of her, beckoning to him, reminding him she had nothing on beneath the dress . . . nothing but warm and willing flesh. She moaned in his ear as he shifted from one breast to the next.

"I wish to be having sex with you now," she breathed into his ear. It made a laugh burst out of him and he left her breasts to meet her eyes.

"I thought that was what we were doing," he said, his hand continuing to stroke and fondle her.

"No, I mean I wish for you to be inside me," she explained, wriggling down the wall a little, her hands diving past her bunched up skirts and beyond the waist of his pants. His belly contracted at the sudden feel of her against his bare skin, but his cock leapt eagerly for the touch of her hand. He groaned soulfully as she wrapped her fingers around him with one hand and struggled to work his clothing open with the other. He tried to help her, but they only got in each other's way and he could barely focus as she stroked him from root to tip again and again until he thought he would embarrass himself by the time she got him free. But at last she did, and after that she wasted no time pulling him in toward her, using the vise of her legs to bring him in tight, using her hand to guide him straight to the open warmth of her waiting body. Then between his own thrusting hips and her reaching body, they brought him inside her in a single crash of movement. She cried out loudly and he didn't bother to hush her. He wasn't exactly being quiet himself. He had shouted out at the moment their bodies met, the pleasure of it too much to contain inside him. There was no explaining how it felt to be surrounded by her. It was like a stunning, living sensation that shot through all of his nerve endings at once.

He looked into her eyes and began to thrust into her in rhythmic, hard bursts. He had never seen such pretty eyes before. Their iridescent color was something unique, and they were framed by lashes as lush as the feel of her body around him. She was so warm and wet it was driving him mad. The speed of his thrusts and the violence of them increased. He liked to see the way her body shimmered at the impacts, liked to hear the grunts and cries that erupted from her. He wanted to make her scream out. Yes, even as exposed as they were, potential witnesses or even enemies all around them, he wanted her to cry out, give away their location, let everyone know that he was the one giving pleasure to her.

His hands fumbled past her skirts until he was gripping her by her bare backside, jerking her forward onto him with every thrust. Fire raced through his veins, warning him that he would not last much longer. But he would not have that until he had made her find her full pleasure.

What he didn't know was that Jileana was closer to spinning away with pleasure than he could have imagined. She had felt it from the first thrust, her body designed for passion and so eager to accept it. She was fighting herself to make the act last longer than it might have otherwise. She didn't want it to be over too soon, to be forced to come apart from him . . . to leave him behind. She liked being together with him . . . really liked it. If she had her way, it would never end.

But it had to end. She knew it. She let herself give over to it. She threw her head back and cried out, her entire body tensing as pure fire washed over her again and again.

Jaykun felt her come around him and it blinded him with ferocious pleasure. He surged up into her, plunging into her one last time, and then let the pleasure of it overtake him. He came with a roar so savage it would have frightened away any of his foes had they heard him. Actually, Jileana was quite convinced they couldn't have helped but hear him. Hear them both.

Jaykun's knees gave out and they collapsed to the floor together, their bodies still connected. Jaykun had landed on his knees, Jileana's backside resting on his thighs. Her long legs were settled loosely around him, her skirts bunched up between them as they both panted hard for breath.

"Oh, that was very . . ."

"Yes," he said breathlessly.

"Well, we should . . ."

"Definitely," he said.

"In a minute," she said.

"Yes. In a minute." Jaykun touched his forehead to hers. "You make me forget myself."

"You make me remember all kinds of things, including myself. I had forgotten things could feel like this. In fact, I don't think I've ever felt like this before."

That brought Jaykun up short. He drew his head back and met her eyes. "Jileana, I think I should be clear," he said, tension filling his voice. "I've no space for a woman in my life. My curse makes it so that I will never be free to feel anything for a woman. Nothing will come of this . . . no relationship."

She looked at him a long moment, then tossed back her head and laughed. "Of course not, you silly man! Oh my, as if I ever could! No, no. We can certainly feel much between us. Yes, we can be free to do that. But there is no permanence to this relationship in the least."

Her statements took him aback. The fact that she found the idea of having a lasting relationship with him amusing rather irritated him. It shouldn't of course. He should be glad she understood this was only for the short term. He should feel relieved. Instead he felt put out.

The feeling bothered him. Everything about her bothered him. He stood up in a surge of movement, setting her on her feet and then quickly redressing himself. She took the opportunity to tuck her breasts back into her dress and he tried to ignore the pang of regret it caused. He realized that, if it was completely up to him, he would prefer to have her naked at all times.

A dangerous thought, that. She too would prefer to be naked, if he read her right. Not for lustful reasons, but just because she seemed to dislike clothing. If she had even an inkling of what his thoughts were, she might take to running around the castle completely nude.

Then he would definitely get nothing done, he thought honestly. As much as he had weighing on him, he would spend the next few days obsessing in his lust for her.

And she . . . Would she feel just as obsessed? She acted so passionately and then seemed so dispassionate.

But of course that was what he wanted, he told himself. He wanted no entanglements. She was actually quite perfect for his needs. He would vent some much-needed lust upon her and then send her on her way. They would enjoy themselves together for these three days and then he would see to it she was gone. He had a lot of other things to focus on. First of which was getting the army established in the city well enough that his brothers could return to their homes for the winter. Then he would spend the winter preparing his men and seeing to it the armada was readied. They would manage the city, make it their own, then leave in the spring with the Krizan armada and an army swelled with any Krizan soldiers who remained willing to fight for coin. With every city they took, his army grew larger and larger, until now it was nearly invincible. With these ships they could finally leave the continent and bring the word of Weysa to even more foreign lands. It was more than he could have asked for.

So, yes, he would take a few days to enjoy himself with her. Just a few. After that he would send her on her way.

"Besides," she said, "I have to leave here in three days' time and am not likely to come back for quite some time. I imagine you will be gone by then, moving on to your next conquest."

"I . . . Y-yes, I will," he said, surprised she was thinking along the same lines he was.

"Very good, then." She reached out and patted his

arm. "Now you go find your brothers or whatever it is you have to do. I thought I might go to the kitchens."

"You are hungry?" he asked. "Dinner will be ready shortly."

"Ah. You eat early, before the sun sets. Of course. That would make sense. No, I am just curious about the place where all that delicious food is made. I think I should like to watch."

"Oh. I see. Well . . . enjoy yourself."

She smiled brightly at him. "Oh, I intend to!"

"But you will eat with us, yes?" he asked her, suddenly needing to know when he would see her next.

"Would you like me to?" she asked. It wasn't a coy remark, merely an openly curious one.

"Of course. You should eat with the rest of us."

"Because the bargain we made was only for one meal a day."

"D-don't you want to eat with me—er—us?" He was starting to stammer like a fool, he realized. Damn it, what was wrong with him all of a sudden?

"Of course I do! Thank you for inviting me! I do so love your food when in good company."

"Well, I certainly wouldn't starve you."

"Of course not. I would simply eat in the kitchens if it came down to it." She smiled softly at him then, reaching to touch light fingers across his left pectoral muscle. "But I am going to be much happier eating with you. I enjoy you as much as I enjoy the food."

"I should hope so," he said with a chuckle. "It wouldn't say much for me otherwise. How about from this point on you share all of your meals with me? I mean . . . if that is what you would like." It suddenly occurred to him that she might want to be elsewhere. She really didn't seem to need his company.

The understanding flummoxed him. He should be glad she was so independent. And he was. It was important that she be so. He would not have been attracted to her in the least had she been the needy, clingy sort. Nothing would have turned him off quicker than that. But at the same time her complete lack of need for him rankled somehow. He couldn't explain it. Especially when knowing he should be feeling otherwise.

"Okay, I'll be going now," she said, bouncing up onto her toes to give him a quick kiss on his cheek. Then, with a flounce of flying dark hair, she was off and away, disappearing around a quick turn in the hall.

Jaykun slowly headed in the other direction, finishing redressing his appearance as he went. He barely made it to the next turn before he came up against his brothers, both standing shoulder-to-shoulder and barring his way. He huffed with frustration.

"What is it?" he demanded of them.

"We are concerned about this girl," Dethan said. "Exactly where did she come from? What is her purpose here? Why has she attached herself to you?"

"Don't you find it a tad coincidental that she has chosen to bed the man who has conquered her city?" Garreth said.

"This isn't her city," Jaykun said, pushing past them.

"Well, not by the look of her," Garreth conceded. "She's not Krizan—that much is clear. But there are no other cities for a great many leagues . . ."

"She's from an island and a city called . . . Serenity." He wasn't about to attempt to say the real name of Jileana's home city. His brother's wouldn't have been able to absorb it any better than he had.

"Serenity? What island? The only island within a day's sailing is Moroun. Perhaps she is a spy from Moroun. They have no doubt heard of our advancement toward Kriza and realized they are next in our path once we gain use of the Krizan armada."

"There is another isle . . . Moroun is northeast; her home is to the southeast."

"Another isle? I saw nothing from the battlements yesterday when I was up there," Dethan said.

"Perhaps it was too far for you to see. I could not see it either because of the storms in the distance."

Garreth scoffed and grabbed hold of Jaykun's arm, dragging him to a stop. "And yet you believe her?"

"I have no reason not to," Jaykun bit out.

"You have every reason not to!" Garreth said. "We are in enemy territory. You would be mad to relax your guard for even a moment! It seems to me that someone around here is thinking with his body parts far too distant from his brain. He's letting a sweet piece turn his head and—!"

Garreth was cut off when a solid blow connected with his jaw. The youngest brother staggered until his back hit a wall. Stunned, he rubbed his aching jaw and stared hard at his brother.

"What the fuck was that for?" Garreth demanded to know.

"I . . ." Jaykun's body was full of tension and outrage, but for the life of him he couldn't understand what had driven him to strike his own brother. "Just . . . just stop questioning me about this. I trust her."

"How in the eight hells can you trust her? She's a total gods-damned stranger!" Dethan barked.

"Because she saved my life!" Jaykun bit back.

The announcement seemed to startle the brothers.

"That's right," Jaykun said. "That assassin this morning? She was this close to running a dagger through my eye. But Jileana stopped her. It was a remarkable feat of strength, really, and fast reflexes at that. I've never seen anything more beautiful in my life."

"But Jay . . . you couldn't have been killed. You're immortal."

"I can be killed, brothers," he reminded them both. "A god-made weapon, remember? And anyway, how was she to know that? How was she to know for certain?"

That sobered the entire trio of brothers and they stood quietly for several moments as they absorbed the impact of the understanding. Even Jaykun found himself inspecting the reason why he had come to trust her so quickly. But if he were going to be honest, he would have to admit to his brothers that he had extended trust even before the incident that morning. He had extended trust the moment he allowed himself to fall asleep in bed with her, something he never did. He had never—not once since his release from his curse, which had allowed him to live somewhat free once more—fallen asleep beside a woman. Women were to be briefly used to satisfy carnal needs, and he had not done even that since his resurrection into the world. He did not in any way relax his guard . . . especially not enough to sleep with a woman.

But Jileana . . . She was different. She was brilliant and amusing and sensual and passionate and, yes, trustworthy. He wouldn't explain it any more than he already had. Just thinking about her and all of her qualities had him obsessing about the moment he would get to see her again . . . a desire so strong he was afraid to examine it.

"I don't wish to discuss this any further," he said, turning his back on his brothers and walking away. It seemed of late that everything in his life was filled with Jileana. It was disturbing. But he comforted himself with the knowledge that she was his to do with as he pleased for three days, and then he would gladly send her on her way. There was nothing wrong in indulging himself for a short while, was there? Surely Weysa would not begrudge him this small comfort.

It did seem, however, that his brothers would. They hurried past him and blocked his way again.

"Jaykun, you're not seeing this clearly," Dethan argued. He was hoping that Jaykun would hear him and listen to his advice as he had always done throughout their relationship. Jaykun had always acceded to Dethan because he had always been under Dethan's command or simply because Dethan was the eldest brother.

"I see it all too clearly," Jaykun said. "I see that my two brothers are afraid of a single woman. Dethan, she cannot hurt me even if she wanted to. Even if she is a spy, what good would it do her? Moroun already knows we are coming. It is obvious where we are heading. Once we begin to make peaceful overtures of negotiation, it will be clear to them what we want and what we will do if they don't peacefully agree to build temples in Weysa's name. So if she is a spy, then let her be a spy. It will do Moroun no good. In the meantime, I will be able to enjoy her the way a woman should be enjoyed."

"But wouldn't you rather know if she is playing you, brother? If she is . . . faking it all?" Garreth asked carefully, not wishing to get punched in the face again.

Jaykun smiled. Truly, deep down smiled. "Trust me, brother," he said with amusement in his eyes. "There is no way that woman is faking her pleasure. Now, enough of this. We have more important things to manage at the moment."

Jaykun pushed past them once more and headed down the passageway.

But as the topic finally moved away from Jileana, he found himself obsessed with a niggling doubt. Faking it? Could she be faking it? Could she be playing him? Was it possible she was expertly managing him in order to spy on him and his brothers? His instincts said no, believed that everything about her was exactly what it seemed to be. But his brain had been cursed by his brothers' thoughts and words, and now he found himself calling everything into question.

What if . . . what if she was getting close to him just to find a way to kill him? What if she was spying on behalf of her people? How could he find out the truth? What would he do if he discovered this to be true?

He had no answers for any of it, and it left him completely disturbed.

CHAPTER
EIGHT

All throughout dinner, Jileana got the feeling that Jaykun was heavily preoccupied. He spoke very little to anyone who tried to engage him, and after two attempts to draw him into conversation, she stopped trying. She would not force him to be social with her if that was not what he wished. She was simply content to be spending time with him no matter what his mood. She had never found anyone so fascinating and enjoyable before. Of course a lot of that had to do with how different he was, how alien he was to her in comparison to her own people. Everything about him was a new and fascinating experience.

And, she had to admit, their couplings were quite erotic and satisfying. Oh yes . . . She hoped he felt more social later on, because she would like very much to be able to communicate her passion for him. She had never known such a craving for a male before. Perhaps it was because she had never mated with a man not of her race before; the newness and differentness fascinated her, making more out of it than it was.

But she didn't really think so. That might have been true in the beginning, but any curiosities ought to have been satisfied with a single mating. There would have been no need for another.

But she wanted another. And another. And . . . well . . . as many as she could possibly cram into three days. She was certain of that. She didn't examine the craving too deeply. She had come there specifically to indulge herself in every new experience her time could afford her, and so far she had not been disappointed in the least. Oh, there would be penance to pay when she got back home, and she supposed she should be worried about it, worried about her parents' displeasure over her actions, but she was having far too much fun.

So she spent the meal enjoying all the new foods and tastes, discovering what she liked and what she didn't like, and tried not to worry about anything at all. Besides, worrying did little good. Things would be what they were going to be; worrying about them really served no purpose.

After dinner, Jaykun left without saying much of anything to her. This didn't bother her either because she knew where he was headed eventually. He really didn't seem to have much choice in the matter. She didn't know all the particulars of what happened to him every night, but she knew it was a lonely business and she refused to see him suffer it alone if she could at all help it. True, she could not share his burden or his pain—she couldn't even hope to comprehend it—but she could be there with him when it began and be waiting for him when it ended. So, shortly before dusk, she left the city, walked down the beach to the cove, and found him there, slowly stripping off his clothing and leaving it in a neat pile at a safe distance from where he usually sat. He looked up in surprise at her approach, not having heard her until the moment before she reached out to touch him.

"Why are you here?" he asked and she detected a note of suspicion in the query.

"Because you wish me to be," she said.

"I expressed no such wish," he said.

"I did not say you expressed the wish, only that you have the desire."

"How would you know what I desire?" he asked, his tone quiet.

"Any person with a heart would know that being alone through this makes it all the more painful."

"It is painful for me to know you are watching," he argued.

"Perhaps. Perhaps because you are caring more about me than about yourself. But I would prefer we care more about you than me for these hours to come. You deserve that much, if not more. I cannot give you relief during this, but I can be here for you immediately after. Please. Allow me to do this," she said to him, her voice soft and pleading.

Jaykun reached out to her, touched his hand to her face, his thumb curving up over the apple of her cheek. She had such a beautiful face, such an open expression. It was hard to imagine her being duplicitous. Especially in the face of all she was saying. Still, he would be very vulnerable during these next hours. It was a vulnerability he wasn't sure he wanted to share with anyone. Not even with his brothers, who had suffered similar tortures in their turn.

And yet he had shared it with her these past nights and she was right. Having her here had somehow made it a little easier to bear.

"Very well. Stay if you must."

"I must," she said, reaching to catch the wrist of the hand touching her face and holding him still long enough to turn her head and press a kiss into the center of his palm.

He dropped his hand away and finished undressing. She reached for the laces of her dress and in a quick movement stripped it off her back. She folded it awkwardly, more rolling it up into a ball than anything, and placed the dress on top of his clothing. He looked at her in surprise, then let his eyes run over her naked skin, his thoughts turning instantly carnal. It was shocking to him. Usually by this time of day he was completely obsessed with what was about to happen. But now . . . now all he could think about was how damned delectable she looked. How with every movement she seemed to be telling a sensual story to him. Everything about her beckoned to every part of him. He let his eyes stroke down over her full breasts, her lean flank, and her curvy hip . . . on to the never-ending length of her legs. She was unbearably beautiful. She had to know that, had to know she was tempting him every second of every day. Was this all part of her design? Was it what she had been told to do by someone from Serenity? Did they wish to know if they were next on his list of conquests?

But no. He hadn't even known Serenity existed until she had told him about it. If her people were trying to avoid him, it would be foolish to send someone to point them out to him.

No, he realized with sudden clarity. She was not a spy.

"Come here," he commanded her, beckoning her forward with a sweep of his fingers. She smiled slyly and slid her bare body up against his, the feel of her warm skin almost an erotic torture because he knew he could not have her. In truth, she shouldn't be standing this close to him. As he kept one eye trained on the sinking sun at the horizon, most of his awareness turned inward so he would know the instant he began to burn.

He slowly walked them into the water, choosing his spot, and sitting down with her.

"You will move away the instant I tell you to. No arguments?" he asked of her.

"I do not wish to be burned. I am not foolish."

"Good," he said. Then he cupped her face between his hands, his thumbs shaping the lushness of her lips. "I will not kiss you for fear it will be too distracting, because I do lose my focus whenever I kiss you."

She smiled beneath his thumbs. "I lose focus as well in some ways. In others . . . I feel as though I have never been so keen in my life."

Jaykun appreciated the thought. "I merely wish to look at you. To touch you. Not to arouse you or us, but simply to appreciate the beauty of you. I see so little in the way of beauty in my war camps. Let me just look at you, Jileana."

"All right," she whispered.

And for the next ten minutes she did exactly that: let him look his fill, let him trace over every one of her curves, every inch of soft loveliness she had to offer him. The appreciation was completely nonsexual, although he was aroused the entire time.

"Next time," she said softly, "I will appreciate you."

"Next time," he agreed. Then he drew in a sharp breath. "Go! Now!"

She didn't hesitate. She scrambled back away from him and made it to a safe distance just in time to feel the incredible burst of heat as he exploded into hot, burning light, blinding her before she lifted a hand to guard her eyes. She wondered that he didn't cry out. The pain must have been excruciating. And she knew it was meant to be. He was meant to suffer through this entire torment. She didn't know why exactly, didn't fully understand, but she would. She would see to it he explained every part of what he suffered.

For now . . .

. . . she watched him burn.

*   *   *

Jaykun's body sizzled in the ocean water, juquil's hour having brought his torment to a halt. But he was nothing more than burned bones and charred flesh at that first moment of release. Then he felt someone gathering him close, holding his pain-riddled body, and rocking him gently. He could not see or hear, both eyes and ears having been burned away, but he felt it. Somehow, through all of his pain, he felt it. As he lay there and healed, he felt her holding him. When his ears healed enough, he realized she was singing to him. Her voice was haunting and beautiful, the tone like nothing he'd ever heard before. She was singing some sort of lullaby to him, he realized. Soft and sweet:

The night brings us close,
Holding you dear.
The night brings us close;
The water is clear.
The night brings us close;
Let's see what you hear.

It was as though the song helped him heal faster, he thought. Well, it healed his soul, in any event. She healed his soul. Having her there, hearing her voice, it settled him and made everything easier somehow.

When he had healed enough, he realized he was lying with his head on her breast and she was holding him up out of the water. Aware of his weight and how exhausting that must be for her, he quickly sat up and leaned away from her.

"Shh. All is well," she soothed him.

"I . . . I know. Are you all right?" he asked, his voice a hoarse rasp as his vocal cords continued to heal.

"I am fine. It is not me you should be worrying about but yourself. Here, now. Rest and let me sing."

"But . . ."

"Shh. Rest."

She pulled him back to her breast and he did exactly that. He relaxed and rested and listened to her sing until all of his skin had regrown, replacing the burns with red scars. Now he could feel the stroking of her hand over his shoulder, down his arm, down his back, all the way to his hip, always in the same direction, as if she were soothing a cat, taming it in her lap.

This time when he sat up and leaned away she didn't stop him. He turned his gaze on her. She was lit by the fullness of the moon, her skin silvery in the dark. He felt as if he had never been as intimate with a woman as he was that night, in those hours. And he had loved his wife a great deal. Had been utterly devoted to her. His brothers had teased him for being besotted and had warned him it would make him blind to her flaws. But he hadn't cared. Right up until the moment she had proved them right, he hadn't cared.

But this intimacy was something beyond that foolish, young love. He didn't fancy himself in love with Jileana of course. He would never be that ridiculous over a woman again. But this intimacy meant far more than the foolishness of love imagined.

He grabbed hold of her suddenly, slinging her into his lap until she was astride his thighs, her lithe, naked body pressed close to his, her mouth but a scant inch away from his as his hand thrust into her partially wet hair.

"What do you want of me?" he asked her fiercely, his hands gripping her tight.

"Nothing," she assured him.

"I don't believe you. You must want something."

"Only the pleasure of your company for two more days," she said.

And suddenly he was afraid that two more days wasn't going to be enough. The thought blindsided him, scared him. He pushed it down by kissing her hard and punishingly. She took the heated abuse, absorbing it and his confusion. He felt her wet fingers against his throat and he broke the kiss, gasping for his breath.

"Then you shall have it," he said.

Braxia, the finia of Kriza, was fuming in her lowly bed-chamber. She paced the floor, back and forth, the beads of the belt hanging from her waist clacking together with her every step, her weighty skirts rustling, and her slippered feet scuffing the dusty floor.

"Look! Look what I am reduced to! Sleeping in this . . . this . . . hovel! While that barbarian sleeps in my bed! My luxurious sheets! My back is in agony for sleeping on this rock in this room they have banished me to. The barbarians don't even have the courtesy to give me a place of honor at their table as a defeated but worthy opponent. And now one of their leaders has killed my most trusted maidservant, Sorna! She served me faithfully for years. But at least she gave her life in honor of her mistress. If only she had gotten close enough to kill him!"

"She may well have," Wizol, the city fortunary said, "but he was not sleeping alone last night . . . an unexpected occurrence." Wizol had been ejected from his place in the vaults of Kriza, his ledgers and the city's gold commandeered by the barbarian men. Now he was forced to watch as they pawed through his figures and fondled the coinage he had been responsible for, the greedy pigs that they were. No doubt they would strip the coffers bare.

The truth was, no one was really certain what the invaders were going to do next. Surprisingly, there had been no raping of the women, no mass destruction or pillaging. They had taken the city in an organized, if violent, manner but had kept their kills limited to those who had taken up arms against them, leaving the innocent alone. There was something to be said for that. At least the barbarian leaders had some control over their men. But that control had been Kriza's downfall. That and the fact that Krizans were used to fighting their battles on the sea. They had been so busy looking for enemies approaching from the ocean that they had turned their backs to the real danger.

"What I should have done was pack my armada full and abandon the city. Why did I not think of that? But at least some of our ships were able to escape."

"They will hunt them down, mistress. Their plans to do so were overheard earlier today."

"Tell me something of the whore the barbarian leader took to his bed last night," Braxia mused to the fortunary. "Perhaps we can enlist her to kill him. Given enough coin she might kill him while in the vulnerable throes of rutting."

"What gold? They have taken it all."

"Besides, she is not a whore. She is *prava*!" the finia's maid Bela said shyly.

"A *prava* sleeps in my bed?" Braxia demanded shrilly.

"Yes, oh glorious mistress," the Bela said, bowing deferentially to the finia. The finia liked it when people bowed to her. She never grew tired of it. It was well known that the best way to mollify her when her temper was up was to bow deferentially in front of her and to stay that way until she gave you leave to rise.

"Yes, yes," Braxia said impatiently, gesturing the maid out of the bow. "They truly are barbarians," she whispered in awe of the levels the invaders would sink to. "The *prava* are animals, beasts even lower than these barbarians!"

"That they should consort with one only shows the measure of their depravity!" Wizol said. He was incredibly nervous. If he were caught there conspiring with his ruler, no doubt he would be slaughtered on the spot. So far the invaders had not killed any of the servants or advisors they had come across, merely relieved them of their duties. But that would very likely not be the case if those advisors were found conspiring to kill them. As it was, the guards knew he was there and would likely report his visit to the barbarians.

"Look, it is clear what must be done," Braxia said. "There are three brothers in charge of this army. Kill the brothers and the army dies with them. Without leaders they will fall into chaos. We must do this before they have a chance to gain a true foothold. Then we can get messages to the ships in our fleet that managed to get away and have them attack from the ocean!"

"Attack our own city? But we've escaped with so little damage thus far," Wizol said.

"They will not be expecting this. It is our only choice. But we must kill these brothers. What about poisoning?" Braxia asked.

"They have their own army of cooks preparing their food. Like everything else, they have taken over the kitchens. Perhaps we could manage something, but a Krizan servant now stands out amongst all these ugly alien invaders," Wizol informed her.

"Then we must use assassins. Surely the brothers can be caught alone in some shadow, the perfect time to slip a dagger between their ribs!"

"Perhaps . . . perhaps the *prava* could be bought after all?" Wizol suggested. "We don't know what motivates them, really. Only that—"

"They cannot be trusted," Braxia said fiercely. "They

are dangerous and deadly. Come to think of it, perhaps we should just bide our time. The *prava* has no doubt affixed herself to the barbarian leader. It is only a matter of time before she lures him to his death. It is what they do. They cannot help themselves."

"Yes. A sound plan," Wizol said. "But it might be better for us to take direct action. Now, how shall we go about it?" The fortunary was anxious about being caught conspiring, but he was more anxious about being left to the whims of the barbarian brothers.

"Find a way! Get ahold of some poison, perhaps, something harsh and violent, and seek an opportunity to get it into their food. If you can do that, then all of our troubles will be over. They all eat together, the entire table full of advisors and generals and the brothers as well. Yes?"

"Yes, great and beauteous mistress," the maid said with a bow. "The *prava* as well."

Pleased, Braxia smiled. "Good. This is our plan. We will wait for the opportunity to present itself!"

"Yes, magnificent mistress," Wizol said with a low bow. "It will be done."

Braxia turned a glaring eye on her room; the small bed and the little desk and chair were the only furnishings within it. If all went well, she would be back in her luxurious apartment within only a few days. And to her mind, it wouldn't be soon enough. She had to succeed at this. She simply could not bear the idea of living a life of obscurity, a life of peasantry. She was finia, the grandest being in all of Kriza, ruler of all and commander of its great armada. These barbarians would be made to recognize that if it was the last thing she ever did.

Of course she was grateful to the gods that they had not killed her thus far. It was a good sign in the greater scheme of things. But she would not tolerate this disrespect, being made to live in such squalid conditions, to not even be given the courtesy of dining in the great hall with them.

No. It was very appropriate that all the barbarians should choke and die on their food. At least she could be assured of her own safety, that their rudeness would in the end protect her from sharing the same fate she planned for them.

Still, it would have been a great pleasure to sit at that table and watch them die one by one in front of her very eyes.

Yes. She would have liked that very much.

The full moon made it very easy to see their way back up the beach to the city. The city wall extended all the way across the beach and into the water, and there was a beach gate in both the north and south ends of the wall. Jaykun and Jileana approached the city via the south gate. The wall and its gates were now manned and guarded by Jaykun's men. The gates—what remained of them and the wall after Jaykun's offensive on the city—were closed after dusk to all comers. The only exception to that order was Jaykun.

Once they were past the wall, they walked along the beach to the docks and then walked the wooden planks to the nearest ship. Krizan ships were massive monsters, made for carrying a great force of men. They were not built for speed, so it was possible to outrun a Krizan ship if the winds were in one's favor, but it would take a skilled captain to do so. But once a Krizan ship latched on to its target, the large raiding party was brutal. Krizans were not known for their mercy on the high seas. Quite the opposite.

"They look so beastly," Jileana remarked.

"They are. But that is exactly what I need. A fleet of

beasts that can carry a great force of men over the waters."

"These ships don't seem as though they could carry your entire army," Jileana said doubtfully.

"That is because a third of the ships have gone missing. But we will get them back. We will crew these remaining ships and spend the winter chasing down what rogue ships we can find. Once spring comes, we will be ready to move on."

"Are you certain you can find them?"

"It is hard to miss a ship that looks like this," he remarked. Jileana thought he had a point. If not by the size of the thing, it would be known by its brightly painted colors. Each ship was festooned with all kinds of colors on its carved railings and the spires of its masts. On some of the ships, the decks were painted; on others, the sides were decorated. Each had a style all its own. The ships were unafraid of being seen and it showed.

"You are right," she said with a chuckle.

"Odds are, the ships were poorly crewed and poorly supplied. That means we will find most of them in ports either in Moroun or at some other nearby harbor. Perhaps even your island."

"Oh no. Not my island. You can't get there by ship."

"Every island can be gotten to by ship," Jaykun said with a laugh.

"Not my island. I promise you that."

"Why not your island?"

"Remember the storms that kept you from seeing it?"

"Yes."

"Well, they are always there. They are violent and dangerous, and no ship can make it through them."

"That's . . . I've never heard of such a thing before. Surely the storms aren't there all the time. They must let up every so often."

"They are there all the time," she assured him.

He didn't believe her. If that were the case, how would she have gotten off the island and onto these shores? He found himself bothered by the fib. Then he rethought the feeling. He could understand her wanting to discourage the idea of traveling to her island. He was, after all, an invader in command of a great army . . . one that now included an armada. She was trying to protect her home from him. For some reason that disturbed him. Why should it bother him? It was his job as an invader to seize cities in Weysa's name and he gave no quarter when it came to that. He should be planning to get to her island after he attacked Moroun. He would of course try peaceful methods first; he wasn't a barbarian, after all. Just like he would with Moroun, he would send an envoy to the rulers of her island, requesting that temples be raised in Weysa's name. The only condition was that on the island there had to be more temples to Weysa than there were to any one of the other gods. If they refused . . . well . . . that was when war broke out. From what he had gathered from Jileana, her people worshipped Diathus. It sounded as though Diathus was worshipped to the exclusion of all other gods. Since Diathus was in the faction that warred against Weysa's faction of gods, to take worshippers away from Diathus and gain them for Weysa helped their cause twofold.

But he wasn't focused on anything other than Moroun at the moment. He could send envoys to Serenity at the same time perhaps and then decide in which direction to go. But the idea sat ill with him for some reason. He found himself not wishing to upset her by planning to attack her people. Perhaps he was being selfish too, because he didn't want to disrupt the rest of their time together, or perhaps he truly didn't want to hurt her in any way. The thoughts sat uncomfortably in him. He was a calculating man, a man who was forced to make cold decisions in the name of his cause. It disturbed him to think he was losing that ability just because of a pretty woman.

Two more days, he reminded himself. She would only be influencing him for two more days. Then he would return to his clear-cut way of thinking and decide what to do as far as her island home was concerned. Until then, he would put it out of his mind and not let it come between them.

"Well," he said at last, "I will take your word for it for now."

"Come," she said, taking up his hand. "Come to bed with me," she invited, walking backward, away from him and toward the castle, pulling him along with her. The invitation gave him a fierce thrill of pleasure and excitement. He followed her all too willingly. By the eight hells, she could have been leading him to his death and he didn't think he would care. His vision narrowed completely at the idea of frolicking in bed with her for the next few hours. By all rights he should be getting some sleep and preparing for the big day ahead of him, preparing to face the mountain of work that needed to be done before his brothers could safely leave him. But all he could think of was that he would gladly face a day with no sleep if it meant a night of being ensconced within her.

He followed her to his fate. Once he was in his bedroom with her, she sat him on the bed and moved a short distance away from him. Slowly she undid the laces of her dress and then wriggled out of it, baring inch after inch of luscious skin to his eyes. Soon she was standing naked before him, her dress in a neglected pile on the floor. He was glad of it. He should never have dressed her in the first place. She was too beautiful in her natural state and such beauty should never be hidden away. And yet he knew that if she remained naked as he had found her, he would never get anything done. He simply would keep her in this room, locked away where no one else could see her and covet her beauty for themselves, and where he could make thorough use of her, satiating the rampant passions she so easily inspired within him.

As he watched her approach him, he marveled at her and his reactions to her. Had he ever been so hot for a woman before?

Yes.

He closed the answer off before it could disrupt what he was feeling right then. He didn't want to taint the moment.

And yet . . . he had to be wary. He had to be cautious or he might find himself—

No, he told himself. This was different. This time he was not blindly in love with the object of his lust. She did not and would not have the power over him that Casiria had had.

"Now it's your turn. Don't you simply suffocate in all those clothes?"

He chuckled awkwardly. He wanted to focus solely on her, but these other things kept intruding, these thoughts of Casiria. Why he should think of her at a time like this was beyond him.

Or is it? an insidious voice within him asked.

He shoved all of that aside with a hard mental push and forced himself to focus on the woman approaching him. In the end, it wasn't that hard to do. He had never seen anything so lovely in his entire life. Not even Casiria could compare. And anyway, Casiria was long dead and this woman was very much vital and alive. But on the surface of it, he was glad Jileana was leaving him in two days. It might be dangerous for her to linger any longer than that.

She came to him, reaching out for his hands and pulling him up from the bed. She turned him and gave him a little push until he was at what she deemed was an optimal distance, then threw herself down onto the bed with a flounce of long limbs and ripe breasts. She leaned back on her elbows and raised an expectant brow.

Feeling suddenly on display, he felt awkward again. He shouldn't. He was a man with a destiny, a warrior through and through who had no one to answer to save an all-powerful goddess. He had just cut a swath through an army of men and had seized hold of a foreign city. These were not the actions of a weak or awkward man.

Frustrated with himself, he shrugged out of the vest he was wearing with some measure of violence. Then, with equal temper, he stripped his shirt from his back, leaving himself bare chested before her.

"Very nice," she said lasciviously, her mouth curving into a devilish smile.

Now he was determined to teach the saucy wench a lesson or two, so there was impetus to his actions as he kicked off his boots and stripped away his leggings. He was naked then and he paused to display his fine masculine muscles before stepping forward to reach for her. But she held up a staying hand.

"Not yet," she commanded. "I want only to look at you for a moment. You . . . you are so fine, you see," she explained with a smile. "The men where I come from are so slight. They are sleek and nimble and fast, but none are as big as you are. Nor do they have so many muscles. None so well developed, anyway. I find I like to look at you. I never thought I would like such a big man, but I find myself thoroughly fascinated . . . and thoroughly delighted."

"So I am just to stand here while you look your fill?"

"Well, you could sing if you like."

"Sing? I do not sing."

"Why not? Your voice is so deep and rich. You must make an excellent singer. We have a great deal of singing where I am from. Everyone sings. Although, it is probably not the same kind of singing you might engage in. There has been no music here so far that I have experienced. I would like to hear some."

"Then tomorrow I will hire a minstrel to sing at the late day meal. I will not be singing for you."

"What about dancing? Surely you dance. All men dance."

"I do *not* dance!"

"Why not?" she asked again.

"Warriors fight; they do not dance."

"No warriors dance?"

His jaw clenched. "Not all. Some do. I do not."

"That is so sad."

"How so?" he asked irritably.

"You do not sing. You do not dance. You fight and kill and suffer a terrible torment night after night . . . It seems there is no joy in you to bring you balance. Song and dance are expressions of joy. If you do not express joy in these ways, I am forced to wonder in what ways you do express joy . . . or if there is even any joy to express at all."

He was silent a long moment. He looked away from her. She was so fresh and innocent, so eager to see the beauty in the world. He longed for the days of romanticism and naïveté he had once enjoyed, but they were long gone, torn away by the bitter truths of life.

"The moments I spend in your body are the closest thing I have to joy," he said, his tone hard and factual. There was no danger of her romanticizing the words.

Just the same, she smiled at him, pleased in some way with him. She shifted, rising up onto her knees on the bed and holding out her arms to him. Glad to stop being on display, he stepped toward her, let her arms wrap around his back, and reveled in the feel of her bare body pressing against his chest and belly.

She touched her mouth to his in the gentlest and barest of kisses before pulling back to engage his eyes with her own. "If this is how you feel and express joy, Jaykun, then I am glad to give it to you. I will gladly give you joy at every possible moment. Of course I will try not to interfere in your day too much, but whenever you would like to have sex, you merely need to ask and I will be delighted to oblige you."

Jaykun couldn't help but chuckle at her. "Are you certain about that? What if I decided to lock you away with me for the next two days, coming out only to suffer my penance each night?"

"Oh, could we?" she asked, lighting up and suddenly eager. "Wouldn't your brothers disapprove?"

"Who gives a damn what my brothers approve of?" he bit out. "If I want to indulge myself in you, then I will damn well do so."

"And so you should. Life cannot be all about war and killing and moving from city to city, bringing death and destruction. There must be time, however brief, to indulge in pleasures or passions. Surely your goddess would agree with that."

"You know something, she probably would. She is the goddess of conflict, but she is known for her passionate ways. Perhaps it is the nature of her highly volatile temperament, but in tales she is fierce and demanding of her bed partners. She knows her mind and her desires and does whatever she must to see them satisfied."

"There, now . . . you see? She would understand such passion in you so long as it did not interfere with her need of you. But from what you've told me, as I understand it, you are done campaigning for the winter. You will not be moving on until spring. There is time for you to breathe a little. To look on joy and feel it and express it in kind."

She reached to engage his mouth with her own, wrapping him up in a drugging series of kisses until his head was spinning and heat was blooming all throughout his body.

When he was next able to, he said, "It would be unfair. My brothers cannot go home to their wives until matters in this city are settled, and those matters will not be settled if I am in my bedchamber with you."

"But your brothers will be going home to spend months finding joy with their wives and families. All you are asking for is two days."

He drew back a little and looked at her, looked at the sweet, pretty shape of her face and features as he digested her practical observations. He tried to see ulterior motives in her, tried to figure out why she would push him into this for her own gain, but he simply couldn't figure it out. It made no logical sense for her to want to lock herself away with him. Not unless she was some kind of agent for his enemies, looking to distract him from something important. But that idea also made no sense and could not hold up under scrutiny. If she were there to deter him in some way, she would have let that assassin kill him that morning and be done with him. No. It seemed there were no ulterior motives here that he could see.

"What do you want of me?" he asked her in a sudden, fierce whisper. "What is it that you hope to achieve here? Tell me the truth!"

"Of course I will tell you the truth. I do not lie."

"And if you did lie you would tell me so?" he asked with amusement.

She laughed at herself. "True. It is a claim that can only be proved with actions or inactions. So let me say this: I merely seek enjoyment. My own and now yours as well. That was my whole purpose in coming here. To enjoy myself. I had no idea what form this enjoyment would take, but I see now that it is you. You are the key to my pleasure. I will take advantage of you for it."

He reached to stroke his knuckles down the right side of her face, letting them follow the shape and curve of it. Her skin was so soft. And he knew it tasted sweet.

"Then I shall let you do so," he said after a moment.

She tilted her head, her eyes widening slightly with surprise. "Do you mean that? Do you mean . . . ?"

"That I will lock you away with me for the next two days? Yes. Yes, I will. I will get much aggravation for it from my brothers, but as it stands right now, I would like to drown myself within you. It will end and you will leave in two days, but until then . . ."

"Oh, Jaykun!" she said with delight shining from every inch of her. "Thank you! Thank you so much!"

He grabbed her then and threw her down onto her back on the bed, following to land on top of her.

"You may not be thanking me come this time tomorrow," he growled at her. "You may be begging for a reprieve!"

"If I had money, I would bet against you."

"I will stake you. One Krizan gold sovereign. If you win, you get two gold sovereigns. If I win . . ."

"I will be in your debt. I think that would be a clever bet for you . . . if you were going to win. But you are not. I will enjoy my gold sovereigns."

"Then I have some work to do if I am going to win my bet!"

She squealed with delight when he moved down her body with a suddenly voracious mouth. He went straight down her breastbone, paused to maul a nipple with his lips and tongue, then moved down to her belly, where he kissed and licked and kissed and licked her. As his mouth traveled down, his hands paved the way before him, stroking and petting her, lifting her up to his mouth, pushing her thighs apart so he could settle between them. His broad shoulders brushed the insides of her knees even as his lips brushed down below her navel.

Dizzy from his attack and at a loss as to what else to do with her fingers—since he was, for the most part, presently out of her reach—she buried them in his hair. As though she were the one guiding him rather than she being at his mercy. She was still laughing and gasping at every touch of his mouth and hands, unable to contain the sheer delight she experienced at finding him being playful with her.

Then delight turned to blinding and absolute pleasure as his mouth slid downward, his tongue plowing through the wet feminine folds of the most intimate location on her body. Having him there swept all of her emotions into a maelstrom of delight. His tongue darted and swirled, sought to give her the best of pleasures. She found if she made the slightest encouraging sound, he hummed with answering pleasure. Soon she was throwing her head back and moaning, fierce waves of heated pleasure rolling through her body until she was dizzy with it. How had they gone from simple conversation to this amount of blinding gratification so quickly? she wondered. Had there ever been anything so delightful ever conceived? She thought not.

She burst into orgasm a moment later, her whole body locking up with the sheer force of her pleasure.

"Again," he growled against her. And he repeated his symphony of torturous delight until she called out a second time, every muscle in her body tightening with climax. Then she relaxed with a gusting exhalation, her limbs heavy and unable to move. She was afraid he would once more say "again," but he moved up her body and kissed her with deep, feverish need. All the while, her fingers still gripped his hair and she wondered if she had tried to rip it from his head at one point. She couldn't recall.

"I would like to do that to you," she murmured. But it was clear she wasn't ready to do anything of the sort right then.

"You will be more than welcome. But right now I think I'm going to take my time exploring you. I seemed to have rushed past it all."

"Oh, but I can't move," she said.

"I'll move you if you need to be moved," he said with amusement.

"Oh. Well, thank you very much."

"You're welcome," he said on a chuckle.

He then did as promised, took his time exploring what had to be every inch of her body. He spent, it seemed, an inordinate amount of time on her breasts alone . . . teasing them, toying with them, fondling and sucking and teething until she was hypersensitive to even the slightest touch of his breath upon her. Then he examined each of her limbs with equal care and fascination, his tongue, teeth, and lips tasting every inch of her as he turned her body to and fro as his desires demanded.

Eventually his ministrations had so aroused her that she was chafing with need and energy, all languor forgotten. She pushed at him, rolling him onto his back. She threw a leg astride him, her hot core pressed against him, open and waiting to be plundered by him . . . or so he thought. She moved away almost as quickly as she had arrived, much to his momentary consternation. But then she was kissing her way down his body, exploring every nook and cranny there was to be found, all the while working her way down and down and down. By the time her breath fell against his raging hard shaft he was all but begging for it. He longed for her, longed to be inside her, but he was also feeling far too much enjoyment simply watching her have her way to want to rush it all to an end. Then her tongue darted out and laved the head of his cock boldly and an explosion of brilliant pleasure sang through him. His left hand reached into the thick mass of her dark hair and he found himself guiding her, holding her to him as if she were planning to escape. But nothing could have been further from her mind. She took him in hand, guided him into her waiting and willing mouth. With a single strong suck of sensation, she took him in deep.

Blinded by lust and need, he thrust up against her palate, letting her take as much as she could manage. He tried to be gentle, but it was impossible with the way she was making him feel. Jileana seemed to savor the taste of him, as she toyed with him inside her mouth, her hand stroked the remaining length of him right to the root. Her fingers crawled through the curling hairs she found there, and then she molded and cupped the pliable sac below that root. Jaykun moaned loudly, his fingers crushing her hair violently as molten heat and ready need took hold of him.

"Come here!" he commanded as he dragged her from her torturing ministrations. "I will have you this very instant!"

"You are very pushy," she remarked with a laugh. But she settled astride him once more and took hold of him to guide him up and into her body in a single mutual thrust. She rode him like that in a steady series of sways and thrusts, her proud young body rising up from him so gloriously it took his breath away. He could hardly bear to look at her—that was how beautiful she was. It was almost frightening . . . certainly humbling.

She was extraordinary—there was no doubt about that—and he still hadn't fathomed why she had chosen to enjoy herself with him. It wasn't that he thought so little of himself; it was that he was thinking so much of her. He should have been frightened by that. If he had any sense in his head, he would thrust her away right that very instant and protect himself from any further influence she might have over him. But he did not do that. Instead he let her ride him until he was unable to see straight, until the curls of desire wending through him lashed tightly around him, holding him fast and hard to her. When he came it was with astounding violence, his pleasure torn up from the deepest part of him. She tensed hard around him, her orgasm just as violent and just as deep. She then fell onto him, a boneless, gasping weight, a weight he enjoyed far too much.

Then he forced himself to speak aloud the one thing that was most important between them.

"Two days."

"Two days," she agreed.

And then they fell asleep.

CHAPTER
NINE

"All right, someone has to say something," Garreth said when he and Dethan found themselves eating without their brother for the second meal of the day. Neither had to wonder where Jaykun was or what he was doing. Although the castle was made of stone, the doors were not and sound traveled far too well along the corridors of the living quarters. Their brother's marathon sexual escapade was being announced far and wide.

Not that they really begrudged him his slice of happiness. The gods knew Jaykun saw so little of it. But there were things to be done, and on a more selfish bent, it made the brothers miss their wives even more than usual.

"This has been a hard campaign," Dethan said with a sigh. "I long to see my newest child."

"Children are well and good, but I miss the comfort of Sarielle's embrace. And every day he wastes in other pursuits is a day longer I am away from her," Garreth grumbled.

"Hush, now. This is our lot. We spend the summers on the campaign trail, as we agreed with Weysa and Mordu, helping our brother, and in exchange we get to have our loves and our children all the rest of the year. I am endlessly grateful for the time I have with Selinda. I can remember what it was like, not that long ago, when I had to face the same fate Jaykun now suffers— tortured night after night, beholden to my goddess all the seasons' turnings. My children would have had a stranger for a father, one they knew only in the winters. No. I will not bemoan my lot. Nor will I begrudge him what little happiness he can find. I tried that with you and it only caused us trouble."

"But ... he must stay focused," Garreth said with agitation. "It is only by keeping focus that we can hope to find what we wish to know! We have been scouring this continent, taking over city after city, exploring the tales of the gods known to each tribe—only in this way can we hope to discover Maxum's prison. Gods know Sabo will not give away the location. He may have let slip that Maxum was buried in soil, but he will never tell us where. We must try to find him."

"And do what if we find him? Dig for him? Only Sabo knows how far down into the ground our brother is. Only Sabo will release him. We are better off trying to make amends to Sabo."

"We cannot do that as long as he is part of the faction that wars against Weysa. Even so, even if there were no war, Sabo thrives on the pain and suffering of others. Why would he wish to bring an end to ours?" Garreth asked.

"I do not know." Dethan released a pained sigh. "I am a mortal man fighting in a war between gods at the side of my immortal brothers. I am the most fragile warrior here yet still I fight. I will do anything in hopes that we will one day be granted the boon of our last brother's freedom. Until then, we search for his location in tale and story. Somewhere in the annals of stories and histories of some race on the face of this planet is the clue to our brother's whereabouts. To that end, today I am going to seek out the library and the Krizan scholars, provided they have any. These are a coarse people. Education is not high amongst their charms. Let Jaykun spend himself on this woman for a day. There are other things to be done without him."

"Very well. Then I shall occupy myself in a like manner. I will continue to manage the details of this household, making certain we are firmly settled and dealing with the matters of prisoners and malcontents. This government will need to be rebuilt. I realize Jaykun has the whole of the winter to do so, but I want to make a good start before you and I must leave."

"Agreed. So we will meet back here for supper?" Dethan said.

"We can exchange our progress over the meal. Perhaps our brother might join us."

"He has to eat sometime," Dethan said with a chuckle.

Jaykun used his tongue to fish the jogu berry out of Jileana's navel and she giggled at the sensation. Her laughter threatened to disrupt the remaining fruits he had perched all about her body. He was eating each berry and each slice of melon or fruit meat directly off her skin, then licking away any juice left behind. It was a titillating game . . . but it also tickled and his playfulness made her laugh.

"My dish shakes and trembles about," he noted with a chuckle. "How am I to finish my meal when it threatens to spill onto the bedclothes?"

"Better still, when is it my turn to eat? I am hungry." But it was clear from the heated look in her eyes that she was not speaking about the state of her stomach.

With a sudden growl he swept the remaining fruit off

her body, sending it hither and thither so he could crush his mouth to hers and pin her body beneath him. She eagerly opened her thighs around his hips, her legs locking together across his muscular buttocks, which flexed hard as he drove himself into her.

"I shall feed you thusly, then," he said, his voice low and rough, coming through clenched teeth. "Feed you until you burst with fullness."

"Oh yes!" she cried out, pulling him down to her mouth so she could kiss him for all she was worth. Then she pushed him away, shoved him almost completely off herself, forcing him to roll onto his back, where she straddled him and immediately took him back into her welcoming body.

"Pushy little minx," he said as his hands clamped down hard on her hips and began to help her grind against him, to help her sheathe him in brutal, demanding need. She felt amazing. Miraculous even. He doubted he could ever tire of her. Each time they connected brought him new knowledge of her, made him marvel at how open she was and how unashamed she was about her appetites. Even now, as they played and fought and tangled themselves up in passion, he found himself wanting her ever more strongly, as opposed to feeling content and satiated. Perhaps it was because he knew his time with her was limited, because he knew he had to jam into two days everything he possibly could.

He pushed aside the feeling of dread that accompanied that thought. He had made a bargain with her—with himself—and he would hold to it. Whatever the cost, he would hold fast. But facing that made him angry for some reason and he took it out on her with a punishing, lurching thrust upward that met the downward crash of her imprisoned pelvis. Her spine curved, her hair was thrown back, and her green eyes glowed with fiery passion and the determination to meet his punishment with every bit of matching fervor.

As he struck her across her sweetest spot she began to cry out in an increasing crescendo of moans. Hearing her reach for pleasure was enough to drive him mad, enough to make him raw with need. It wasn't long before his voice joined hers, the chorus reaching a breaking point roughly and quickly. It frustrated him in a way—that she could drive him into a fever so quickly and so easily. It made him forget himself, made him forget every promise he'd made to take her more slowly, to savor every inch and every moment of her. But the nature of their relationship made slowing down almost impossible. They were racing against time. He had so little time and so much he wanted to force into it. He would savor in retrospect; later he would take things out and replay them more slowly. For now, he wanted her rough and hard.

She came first, with a scream of pleasure that cascaded into smaller shouts. He exploded with a roar of his own, feeling as though his very soul were pulsing and jetting out of him and into her with his final thrust. She collapsed upon his chest, her breasts crushed between them, her breaths panting hard and wild and loud against the side of his neck and shoulder. He thrilled to hear it, longed to hear it go on forever.

No. Not forever.

Just two more days. Only that. Nothing more.

Nothing more.

Dremu skulked his way toward the kitchens. No one paid him any mind except to maybe shove him out of the way. But it was something he was used to. He was considered to be lower than the lowest of his kind. If half-breeds could be called his kind. He was the mis-

shapen product of an unfaithful Krizan woman and, it
was rumored, a gypsy man who had traveled with the
minstrel caravans. Oh, his mother had been properly
wed to a Krizan man—a good, solid farmer from the
hardland farms just beyond the Krizan city walls. But
when Dremu was born, it had been more than clear that
she had been faithless. His teeth were straight and even,
all within his mouth instead of tusking up over his
upper lip as a purebred Krizan's would. They were so
small he could not even cap them in gold or gems. His
skin was a sallow sort of tan color, nothing like the
typical ruddy Krizan complexion. And he was of an un-
healthy, lean sort of build, lacking the true beautiful
bulk of his people.

He was a half-breed and it showed. His mother had
died for her faithlessness, as per the laws of Kriza, and
he had been left on the beach, exposed to the elements,
squalling and vulnerable. Then he had been retrieved by
a couple so desperate for a child that they had been willing to overlook his ugliness and mixed birth.

So at the very least he had grown up loved by his
adoptive parents.

But he had grown up hated by everyone else in the
city. They called him a *trega* half-breed. Kicked dirt at
him and spat at his feet. The idea of him ever being accepted by a Krizan woman was ludicrous, so he lived
alone now that his parents were dead. He bunked in
stables or dark places where he would not be noticed
too easily. He worked in the shadows doing whatever he
could, whatever they would let him do.

But today his *trega* appearance would serve him well.
He gripped the small leather pouch in his hands for all
he was worth, scurrying like a rat toward the food in
the kitchens. All he needed was the right moment. A
single right moment. Then he would be given, for the
first time in his life, one gold coin in trade for his day's

work. He had been promised it by the finia's fortunary. One gold coin that would allow him to finally leave this horrid city where he was so thoroughly rejected day after day. He could afford to leave, could go onto the road where travelers from different lands were found all the time. His differences would be expected there, not questioned. He didn't know what he would do exactly, but at least he would be able to find work or earn his way in fair trade. It couldn't be worse than this life. Nothing could be worse than this life in Kriza.

He had of course toyed with another idea. Perhaps he could join the *trega* army. Perhaps his looks would go unremarked in a group of men and women who all looked so different from one another. He had never seen such a mix of races before, so many different types. Skin of blue, eyes of yellow, hair of green. This one looked one way and that one another. He would blend right in with such a noise of races. But for all that he could be one of them, the *trega* frightened him. They were a warring lot, made to kill others. He wasn't able to lift a sword, so what could he possibly do in an army?

It left him little choice, really. He could take his chances trying to find something to do in the *trega* army or he could be loyal to his people, earn his gold coin, and be on his way.

Even though his people had never been loyal to him.

Dremu ducked into an alcove just outside the kitchens, pressing his back against the wall and breathing hard in a panic. He shouldn't do this. He had never killed anyone before. He didn't have it in him! He clutched the leather pouch so hard his nails dug into the soft skin of it. He needed that gold coin. Desperately needed it. Needed it more than he had needed anything in his scraping, needy existence. One gold coin for the price of . . . death.

He glanced into the kitchens. They were abustle with

preparations for the evening meal, loud and boisterous cooks singing as they worked. All Krizans had been banished from the kitchens; only *trega* were allowed. It was why he was the only one who could do this thing.

He loosened the drawstring of the pouch and peeked at the white powder inside. He was careful not to get any of it on himself. If he should accidentally ingest it, he would be dead within seconds. One sure way of ending his quandary as to what to do with his life. He looked around for something he imagined everyone would be eating. He needed to slay as many with one blow as was possible. As soon as one fell, the others would know and would stop eating. But the most important thing was to get the leaders. That was his goal: to kill the *trega* leaders as directed by the fortunary. The fortunary had even been so kind as to provide the poison.

Kill them or join them.

In the end, it was the guarantee of that gold coin that made the choice for him. The *trega* had made no such offer and likely wouldn't even if he went to them and exposed the poisoning attempt. They were, after all, barbarians . . . weren't they?

No. He must have his gold. Then he could run away or even . . . even join the army anyway! How would they ever know it was him? If he snuck in and out fast enough, if he escaped unseen, how would they ever find out?

They wouldn't. They simply wouldn't.

With a deep breath, he moved quickly into the kitchens.

Soup. A pot of soup. It was the first thing he saw that he knew he could dissolve the powder in unseen. He walked up to it, looked furtively left and right, waited until no one was paying any attention, then dumped the white powder within it. He hastily stirred it in using a large wooden spoon he found nearby. Now all he could do was hope no one tasted the soup before it was served. But he had done his part. All they had to do was die. One or all, the fortunary said. Whatever he could manage. One death at that table or all. One death would earn him the coin . . . All would earn him more, he had said.

More! Imagine more than a single gold coin! It was more than he could ever hope for!

He hastened away from the pot of soup before someone could see him there. He found a shadow to hide in just outside the kitchens and kept his eyes glued to that pot of soup. He now had to keep someone from tasting it before it was served. That was all he had to do. So he sat in the corner and he prayed to Hella, the goddess of fate and fortune, that she would be with him this night.

Dethan sat back in his chair at the dinner table and exchanged a look with his brother, who was seated across the table from him.

"I don't think he's coming," he said with a chuckle.

"Coming is not his problem," Garreth quipped dryly.

Dethan laughed aloud at that. "Let us eat without him," he said as a bowl of soup was placed in front of him. "No reason we should starve just because he prefers to. Unlike my two brothers, I must eat to survive."

"Tch," Garreth scolded. It was not widely known that the brothers were immortal. Nor was it widely known what Jaykun suffered each night. There were rumors and such, to be sure, but that was amongst the troops, not amongst their enemies.

Dethan ignored his brother's admonishment and picked up his spoon. "I was in the library most of the day and you wouldn't believe the stories I found. Most of them are in Krizan so I could not read them for myself, but the scholars were surprisingly helpful about the local legends. There was—"

"Good evening, brothers!"

Garreth and Dethan looked up at the jovial greeting. Jaykun entered the room and clapped Garreth on the back as he passed by him. He flung himself into his chair at the head of the table and beckoned to Jileana so she might sit beside him.

"Good evening, brother," Dethan greeted in return, a grin on his lips. "We didn't think to see you."

"Ah. Well. I find I am famished!"

"Is it any wonder?" Garreth muttered.

A servant put two more bowls of soup on the table in front of Jaykun and Jileana. As was the common manner, no one ate until the most senior of the group began to eat first. Now that Jaykun was here, that fell to him. He picked up his spoon and so did Jileana.

Jileana, unaware of the fact that she was supposed to wait, scooped up a spoonful of soup and brought it to her lips. She was starving, having eaten nothing but fruit for the whole of the day.

But the very instant the soup's aroma hit her nostrils she blanched and cried out.

"Cogzinia! Don't eat it! It's poison!" She grabbed Jaykun's bowl and threw the hot soup onto the floor.

"What in the eight hells?! Jileana!" Jaykun protested.

But Jileana had leapt onto the table and was shoving the bowls of hot soup away from whomever she could reach.

"It's cogzinia! It's a shellfish from the ocean that's pure poison! Why are you eating this? Surely you don't mean to eat this!"

"Jileana!" Jaykun reached for her and dragged her down from the top of the table. "It's all right!"

"No, it's not!" she shouted into his face.

"I mean it's all right, we won't eat it. Here, now! Be

calm!" He caught her face between his hands and was shocked to see how stricken she looked. He had never seen her so upset. She had always been so calm . . . unflappable. For something to upset her, he knew it must be true.

"How do you know what it is?" he asked her gently.

"I can smell it. Can't you smell it?"

"No. We can't." Jaykun looked at Dethan and sudden panic rose up in him. "Did you eat any, Dethan?" Garreth and he were immune, but Dethan . . .

"I was about to when you arrived. But no," he assured, "I did not eat any."

"Thanks be to the gods," Jaykun exhaled. "Any of you others?" All the generals shook their heads and were grateful they had observed common courtesies. They all turned an appreciative eye on their leader's woman. "We are very fortunate, then. I thought our people were in charge of the kitchens."

"They are. Someone must have gotten past them," Dethan said.

"From now on, brother, you do not eat until we have tasted your food first," Jaykun said to Dethan. "We will get to the bottom of this. I will not have this."

"We need control of this city," Garreth said darkly. "It's time we settled some things here."

"We will," Jaykun agreed. "The people must learn that their lives will be made better by our arrival, not worse and not more troubled. We will begin to make proclamations the day after tomorrow. We will spend tomorrow drawing them up."

"It will be good to have you with us again, brother," Dethan said, amusement touching his tone. His heart was still racing as he thought of how close he had just come to making his wife a widow, his children fatherless. The idea sickened him. Yes, his brothers would care for his family as if they were their own, but he did not want Selinda to suffer the loss of him. He knew exactly what it would do to her. As strong as she was, she would find it difficult to survive without him.

He owed a debt to this woman who had latched on to his brother. "Jileana, you have the gratitude of my wife, my children, and myself," he said to her gravely.

"I am grateful. So grateful," she said, tears welling in her eyes. "When I think of what might have happened . . ."

"Hush. All is well now," Jaykun soothed. "Let us find something safe to eat. Some fruits and cheeses perhaps. Cured meats. I will eat first, then you will share my plate. I'll not have you harmed in any way. You have saved the life of my dearest brother and have become precious to me because of it. Come. Sit beside me while this is all cleared away."

"Very well," she said, letting him sit her back down in her chair beside him. "Very well."

The table was cleared and reset, this time with foods deemed safer. The meal went long as everyone ate more cautiously. But Jileana sensed no other poisons in the foods brought to her. Eventually she began to relax and found herself cautiously enjoying Jaykun's company once more.

Jaykun was feeling the guilt of his unbridled day. He had responsibilities and he had ignored them all day. He could not afford to do so a second time, as much as he was craving another day in bed and in Jileana's body. He would have to be satisfied with having her for the night. As it stood, dusk was fast approaching and they would barely have time to make it to the cove.

They left the table and traveled on horseback this time, sharing a saddle as they raced the beast down the beach in order to beat the setting sun. Jaykun barely had time to tether the animal and strip off his clothes before his curse was searing through him and scorching him with blinding agony. He had known such pleasure all day that, in contrast, his torment seemed to be especially brutal.

When it was over he shuddered with the pain of it, crying out through clenched teeth as the salt from the ocean waters penetrated his raw flesh. Jileana gathered him close again, drawing him gently into her lap as she softly began to sing to him once more.

CHAPTER
TEN

"**D**amn her! Damn that *prava* bitch to the eight hells and let her burn!" the finia raged. "Damn that *trega* whelp! He will get nothing from me for his failure! You should have known better than to trust a half-breed whelp!" Braxia glared at the fortunary. "And now there will never be another chance to get at them that way. They will be especially cautious. We must do something before they get further entrenched in my kingdom!"

"Then that only leaves us the choice of a slip blade," Wizol said, making certain to bow low to her. In her present state of temper it was wisest to remember his deference. It wasn't beyond her to beat a servant within an inch of his or her life. Luckily, he was needed.

"Then do it!" she screeched. "Do it, do it, do it!" She swung out and cuffed him hard on the head. "Send that *trega* whelp to do the job and tell him if he fails me this time it will mean his life!"

"Surely you don't mean to send him to do it," Wizol ventured, making certain he remained in a low bow. "This requires an expert hand, beauteous one."

"Then find me one! Now! Meanwhile, that *trega* half-breed can redeem himself by killing the *prava*. She dares to sleep in my bed and defies our plans to win back our kingdom? She is an abomination, plain and simple, and she should be killed. Make sure the boy understands. Kill the *prava* bitch and he will have his gold coin."

"Yes, mistress," Wizol said in a quiver of words. Then he picked himself up off the floor and scurried out of the room.

Dremu met up with Wizol shortly after the fortunary left the finia's rooms. Wizol relayed the new orders and left Dremu shaking in indecision. He did not know what to do. He was in danger either way. If he disappointed the finia, he was certain he would meet his death. If the *trega* were to discover what he had tried to do, he would be killed for certain. The invader brothers were ruthless soldiers, killers to be sure. There would be no forgiveness there. Dremu was afraid he had made the wrong choice when he chose to poison the brothers. He should simply have joined their army. He was not a soldier, not a killer, but surely there was something a willing man like him could have done.

Again he faced an impossible choice, if he did as the finia asked, he would become a killer. He had no future otherwise. But how would he kill the *prava* female? She had already foiled his last attempt and she was a creature of mystery to Dremu. It was said the *prava* had great mystical powers. How was he supposed to get close enough to her to kill her? And how does one kill a *prava*?

Dremu scurried into the first dark hiding spot he could find—an alcove full of brooms and buckets. He crouched down into a quivering ball of flesh, curled into himself, and closed his eyes. He needed to think and to sleep. No one should bother him here. No one should be able to see him behind the brooms. He would sleep and he would think.

Oh sweet gods, was he actually going to do this terrible thing? Was he going to kill a woman? And how would he do so without alerting the brother she bedded with? Oh, by the gods, there had to be a better way. There had to be!

Despite his upset, the exhausted Dremu finally found it within himself to fall asleep.

Jileana was well loved.

Her physical body was, in any event. She was lying in bed, her limbs languorous and exhausted, her eyes trained on the magnificent body of her lover as he went about getting dressed.

"Must you leave?" she asked, trying not to sound too demanding of him. She recognized he wasn't the type of man who would care to have a woman make demands of him that he wasn't readily willing to give in to.

He smiled though, his gaze sliding over her naked body as it lay on display in his bed. She was on her stomach, a pillow pulled up under her cheek, her fanny exposed, and her crossed ankles lifting up toward her backside and then dropping back down onto the bed, lifting and dropping as she bent her knees rhythmically.

"I want little more than to stay in bed with you on our last day together, but I cannot risk letting my responsibilities slide. I must spend this day with my brothers, coming up with the proclamations that will put this city at ease and hopefully settle the matter enough to dissuade any more attempts on our lives."

"Proclamations will not make the Krizans love you."

"No. But it is a start. And over time they will come to appreciate my rule. I hear the finia was something of a tyrant."

"Indeed she was. I have heard many tales that would shock and appall you."

"Nothing shocks me any longer." He frowned. "You would think they would be more grateful, then."

"Change is not easy. And you are right; they have no idea what your intentions are. For all they know you will be worse than their former leader." She lifted her head from the pillow. "How will you begin to engender trust?"

"I don't know. It is different for every city. Usually in a city run by tyranny it is best to hold open days of hearing disputes and begin to make fair and equitable solutions to common troubles. Word of these things will spread and eventually the people will come to realize they will be dealt with fairly."

Jileana smiled. "That is a brilliant maneuver! I am most impressed."

He chuckled as he belted his trousers. "Hopefully the Krizans will be just as easy to impress as you are."

"I have every faith that they will come to love you." She smiled as she turned, rolling over slowly onto her back as she ran an inviting hand up from her hip to her waist to her ribs and eventually to embrace her breast. "They will feel just as stimulated by your attentions as I am. They will know what a very good man you are."

Jaykun growled. "Stop that," he scolded as he snatched up his shirt. "I must go to my brothers and you know it makes me mad with lust when I see your hands on your own body."

"Do I?" she asked archly. "I don't know what you mean."

"Jileana," he warned.

"All you have to do is get dressed and leave. I am not stopping you."

But she was stopping him and she knew she was. He was overwhelmed by his lust for her in a way he had never experienced before. With Casiria it had been about love and devotion more than it had been about lust. In truth, Casiria had not enjoyed bed sport as much as Jaykun might have wanted her to. Oh, they had had their intimacies, but never had it reached this level of insatiability.

Jaykun pushed the comparison aside with irritation. Why did he keep comparing Jileana to Casiria? They were nothing alike. Casiria had been fair, blond, blue-eyed, and pretty. Jileana was a dark, sultry beauty nearly half a foot taller than his diminutive Casiria had been. Jileana was strong and vital; Casiria had been fragile and delicate. He had treasured Casiria and protected her at every turn. With Jileana, it felt as though she were the one doing the protecting. She had certainly saved everyone at the dinner table from terrible deaths last night. When he thought of how she had scrambled down the table, tipping over bowls of soup, he knew Casiria would never have made such a spectacle of herself. She had been a lady, demure and modest, everything opposite of the bold Jileana.

Casiria also would never have lain naked in bed trying to tempt him back into it by touching her skin as Jileana was now doing. He watched as she pinched her nipple, pulled on it a little, tempting him with the memory of how she felt under his touch. She was so hot, her skin the softest and smoothest he'd ever felt. He found himself quite addicted to the feel of it.

Then her free hand came into play. It began at her other breast, then slowly progressed down the length of her torso until her fingers were scraping through the curls on her mound and then slipping between her nether lips. She gasped softly at the sensation and her eyes rolled closed.

"Go on," she breathed. "Be on your way if you must. I have plenty to keep me occupied without you."

Jaykun was rooted to the spot, his cock hard and throbbing since the moment he'd first seen her touching her own skin. He could hear his pulse in his ears, and his hands had halted in the action of putting his shirt on. Now all he could do was watch raptly as she touched herself, her long body sliding restlessly amongst the bed linens, every curve curving, every arch arching. Her hair was a dark cloud beneath her head; her lips flushed red as sounds of welcoming pleasure moaned from between them. He ejected a sound of frustration as his body locked with tension and outright craving.

Damn her anyway! He should be tired of the tempting little witch by now! Instead it seemed his need for her expanded exponentially. Every time he had her, he had to have her again. It was too much. It was frightening. He could not afford to lose himself like this with a woman. Not now, not ever again. And not just because of the pact with his goddess, Weysa, who expected him to devote himself completely to her, but because he had learned the lesson long ago, that to lose oneself to one's passions was a dangerous, deadly road. A painful one he had no intention of ever walking down again.

And yet . . . and yet he could not seem to make himself turn around and walk away from her. She just looked too delicious lying there pleasuring herself. He simply could not abandon all the promise filling the room just as her increasing moans were filling it.

"Damn you, you wicked little wench," he hissed, his hands suddenly stripping his shirt from his body. He threw it down with no little violence, then unfastened his belt as he stormed up to the side of the bed. She reached out, placed a foot in the center of his chest, and stayed him from getting into the bed with her.

"I did not say you were invited," she said breathlessly.

"It's my bed," he pointed out gruffly. "And I claim everything that lies within it."

"Hmm. I suppose that is your right, after all." She lowered her foot and smiled at him with knowing victory. "Aren't your brothers awaiting you?" she asked.

"They will wait a little longer."

"A little?"

"Don't press me, woman. I do not like to be managed."

"I think you like it more than you think," she said, reaching to fondle the rock-hard flesh between his legs. "Yes, I'd say you like it a great deal."

"Hot little bitch," he hissed. "You toy with danger when you toy with me."

"Then I must enjoy danger," she said, "for I love nothing more, it seems, than to toy with you."

"So it would appear," he ground out as he pushed himself into her touch. To feel her touching him while she still touched herself was beyond pleasurable. The teasing war of their words only added to his gratification.

"Enough!" he snapped out after a minute of letting her touch him. "I *will* have you, then I *will* leave you."

"Of course," she murmured breathlessly. "As you wish."

"Damn right as *I* wish. It is because I wish it, not because you wish it."

"Of course," she said, her hand sliding down the front of his trousers.

"Gods damn you, Jileana!" he ground out as he surged into her caresses again and again and again. Then suddenly he barked out a sound of frustration, grabbed hold of her by both shoulders, and gave her a hard shake. "You do not control me!"

"I would not want to control you," she assured him.

"You could have fooled me," he said fiercely.

She tilted her head and looked at him with genuine, softening surprise. "You mistake me, then. All I want is to give you pleasure, to make you happy. If this does not make you happy, then I will stop immediately."

And stop she did, withdrawing from him quickly.

Feeling instantly bereft, he hastened to keep her from leaving him. "No! I didn't mean . . . I didn't mean you didn't please me. Only . . . only that perhaps you please me far too much at times."

"Is there such a thing as too much pleasure? There are so many hard and harsh things we have to live with every day. Can we not live happily with pleasure as a means of counteracting all that hardness?"

Bemused, he smiled at her. "I never thought of it like that before." It was an idealistic attitude, one very much in keeping with the woman he had begun to understand. She was right. Their time together was growing short. What harm was there in giving in to his impulses when they did indeed give him some much-needed pleasure?

He didn't need to argue with himself a moment longer. He simply grabbed hold of her, pushed his mouth onto hers, and kissed her with all the ferocity he could muster.

"Very well. We will have this your way," he said roughly. "But after this I *will* go to my brothers."

"Yes. I know," she said.

"Swear to me now you will do nothing to interfere with that further."

"Nothing at all," she vowed.

"Ah, damn you . . . I don't believe you for a second."

"And so you shouldn't." She laughed. "For I am most untrustworthy when it comes to this."

"So be it. A contest of wills, then."

"Ah. A challenge."

"Yes."

"Well then, you should know . . . so far you are losing."

"And yet somehow losing feels very much like winning." He chuckled.

After Jaykun finally managed to join his brothers, they got a great deal of work done. Unfortunately, his brothers caught him daydreaming about long silken limbs and mysterious green eyes on more than one occasion and they had fun taking turns teasing him.

"So I suppose we won't see you for several more days now," Dethan said as he pushed back from the table and stretched. They had been working the entire day, and for men of action, sitting for hours on end was never a preferred activity.

"No," Jaykun said with a slow shake of his head. "She leaves tonight."

His brothers exchanged looks across the table.

"So you needn't fear me losing sight of my purpose," he barked out further. "I know that's what you've been thinking behind my back."

"Not at all," Garrett denied. "We would never begrudge you any happiness. There is no law in this that says you cannot have a woman by your side. It's just that . . . Well, war camps are not safe places. You would not want your woman to follow the camp. That means leaving her behind for all but the winter months. It is an untenable situation and we—"

"Stop. It doesn't matter. She will be gone and that's that," Jaykun said, holding up a hand to fend off any further words from his brothers.

"It doesn't have to be. If you care for the girl—"

"I feel nothing for her," Jaykun said harshly. "We have enjoyed our time together and that is the end of it." He stood up and pushed away from the table and the eyes of his brothers. He turned and walked out of the room, his gait swift and determined.

No, he told himself, he felt nothing for the girl. She was delightful, yes, pleasurable to be sure. But there were no actual feelings to be had. After three days? That was a ridiculous concept. People did not form attachments over three days' time.

Or at least they shouldn't. He had fallen in love with Casiria on sight. He had known nothing about her and yet fancied himself in love immediately. It was pure proof that he had been both young and foolish. Only the young made such fantasies in their minds. The young, who had no experience in the ways of the world. Jaykun had faced many hard truths since then.

No. Wait. It was wrong to say he felt nothing for her. Of course he felt something. She was an incredible woman with a wonderful personality. Beyond the sex, she had always been a delight, with bright humor and gentle wisdom. To say he was untouched by her was a lie.

But she must go, he told himself sternly. She was too much of a distraction. He would get nothing done if she remained close by.

And yet . . . these past hours had proven that she would not escape his thoughts so quickly. His mind had turned to her again and again. Who was to say that distraction would stop just because she was gone? Perhaps . . . perhaps he needed her to stay a short while longer. Long enough for him to work her free of his system. Surely he would grow bored of her after a while. The passion would run its course and that would be the end of it. If she left so soon, it was possible he would simply find himself obsessing about that which was gone.

No. He was in control of this, in control of his thoughts and desires. He was . . .

He thought back to the way she had been just hours earlier, lying in his bed with her hands on her own body, filling his head and body with fast, searing heat. Who was he kidding, he thought painfully. She was under his skin. Utterly and completely. He had sworn no woman would ever be able to do so after Casiria, but here she was just the same. He was not in love with her . . . No, there he drew the line. He would never love another woman. But this woman was too uncommon to simply let her slide out of his life without at least trying to figure out how to manage these passions. Either that or he should let her go, bear the brunt of whatever came to be, and move on with his life.

That was as unpalatable as the poisoned soup would have been. He did not want to think of it. But he should force it on himself. He should take the bitterness in and let this passion die.

Damn her and her wicked eyes, her bountiful body, her searing, passionate nature. Damn her. He couldn't do it. He couldn't let her leave. He looked at the sky through a nearby window and knew the evening meal was almost upon them. He had to find her and speak to her before then. He would ask her to stay. Just a few days more. Just long enough to . . . to . . . to whatever. To figure this all out. To work it through. Three days simply wasn't enough time.

And now that he realized he was going to ask her to stay, he grew excited. His pace picked up as he headed for his rooms, hoping she was there. Yes. Just a few more days. That was all he needed.

He burst into his rooms and found her asleep in the bed. Dead asleep. She didn't even stir at his exuberant entrance. It made him chuckle. For all of her seductive ways, she was just as worn out by their lovemaking as he was. Perhaps it was because they had been trying to cram so much into so little time. Perhaps with a relaxed atmosphere things would calm down and be quieter.

He sat down on the edge of the bed and reached out

to touch her bare back. Her skin was cool, the days having grown steadily cooler and the nights following suit. Winter would be upon them soon. Perhaps he could have her for the winter. Just until he had to move his army onward. Yes. That was a fine idea. Surely by the time winter was over he would have grown tired of her.

"Jileana," he whispered into her ear. "Wake up." He gave her a nudging shake. She made a complaining sound and weakly tried to push him away. "Come, now. It's time for dinner and we must talk."

She opened an eye then and looked at him. She groaned and rolled over, away from him. "No. Don't wanna talk. Don't wanna eat. Wanna sleep."

"Come on. Up you go!" He reached out and smacked her backside hard.

She yelped and sat up, her entire body bristling. "Ow! Hey! That's not fair! First you wear me out with your unending appetite for sex, then you wake me up."

"Um . . . the unending appetite for sex was you," he pointed out.

"What?" She seemed to think about it. "Oh. Right. Sorry."

"Don't be sorry," he said with a chuckle. "I like your unending appetite for sex."

"Yes, I seem to recall that," she said with a grin.

"Jileana . . . I want you to stay. At least for a little while. I find three days to be woefully insufficient when it comes to learning about you. I . . . I should like to get to know you better."

Her iridescent eyes brightened and she smiled. "You would?"

He smiled back. "I would."

"Oh, that's so nice," she said. "But I can't stay."

"You . . ." Jaykun was taken aback. It had not occurred to him that she might not want or be able to stay. He hadn't realized that their three-day timetable might be restricted for a reason on her part. "But surely you can put off whatever business you have for a few more days," he found himself saying. "Or perhaps you can come back when you are done."

"No. It's nothing like that." She gave him a wan smile. "I must go home. You see, I wasn't supposed to come at all. My family is probably wondering what happened to me. Or they may have figured it out and are likely quite cross with me. Either way, I must return home."

"Well, maybe if you go home and tell them where you are, surely then you could come back and—"

"No. My family is not very understanding about these things. You see, where I come from a daughter does not leave her father's house until she is bonded with her husband. I may be rebellious enough to leave for seven days, but any more than that would be disrespectful to my father. And hurtful. I would not do that to him." She brightened then. "But you could come with me. I know you would like it in Serenity. And it would give you the opportunity to discuss with our leader the possibility of erecting some temples in Weysa's name. That is, after all, your purpose, is it not? You did say you first would try peaceful methods over war. I do not know how successful you will be, but it would not hurt to try."

"No, you are right. It would not hurt to try."

But if he failed, then what? Then he would make war on Serenity and Jileana's people? He found the idea surprisingly distasteful. He scoffed at himself. A warlord who did not want to make war? What was wrong with him?

He didn't want to admit it, but the idea of going with her to Serenity and spending more time with her under the guise of diplomacy was more than appealing. He could do two things at once. His brothers could manage without him for a little while, couldn't they? Just a few days?

"Very well. I shall come with you as an ambassador in Weysa's name. My brothers can manage here for a little while. Can you give me a day to prepare?"

"No. It must be tonight. Tonight or a moon from now. That is your choice."

"A moon from now? Why are you pressuring me so? I do not understand what one day has to do with anything!"

"You will once I show you the way to my people. Please. Tonight or a moon from now?"

"I see. You have a ship leaving tonight," he murmured.

He couldn't wait for a moon from now. His brothers would be gone by then and there would be no one to manage the city while he went on an ambassadorial mission. He did not like to be so pressured; it was probably very unwise of him to allow it. There was no time to prepare.

"I would need to get a guard together. I cannot go to a foreign court with merely the clothes on my back and no one to protect me."

She laughed at that. "Jaykun, you do not need protecting. You are immortal."

"What? H-how did you know . . . ?" he stammered.

"You burn yet do not die. I therefore guess you to be immortal. Am I wrong?"

"No. You are not wrong," he said, relenting. "I *am* cursed. I *am* immortal. And I will suffer that curse until the end of time. That is the way of it."

"Very well. So you are immortal and do not need protecting."

"Immortality does not protect me from imprisonment."

"Jaykun, you have my word. No harm will come to

you. You will be a free man in our court. We have guests very rarely, but when we do, we treat them well. It is an exceptional thing, to be extended an invitation to Serenity. I hope you appreciate it as such."

"And you are certain your court would welcome me?"

"As certain as I can be. Come . . . come with me. I would like for you to meet my mother and father. I think you would enjoy meeting them and they would enjoy you as well. You are an intelligent man and my mother does appreciate someone handsome to look at."

That made him chuckle. "And does this mean I get to stay in your bed? Or will the rules change once we are in your home?"

"Well, some rules will certainly change, but being in my bed will be, I'm afraid, a requirement of your visit."

He laughed at that. "Very well, then. Let me discuss it with my brothers and pack some belongings. Then I will make my first diplomatic mission to Serenity."

"The first of many, I hope. We worship Diathus almost exclusively, but it is perhaps unwise not to appreciate all the gods. We should not give insult through neglect."

"Even if you raise just a few temples in Weysa's name, I think I can be satisfied."

"You will have to be. War on Serenity is impossible. Diplomacy is your only option. But I should like to give you the opportunity."

"War is impossible? How so?"

"You could never get your army to Serenity. There is but one way there and it is heavily guarded."

"It is an island and I now have an armada."

She laughed at him. "Your armada will mean nothing. Serenity is impenetrable. The storms, remember? You will see. You had best hurry. Dusk is approaching."

He smiled at her, then called for a servant.

CHAPTER
ELEVEN

It was very nearly suppertime. Jileana had packed her second dress with Jaykun's belongings. She had grown to like it very much and she didn't have the heart to leave it behind. Besides, she might need it again someday . . . provided it lasted long enough for her to use it again.

Once that was packed, she wandered around the castle for one last look at everything. She had much to tell everyone once she got home and she didn't want to forget a single detail. From the crotchety old cook who baked the bread she loved so much to the way the wind felt as she stood on the battlements of the castle. She was up there now, walking slowly around so she could see everything in all directions, including the stormy clouds that hid Serenity from sight.

She heard a sound behind her and, startled, swung about. The body that lunged at her was built as she was built, about the same height and weight. But because she was taken off guard, when he plowed into her, he sent her sprawling backward. He followed her every inch of the way down, then clambered up onto her body, straddling her. His hand swung upward through the air. Dazed from striking her head, she barely registered the knife in his hand. He stabbed down.

But just before the weapon would have pierced the flesh of her breast, the man drew it back. That was when she registered that he was shaking like a leaf and . . . crying.

"Please don't—" she began hesitantly.

"Shut up!" he yelled into her face. "I have to kill you! It's my only choice!"

"No. It isn't," she said calmly, soothingly. She could tell this man—this boy, really—was no killer. He was perhaps desperate enough to kill—it was written on every ounce of his body—but he was no stone-cold killer. This boy would be torn by tremendous guilt for the rest of his life if he succeeded in killing her tonight. Not that he could anymore. He had lost his advantage of surprise and she could easily overpower him and take the knife.

"What do you know about it, *prava*?" he spat. "You don't even belong here!"

"Perhaps not. But you don't belong here with a knife in your hand."

"You don't understand!" he shouted into her face. "I am a *trega* half-breed in a city of people who take one look at me and spit in my face. I make my living shoveling dung or digging ditches or scrubbing the sewage pipes. I am dirty all the time, starving all the time, lacking for a bed all the time! I need this gold piece! I need it to get out of here!"

"There are easier ways of getting gold," she said gently. Gingerly.

"Not in this city! Not for me! Not for *trega*!"

"But don't you see? The city isn't going to be run by Krizans any longer. The *trega* have come and will rule this city for many years to come. *Trega* will infiltrate every part of it, live here, and build businesses here.

Businesses that will need strong, hard workers. You will no longer be an outsider. You will be a part of the new order and the old will be brought down."

"But . . ." He hesitated and looked around himself nervously. Then he gripped the knife tighter and drew it higher. "You don't know what you're talking about! Just shut up!"

"Can I at least know the name of the man who is going to kill me?" she asked in a calm and strong tone.

"What for?" he asked.

"Where I come from, knowing the name of our killer allows us to forgive him so we might enter the heavens with a light heart and no malice. If we hold those feelings into our death, we risk becoming a shade, doomed to walk the world, haunting it for eternity. Though I feel no malice toward you at the moment, I want to be certain my heart and soul are cleared.

"I . . ." He swallowed. "Dremu. My name is Dremu."

"Dremu, you don't have to do this. There are better ways. Dremu, I promise you. I can find an alternate solution for you."

"Sure." He scoffed. "You say that only because I'm going to kill you!"

"You aren't going to kill me. If you were, you would have done so already."

"I am too! You just . . . Stop talking to me!"

Jileana suddenly moved, one hand snatching the wrist of the hand holding the knife, the rest of her strong body bucking him off her, over her head, and hard onto his back. She leapt after him, his wrist twisting until he cried out and dropped the knife. The knife was in her hand an instant later and then it was she straddling his body and holding the knifepoint to the top of his throat. He swallowed hard beneath the blade, his eyes wide and wild, panic in every inch of his body.

"Now you listen very carefully," Jileana said. "Are you listening?"

He gave a ginger little nod, aware of the knife tip that was just shy of breaking his skin.

"There are better ways to earn gold and I am going to prove it to you. In fact, you don't need gold at all to make your way in the world, live comfortably, and eat and have a bath whenever it pleases you. Besides, you are no killer, Dremu. You know it as well as I do."

"B-but if I fail, the finia will beat me or order my death. I cannot stay here! She will find a way to punish me for failing to do as she demands!"

"Ah. So it is the finia who is behind this. Thank you. I was wondering who it might be. It was so clearly not your own idea. Tell me, Dremu, what do you know of my people?"

"Only that you are to be feared, that you are deadly and dangerous and that I should run in the other direction if I ever lay eyes on one of you."

"Hmm. Then you know we are powerful and we are able to do things no one else can, yes?"

"I . . . guess so."

"Then will you believe me when I say I have the power to make your life better?"

He swallowed again, nervous and confused. Dremu couldn't understand why she had not killed him the moment she got the advantage of him. He couldn't understand how she was talking about giving him what was, for all intents and purposes, a reward. For that is what it would be. A life as described by her was all he had ever wanted, so it would be the ultimate reward from his perspective. Why? Why would she give that to him after what he had just tried to do to her?

"I do not believe you, but I am willing to put myself in your hands and to see what comes of it. After all, it's clear you have the upper hand and can do what you wish with me. You would be within your rights to have me killed to answer for my crimes against you."

"No one is going to die tonight. Not you and not me. But you will learn to live . . . and to trust. Now come." She pushed off him and gained her feet. She held out her hand to him and helped him up.

"What is this?"

Jileana whirled about at the sound of Jaykun's demanding voice, quickly hiding the knife behind her back and standing between Dremu and Jaykun. "Jaykun! What are you doing up here?" she asked with a bright smile.

"Looking for you," he said with a frown. "And here I find you with this boy?"

"Oh! You mean Dremu?" She laughed, hoping she didn't sound nervous. Clearly Jaykun had seen her sitting astride Dremu. Now he was angry and distrusting. He was . . . jealous. Yes, that was it! The temper in his tone and the aggressive tension in his body . . . He was jealous! "Dremu and I have just met. He was telling me something very interesting about the finia. He claims it is she who has been behind the attempts made on your lives."

"And how does he know this?" Jaykun asked.

"He . . . he overheard someone talking in the halls," Jileana lied with an inward wince. She was not a very good liar, but she did not want Jaykun to punish Dremu.

"The fortunary," Dremu piped up meekly.

Jaykun absorbed this with stony silence for a moment. "Very well. We'll handle the finia."

"Dremu will be coming with us tonight," Jileana added hastily. "I am in need of a good servant and he was wanting a change of scenery."

"Oh. I see," Jaykun said slowly.

"Are you ready? We should be leaving as soon as possible for Serenity," she said.

She heard Dremu inhale sharply and then another of those nervous gulps.

"Are we not going to eat first?"

"There isn't time to eat, travel, and get you somewhere where you can . . . before dusk," she said, moving past Jaykun briskly, hiding the knife in the folds of her skirt as she did.

Jaykun appreciated her discretion, that she wasn't going to tell everyone she met about his curse. He narrowed his eyes on Dremu and felt doubt swirling around inside him. He could have sworn she had been astride him, a position that was not easily achieved if they had just bumped into each other. It had seemed more blatantly sexual to him. Why else would she . . . ?

He caught himself in the thought and the emotion accompanying it. What did it matter to him what she may or may not have been doing sexually? They had no commitment to each other, no ties. If she wanted to fuck his entire army, it should make no difference to him.

But damn, it did make a difference to him, he thought as he followed her back into the castle and down the stairs. At the very least she could wait until such time as they were done with each other.

But she was such a free spirit, going wherever she wanted to go from one moment to the next. It was one of the parts of her personality that drew him so inexorably toward her. But he found he was not of a mind to share her with anyone. The whole point of him going on this trip so precipitously was so he could spend more time with her.

The thought made him stop in his tracks. Wait. No, he thought. He was going to Serenity as an ambassador, in order to begin negotiations for erecting temples in Weysa's name. That was the main reason for going. He was not going just to be with a woman. He was not leaving a newly conquered city—which needed him to take the reins of it desperately—in his brothers' hands at such a crucial time just so he could—

"Jaykun? Is something amiss?"

He blinked and realized Jileana and Dremu were looking at him curiously. That was when he realized he had come to a halt.

"No. Nothing," he muttered, pushing past them and moving on.

"I-I-I don't w-want to go to Serenity," Dremu whispered to Jileana. It was clear he was terrified by the thought.

"Either you come to Serenity," she whispered back, "or I tell him you tried to kill me. It is your choice. Previously you said you had no choice but to kill me. Well, now you have choices. Live with me or die by him. Which do you choose?"

Dremu gave her a look. "Live of course," he said. "Who would choose to die? But . . . Serenity? I have heard stories . . ."

"Most of which are probably lies or exaggerations. Don't worry. It is a very nice place. You will learn to love it."

"But how will I be able to—?"

"Trust me," she said softly, reaching to squeeze his forearm. "You are under my protection and guidance. All will be well."

Dremu took a deep breath and nodded.

"Jaykun, Dremu can carry any belongings you wish to bring with you. He will act as servant for you."

"I have my own servants. I will bring one of them."

She moved up to him and put a hand on his arm to draw him to a stop. "Dremu and no others."

"Why?" he demanded to know.

"Passage to Serenity is limited and I must choose very carefully who to bring. You and Dremu may come; all others must stay."

Jaykun didn't like it. Why was she suddenly taking an interest in this person she had just met? It didn't make any sense to him.

But the fact was that the passage to Serenity was controlled by her, and as a visiting dignitary, he had to be the one to accede to whatever Serenity's customs were . . . for now. That might change later if he found the people of Serenity intractable about building the temples he requested. But he did not wish to consider the ramifications of their potential refusal. Not at present, in any event. He had more than enough on his plate as it was. He would have put this trip off if not for the limitations on their travel. He chose to ignore the voice in his brain that whispered he could have just as easily done this in the springtime as now.

"Very well. Have it your way," he muttered to her. Then he led the way to his rooms. Sitting on the floor was a small trunk. He pointed to it.

"Take that, boy. You will be in charge of my belongings. If anything happens to them, it will be your head. Understood?"

"Yes, my lord," he said, and with all haste he went to fetch the trunk, lifting it with a small amount of difficulty but managing without complaint in the end.

Jaykun turned to Jileana. "I need to say goodbye to my brothers and manage this news about the finia. Shall I meet you at the docks?"

"No. Not the docks," she said with a shake of her dark head. "The cove."

"The ship is anchored near the cove? Why does it not just come to the docks?"

"All will be explained. Just meet me at the cove."

"Very well, then," he said, reaching to ring her about the back of her neck with one strong, demanding hand. He jerked her close and seized her mouth with his, laying claim to her in front of the other male, making certain Dremu knew who owned her affections at that time. He tried not to examine the proprietary impulse too closely as he let her go slowly, taking in the smile she gave him and feeling the better for it.

Then he took his leave of her and headed for his brothers in the dining hall, the servant following steadily behind him.

"Well, brothers, I am off. Do I look the diplomat?" he asked, indicating himself and the finer than usual clothing he was wearing.

"Every inch," Dethan said.

"Jaykun, I must protest again," Garreth said. "Now is not the time for you to leave."

"No, it is not ideal," he agreed. "But if I do not go now, I will not be able to until the summer when you return, and by then I hope to be laying siege to Moroun or perhaps one of the cities on the far continent. No. Now is the better choice."

"Methinks you are thinking more with other parts of your body than with your brain," Garreth said with a frown.

"Enough!" Jaykun said, slamming a fist down on the table. "I will not listen to you and your half-conjured ideas as to my motivations in this. Just . . . just manage this city for the next few days. That is all I ask. Please."

"You know we will," Dethan said soothingly. "Whatever your reasoning, we are here for you, willing to do whatever is necessary. Now be off with you. All is in good hands here. You can be assured of that."

"Thank you, Dethan," Jaykun said with a sigh. "Garreth, forgive my temper."

"You do not like to be questioned. You never did. Which is no doubt why I always questioned you," Garreth said with a chuckle.

"No doubt," Jaykun agreed, smiling. "See you in a few days, brothers! Try not to foul up my city in the meanwhile." He turned toward the door, caught sight of Dremu, and belated remembered to tell his brothers about the finia. "Oh, and you should know that it is the finia behind the attempts on our lives."

"How do you know this?" Dethan demanded.

"This boy overheard the fortunary giving commands," he said, nodding to Dremu.

"I thought the finia was under guard," Garreth said.

"I allowed her limited visitors," Dethan said. "I thought the fortunary would be harmless enough. It isn't as though he were her vizier or her head of guard. I see now my error."

"It is not our way to imprison the leaders of the cities we conquer," Jaykun said. "They are usually harmless enough without gold or armies or advisors."

"Usually. Perhaps we have been too lax with our methods," said Garreth.

"It has worked for us in the past," Dethan said. "The finia is the exception, not the rule."

"Very well. The finia's life is forfeit. And the fortunary will fare no better. Are we agreed?" Jaykun said.

"We are agreed," Dethan said. "Now you best get going. You need to be on that island before dusk."

"I am well aware," Jaykun said dryly.

"And no dallying on the ship! This is a diplomatic mission! Some comportment please!"

Jaykun rolled his eyes and turned his back on their laughter, heading out of the castle and toward the cove.

CHAPTER
TWELVE

The sun was quite low in the sky by the time Jaykun and Dremu reached the cove and it was making Jaykun nervous. There was no way, he thought, that they would make it to Serenity in the hour before dusk and also be able to find a safe place for his curse to come upon him. The island was just too far, and given the wind of the moment, they wouldn't travel fast enough. The last thing he needed was to be on a wooden ship when the curse struck. It would immediately be burned to cinders and ash.

He would simply have to tell Jileana that they could not leave until after juquil's hour. She would not like it—for some reason she was in a desperate hurry—but there was nothing to be done about it.

As they approached the cove, he peered out over the water in search of a ship. There were none to be found anywhere on the horizon. No dingy was rowed in and waiting for them. All he could see were the rocks of the jetty and a colony of seals and morari sunning themselves atop them.

As he entered the cove, he saw Jileana standing there waiting. She was completely naked, holding her dress folded in her hands. Jaykun sucked in his breath at the sight of her. He had truly never seen anything so beautiful in his life. Her skin was warm and dark, her long hair streaming down her back in a silky black cape. He balked at her nudity, however, in front of this other man. He walked up to her, shielding her from the servant. But luckily for him the boy had averted his gaze and was nervously trying not to look at her. Good, he thought. He didn't want this Dremu to look at her. He didn't want anyone to look at her when she was like this.

But she walked around his shielding body and presented her dress to the boy. "Put this in the trunk as well," she said.

Dremu hastened to do as she asked, dropping the trunk on the sand, opening it, and shoving the dress inside.

"You are not going like this, are you?" Jaykun demanded.

"We do not wear much in the way of clothing in Serenity. It is too confining and drags us down. You may want to remove your clothing as well."

"I will not! I'm not going to present myself naked in a foreign court!"

"As you wish," she said simply. "Dremu?"

"N-no, my lady. I-I am fine like this."

"Very well, then," she said breezily before Jaykun could work himself up over her inviting a servant to get naked with her. "Let's go!"

Then she ran into the water.

Jaykun just stood there and stared after her, at a total loss. Where in the eight hells was she going? Did she expect them to swim all the way to Serenity?

"Come on!" she called out gaily.

"Jileana, what in the eight hells are you doing?!" Jaykun shouted out to her.

"It's here. Under the jetty. Come on!"

Under the jetty? Jaykun wasn't sure he had heard her right. But sure enough, she dived downward.

That was when he began to realize there was a lot more to this than had been immediately apparent to him. Things began to click: Finding her naked on the beach. The way she had said he couldn't get to Serenity by ship. The way she had treated everything like a new and wondrous experience . . . as if she had never experienced the world before. The fact that there had always seemed to be something a little . . . otherworldly about her.

He suddenly began to strip down, disrobing faster than he ever had before in his life, throwing his clothing and boots at the hapless servant, who stood quivering at the water's edge with his trunk.

The instant Jaykun was naked, his heart racing with a combination of fear and excitement, he plunged into the water and chased after her. When he reached the place where she had dived down, she popped back up, her hair slicked back and a laughing smile on her face. The water was cold but not frigid and he felt very exposed being naked with her.

"What are you?" he demanded of her.

She smiled again. "The Krizans call us *prava*. But that is a derogatory name. You would probably call us selkies. These are all my people." She indicated the seals diving from on the rocks, entering the water and swimming down beneath the jetty. "Look. See?"

She dived under the water and he watched as she swam around him, her long woman's body suddenly changing shape into that of a sleek seal. She surfaced again croaking out a happy sound, dived back under the water, circled him again, then came up as the woman he had come to know.

"Beneath the water, built into the jetty, is the portal

to my home. To Serenity. You have to swim down and through it. Come on, Dremu!" she shouted out.

Dremu stood uncertainly at the water's edge, holding the trunk in his quaking hands.

"B-but the trunk, my lady!"

"It will be as nothing in the water," she said.

Then she lifted a hand, rotated it in a circular motion, and the trunk became light as a feather in Dremu's hands. Stunned by this magic, and swept along in the current his life had been caught up in, he found himself splashing into the water. He had to follow. He had to. He was finally going on an adventure, an adventure no one else would ever be able to lay claim to. *His* adventure. It was an amazing thing . . . It was better than gold.

Jileana waited until Dremu and the trunk had joined them.

"You will be able to see the portal straight away. It glows. Just follow me through it!"

She dived down and the men had only two choices: follow or go back to shore. Of course, each for their own reasons, they chose to follow her.

Jaykun felt as though his life had suddenly become completely surreal. He should really give this some thought. He shouldn't merely jump in without thinking of the consequences. But, he realized, that was exactly what he had been doing ever since he first met Jileana. Jumping in with both feet and letting himself be swept away with hardly a thought to the consequences. It was probably because his life was so written out for him already. He had a role to play and no choice but to play it. He was slave to the whims of a goddess. At least in this small thing he was able to make a free choice, to choose to go or not to go. Oh, he had cloaked it in the cape of diplomacy, telling himself it was still in Weysa's best interest, but in the end . . . in the end, it had been about what he wanted. And what he wanted was her: Jileana. He didn't know how long he wanted her, but he wanted her now to the exclusion of all else.

He gave the briefest thought to his brothers. But he pushed that concern aside as well and dived down beneath the blue waters.

The water was not crystal clear, not like he had seen in his travels along the southern continents, but it was still clear enough for him to make her out as her sleek body dived down and swam along the rocks. The rocks turned to coral almost immediately as they swam downward, and it was only a short distance before he made out the glow of the portal. Excitement coursing through every last one of his veins, he swam down along the peach-and-russet-colored coral, swam through a school of little fishes, and then came to a halt in front of an archway of rock and coral that glowed blue along its edges, each end of the arch rooted in sand on the ocean floor. As he watched, several seals swam through the portal, disappearing in a bright flash of light. He could see them swimming away on the other side.

In fact, on the other side the water was a completely different color. Or rather, it was much clearer. The coral was a different color as well. It was red and tan. Schools of brilliantly colored fish were darting around, disappearing from view when they should have just been showing up around the other side of the archway. Jaykun was curious as to what the portal looked like from the back, but he had been holding his breath for quite a while and his lungs were beginning to ache. True, he could not die from drowning, but it would not be a pleasant sensation to drown over and over again. Besides, Dremu was not so fortunate.

Almost without thought for them, Jileana swam through the portal in a brilliant flash. Then she stopped and waved them onward. Figuring he had only two choices, to go forward or to go back, he decided to go where the most appeal lay. He swam through the portal.

It was the strangest sensation . . . almost like touching lightning. Only not as violent as he imagined that would be. Also, the temperature in the water was radically different from one side of the archway to the other. It was much warmer on this side. The moment he crossed through, he saw Jileana dart upward, her body moving so fast it was amazing. He followed her readily, very much in need of taking a breath. He only spared a glance backward to see the servant swimming through the archway, the trunk dragging behind him in one hand. Everything within it should be wet, ruined, and heavy, but the servant was pulling it along as if it weighed nothing at all.

He and Jileana broke the surface of the water together and drew in breath. She waited for Dremu to surface. He did, spluttering and gasping. She laughed with delight.

"You did it! You both made it! Wonderful! Look! There's Serenmitazahmiktubarinaty! My home!"

She pointed to a sheer cliff only a short distance away. The inlet was like nothing Jaykun had ever seen before. It was a city constructed of fossilized coral, honeycombs and caves leading from surface to surface, level to level, from high at the top of the cliff to down at the water. Even from a distance he could see people climbing up the cliff walls in order to go from one level to the next or, in some cases, simply leaping off and diving with hurtling speed into the water below.

Jileana began to swim toward the coral city, her streamlined body moving fast. It was clear she was happy and eager to get home. The trunk was floating in the water, the servant clinging to it desperately, as if his life depended on it. Jaykun had to give him credit for his bravery. There weren't many men who would jump into a situation like this unprepared and unarmed. He still couldn't believe he had done so himself. But if he hadn't, he wouldn't be seeing all he was seeing, experiencing all he was experiencing . . . and he wouldn't have traded this moment away for anything. He had never felt so alive, so brave and daring, so strong in the face of his fear of the unknown.

"Come along, little fellow. We best be following her," he called to the servant. "Can you manage with that?"

"Y-y-yes, my lord!"

"Very good! Our adventure awaits!"

Jaykun took off after Jileana. She was like a fish, darting from one place to the next, until they reached the clear blue-green waters of the inlet and were only a few feet away from the place where the coral cliffs met the water. That was when he saw that the caves and cubbies continued below the water's surface and the water was teaming with people deep down, beyond where he could see. The coral beneath the water was not fossilized, dead and dry; it became a living, breathing jungle of life that teemed from its every pore.

And every last one of the population was either naked or wearing the briefest bit of clothing to cover their sex. The women were all bare breasted, the men bare chested.

Jileana swam to the nearest cave and led the men inside. There were shelves immediately to the left and right, and Jileana hauled herself out of the water and onto a shelf. Jaykun followed suit. Then he looked around to see about half a dozen eyes staring at him in surprise.

"Jaykun, these are my people." She introduced them with a wave of her hand. "This is Kino," she said, pointing to a darkly tanned, leathery looking older woman. "Kino has been serving my family for generations. Dremu, you will stay here with her and she will help you get our belongings to the upper level where I live."

"Oh, mistress," Kino said, tsking hard. "Your fadder be sorely mad wid you. You know he don't like da idea of you goin' to da Overworld. No, mistress, not at all. He told you no go, but you go anyway. He be hoppin' mad."

"I figured as much," Jileana said with a sigh. "But I will deal with that later. First we must see my mother."

"She no much happier wid you dan your fadder is," Kino said with a raspy little chuckle. "You done steamed quite a lotta people, you done."

"I know, Kino. I know." Jileana leaned forward and kissed one of those leathery cheeks before looking at Jaykun and winking. "Come on. There isn't much time. We have to get you somewhere . . . safe."

That was when he realized, with no little surprise, that for the first time in as long as he could remember, he had forgotten the time of day, lost track of it, been completely free of the knowledge of his curse. It astounded him. Ever since the curse had begun he had spent every waking moment fully cognizant of it, always aware of it and aware of the time of day. Always plotting exactly where to go that would be safest and farthest away from everybody else. For these past minutes he had been free of that weight.

But now it came crashing back into him and he felt a rising sense of panic. He didn't know where he was, didn't see any kind of beach that would be a safe distance from everyone else. His curse would begin and all of these people would see him burn. It was the last thing he wanted.

Jileana dived back into the water and slipped away from him, going down deeper this time. He took a breath and followed her even though a visceral part of him was saying they were going in the wrong direction.

He needed to be isolated on land . . . else he would have to burn in the water in the middle of the ocean. Burn and drown at the same time. Burning was bad enough, but to drown on top of it? It was more than he thought he could bear. True, that was exactly what he would have been forced to do as they crossed the oceans in his armada—swimming safely away from the big wooden ships—but he had not come to terms with it in his mind, had not yet prepared himself for it.

He followed the woman who darted and danced through the water as if she had been born for it, and he supposed she had been. She swam almost as fast as she had in her seal form, or so it seemed to him as he tried to keep up with her. He was a strong swimmer, but she was stronger. She had to stop and wait for him on more than one occasion. Finally, she brought them into one of the coral caves, and taking his arm, she pulled him up into a pocket of air. He gasped for breath and she smiled at him.

"Only a little farther in," she said, beginning to swim toward the back of the cave. Then, after a moment, he began to see a glowing light. Not that there were fires, he realized as they drew into what looked like grand private living quarters, but the walls themselves were phosphorescent. Jileana pulled herself out of the water and onto a shelf, then she reached out a hand to him and helped him to do the same. He was beginning to realize why she was so strong. If the people of Serenity swam and climbed constantly in order to get from one place to the next, it only made sense that they were fit creatures.

She stood up and walked to the rear of the cave, leaving him with little choice but to follow. He was beginning to feel itchy, though, itchy with the worry of the setting sun. The cave seemed isolated, but then he saw a woman at the back of the cave.

She had hair as red as blood and it was braided down her back in a thick rope that reached the backs of her knees. There was a circlet of golden wire braided into it around the crown of her head. She was nude except for a small sarong knotted at her hip. She was tall and slender, as fit as Jileana was—as everyone seemed to be—and as she turned to look at them, he was instantly struck by the fact that she was nearly Jileana's twin.

"Mother!" Jileana greeted the woman, her bare feet slapping against the cave floor as she hurried into her mother's eager embrace.

"Jilly, you naughty child! Your father is beside himself! You know he forbade you to go to the Overworld. When he realized where you had gone he was furious!"

"I'm surprised he didn't come after me," Jileana said as she hugged her mother.

"Creasus couldn't afford to be away. The grots have been grumbling with discontent. He sent Lalo after you, but in the end, it was the clutch that kept an eye on you. After all, you came back every night where they were able to see you."

"The grots are sea creatures that live in a small settlement nearby. The clutch is the collection of seals and morari sitting on the jetty of the cove," Jileana explained to Jaykun. Then she turned back to her mother. "It was one reason why I returned to the cove each night. I knew the clutch would report back to Father that I was well."

"That was not all they reported," Jileana's mother said as her attention turned to Jaykun. "Is this the man who burns?"

"Yes, Mother, it is. His name is Jaykun. Mother, we don't have much time. He must burn every night from dusk to juquil's hour. It is a curse. I was hoping that you could help."

"Oh no, dearest. This is obviously a curse of the

gods," she said as she inspected Jaykun carefully. She shook her head. "I cannot touch it."

"I didn't think you could. But I was hoping you could help him stay below the waters."

"Oh! Yes, of course I can. Come here, young man."

Jaykun lifted a brow at that. He was not a young man by any stretch of the imagination. True, his immortality had frozen him in the prime of his life and looks, but he was over two centuries old, most of that spent chained to a star in torture. There was nothing young about him.

Still, he moved closer to her.

"My name is Ravi. I do not want you to be afraid."

"He is a very brave man, Mother."

"He would have to be to gain my daughter's respect and trust. Jilly would not bring just anyone into our world. There are strict rules about that, Jaykun."

"Then I am honored," he said.

"He is an ambassador, Mother. He wishes to speak with the empress."

"Ah. Well, that should be very interesting. But first let us make it so you can move freely about amongst us."

Ravi then placed both hands on Jaykun's chest and closed her eyes.

"We haven't much time," Jaykun said, tension ratcheted up in his voice. "The curse is coming."

"Yes. I feel it," she murmured. "You will feel a tingling sensation, Jaykun, in your chest. That only means the spell is working."

"*Spell?*" he asked tightly.

Then, as promised, his chest began to tighten and tingle. Suddenly a jolt of energy jumped from Ravi's hands and into his chest. Startled, he stepped back, away from her.

"There. It is done."

"What is done?" he demanded to know.

"It is an osmosis spell. From now on your body will draw air from the water. You will no longer need to breathe as you would on land," Jileana said, reaching out to put a comforting hand on his arm. "Now you can choose any spot on the ocean floor to burn without drowning as well. You can move freely from land to water like the rest of us do. You can hear and speak beneath the water. You can live in my world."

Stunned, Jaykun didn't know what else to do other than to thank her with a murmur of politeness.

"I believe your friend is a bit shocked by all he is seeing and hearing. But you haven't much time. Take him to the juna cave. There will not be anyone there and that should protect everyone from the burning."

"How did you know . . . ?"

"Mother is a sea witch. *The* sea witch. There is no one more powerful. My magic is nothing compared to hers."

"*Your* magic?"

"Oh, minor spells," Jileana said breezily, waving the query off. "Like the one that made the trunk lighter and waterproof. Now follow me. We better swim fast." She gave her mother a swift kiss on the cheek. "I will be back later!"

She ran away and leapt into the water. Jaykun hastened after her.

The first thing he noticed was that he could draw in a breath as easily as if he were on land . . . only he wasn't breathing through his mouth and nose. It seemed to enter him from all around him, as if his entire body was breathing. Then Jileana turned and said to him, "This way!" and he heard her as clear as if she had been speaking to him above the water. He was stunned and fascinated, but he didn't have time to enjoy the new experience. They were just swimming into a large cave some distance away from everyone else when the burn began in the center of his chest. He shouted out in warning to Jileana, and she hurriedly swam away to a safe distance. Within moments the water around him was boiling with heat and his body was wrenching and burning just as badly as ever. The pain was extraordinary. Blinding and searing.

And so, once again, the curse was fulfilled.

CHAPTER
THIRTEEN

Once Jaykun was able to swim again with only a modicum of pain, Jileana led him back to the surface. It seemed the selkie city extended as deep below the surface of the water as it soared above it, making the city quite vast indeed. Even though now it was dark and quite late, there were many selkies moving about. Jileana led him to the cliff face of fossilized coral, and using the porous surface for handholds and footholds, she began to climb up as easily as though she were climbing on the rungs of a ladder.

His hands and feet were still raw with burns, and this made it difficult because the coral was quite rough. But he did not complain. There was nothing to be done about it so complaining served little purpose, in his mind. He had suffered much worse agony and this was light in comparison.

Jileana led him up to a level of the coral that was quite a healthy distance from the water's surface. On this level the coral had been smoothed to create a surface for walking normally. There was a ledge about the width of a road that ran the entire length of the cliff face. Along this road was a series of caves—some completely dark, and he was unable to determine what was in them; others had light glowing warmly within that showed selkies sitting or sleeping or in leisurely pursuits. One selkie he saw was reading; another was working fibers to make a net. It seemed so normal, so homey, just as what one would find in the many rooms of a castle, only here there were no doors and all was on display for anyone to see who might be passing, so long as the light was on, that is.

The source of their light seemed to vary. Some used candles, some lanterns. Small fires built close to the entrances of caves shed light nearly to the back of the caves; it all depended on the size of the cave in question.

However, most of the caves were lit from what seemed like the walls themselves. When Jileana led him into one of the larger ones, he was able to touch the wall where it glowed.

"It is a phosphorescent ink," she explained. "It comes from the ink glands of the kilmari fish. We catch them and milk the glands, then paint the walls as you see. The ink only needs to be refreshed about three times within a full turning. It is what most of us prefer to use. The fires are fueled by charcoal, not wood; as you can surmise, wood is in short supply and becomes too damp here to be useful. The coal is mined from enriched caves a bit farther down on this side of the island." She took his hand and led him deeper into the cave. "This is my home. Or rather, my father's home. This entire ledge houses my father, my brothers, and their families. My mother lives below the water's surface. She and father have not been together since my birth. She is the most powerful sea witch ever to live," she said with obvious pride. "And my father is the greatest warrior."

Jaykun chuckled at that. "You are their child. Of course you would think that."

"Perhaps," she said with a sly smile. "But any one of the selkies will tell you the same. My father is commander of the empress's army. Many great warriors follow him."

"I thought Serenity was immune to invading forces. Why would you need an army?"

"We are immune from human invaders," she qualified. "We have other enemies who are constantly nipping at our heels like rabid little mongrels."

There was true venom in her words and he felt it eddying off her. The selkies clearly had some troublesome enemies.

And oddly enough he felt the urge to help her . . . to help them. He didn't know anything about these enemies and he barely had a clue as to how to navigate in her world, but just the same, the urge to be of some kind of help to her was overwhelming. The desire, as powerful as it was, confused him, so he shoved it away from his most ready thoughts. Instead he tried to focus on where he was, on all the things he was seeing and learning.

In the end, it was not hard to do at all. He felt like he had the eyes of a child, dazed with wonder at everything he saw. She brought him deeper into the cave and he saw it went back much farther than he'd first thought, taking a turn before ending in what looked to be a bedroom. He assumed this because on the floor was a pallet. At the base was a six-inch thick layer of sand, presumably to add softness. Covering the sand was a woven mat of some kind. Then there were layers of soft animal skins. He crouched down and fingered one of the skins thoughtfully.

"So you hunt on the island, then?"

"We do, but rarely. Only for what we need. We rarely eat the meat of the animals, so we mostly hunt them for their skins."

"I know you don't eat the meat. You were so fascinated by the foods we eat, it was clear you didn't experience food from game or grain. So what do you eat? As we speak of food I grow hungry."

"Of course! You didn't eat this night. For that matter neither have I. I had almost forgotten. Here, let me show you how we eat."

She took him back out to the main body of the cave. She picked up a container. The hollow drumlike object seemed to hold bones or stones in its center. When she shook the drum, it rattled loudly. Shortly after she put it down, a young girl appeared and dropped to her knees before Jileana, bowing her head.

"What may I do for you, my mistress?"

"Sana, this is Jaykun. He is my guest. You are to get him anything he needs if it is possible. He knows little of our ways and you are to help him become acclimated to life here. For now, we are hungry."

"Yes, my mistress. I will prepare a meal for you." The young girl stood up and hurried away.

"Sit. Relax. We have had a long day," Jileana said invitingly as she sat down on the smooth cave floor and patted the floor beside her. Jaykun took her invitation readily, taking the seat beside her. She was smiling at him, looking soft and beautiful to his tired eyes. There was something decadent about having her completely naked all the time. He could reach out and touch her any way he liked at any time he liked. There was no confining clothing to get in his way. He had free access to all of her dark and beautiful bare skin. He quickly tried to quell those compelling thoughts because his lack of clothing allowed it to be all too obvious when he found her arousing. Still, his restraint came too late and she leaned into him with a chuckle. Her hand came to rest on his chest, her fingers drifting silkily down his breastbone.

"Food first," she admonished him. "Then we will settle all other appetites."

He gave her a low, short growl. "I cannot help it if you are so unbelievably delicious to my eyes. Especially if you run about indecently lacking in clothing."

"Clothing is highly overrated. It weighs a body down and tangles it up. It is impractical."

"Yes, I can see that, considering how you live. But you have spent the past few days learning and adapting to living in my world. Now I will be given the same opportunity in yours."

"And are you looking forward to that?" Her gaze drifted from his. "I know I offered all of this to you without any warning. I must say, you have taken very well to it."

"Before I was cursed by the gods, I roamed this world with my brother, doing what I am doing now, only voluntarily rather than being indentured to it as I am now. I traveled far and wide, and in those travels I saw things, many wondrous and magical things that you could never imagine. The adventure that gained me my immortality alone is quite a story. It taught me long ago to be aware and to be flexible. I should have known there was something about you . . . something different and magical. Actually, I did know. I simply was so taken with you that I didn't allow myself to see what was right before my eyes."

"It was not my intention to trick you. I didn't know what you would think of me. I had to protect my people. The Krizans know of us, but no others, really. We are mostly thought of as beings of myth or legend. It is best that way. Almost none know of the portal. Fortunately, the portal between our worlds is only open for the span of the week of the full moon. The three nights waxing, the day of the full moon, and three days waning. As soon as the moon wanes three nights the portal closes until the next moon."

"That's why we had to go tonight. It was going to—"

Jaykun took a breath in harshly. "Are you saying the portal is closed now? Closed until the next full moon?"

"Why, yes. Is there something wrong with that?"

He reached out and grasped her arm, giving her a little shake. "I was only supposed to be here a few days! You mean I am trapped here until the moon turns full again?"

"Trapped? This is no prison, Jaykun," she said sharply, her eyes attaining a wounded appearance. "You will be treated as my honored guest. I don't think you appreciate the rarity of the invitation I have extended to you. I warned you . . . tonight or a month from tonight. I said it more than once."

It was true. She had said it more than once; he simply had not understood her. Had not understood the limitations involved. From her perspective they had been obvious.

The truth was, he should never have come in the first place. He should have remained focused on his newly won city. He should have focused on getting his brothers home to their wives. Instead he had foolishly and selfishly chased a woman into another world. Looking back now he couldn't understand why he would do something so headlong. Why? Why had he done it?

He looked at Jileana and he knew why. Because he had been unable to reconcile the idea that she would leave him so soon after he had just gotten to know her. He had not been ready to let her go. He couldn't explain it, but he had not been ready.

And now his brothers would suffer for it. It would be a waning now before they could leave for their homes, forcing them to travel in the growing colder weather. That and they would worry about him when he did not return after the few days' time he had told them he would be gone. The term "worry" was perhaps an understatement. They would be aggressive as they searched for him, taking ships into the storms that surrounded Serenity, not realizing that the island was magically protected against all human intruders.

"Is there no other way out of here?"

"There are only the moon portals to the Overworld. Your world."

"That's what you call it? The Overworld?"

"Yes. And the ocean is the Underworld. Serenity lies between."

"And no ships can ever make it through the storms?"

"Never," she assured him. "Ships that try are either turned back or completely destroyed. It's madness to even try."

"How many moon portals are there?"

"There are several throughout the oceans, but to go through them would mean traveling a distance from here. The portal we went through is the closest one to the actual Isle of Serenity. Ah. Our supper," she said when Sana returned with a plate of multicolored food on it.

"Wonderful. I have missed this," Jileana said with eager anticipation. "Your food is delicious—don't get me wrong. But this is so much more delicate and varied."

"What is it?"

"It's fish of course," she said, reaching for a yellow fleshy strip of meat. That was when he realized it was raw.

"You . . . you don't cook your food?" he asked, trying hard not to sound horrified.

"No. We simply debone it and eat it as nature intended it to be eaten. Try it. I promise you, you will like it. Try the orange one. It is delpi fish, a sweeter, fattier fish. It simply melts on your tongue. Go on, try it," she urged him. "If you like, you can wrap it in seaweed or kelp. Like this." She demonstrated, rolling the fish up in the seaweed and then popping it in its entirety into her mouth. "Mmm."

With a brave, steady breath, Jaykun imitated what she had done, and after only a moment of hesitation, he popped the fish into his mouth and began to chew. To his surprise a burst of salty sweetness washed over his tongue. He had never eaten raw fish before; he had never realized it could actually taste good. Fish had always been one of his least favorite dishes, the flesh of it always so dried out from cooking, in his opinion. But prepared like this, it was lush and juicy and so surprising.

Jileana laughed at the expression on his face. Try the purple one. It is more tart. We cradle it in kofi leaves, which are sweet, to offset the bitterness. Like this." She demonstrated, laying the flesh in a cuplike leaf with purple veins running throughout it. She took a bite, then offered the rest to him.

Before he knew it, they had cleaned the plate of every last piece of fish and all the leaves and seaweed. More than satisfied, Jaykun sat back with a sigh and smiled at her.

"I can see now why our foods seemed so different from yours."

"I am afraid you have a greater variety than we do. But our food is still delicious and there is plenty of it. The ocean is a trove of different kinds of fish and even we have not experienced them all. But we do have our favorites."

"I think I liked the orange one best."

She laughed. "Most children love that one."

"Are you saying I have the palate of a child?"

"You can take it that way if you like. But the delpi is a sweet-fleshed fish and that appeals to children. But it happens to be one of my favorites as well, so believe me, I am not judging you."

"Well, I will take some consolation in that. So . . . now what do we do?"

"We sleep. It is late. You still need to heal and rest some more. I have a bed, as you see, or we can sleep in the ocean. There is nothing like sleeping in the water, your body floating free."

"And risk being drawn out to sea? No, thank you."

She laughed again. "We tether ourselves so that doesn't happen."

"I think I will stick to the bed. It is what I am used to," he said, moving over to it and sitting down upon it. She rose and came over to him, doing the same. She leaned into his side and reached to catch his mouth with her own, giving him a slow, searching kiss.

"Mmm. I don't foresee much in the way of rest if you continue to kiss me like that."

"Don't worry. I will let you sleep . . . for now. We have had a big night and it is much to absorb." She smiled at him and fingered a strand of his hair, smoothing the curl of it. "There will be much to see tomorrow and I must introduce you to the empress. Just remember, she is a woman of great logic. She will want to be reasoned with in an intelligent manner. But like any monarch, she can be pushed too far. She will not tolerate someone telling her what to do."

"I am usually a bully when it comes to this, forcing Weysa's will upon people. It is my duty to do so. The goddess would not give any quarter and neither must I. However, since there is no way I could bring an army here to bully your people, I will have to be content with using diplomacy. I will be satisfied if I can get your empress to raise even one temple to Weysa."

"It is a reasonable goal. I don't see how she can refuse."

"I will ask for more of course and settle for less. I will approach this as a bargaining would be approached."

"Just be careful. Don't be greedy."

"No. I won't. Stop fretting. I have done this before," Jaykun assured her.

"Very well. Now come to bed. Sleep." She moved to draw him into a reclining position. Once he lay down, she cuddled up along his side and rested her head on his shoulder.

She closed her eyes, and with a deep sigh of contentment, she fell asleep.

CHAPTER
FOURTEEN

Jaykun awoke to a heavy, strong punch slamming into his chest. He was grabbed by both arms and hauled up onto his feet. No mean trick considering his size and weight. Still disoriented, he shoved at the man who was manhandling him and became aware enough in time to throw up an arm and block the roundhouse punch aiming for his head. Instinctively he countered the attack and sent a crushing punch into his attacker's jaw. The man, of equal build and strength to Jaykun, staggered back under the force of the hit. He recovered quickly, though, and lunged forward with renewed fervor.

But suddenly Jileana was between them, shoving the other man away with all of her strength and standing protectively in front of Jaykun. "Silan, enough! Enough of this!" she barked at him.

"What is he doing here?" Silan demanded of her, his big body lunging forward threateningly. But she pushed him back again and Jaykun realized Silan allowed it because he didn't want to hurt her. "In your *bed*?"

"He was sleeping. And I had hoped this morning he would be making love to me. But you have ruined that!"

"Good! You are an unmated woman, Jileana! This is highly improper!"

She sighed as if in exasperation. "Silan, you are the most uptight and prudish selkie ever to be born on this planet. That mode of thinking is so far out of date it has a grizzled old beard. And even if it were a reasonable thought, why would you try to resolve the issue by throwing punches? Honestly. Are all my brothers this pigheaded?"

Ah. Brother. Well, that explained things a little more clearly to Jaykun. For a moment he had been afraid that Silan was her lover and Jaykun had inadvertently found himself in the bed of another man's woman. In truth, he didn't know enough about Jileana to know if stringing two men along at the same time was something she would do. But the thought sat ill with him. No, he realized, he did know her well enough to know she wasn't the sort to do something like that. She was a decent and honest person. He had gotten that much of a sense of her.

"Your sister is an adult capable of making her own choices," he said to Silan. "She is a sensible, intelligent woman. It is her choice who she decides to consort with, is it not?"

Silan seethed, growled, and clenched his fists as if he were trying to use every ounce of his self-control to keep from ripping his sister away from Jaykun and lunging for Jaykun's throat.

Jaykun smiled. Let him try, he thought. He would be in for a rude awakening. Jaykun was not easily brought down.

"Silan, enough," Jileana again barked at him.

"Where have you been?" Silan demanded after turning his attention back to her. "Do you know the state you've put Father in? You've been to the Overworld, haven't you? That's where *this* is from, isn't it?" he demanded of her, jerking his chin in Jaykun's direction.

"Silan, stop being rude!" she snapped, losing her temper. She placed a hand at the center of her brother's chest and shoved him hard. "Yes, I've been to the Overworld." She shoved him again. "And yes, he is a human." Another shove. "And yes, he is my lover. And *yes,* this is none of your business! Now, you either let me introduce you properly and civilly or you leave right now."

"Fine. I'm leaving. And I'm going to tell Father what you've done."

"No, you aren't! You are going to allow me the courtesy of explaining myself to Father without your interference and prejudiced opinions!"

"Just try to stop me," he dared her on a sneer. Then he turned on his heel and marched out of the cave.

"Damn. I'm sorry," she said, turning to face him. "Truly sorry for my brother's deplorable behavior. Your welcome here should not be like that."

"It's fine," Jaykun assured her as he pulled her closer. "He's not the first brother I've met who disliked a man courting his sister."

"Is that what this is? Courting?" she asked with a tease in her tone. "It feels so much more sordid than that."

He laughed. "Perhaps. But you are worth more than a cold, thoughtless tumble. I cannot promise you much, but I can promise you that."

"Why, Jaykun, that's practically romantic," she said with a laugh. "Now come, let's break our fast, and we can go see the empress and then my father. Hopefully we can attend him before my brother poisons him too harshly against you."

"Then perhaps we should attend your father first and the empress next. I do not wish for your father to think too ill of me. It's bad enough that I am committing egregious sins with his daughter."

"How funny humans are, that love is a sin."

"Well, love is not so much a sin, but a man using a

woman for sex with no thought to making her a wife is apparently frowned upon in polite society. It is different from culture to culture of course, but it seems to be a trend throughout all the lands I have been to."

"It is like that here in some respects as well. Or it was. Some people prefer the old ways, but the younger ones are more free-spirited like I am. My father will have to accept that about me. And he has . . . for the most part. But my brothers are another matter. They are overprotective of me. Severely so in Silan's case."

"Well, I do not wish to incur the wrath of any of your brothers or your father. By the by, how many brothers are we talking about?"

"Only six."

"Six!" Jaykun choked out. "And all are overprotective of you?"

"No. There is a fair enough balance between those who are and those who are not. I mean, to some extent they all are, but some of them understand that it is my life to live as I see fit. So long as you do not harm me, you have nothing to worry about from them."

"And how many are zealously overprotective like Silan?"

"Silan is in a class by himself. However, there are two others of a similar bent. Not quite so fanatical, but similar."

"Lovely. And the other three are more fair. Well, at least they are split in twain and not all will be wanting my head on a platter."

"Don't worry," she said, patting his chest. "We'll be fine. You'll be fine."

There was the sound of a throat clearing behind her and Jileana turned about to see Dremu standing there awkwardly.

"Dremu! I forgot all about you! I am so sorry!" she exclaimed.

"It's all right, my lady. I found a place to sleep with some of the other servants. They got a cave just for those who are coming and going as guests. It was nice. Nicest place I've slept in a long time."

Dremu put the trunk he'd had tied to his back on the floor of the cave. "I checked," he said. "Not one drop of water got in."

"It was a part of the spell I cast. It makes things light and waterproof. It helps when we have to travel here and there with things we don't want to get wet for whatever reason. Though I must say it isn't something that comes up often. We usually don't mind getting things wet. Now come on. We have a busy day ahead. Dremu, you can follow Mishka around today. She is a serving girl who works here. Follow her lead and you will learn what is expected of you."

"Yes, my lady. Anything you want," he said, bowing low to her.

"Enough. I am no empress in need of kowtowing," she scolded him, lifting him up straight. "I am just a woman trying to give a man a new way of life. When you are used to life here you can decide what you would like to do. You will earn coin and you will find people here friendly and accepting. Perhaps even fascinated by who you are. Later I will bring you to my mother and she will cast magic on you that will allow you to breathe underwater. It will be necessary if you are going to be living here."

"A s-s-spell?" the man said nervously. "Oh, I don't—"

"Dremu, you have been so brave so far already. Surely you have seen mages. A sea witch is no different. Although, I daresay my mother is far more powerful than the average mage. She won't hurt you. No one will hurt you while you are under my protection. If anyone misuses you in any way, you let me know immediately."

"Yes, my lady," he said with a tremulous smile.

"Now, I'm sure everyone is hungry. So let me fetch something for us to eat."

"Oh no, my lady! I can do it! I already know where the . . . kitchen is. Or rather, the cave where they prepare the trays." He turned to Jaykun. "It's not really a kitchen so much because there's very little cooking done. But you should see these huge cauldrons they have where they boil the fishes sometimes. The fishes in shells, that is. Like crab and such. I never had crab before last night. I've never tasted anything so good. Anyway, let me go get it. I'll be back in a shake." Dremu turned and dashed off, heading out of the cave.

"Well, he's excited to be here," Jaykun said with a chuckle.

"And you aren't?" she asked archly, a brow lifting.

"Oh, I'm excited all right. But it has less to do with being here and more to do with what I'm seeing right now," he said, sliding a lascivious look down the length of her body.

"Stop!" She laughed. "Time enough for such things later. Dremu will be back quickly."

"Then I shall have to be quicker!"

She squealed when he grabbed her up off her feet and threw her down onto the bed.

After gorging himself on her and then breakfast, Jaykun followed Jileana out of the cave and, with a harrowing dive off the cliff face, into the water. As they swam downward, Jileana changed back and forth between woman and selkie seal, playfully swimming across his path each time she did. She was quite beautiful in both forms, Jaykun thought. Her body was sleek and dynamic, fast and incredible. He found himself thinking how easily he could get used to her being around. But he quashed the thought instantly. They were from different worlds. He could never live in this world and she would not likely want to live in his. And in any event, in both worlds he was a cursed man. A man with a mission in life that did not leave room for things like relationships with women. As it was, he was letting things get too far out of hand, letting his desire to be around her cloud his better judgment and get in the way of his goals. Now his brothers would have to cope with the aftermath of his rash choices. They would be forced to wait another three weeks for the moon to come full before they could go home to their families for the winter. He felt very guilty about that actually. He had been selfish and his brothers would pay the price for it. He wasn't kidding himself any longer. He had come here under the guise of diplomacy, but the truth was, he had not wanted to leave Jileana's company. He had not yet been prepared to do that. Their time together had been too short. But now he would have her for the better part of a month, until the week of the full moon, and he found himself glad of it. He should feel worse for it, he supposed, but he couldn't make himself hang his head with heavy regret. He enjoyed being with her too much to come by too much guilt honestly.

They went deep into the water, but he did not feel the pressure of it. He should have, but he didn't. He imagined that the sea witch's spell must have something to do with it. As they went down, they passed a great many other people. To his shock, there were more than just selkies. There were morari and mermaids and mermen.

When they reached the seabed, there was a vast plain of white sands that led to a golden gate. They swam through the gate and along a busy byway toward a huge coral reef. Only this coral had been shaped like a castle, built and grown into grand rooms and apartments, more of the caves dotted along every inch of it. There were selkies everywhere and all of them turned to watch him go by with more than a little curiosity. A selkie in human form looked no different to him from a human, but they had no such trouble telling that he was not a selkie.

"It's your smell," Jileana said when he remarked upon it.

"My *what*?"

"Your smell. Selkies have a very sensitive sense of smell and we know what other selkies smell like. You smell human. It's not a bad thing"—she laughed when he gave her a look—"just different."

"Oh. Good. I was worried I was offending people for a minute there."

"Well, to be honest there are those who will be offended by your presence. Some selkies are purists. They think humans are trouble and they should be kept away from us at all costs. It is why we do not often allow humans to come to our world."

"Have you . . . have you done something you will get in trouble for?" he asked her.

"Oh, I don't think so," she said. "You are here to see the empress on a matter of diplomacy. You made the request. How can I refuse it? I really don't have the authority to decide who should or should not see the empress. That is for her alone to decide. If she finds you offensive, she will send you away herself."

"Wonderful," he said dryly. "So she might kick me out the moment she lays eyes on me?"

"She might, but I doubt it. Our empress has always had a fascination with humans. I think she will be entertained by you."

"I hope so," he replied.

"Well, you are about to find out," she said as they neared a soaring archway. On either side of the archway were guards, each armed with swords of what looked like sharpened shell. They were long and curved and very deadly looking. Even being immortal as Jaykun was, he did not like the idea of being on the receiving end of such a weapon. The guards swam forward and impeded their progress.

"What is your business here?" one demanded gruffly.

"This man wishes an audience with the empress," Jileana said firmly.

The guard laughed. "Everyone wishes an audience with the empress. What makes a human so special that our empress would want to bother with him?"

"It is not for you to decide whether he is special enough to see her. He is here on a matter of diplomacy. He is to be treated like any other ambassador and be given all the same courtesies."

"It is our job to make certain no one wastes the empress's valuable time." The guard sneered at them. "And I say no human deserves that time."

"And when I tell my father, the captain of the empress's guard, that you refused to let his daughter pass into the empress's hall, what do you think he will say?"

The guard seemed to blanch at that. The second guard gave the first guard a shove in the arm. "Idiot," he said. "I am sorry, Jileana. He does not recognize you. He is new to this watch. Be warned, however. The empress is not in the best of moods today. But perhaps you will provide some entertainment for her," he said thoughtfully as he gave Jaykun a once-over.

"I don't know if I should take that encouragingly or not," Jaykun said dryly in response.

"Come on," Jileana said, urging him forward. "There is only one way to find out."

With that, they swam past the guards and into the empress's great hall. The room was filled with people, all of them congregating in groups. But almost every conversation stopped as Jileana and Jaykun passed. They proceeded to the head of the room, where a woman was swimming back and forth in an agitated sort of pacing as a man spoke to her from a distance of about ten feet.

"No!" she said suddenly and sharply. "I have had enough of Horgon's excuses! Tell him he is to come to me immediately or risk my unending wrath! I will not stand for this!"

"But . . . Your Majesty . . . Horgon is a true and loyal subject. He would never do anything to incur such a negative emotion. He only wishes to please you in all things," the man said, bowing his head to her.

"Ha! He only wishes to give me pains in the stomach! He wishes to be emperor himself! I know he plots my downfall every chance he gets. Tell Horgon to appear here before me by tomorrow evening or I will have him dragged here in rusted chains!"

"Yes, Your Majesty. Of course, Your Majesty, he will make every effort to please you. I shall have him sent for immediately."

"See that you do!" she snapped. Then she waved him off with a sharp motion of her hand. After a moment her attention drifted toward Jileana and Jaykun. "What is this?" she asked with a frown.

"Majesty," Jileana said, swimming forward. "This man is Jaykun, the ruler of many cities in the human world. He has come with a request, if you are so inclined to hear it."

The empress's brow rose. "You have come to a very strange world, human. Not many have the bravery for such an adventure. I will hear your request since you have come so far to make it."

"Majesty," Jaykun said, "I come with a personal request from Weysa."

There were gasps and laughter from the room around them. The empress joined with a laugh of her own.

"You speak for a goddess?" she asked.

"I do," Jaykun said. "I am Weysa's champion. I have been sworn to do as she bids me and she bids me to bring word of her to every land I go to. My request is simple. Weysa asks that you remember her. That you remember conflict is the predecessor to peace. That all problems are resolved through her. She asks that you remember her in temples and prayers to her."

The empress looked at him intently for a long moment as she digested this. "And how do I know you speak the truth? How do I know you are truly Weysa's champion? For all I know you are just a human man with delusions of grandeur."

Jaykun was silent for a moment, then he looked around the room. He saw a guard standing beside the empress's dais and went over to him. He spied a dagger at his belt—one made of the same sharpened shell.

"May I use your dagger?" At the guard's dubious look, Jaykun promised, "I mean no one any harm. You may stand behind me with your sword at the ready if it pleases you. I will remain at a distance from your empress."

The guard looked at the empress and she gave him a nod. The guard removed the dagger from his belt and handed it to Jaykun. Then the guard drew his sword, coming to stand behind Jaykun, the weapon at the ready. Jaykun kept a respectful distance from the empress but stood where she could easily see him.

"If I prove I am who I say I am, then will you heed the words of my goddess?" he asked her.

"If you can prove it, I will weigh your words most seriously," she assured him.

"Very well."

With a powerful movement, Jaykun stabbed the dagger into his chest and into his heart. The entire audience reacted in shock as he yanked the blade out and a cloud of red blood swelled within the water. Jaykun threw the blade down to the sandy floor and looked at the empress. She was wide-eyed with shock and surprise. She waited for several beats of his heart before she realized he wasn't going to fall aside and die before her.

"Remarkable," she said after a moment. "You cannot be killed?"

"Not by ordinary means, no," he said. "As I said, I am Weysa's champion. I am immortal so that I may do her bidding in this world. Now will you consider my request?"

"Most readily," the empress said, still sounding very impressed. "I dare not incur the wrath of such a powerful goddess. But I feel I must warn you. As ocean dwelling people, we are loyal to Diathus. I cannot see many of us going to a temple for Weysa. Although, perhaps we would be wise to since the hand of the goddess herself has come to beg prayer from us."

"I only ask that you raise five temples in her name. Whether they are prayed at is a matter left to your people."

"Five! I will raise two and no more. We do not wish to anger Diathus, after all. If her people were to turn on her . . ."

"I do not expect you to turn on your patron goddess. Believe me, if there is one thing I understand, it is what it feels like to know the wrath of the gods. I only hope that you will broaden your prayers . . . to spare some thought to Weysa. Three temples in her name. Three and Weysa will be satisfied."

The empress thought on it a moment, then conceded with a nod of her head. "Three temples. This is all you ask? How am I to know you won't come back and ask for more later? Or ask for other things?"

"I speak for my goddess. If we agree on three, then

three will be all Weysa asks. And there is nothing else I want from you or your people."

"So you say." She narrowed her eyes on him for a long moment. "Very well. I will agree to your temples. However, we cannot start work on them immediately. There are more pressing concerns at the moment."

"I will be satisfied with your promise of the future. Let us say that construction will begin before the next full moon?"

She thought on this a moment as well. "Very well." She raised her chin and called out in a high-pitched sound that cut through the water.

An instant later a man hurried up to her and bowed his head. "Yes, Great Majesty, what can your humble servant do for you?" he asked.

"You will see to it that three temples are raised in the name of the goddess Weysa. They do not need to be too large or too prominent, but I wish them to be where the people can see them as they pass. One in the upper caves, one in the lower caves, and one on the path to my palace." She raised a brow at Jaykun. "Will this suffice?"

"Yes, Majesty. It is exactly what I would have asked for. You are thoughtful and generous."

"I am not in a position to anger the goddess of conflict," she said grimly. "The gods know I have enough of it here."

"Trouble, Majesty?" Jaykun asked.

"Always trouble. I have a room full of courtiers plotting my downfall or their own advancement at every turn, and I have those who don't attend me at all because they do not respect my rule. And that is to say nothing of my kingdom's outside enemies." She eyed him a moment. "You rule many cities. Perhaps you have some insight that can help me to manage the unruly beings that surround me."

"Perhaps I do. I will be here until the next full moon, Majesty. You may avail yourself of me and any advice I can impart to you at any time you choose."

She narrowed her eyes and considered him. Then she smiled. "Come. I would talk with you awhile." She turned her back on the room and swam away, down a corridor. People Jaykun could only assume were servants quickly moved out of her way and made obeisance to her. She didn't seem to notice them as she led Jaykun and Jileana to a room deeper within the castle. Once there, she pulled two combs from her hair and let the mass of it float free. She sighed in contentment as she scrubbed her fingers through it. It was a rich red color, deep and dark, and Jaykun imagined it would have coppery highlights in the sunshine. She was a fit woman, like most he had seen, with small breasts and strong legs. He didn't think she was pretty—that was too girlish a thought. She was handsome and serious, but she was not old. She looked as youthful as Jileana did, but her air was one of much deeper maturity.

She turned to look at Jileana and Jaykun. "There are two things plaguing my reign at the moment. Well, two major things. There are dozens of little things as well, I assure you."

"Something I know very well," Jaykun said with a smile of sympathy.

"The first is Horgon. He is a selkie of great influence and power amongst my people. There are even those who believe he should be emperor. Little plots are constantly at work toward that endeavor. It is never ending."

"Does he have a claim to your throne?"

"He does. He is my cousin and next in line to inherit if I do not bear any children. He commands a great deal of respect and favoritism amongst my people. There is probably a plot to put him on the throne as we speak." The empress clenched one hand tightly in the other for a moment, her temper and stress at her words clearly reaching a high point. "He even has loyalties from amongst my standing army. Jileana, I know your father is loyal to me, but I would not put it past Horgon to take troops from under your father's purview and turn them against their own kind in a civil war simply to put himself on my throne. Sometimes I think to myself . . . just let him have it. If it means keeping brother from killing brother, simply give in and let him have the throne."

"And why don't you?" Jaykun asked.

Her eyes flashed with anger. "Because he is a cruel and sadistic bastard. If he had that much power, he would subjugate and ill-use every person within his reach. The people would suffer . . . whether they realize it or not. Those who are loyal to me understand what the alternative is truly like. But there are those who know of his cruelty and still wish for him to rule because they think he is stronger than I, think he could better stand up to our enemies. Which brings me to the second issue that plagues me and my people."

"One particular outside enemy?" Jaykun asked.

"Yes. The sirens."

"Sirens?"

"They are sea creatures like us," Jileana explained, "only they live more like humans in the Overworld do. They eat fish like we do but also hunt animals on the island and cook them for their sustenance. They live in huts along the beach on the other side of the island."

"They own the other half of this island. There is a very distinct border, one that was agreed upon many years ago by our forefathers," the empress said. "Lately there have been instances where hunting parties have been found on our side of the border and skirmishes have broken out between them and my guards. My guards are posted along the border, you see. They cannot cover every inch of it every minute of the day—there simply aren't enough of them—and the sirens look for weak spots and plan incursions. The siren roja, their leader, claims they are just hunting parties who have gone astray, but I believe they are testing my borders for a darker reason. I have an ambassador and aides in her court and she has hers in mine. 'Ambassador' and 'aides' being the kind words for spies. They know of the trouble I am faced with because of Horgon, and I feel certain they are simply waiting for the opportunity to strike us when we are weakest. They want to oust the selkies from this half of the island. I am sure of it."

"Why do they want to do that when you have enjoyed peaceful borders for so long?"

"The hunting on their side of the island has grown scarce," Jileana explained. "I suppose the wild boar and deer and smaller animals know where they are safest. Our side of the island is rich with the meat they desire."

"So it's resources they want."

"They do indeed."

"So why not let them hunt on your side of the island?" Jaykun asked. "It's not as though they are going to stay and take it over. You don't use the meat from the animals very often, as I understand it. Let them have controlled hunting parties. Have them put together a hunting party and have selkie soldiers accompany them on their hunts. If you do this, they get what they need and it keeps the peace between you," Jaykun said. "They won't need to take the resources they are freely given. At the end of the hunt the party is escorted back to its side of the island and that is the end of it."

"Why . . . I . . ." the empress said with some reluctance. "In truth, I never thought of such a thing. We've always been so militant about protecting our borders. It's what we've always done. But as you say, if I give them what they want . . . then there is nothing for them to take by force."

"Exactly."

"They still want the entire island to themselves," the empress said with a frown. "The sirens and the selkies have never cared much for one another. There is much hostility there. It will be very hard for hunting parties to get along. I shall have to choose tolerant guards. Those with slow tempers . . . those who can take insult and abuse without losing their tempers. I am sure the sirens will be very provocative at first."

"Especially if they have no love for the selkies," Jaykun said. "They will not like being controlled in the hunt, but over time they will get used to the way things must be done. Or so one would hope."

"This is remarkable," the empress said. "Only ten minutes in your company and already you have been more useful to me than my entire cadre of advisors has been for months. But I still fear giving them this concession. I feel if I give them a little they will want to take much more. This is why the hunts must be controlled."

"You decide when, where, and how much. It is entirely by your good graces. And if you go to the siren roja with this, you will be seen as generous. Is there something you desire from them in return? This could be used as a bargaining tool. A piece of leverage."

"No. The only thing I want from the sirens is for them to stay on their side of the island and to leave my people alone."

"Then make yourself appear to be the better and more generous ruler. Surprise them with this generosity."

"Yes. Yes, I think I will," she said with a slow smile. "I will contact your father at once, Jileana, and have him choose from his guard those who can immediately be sent to lead a siren hunting party. I will send them to the siren court straightaway as a gift to the roja. Then we will see about scheduling more parties more regularly." She smiled again. "Now, if only you could solve my problems with Horgon so easily."

"I have a solution," Jaykun said, "but it is a cold-blooded one and you will deprive yourself of an heir."

The empress blanched. "You mean have him killed."

"Yes. Your reign is under threat. You must remove that threat or it will be hanging over you for all of your days . . . perhaps leading to your own death. Because I promise you, if he is as cruel as you say he is, he will have no qualms about killing you in order to secure his reign if he should overthrow you."

"Gods, you are cold-blooded," the empress said in a heated rush. "I do not think I can bring myself to that. To order a man's death just because of what he might do. I cannot bear the thought of making myself just as cold and cruel as he is."

"Then your only recourse is to tolerate him and try to remain one step ahead of him."

"Which is exactly what I have been doing all along."

"Perhaps with this new agreement with the sirens the people will see your power and benevolence as a ruler."

"Or they might feel more threatened by the idea of siren incursions on our territory. It might be just the thing Horgon needs to rally the people against me."

"One thing at a time, Majesty. Quell the siren threat first. Deal with Horgon afterward."

"Yes. Yes, you are right." The empress smiled at him. "I believe you are going to be my new favorite. My favorites call me Jalaya. I will enjoy 'Majesty' on most occasions, but when we are speaking in private like this you will address me by my given name."

"I am honored, Majesty," he said, inclining his head in respect to her, then corrected himself. "Jalaya."

"You must have evening meal with me tonight," she

said eagerly. "We eat at dusk on land in the communal caves on the lowest level of the cliff wall. My cave is on the far left. Jileana will show you."

"Your pardon, Majesty, but I must decline," Jaykun said hesitantly. "I am . . . spoken for from dusk to juquil's hour every night. Perhaps your midday meal today?"

"Very well," Jalaya said slowly, her eyes narrowing on him curiously. "In what way are you spoken for?"

"My goddess makes demands of me," he said. "There is a price to be paid for the immortality I have shown you. My goddess speaks and I must listen."

"Yes. I see that you must. Very well, I will see you at midday meal. Jileana, see that he is there."

"Yes, Majesty," she said.

Jileana took Jaykun's arm and pulled him away from the empress. But he stopped and looked back at Jalaya.

"Majesty, demand Horgon's attendance at the midday meal tomorrow. Tell him to come or he will be thrown into prison. You do have a prison, I take it?"

"We do. Any selkie who breaks the law is chained to the bottom of the ocean. They can swim only to the end of the tether and must live under constant guard. Their freedom is taken from them in a way that can drive a selkie mad."

"We value our freedom and the ability to swim swift and free more than anything else," Jileana said.

"I can imagine you would," Jaykun said. "Very well. Tell him to come or be chained—those are his only two choices. And make sure you send a contingent of guards to escort him to your table. He must obey you, just as any other subject must obey you. It is time you put him in his place."

"But will that not anger him?" Jalaya asked.

"I am counting on it. Let us see what he does when he is provoked. It will tell me just how far he is willing to go. It should make for some interesting conversation at the table at the very least."

"Indeed it should," Jalaya agreed. "Very well. I will send word immediately that he is to obey me. You are right. It is high time he and others like him be put in their place in all respects. You know, I have ruled successfully for quite a long time, but sometimes it takes the vision of an outsider to see things more clearly than those of us who are too close to the problem."

"Also, we are very different rulers," Jaykun said. "You are more peaceable. I am not above stirring things up."

"Perhaps that is a weakness of mine," Jalaya said with a frown.

"Not at all. Peace is to be valued above all else. It is what should be strived for. However, by not taking more definitive, forceful steps, your peace is threatened at any given moment."

"It is something to think about, in any event," Jalaya said, her frown fixed.

"I can just as easily learn patience from you," Jaykun said, "as you can learn violence from me. So we will see you at midday meal?"

"I look forward to it," Jalaya said.

"We are off to see my father," Jileana said. "Shall I tell him to attend you afterward?"

"I will send a separate messenger, but thank you."

"As you wish, Majesty." Then Jileana pulled Jaykun away once more.

They left the palace in relative silence, each busy with their own thoughts. "I know a lot of the selkies will be upset by the idea of siren hunting parties on our side of the island, but there are those who don't hate the sirens."

"Tell me more about them, Jileana," Jaykun said. "I

have heard stories of sirens . . . how they can lure a man to his death with the sound of their voices. Is that true?"

"It is. The sirens sing almost constantly. It is in their blood to do so. The selkies are immune, but humans are drawn to the song of the sirens. Usually it's sailors, and they are lured into the storms that surround the island where their ships are invariably destroyed and the sailors are doomed. The sirens go to the edge of the storms and sing for them, then plunder the broken ships once they have sunk. You would not be immune to the siren song. A siren could enchant you into believing you were in love with her and use you as she wished. The sirens use the portal on their side of the island in order to find human mates to sire their children. You see, the sirens are all female. They birth only female children. If they wish to become impregnated, they go to the Overworld and lure human males into their beds."

"I understand."

"When the Krizans call us *prava,* they mean any of the sea creatures and often they mistake selkies for sirens. Sirens are much more . . . Well, they are more disruptive. They don't care if a human male is already in love with someone else. If a siren wants him, she will take him and then leave him to pine for her for all the rest of his days. She would never do what I have done. She would never bring a human male back to the island with her. You must promise me you will never leave the cliffside, that you will never venture into the island forest," she said with passion. "I . . . I don't want a siren to have even the slightest chance of being able to sway you."

"Don't worry. The last thing I want is to spend my immortality longing for the love of a siren."

"Good," she said. "Good."

CHAPTER
FIFTEEN

Jaykun swam behind Jileana, following her to a part of the coral reef that was surrounded by sentries. There, armed men were busily swimming back and forth, coming and going from a central point. Jileana led him to a muscular dark-haired male swimming about, giving orders to the men.

"Kurn, I want you and the sixth regiment to relieve our men at the border. The siren incursions have increased of late. We want to be on the lookout before they get too bold. Drato, you can take your men and change the guard at the chains. Lesun, your men can relieve the palace guards."

"Yes, sir!" they all replied briskly before heading off in three separate directions. The male then turned and met Jileana's eyes.

"Daughter!" he snapped, a frown warring with the relief in his eyes. He swam over to her and Jaykun noticed Silan shadowing his father. "I was worried sick! You worried your mother as well!"

"Father, you know Mother is not the one who frets about me. I've already seen her and she didn't look all that worried to me."

"That is not the point! You went to the Overworld! *Alone*. And you've brought back some human pet."

"Father! He is not a pet! He is a man just as you and my brothers are men! I won't have you insulting him!" she said sharply.

Jaykun smiled at her from behind her back, where he was waiting at what he deemed a respectful enough distance. Jileana must deal with Creasus in her own way, he realized. He should not interfere, even though he wanted to very much. He found he did not like to see her upset. It was a strange sort of sensation, realizing that he cared about her feelings to that degree. When exactly had that happened?

Jaykun pushed the uncomfortable realization aside and paid attention to the discourse Jileana was having with Creasus.

"You should never have gone without at least telling us where you were going. Without some kind of an escort," her father was saying sternly.

"If I had told you where I was going, you would have tried to stop me. Possibly even locked me up in the chains until the full moon had passed."

"I would never do that," Creasus said, looking offended. "I would have tried to talk you out of it, yes, but the chains? I wouldn't wish the chains on even my worst enemy. They are a necessary evil, but I would not wish it on anyone."

"And if I had taken an escort, he would have curtailed my exploration of the human world. This way I got to see and experience absolutely everything. It was simply amazing, Father! It was so exciting! And the food! You should taste the food!"

"Thank you, Daughter, but I have been to the Overworld. I am well aware of what it is like. Just as I am well aware of how dangerous it is."

"You should never have gone! You could have been

hurt," Silan barked at her from over his father's shoulder. "You should have taken Barban with you."

"Ha! I went to the Overworld to escape Barban!" Jileana said with fiery spirit. "He thinks he owns me and you do nothing to discourage that notion. When are you and Barban going to understand that I am not his. I am not going to be his bride no matter how much he wills it to be so. No matter how much *you* will it to be so."

"Barban comes from a great selkie house, steeped in the traditions of our ways. He would never have disrespected you the way this human beast did when he shared your bed. Father, you must talk some sense into her. Can you not force her to behave herself?"

"Force me!" Jileana scoffed. "I will listen to reason when reason is spoken, but if you think to force me to your will, then I promise you, you will lose me. I won't be forced into your idea of what a proper and good sister should be."

"Jileana! When are you going to see it is for your own protection? There are dangers out there! Especially in the Overworld! At least here, amongst the selkies, you are safe."

"It is just as dangerous amongst the selkies as it is in the human world. We have our enemies just as they do. I could easily run afoul of a siren or a sea beast or any number of things. Barban being one of them. You will not listen to reason when it comes to Barban. You think he is this great, respectful warrior? Well, I tell you I have seen a different side of him. A side you would not like. At least my human pet, as you put it, has treated me with care and respect the entire time I have known him."

"Respect? You call being in your bed respectful?"

"Silan, stop it! I am not some virginal child who cannot decide these things on her own! You are suffocating me! And I promise you, the more you suffocate me, the more I will fight to be free of you. You have made living here all but unbearable. Is it any wonder I wanted to escape to the Overworld?"

"Jileana." Her father spoke up in a kinder and gentler voice. "Your brother is simply worried about you. He loves you and cares about your well-being."

"Well, he needs to care a little less," she said angrily. "Father, I am sorry I worried you. But I was curious about the Overworld. You wouldn't believe the things I saw. And Jaykun"—she gestured to Jaykun, who had moved up against her back in support when she had grown so violently upset—"Jaykun is a remarkable man. If you would just take the time to get to know him, you would see that."

Silan scoffed. "He is a human. There is no such thing as a remarkable human."

"Oh! There is simply no talking to you!" Jileana cried out in exasperation. "Jaykun, you have no idea how fortunate you are to have brothers who do not try to force their will upon you."

"Well, not force . . . but they do try to exert influence over me. They certainly aren't obnoxious about it," he said with a pointed look at Silan.

"Why, you little—" Silan lunged, his hand going to his sword.

But his father stopped him with a hard hand in the center of his chest. "Enough, Silan. Why don't we get to know this human a little before we make rash judgments about him? Yes, I am inclined to agree with you that humans are nothing but trouble, but if my daughter sees something special in this human, then I have to ask myself what that specialness is. I have to ask myself why she risked bringing him here. My daughter is not a foolish woman."

"She is a child who has behaved rashly and stupidly!" Silan barked.

"Enough!" Jaykun roared suddenly, stepping around Jileana and facing off with her brother. "I won't stand here while you continually insult your sister! She is a good woman with a fine heart and a happy soul. Would you sully it with such disparaging thoughts about her? Will you continue to hurt her with these cruel words? No. I will not allow it!"

"You will not allow it?" Silan roared back, this time drawing his sword as he lunged past his father. "Who are you to interfere in this family?!"

Silan made it past his father this time, and it wasn't lost on Jaykun that the father purposely moved out of the way to let him.

Fighting underwater was a skill he'd never had the opportunity to develop, and Silan had done so for what Jaykun assumed was all of his adulthood. In that way Jaykun was outmatched. But Jaykun was still a warrior of some renown, and his strength and skill were nothing to be disregarded whatever his disadvantage. Silan's sword slashed through the water connecting with Jaykun's arm as he threw it up to block the other man's swing. Once again his blood clouded the ocean waters. The sword Silan used was sharper than any Jaykun had encountered before. Silan's blade hit straight to the bone and Jaykun had to grind his teeth against the pain. But he took advantage of the other man's overconfidence that the blow would leave him cringing in a ball of pain. Silan didn't realize that Jaykun bore far more excruciating pain for hours every night. The cut of a blade into his flesh was child's play compared to his flesh roasting from the inside out.

Jaykun reached out and grabbed the other man around his throat, yanked him forward, and used the only weapon he had: his head. He cracked his skull hard against Silan's, sending Silan into a stunned twirl.

"Stop it! Stop this right now, Silan, or I swear I will go to the Overworld and you will never see me again!" Jileana cried out.

Floating back dazedly, Silan put a hand to his ringing head and looked angrily at his sister. "You wouldn't dare!" he hissed at her.

"Wouldn't I?" she retorted, moving to Jaykun to touch the injury to his arm with gentle fingers. His arm was hanging almost uselessly at his side, but it would heal in time. Faster with Jileana's tender care. "Are you all right?" she asked worriedly.

"You know he can't hurt me," he reminded her gently.

"That's untrue. I know this hurts a great deal. Pain and death are different matters. Father, keep Silan under control or I swear it will be the last you will ever see of me."

"You would give up our beautiful world just to be with this inferior creature?" Silan ground out in disbelief.

"Jaykun has nothing to do with it. He has made me no promises of a place in his life. Quite the opposite, I assure you. No. If I leave, it will be because of you and others like you who are intent on driving me away. This world holds little beauty in it so long as you have a hand around my throat and suffocate the life out of me. Father, you are little better. You give him free rein. You even encourage him. The only one who seems to understand this is Mother." She swam away from them, pulling Jaykun along with her. "Until you learn how to better behave, you will keep your distance from me! You are not welcome in my home room, Silan! Do you understand?"

"Father! Are you just going to let her leave like this?"

Jileana's father just gave a silent shrug of his shoulders. "She will do as she pleases whatever I say. We will see her later tonight. We can discuss it further then."

"Discuss?" Silan said in disgust. "What is there to discuss? You are her father and she lives under your roof. She must do as you demand."

"Silan, I said we will discuss it later!" Jileana's father said, raising his voice in temper.

Silan subsided at last, but it was obvious he was none too pleased about it. He glared mutinously at Jileana and Jaykun the entire time they swam out of sight.

"I'm so sorry," Jileana said after several minutes, her voice low and contrite. She hovered over Jaykun's injury, speaking a soft magic to stop the bleeding.

"There is nothing for you to apologize for," Jaykun assured her.

"There is. Silan's behavior is inexcusable. He thinks he owns me. He thinks he can map out my entire future for me . . . that it is his right to do so."

"Clearly you have other ideas."

"Yes. I do. I wish I did not live under my father's roof, but I cannot leave until I am mated. You see, each level of the caves is occupied by a specific house of the nobles. The higher the caves, the higher the nobles' standing in the eyes of the empress and the court. My father comes from an ancient bloodline, almost as ancient as the empress's. That and his role as captain of the empress's army puts him high in the houses. It also makes his daughter a valuable item. For as long as I can remember, men have tried to win me over. Win me so they may enter my father's great house."

"Barban?"

"He is but one. The most persistent one. Mainly because my brother has made it clear that he would be very much in favor of the match. My father has done nothing to discourage it either."

"And when do they consider your wishes in the matter?" Jaykun asked.

"They never do. They never will."

"Is that why you came to my world? To be free of them, if only for a little while?"

She nodded and then swam upward, her hand holding his, her feet kicking in strong, graceful strokes. Not another word was said until they broke the surface of the water and took strong breaths of the air. Jaykun did not need to breathe air while underwater, but it still felt more right to take in the air through his lungs. More natural. The habit of a lifetime.

"I wanted to know what it would be like away from them. I knew it could only be for a week, until the moon waned, but still, a week of reprieve from this was like the richest of gemstones would be to someone of your world. Priceless and coveted. To me, anyway. Most selkies want nothing to do with the Overworld. They are afraid of it. Here the selkies are protected from all outsiders. The only dangers here are the sirens and perhaps a few civil factions trying to go to war amongst themselves, as you learned from the empress. Maybe a sea beast here or there, or the grots. The selkies think the world of man is the root of all danger and all evil. They don't see beyond that. They don't see that there is just as much danger here as there is there. And your world . . . your world is so diverse. Oh, I know I saw only some of it . . . but that's the adventure of it. I've seen only a small part of it. I want to see more. I want to see all of it! And I know it would take me a lifetime to do that. But what a lifetime that would be," she said wistfully. "So full of adventure and newness at every turn. It's the life that you have, isn't it? It's what you do. You go to all kinds of lands and see many strange people and places. I envy you your life."

"Do not envy me," Jaykun said harshly. "My life is nothing you would want for yourself."

She cocked her head and narrowed her eyes on him. "I know parts of it are unbearable," she said. "I am not ignorant of that. But surely you must enjoy some of it. You must take some kind of pleasure in it."

The truth was, he hadn't taken much pleasure in his life lately. He had borne it. Had walked numbly through it, doing what he was required to do. The only joy he'd had was being with his brothers again. But even that was curbed by the knowledge that there was still one brother missing, one brother living in unending torment somewhere, buried deep within soil and bedrock in a place unknown to them, suffocating and being crushed under the weight of the world again and again and again. It made Jaykun's nightly torment seem trivial in comparison.

Until he had met Jileana. Suddenly there was light in his world. A type of pleasure that he had all but forgotten. The type of pleasure that could make a man afraid. Afraid to lose it. Afraid to believe in it. He suddenly turned from her, unwilling to look at her. He had nothing to offer her. He had nothing to offer anyone, least of all himself. His life had ended with a single swallow of forbidden waters and this . . . this *existence* had sprung up in its place. He had thought he wanted immortality. Now all he wanted was to live a normal, peaceful life . . . and to die a normal, peaceful death.

But his wants weren't worth thinking about. His was a cursed existence and nothing was going to change that. Certainly not by wishing his life were otherwise. All of his wishes had long since been superseded by the wishes of another . . . of a goddess.

Jaykun began to swim. He could see the cliff face in the distance and he aimed himself toward it. The churning of his arms, the force of propelling himself through the water, made his heart pump harder and faster. He needed it, needed the violence of it. He didn't know if she was following him, didn't really care in that moment. All he knew was the need to move hard and fast however he could, and it was difficult to do that in the water.

So he swam. Arm over arm over arm. Swam until his body hit the wall of the cliff face. Then he dragged himself onto the nearest ledge, and he would have begun to climb just as blindly as he had swum, but suddenly there was a great weight on his arm and he was being dragged about until he was looking down into her concerned face.

"What is it?" she asked him. "Jaykun! What is wrong?"

He was heaving for breath, water streaming from his hair still, his body being baked by the brightness of the sun. Off in the distance he could see the wall of grey denoting the storms that protected the island, but where he was standing was as clear and warm and sunny as any high summer day. He found himself inanely wondering if the seasons turned cold in this idyllic place where people lived in the cool waters and ran naked under the sun.

"Does winter ever come here?" he asked.

"What?" she asked, surprised and confused by the question. "What is winter?"

"Does it ever grow cold or snow here?"

"It is always the same here. The storms come from time to time. What is snow?"

He smiled at that and looked down into her pretty, upturned face. He reached for it, touching gentle fingers to the sweet curve of her cheek. "Snow is when the rain freezes and turns to ice."

"Oh. Mother can make ice. She has a spell for it. I think I might know it. Does it fall in big blocks, or is it small like drops of rain?"

"Small like the drops of rain. You've never seen snow?"

"No. It sounds painful."

"No. Snow can be light and soft, and it can be very beautiful."

"Oh. I would like to see snow," she said with a beatific smile. "When does it come?"

"With winter. You see, where I come from, in the Overworld, we have seasons. Four of them. Summer, which is warm and sunny like this. Autumn, when the air grows colder and the leaves of the trees die and fall off in preparation for winter."

"They die? Oh, that sounds terrible," she said with a frown.

"They have to. But don't worry. The trees are only going to sleep a little while. That is when winter comes. It grows cold . . . so cold your breath freezes on the air. Then soft snow comes and lays white over everything. Every road, every house, every tree . . . until all you see is a great, vast, blinding blanket of white. The children come and play in it and their laughter can be heard for great distances. We build fires and stay warm next to them. Men and women cuddle up close for warmth and make love to bring fire to their blood." He reached for her and drew her close to his body, demonstrating by holding her close and warm.

"Oh," she breathed, "that sounds wonderful."

"It is. There's nothing like it in the world. And then the snow melts and spring comes. The trees wake up and grow new leaves. The flowers bloom and fill the air with the smell of freshness and new life. Then summer comes and it all begins again."

"Snow. I want to see snow," she said excitedly. "Why has no one ever told me about this before?"

"So you've really never been to the Overworld before this?"

"Never. I was too young. We can't pass through the portal until we're of a certain age. It keeps our children from passing through unexpectedly. The storms keep us in just as they keep others out."

"And you just reached this certain age?"

"Well . . . no . . . it was a few years ago. But I confess, it took me a while to be brave enough to venture through the portal. But once I did I saw you and thought what a wondrous world it must be, to have such people in it that they burn like the stars. After that I wasn't afraid."

He laughed at that. "Had anyone else seen me they would have been terrified of me."

"Well, I wasn't. I thought you were beautiful. That was before I understood how much it hurt you, though. I don't think it's beautiful any longer."

He realized then how beautiful he thought *she* was. Not just aesthetically beautiful, but straight through to her very core. And in his world, a world ugly with war and political machinations and people bent on killing one another, that meant a great deal to him. It was something incredibly rare and special. Sure, she was a selkie and that made her rare to begin with, but it went beyond that. He couldn't remember the last time he saw such beauty. Real beauty—not a beauty he had created in his mind, blinded in every way to the flaws within. He could see her flaws—things like her impulsiveness and her stubbornness. He was not imagining her to be something perfect and beyond reproach, and he was glad of that. It told him he was truly seeing her. But at the same time it scared him, truly rocked him to his core. He didn't know what to do with these feelings. They had no place in his life. He could offer her absolutely nothing of value and she deserved to be given everything the world had to offer her. She deserved better than him.

CHAPTER
SIXTEEN

Jaykun forced himself to let go of her, to turn away from the comfort of Jileana's arms around him, and he picked his way over to and then up the cliff face, using handholds and footholds and all the strength in his body to propel himself upward in hard surges of movement. It was what he liked to do when he was troubled. He liked to force his body into activity, sometimes until he collapsed with exhaustion. He didn't see that being possible here, so he took advantage of what he could when he could. He climbed all the way to the uppermost level of the honeycomb of caves and then a bit farther until he was standing at the very top and looking down upon the entirety of the selkie world. He breathed the air in deep, only partly aware of Jileana coming to stand beside him. Then he turned around and faced the island itself and for the first time saw the sprawl of lush trees and vines, and heard the chittering of insects and the rustle of wild things in the underbrush.

"So this is what the sirens want so badly," he said. "I can see why."

"Yes, it is very beautiful, but it is also very dangerous. I wouldn't want you to go into the island. If you should come upon a siren . . ." She bit her lip anxiously. "Promise me you won't go in there."

"I have no reason to go in there and I am not foolish," he reassured her, reaching to brush a soft thumb over the rise of her cheek, his fingertips lingering in her hair. "I promise you, I will be careful."

"Thank you," she breathed. "I wouldn't be able to bear it if you were lured by a siren and were . . . It is a false love and the sirens don't care about the suffering of the men they leave behind. They don't care about them at all. All they want is a means of getting their daughters. Otherwise, they have no use for men."

"The selkies sing too, yes?" he asked suddenly. "I seem to recall hearing you sing and it being somewhat . . . otherworldly."

"We do. We sing to cast certain spells. Like the healing spell I sing for you each night to help speed your healing."

"I knew you were doing that. Somewhere inside me I knew, because I was healing faster and with less pain than I was before you came along."

"Diathus loves her selkie children. She has given them the sea witches—selkies like my mother and me who can cast certain magics. You could say we are Diathus's priestesses."

"Like our mems. Our mems are priestesses for the other gods. They have healing gifts and other abilities as well. We also have mages, but they are not as connected to the gods as the mems are usually. Are the sirens the children of Diathus as well?"

"No. Though they live near the water, they turn away from Diathus. It is Jikaro, the god of anger and deception, whom they worship."

"Jikaro is part of Xaxis's faction, as Diathus is." At her questioning look, he explained about the war between the two factions of gods.

"This war between the gods is a terrible thing," Jileana said, shaking her head, "and it is dangerous for us to get involved."

"I cannot help but be involved. I have been commanded to interfere on Weysa's behalf. I wish I could live in ignorance of the war like so many people do; it would make for such an easier, more blissful life. But that is not to be and I have not been that lucky. But I asked for my own fate. I deserve nothing less."

"How did you ask for it? Are you going to tell me why it is you must suffer so?"

He looked into her eyes and gave her a grim smile. "I thought I could force the hand of the gods. I took from them something they were not willing to give. My brothers and I drank from the Fount of Immortality without the permission of the gods and we have been punished for it. I spent untold years chained to a star, burning endlessly like a molten cinder. I have since been freed of it, but as you see, it is my lot to be reminded of my punishment every night so I will not forget where hubris can lead."

"Jaykun," she said softly. "When will it end? When will it be enough? You have spent years suffering . . . When will the gods be satisfied? I cannot believe they are so cruel!"

"Believe it. You see it night after night with your own eyes."

Jaykun dropped to the ground, sitting at the very edge of the cliff, letting his legs dangle in the open air over the side. Jileana joined him, doing the same.

"I know I do," she said then, "but I also believe the gods are capable of great benevolence and forgiveness. I have to believe that. They have forgiven me so often. . . . Why can they not forgive you?"

"Forgiven you?" Jaykun asked, his fingertips on her

soft, beautiful face once more. "What could you possibly have done that would anger the gods?"

"I . . . I am defiant of my father when I should be a better daughter. I fight with my brothers endlessly. We have always done so for as long as I can remember and it should not be so. I love them, I do, but I just can't seem to get along with them. It must be some intrinsic fault of mine. I am stubborn and willful. And I . . . I am ungrateful of the safe haven Diathus has provided for the selkies. I . . . I dream of leaving this place, of finding a home in the world of human men and women, of adventures beyond the safety of these caves and waters."

"Hmm. These are grievous sins indeed," Jaykun said gravely. But his eyes were lit with humor and she could see it.

"You mock me," she scolded him with a playful push against his shoulder.

"No, indeed I do not. I can very clearly see why you would require forgiveness. But I can also see that if you were not so driven I . . . I would never have gotten the opportunity to see and know you. So you must forgive me if I do not mind your sins."

She gave him a sly smile. "This is very true," she said. "Very true indeed. So you are saying that you are glad to have met such a wantonly disreputable female such as myself?"

"Very glad. And if you are disreputable, what does that make me? I have sinned far more grievously than you ever will." He said the last more seriously than he had intended. But it was a serious topic, despite their making light of it. It was the be-all and end-all of his days. Everything he did, everything he was, was because of the sins he had committed against the gods. The only thing he had that did not touch upon that taint was . . .

Her. Somehow he had earned the gift of her. A blessing amid his curse.

The thought of squandering that blessing scared him. Truly terrified him in a way nothing else had been able to ever since he had been rescued from the chains of that star. When one was immortal, one's fears tended to evaporate. All fear, it seemed, was rooted in the fear of death. When it boiled down to it, a fear of heights or a fear of snakes or any such fear was a fear of being killed. Death was a frightening thing. An unknown thing. Take away that fear, take away death, and suddenly very little was frightening. At least that was how it had been for Jaykun. Now that death had been taken out of the equation, he felt he was nearly invincible and he feared almost nothing.

But the one other thing that terrified him was the mercurial nature of the gods. Their moods and tempers were the stuff of legend. If anyone could touch him, it would be the hand of a god. To be specific, a goddess. Weysa would look upon anyone who might interfere in his punishment with a hostile eye. She would feel threatened by any woman who came too close to him. She had already released his brothers from their curses, and as long as there was a brother to replace them and she had a warrior to fight in her name, she was content. But if for any reason she thought Jaykun might be swayed from his course and purpose . . . well, it was quite possible she would simply rid herself of the threat and be done with it.

So it was key that he manage his emotions and his desires with a strict hand. He did not think Weysa would begrudge him female company, so long as he played by the rules and kept his heart out of the game. And that was exactly what he would do. He would enjoy Jileana for whatever time they had left together, then he would put her aside and focus on the next city he was destined to lay siege to. Weysa couldn't possibly ask anything more of him.

Well, actually she could, but he hoped this would be enough to keep her satisfied.

"I think your sins should be forgiven. You suffer for them nightly, and it is a cruel thing. When will it be enough? When will you earn reprieve?"

He shushed her nervously, looking around them as if there might be someone spying on them and hearing her words. "I deserve every moment of my fate. Do not question the will of a goddess."

"I will question it," she said stubbornly. "There has to be a point when they must forgive you for what you've done and release you from this awful curse. Otherwise, to do this indefinitely makes them purposefully cruel and sadistic, and I don't like to think the gods are sadistic. I prefer to think of them as kind and benevolent and perhaps a little strict when it is called for . . . but this . . . this is just merciless and brutal."

"Enough. Do not speak of this anymore," he said, harshly gripping her by her forearm and giving her a shake. "You do not know what you are daring and I will not have you endangered! I couldn't bear it if—" He broke off and looked away from her.

But she smiled as she realized what his unspoken emotions were. He did not want to see her hurt. He cared about what happened to her. The understanding made her feel light and dizzy inside, and she didn't even understand why it should matter so much. But it did matter. It mattered enough to make her feel good, and that meant something. She didn't know what exactly, but it did mean something.

She considered that she might be falling for him. It was a strange notion for her because she had never fallen for anyone before. She had never really wanted to. She enjoyed everyone, for the most part, equally. She didn't really think more or less of one man over another.

But she liked Jaykun a great deal. There was much about him that impressed her. He was brave and strong. More important, he was cunning and intelligent. She had seen it in the way he solved his problems and the problems of others. He was never overbearing like Silan and Silan's friends often were. Friends who thought they had a rightful claim on her. She frowned as she thought of Barban. She had not come across him yet since she had returned from the Overworld, but she would easily bet that Silan had reported her behavior accordingly. It was only a matter of time before Barban sought her out and made his displeasure known. It was a confrontation she was not looking forward to.

But thinking of Barban only served as a contrast to how much pleasure she derived from Jaykun's company. She had not known him that long, really, but even so, she felt she knew him better than any other man she had ever known. And considering how many brothers she had, that was saying something. Then again, comparing any man to her brothers was likely to make that man come out ahead of the mark. Her brothers did little more than aggravate her.

"All right," she said, refocusing on the conversation at hand. "I won't speak of it any further," she said to him, laying a comforting hand over the one gripping her arm. She then leaned her body against his again and reached to kiss him softly and slowly on his cheek. When she pulled back he was looking at her bemusedly.

"What was that for?" he asked.

"Do I need a reason now to kiss you?"

"Of course not," he said. "It just seemed . . . different."

"It was different, I suppose. It was my way of beginning to lure you into my bed again."

His right brow shot up. "Is that so?" he asked. "Well, then I rather like different."

"I somehow thought you might," she said with a chuckle. She leaned in again and kissed the corner of his lips. Then her next kiss fell dead center on them. Jaykun's hand drove into the wet tendrils of her hair and held her head as his mouth seized hers suddenly and fully. The kiss lit a fire deep in her bones, heating her until all of her skin was flush with it. Between that and the sunlight, she felt as though she had never been so warm. But the truth was, she had . . . as she had sat close to him while he burned. Now he was burning her in a completely different way. This way was from the inside out. She had had sexual experiences before—Jaykun had not been her first—but they had been so cold in comparison. He was so much more passionate than her selkie lovers had been, somehow more alive than they were. Perhaps it was because she saw him through the eyes of her adventurous soul, but she didn't think so.

She slid herself around into his lap, and for a moment her backside dangled in the air over the cliff as she straddled his legs and seated herself across his thighs. He anxiously locked his grip at her hips, drawing her in tight and close at the fear of her possibly falling over backward, down the long cliff face, and into the water.

"Don't worry," she whispered across his lips, "I'm not going anywhere. You won't be rid of me that easily."

"That's just it. I'm not looking to be rid of you at all. Just the opposite, I find."

She smiled at that and shifted herself as close to him as was possible, chest to chest, sex to sex, and snuggled in tight.

"There, now. See? I'm not going anywhere."

"Yes, you are rather . . . secure," he said as he nuzzled her ear beneath her hair. "But I'd much rather you be safer than this. After all, only one of us is immortal."

"Mmm . . . after a fashion. I won't grow any older. Selkies never do. So I'll never die of old age."

"But you can die from falling off a cliff," he said dryly.

Jileana leaned back in his lap until her hair was dangling out in the open air beyond the edge of the cliff.

"This cliff? I've dived off this cliff before."

"Good gods," he breathed, jerking her back in tight to his chest. "You're insane. I'm immortal, but it still hurts to hit that water wrong. I'd likely break every bone in my body."

"You likely would since you aren't natural to diving. But we are. It's like second nature. There's something inside us that makes us hit the water just right every time. Accidents do happen of course, but it's rare."

"I think I would prefer it if you don't do that while I'm watching. Come, let's go where it's safer."

"No!" She tensed her body and stayed him from getting up. "Let's stay right here. Just like this."

She gripped his strong shoulders with both hands, and with a flex of her limber thigh and abdominal muscles, she undulated her sex against his, rubbing him hotly in her wet kiss.

His heart pounding, blood filling his cock, he gripped hold of her wicked hips. He glanced beyond her, out into the open air and down, past all the levels of caves and at last the water. His entire lower body tensed, as if he could cling to the ground beneath him and make it more safe somehow. But the fact was, it wasn't safe at all . . . and that was what was making his heart race and his blood burn.

He reached up, grabbed a fistful of her hair, and controlled her head as he crushed his mouth onto hers. He invaded her mouth with his tongue, lapping at the heady flavor of her. She was beyond delicious to him, and he savored every second of his tasting of her. He let go of her hip but did not lift his hand from her body for even a second. He wasn't going to risk anything with her—at least not more than he already was. But he had to admit there was an immeasurable excitement to be found in what they were doing. Which was no doubt her entire purpose. He ran his free hand up along the curves of her side, the hand in her hair clenching tighter as he embraced her full breast. All the while, he was kissing her as if he were starved for her. And he was. It felt like forever since he had been inside her, and he was definitely willing to change that . . . even if it was while she dangled over the side of a cliff.

Jileana kept her hands busy as well. They left his shoulders and brushed down over the tight swells of his pectoral muscles, her thumbnails scraping at his nipples in taunting little flicks. Then, while her left hand remained at that particular task, her right continued down over the ridges of his abdomen and farther down until her fingers were scraping through the wiry hairs where their bodies met. She lifted her hips just enough for her hand to reach between them and take hold of him. He sucked in a breath, then released it in a growling groan of pleasure. He wanted to lift up into her touch, but he dared not move an inch lest he topple them over the edge. Instead he was forced to let her do all the work, let her stroke him tightly until he was beyond hard for her. She alternated stroking him with her hand with rubbing him against the wet flesh of her sex. Then she rose up in his lap, trusting him to hold on to her, and offered her breast to his lips. He took her in between his teeth, sucking at her urgently until she gasped from the punishment. But she deserved to be punished, he thought. Look at what she had him doing. Look at the risks she was willing to take. He was beginning to realize that she had very little in the way of a self-preservation instinct. It was obvious in everything she did. She was utterly fearless . . . and she even sought out trouble aggressively. Oh, she didn't mean to get into trouble, but she did nothing to lessen her chances of it and she put herself into situations where trouble was just as likely to occur as not.

Through with punishing her, he gentled to teasing flutters of his tongue around her hard, distended nipple. The gentler undertaking made her moan with pleasure just as the rougher one had. Her free hand crawled through his hair, clutching at his scalp.

Finally, after he had left her breast in trade for the side of her neck, her shoulder, and then her opposite breast, she rose up once again and guided his shaft into the waiting embrace of her body. She lowered herself onto him slowly, bringing him snugly into her with small undulations of her hips. His hands rocketed to her hips, holding her and guiding her as he exhaled in a gusting groan of pleasure.

"Ah gods, how you *feel*," he said between clenched teeth. He could not thrust up into her as he would like, not without risking the worst, so he was forced to let her ride him as she saw fit. It was frustrating and erotic at the same time. His blood was pumping through his every vein with brutal force and he felt as though he could barely catch his breath.

As for Jileana, she was loving every minute of her control of their pleasure. She rode him in slow, wicked, torturous moves until she had built up to short, quick undulations of her hips. Their mouths touched, but only enough to exchange hard, rapid breaths. She trusted him to hold on to her, to keep them rooted to the cliff's edge while she gave in to her need with absolute, heart-stopping abandon. She threw her head back, then slowly curved her body backward over the abyss, her hair hanging in the open air, only his hands around her rib-cage anchoring her to solid ground. She came back upright at his insistence and once again focused on the movements of her hips. It was more than she could bear, her heart pounding with the thrill of the danger she was in at every instant and the even more ecstatic thrill of having him inside her. Danger was one thing . . . but it was nothing . . . nothing without the thrill of having Jaykun. Nothing could compare—only enhance—what was already there, making it so much more. Jaykun was wild. Having him like this was wilder.

She launched into orgasm, knowing she was free to do so, free to let her body spasm and curve, to throw her head back . . . all with complete abandon and trust that he would not let her go, would not let her fall.

To be given that trust made a huge impact on Jaykun. It was an erotic high all its own. He had to force himself to wait, however, force himself to keep control until she had gone limp and he could pull her back into balance against him. Then, with her help, he was able to release, to let his orgasm be birthed. But it was a controlled passion. He dared not forget himself for even an instant.

The moment he had recovered his breath he pushed away from the cliff's edge and rolled them onto solid ground. He had her on her back beneath him and was settled between her thighs as he looked down into her face. She looked mightily self-satisfied, proud of herself for her achievement. He couldn't help but laugh.

"You seem quite content," he said.

"I am at that. However, one could always use more contentment."

He laughed again. "If you were truly content, then you would not want more. But I can see I have somehow come up short. I think I shall have to remedy this."

"You shall, but not right now," she said, giving him a little push. "We have to get to our midday meal."

"Must we?" he asked, dipping his head and nuzzling the crook of her neck.

"Yes! We must! Stop that." She laughed.

"Very well. But I will be readdressing this matter at a later time," he said just before he surged to his feet and held a hand out to her. She took it and he pulled her up to her feet as well. When she moved to the edge of the cliff, he snagged her hard about the arm and pulled her back. "Don't even think about diving off from up here. I am sure you would be fine, but I'm also sure my heart could not withstand the terror of watching you do it."

"But it would be so much faster," she said hesitantly.

"Please. For me," he begged her gently.

"Very well. We can climb down to the dining level." But it was clear she was only mollifying him; she would have chosen to dive off had it been up to her. The thought was absolutely harrowing to Jaykun. He was not a cowardly man by any stretch of the imagination, but still . . . it was a long way down to the water and he had tempted fate enough for one day.

CHAPTER
SEVENTEEN

The midday meal was a gathering of all the nobles of the court, including Jileana's father and five of her brothers, Silan, Lalo, Misan, Kidas, and Gruen. Lalo, Misan, and Gruen seemed a little more laid-back than their surly elder brother, Silan. The jury was still out on the remaining one who seemed to be watching him with sharp eyes. Jaykun watched the proceedings around him quietly and with a careful eye. He decided he liked her brothers after only a short while of watching them. They were clearly careful and thoughtful where their brother Silan was headlong and headstrong.

Also amongst the attendants was a beautiful woman with sea-green hair and fey features, including pointed ears. It was instantly obvious, even to him, that she was not a selkie. And when Jileana's eyes settled on her, she went hard with instant tension at his side.

"Oh no!" she cried softly. "I had forgotten!"

"What is it?" he asked her quietly.

"The siren ambassador!"

At her words he began to share her tension. The idea that this woman could open her mouth, sing a few notes, and ever after hold him in a thrall of love made his soul go cold. He had been in the thrall of love once before. He would never wish to be so stricken by that emotion again—and left blind to the faults of his partner because of it. He did not want a woman to have the power to manipulate him at her whim. He could think of no worse fate.

"We must visit my mother after this," she said anxiously. "Surely she has a spell that can counteract the effects of a siren's call."

"A wise plan. I am not comfortable being within earshot of her."

"For now it is best we do not draw any attention to you," she said.

But as luck would have it, attention quickly turned solely to him. Jalaya was utterly fascinated by him and would hear nothing from anyone else at the table. The "table" was a cleared, raised platform of stone around which everyone sat cross-legged. Servers circled the table with trays full of various selections and allowed for each individual to choose what they wished and how much of it they wished.

Jalaya focused completely on Jaykun, laughed at him, lavished him with her attentions. It wasn't long before Jileana realized Jalaya was flirting with him—and an even shorter period of time before jealousy set in. It wrapped itself hard and fierce around her heart and she shocked herself with the level of hostility she suddenly felt toward the empress. What was wrong with her? she asked herself. She had wanted Jaykun to find a useful position in the empress's attentions, had she not? Had they not come here with the sole purpose of striking an accord between Jalaya and Jaykun?

But an accord was one thing, a flirtation something else entirely. Did the empress not see that Jaykun was hers? But if the empress decided she wanted Jaykun, what power did either of them have to refuse her? It was her court, her power, her rules. They would merely be pawns in her game.

Suddenly Jileana wished she had never brought him here. It would have been better if she'd just stayed in the world of humans for another month than risk him to sirens and bring him to Jalaya's attention. Gods, what had she been thinking?

She had been trying to hold on to him at any cost, she realized with dawning comprehension. They'd had only three days before she brought him here, and she had not been ready to let him go. She had swiftly become addicted to having him in her life. She had felt changed ever since meeting him. At first she had thought it was because the Overworld was so different and new—so exciting. But now she realized he had been a key factor in that excitement. Oh, she would have found everything to be just as wondrous but her pure passion had been all Jaykun's doing.

The understanding left her a little shaken. She had known things with Jaykun were different—exciting and more than a little bit wild—but this was the first time she had considered there might be more to it than just simple good feelings and good times. It was the first time she had considered there might be any depth to the relationship beyond what they were feeling at any given moment.

But what truly made the comprehension dreadful was the understanding that Jaykun would never want anything beyond what they were already sharing. She didn't know why he closed himself off, but he most definitely shut down whenever it came to his emotions. Perhaps it was because of his curse, because of the limitations set upon him by Weysa. Yes, she was sure that was it. He was not free to give himself, and so he did not wish to engage in any behaviors that might bring another's feelings into the mix, that might leave someone else vulnerable and hurting, because he was unable to give himself completely.

But Jileana did not need completeness. She did not need all of him in order to be happy. She would be content with exactly what she had right now: time with him, in his arms and in his bed. True, she knew his attention to her could not last; he had a duty to perform and he could not be swayed from it, be it for circumstance or for his honor. He would honor his bargain with Weysa until the end. Were he free of the curse tomorrow she believed he would still fight in Weysa's name and for her cause. He was a warrior at heart and a principled one at that.

And Jileana would follow him. She knew in a heartbeat that she would leave her world, leave all of her friends and family behind, just to follow Jaykun into the world of humans. And she knew his goals might take him far from the ocean, that she might be cut off from all ocean water for long periods of time—months . . . maybe even years—if she followed him. Still she did not care. She would not mind. She would easily trade away the comforts of the ocean for the comfort of his arms.

But right now there was a danger far more serious than being separated from the ocean. If Jalaya formed an attachment to Jaykun, if she set her sights on him, there would be a great deal of trouble to be had. And now Jaykun was stuck within Jalaya's reach for the next three weeks. How were they to avoid her, and avoid her attentions?

Disturbed, Jileana found herself leaning into his body, settling her weight against him, and setting her chin on his shoulder. To her pleasure, he reached up and buried a warm hand in her hair, petting her absently as he talked with the empress of the selkies. Whatever Jalaya's intentions were, Jileana took comfort in the thought that it was very unlikely that Jaykun would go along with those intentions. Not unless he was given no choice. And maybe not even then. She simply did not know. The best idea would be to remove him from the equation as often as she could. But she didn't see how that was possible. It was a dangerous quandary for them to be in.

"Tell me . . . are all human men as intelligent as you are?" Jalaya was asking him.

"No. Not all. Haven't you ever been to the Overworld?" Jaykun asked her.

"I have . . . once, when I was very young. I spent a full month in the world of men. I wanted to see what it was like for myself. I also was trying to escape the demands of my family." The empress gave Jileana a knowing wink. "But that was almost two hundred years ago and I was not impressed with men at the time."

"In some ways men are greatly different than they were two hundred years ago; in others they are ever the same." Jaykun was silent a moment. "I do not think you would like the Overworld much. This place is idyllic compared to the Overworld. Were I another man I might never wish to leave."

"But you are not that man?" she asked curiously.

"No. I have too many responsibilities awaiting me in the Overworld. My brothers as well. And I am bound by my goddess to serve her. Also, I search for my lost brother."

"Lost brother? How was he lost?"

Jaykun hesitated. His first instinct was to avoid talking about his curse and what he and his brothers had done to prompt it. But this was not the Overworld. It was a different place, a place set apart from the world of humans. In the end, he gave her a quick retelling of the tale, ending with each cursed brother's fate.

"Each of us was consigned to punishment by a different god. Weysa thrust my brother Dethan into the bowels of the eight hells. Hella chained my brother Garreth to a frozen mountainside. Lothas chained me to a star, and Sabo buried my brother Maxum beneath the soil. Maxum is the only one who has not been freed from his curse and we search for him everywhere we go."

"And what will you do if you find him?" Jalaya asked him, suddenly seeming less open to him, less flirtatious. Her body language had changed significantly. This hardly surprised Jaykun. It was nerve-racking, no doubt, to be close to someone who was so damned by the gods. It amazed him that Jileana did not react similarly. Perhaps it was for the best. He had not been blind to Jalaya's flirtations and interest. He had just avoided opening a tricky can of worms.

"Bring him up out of the ground. Hope that we can free him from his curse somehow. We haven't thought that far ahead. We must find him first before the rest can be worried about."

"True," she murmured. Then suddenly she was rising to her feet, forcing her courtiers to stand hastily in deference to her. "Jaykun, I will have you come to midday meal again tomorrow. I think it will be interesting to see how you take Horgon's measure and how he takes yours."

"I will be honored to do so, Majesty," Jaykun said with a deferential nod.

The empress left, and those at the table sat down and finished their meals. But it quickly became apparent to Jaykun that Jileana had lost her appetite as well as her usual vivacity.

"Are you well?" he asked her after a few minutes of watching her.

"I . . . I will be better once we have seen my mother and I know you are protected from the sirens' call."

"Then let's go to her now. I won't have you worrying," he said, rising to his feet and holding his hand out to her. She took it immediately and rose as well. They walked out of the dining area and onto the open ledge. It was a short dive to the water and they prepared to make it.

"Leaving so quickly? And before I have had time to make your acquaintance?"

They turned together at the address, which was followed by a musical little laugh. There she stood, the siren herself, her green hair flowing all around the slim planes of her nearly boyish body. Unlike Jileana, she lacked the curves that would make her markedly a female. She had small, nearly nonexistent breasts, but her features were everything fey and feminine. Other than the hair on her head, she had no other hair on her body, except eyelashes that were green as well. She had no eyebrows to speak of. There were swirls of tiny white spots on patches of her skin, almost as though they were there in place of the hair that was missing from her body, and her nails, on both her hands and her feet, had a purplish tinge to them.

"We have somewhere to be," Jileana said with poorly veiled hostility as she stepped protectively between Jaykun and the siren.

"Please, little one," the ambassador said with a lightly scoffing laugh. "If I want him, the placement of your body will do nothing to protect his ears."

She turned her attention to Jaykun. "I am Falin," she introduced herself, holding up a palm in respectful greeting. "Do not be afraid I will enrapture you. It is clear you are the empress's favored companion and I will not risk war between the sirens and the selkies simply to win the attentions of a man."

Jaykun took her measure for a moment and then realized she was telling the truth. Clearly the siren leader had chosen well when she had chosen her ambassador.

"It is a pleasure to meet you, Falin," Jaykun said, holding out a hand to her. She looked at him with ice-blue eyes a moment, then took his hand in hers. Her skin was smooth and cool under his touch. "I am glad you will not attempt to enthrall me. You might make me love you, but I would kill you for it."

"You would love me too much to want to kill me."

"I have killed things I loved in the past," he said quietly. "And in any event, it would not be true love, merely an illusion. Illusions can be broken."

"No one can break the lure of a siren's call," she said almost apologetically. "But it might surprise you to know that many sirens do not use their song to call a mate to them. We prefer to know we can obtain the affections of a man without thrall. There is more of a victory to it that way. The thrall is often a measure of last resort. It can be as hollow for us as it is for the subject. Although, the subject does not feel hollow."

"No, just abandoned by love once you are through with him and discard him."

"Mmm. True. We have little use for men outside of breeding partners. All the more reason we do not like to use the thrall. We are not cruel, you know. We are not all selfish. No more than those of any other culture."

Jileana released a snort, the sound making it clear she didn't believe the siren in the least. It was a sentiment of pure prejudice and the first time Jaykun had seen a behavior like it from her. She was so open and warm and inviting in all other ways, it was almost alien on her, to see her acting so caustically.

"Well, I am comforted by your assurances," he said amiably.

"I have never seen a man in the selkie court before. I am sure there have been men brought across the portal before, but none have made it into the empress's purview during my stint in her court, and I have been here for several decades. Indeed I have been here so long I am accused by my people of being more selkie than siren."

That made Jileana frown. "The sirens act with prejudice against you even though you are here on their behalf?"

"Some see me more as a traitor than as an ambassador. We have very narrow-minded peoples on both sides of the island. You see, I am not entirely welcome here, and I am no longer entirely welcome amongst the sirens. So I find myself without a homeland."

"And yet you are supposed to negotiate between our peoples?"

"The selkie queen and the siren queen view me as useful, and in the end, that is all that matters. As long as I can relate the truth of their words without prejudice to cloud the issue, then I am still of use to them both."

"Spoken like a true diplomat. Both courts are fortunate to have you," Jaykun said.

"I hope so. As long as I can be useful, I will continue to serve. The day I no longer feel that I am is the day I will return home and try to find my place back amongst my people. Perhaps I will then mate with a man and have a daughter."

"It is a wonder you don't do that now," Jileana said. "Couldn't you have a child even while in service?"

"And raise her where she would be despised just for being a siren? Do you think that wise?" Falin asked knowingly.

The grim set to Jileana's mouth was all the reply that was needed.

"Well, perhaps things in the future will change," Jaykun said. He did not elaborate since he wasn't sure if the empress had told the siren ambassador of her plans yet. It was not his place to do so. Nor did he want any of the credit for the idea. It would have more value if it was perceived as having come from the empress's own mind. He only hoped that a new accord with the sirens would mean a positive future between selkies and sirens. Perhaps, with time, prejudices could be set aside and a trust could be established between the two peoples.

"Perhaps it will," she agreed.

"But what is it you want of me?" he asked her directly. "Or is this just a desire to get to know me?" It was obvious by his tone that he did not believe that was all it was.

"I have no immediate need of you," Falin said. "But who knows what the future holds? So it is in my best interest to get to know you a little. To find myself on your good side, as it were."

"Ah. More marks of a good diplomat: Always keep channels open for future use. Make no enemies and make many friends."

She smiled. "Exactly. But that does not make my friendship seem any less sincere, I hope."

"Not at all," he assured her.

"Good. Then will you walk with me awhile?"

Jaykun hesitated. He could feel the anxiety emanating from Jileana. She was afraid. Afraid of him being exposed and vulnerable. He didn't know what it would take for a man to fall under the thrall of a siren. A single note? A refrain? An entire song? What did it take?

He was not inclined to find out the hard way.

"Thank you, but we have somewhere we need to be," he said. He could feel the relief washing through Jileana. He almost chuckled. He wondered again if she realized how easily she could be read. The siren's knowing smile only solidified that understanding. But clearly Jileana didn't care. All she cared about was getting him away from the siren as swiftly as possible.

"Until another time, then," Falin said before turning her back to them and walking away.

Jileana did not sigh with relief, however. She would not be content until Jaykun was out of earshot of her. To that end, she grabbed his arm and pulled him off the cliff ledge, sending him down into the water gracelessly. She didn't give him time to get into a proper diving position, but luckily the dining cave was only a short distance from the water. Unlike her, he did not have an inborn righting mechanism that allowed him to hit the water perfectly each time, so his landing was a little rough.

Once they were beneath the water, she immediately cut a path ahead of him, swimming down toward a familiar cave: the cavern of her mother, the sea witch. It was clear that Jileana's magic was rudimentary at best, especially compared to her mother's. She did not have the ability to protect him from the sirens' call.

"I'm sorry," her mother said with a concerned little frown some minutes later. "There is no protection against the sirens' call, save deafness. I could take away your hearing, but—"

"No!" Jaykun cut her off sharply. "That is definitely not an option."

"Then you have no recourse other than to trust the siren at her word."

"Trust a siren?" Jileana scoffed at the notion.

"Why do you distrust them so much? Why all this open hostility?" Jaykun had to ask her. "Is it just a general racial prejudice or have you been slighted personally in some way?"

He could hear her grinding her teeth, could see her temper simmering beneath the surface. Had he been asked a day ago he would have said she wasn't capable of anger. Now she was literally seething with it.

"I don't want you vulnerable to her! Is that such a crime? I would think you would want the same thing. Or do you like the idea of becoming her puppet?"

Jaykun bristled at the very notion. "I do not. I have been a puppet to love once in my life and I will never be one again."

That seemed to cool her temper, and a wave of curiosity washed over her. "How were you a puppet to love? What happened that has closed you off to the feelings a good and natural love can provide you?"

"There is no such thing as a good and natural love. All love is like the sirens' call: blind and weakening, and a large percentage of it is false."

"That isn't true! Why would you feel in such ways?"

"Why do you hate the siren?" he shot back at her.

She bristled and it looked for a moment like she was going to answer him, but then she turned sharply away from him and with a few quick steps dived back into the water, leaving him alone with her mother in the underwater cave.

"I don't understand," he said with a shake of his head. "Everything I know about her tells me she is an open and fair-minded creature. This hatred toward the sirens baffles me."

"Then perhaps I can enlighten you. Jileana has several brothers, as you may or may not know."

"Yes. I have met them."

"Did she also tell you that one of them was killed while on sentry duty at the selkie-siren border?"

"No, she did not," he said with a deflated little sigh. So that was why there were only five of them at the midday meal.

"There was a raid across the boundary . . . It was long ago before there was a true working peace between the two sides of the island. My son . . . He was a strong warrior. Proud. Unable to back down from a fight. Besides, the sirens don't only take human lovers. They've been known to take selkie males prisoner and woo them into becoming the fathers of their children. At least they did in the past. My son figured he would rather die than become a siren's plaything. And so he did."

"And now your daughter hates the sirens."

"'Hate' is too strong a word. She believes in peace. She knows it was a long time ago. But she does not trust the sirens. Not with the well-being of someone she loves."

Jaykun did not rise to the bait of that observation. He chose to ignore it. Love? What love was there between Jileana and him? She knew what he felt, knew he would never let himself be distracted by fanciful notions like love. She was smart. She had to know it would be an unwise waste of time and emotion for her to fixate on him in such ways. He dismissed the idea outright.

He walked to the edge where the cavern met the water, watching the reflection of the light on the water as it danced along the top of the cavern around him.

"I suppose there are many selkies who have reason to despise the sirens for similar reasons. My solution to the empress's troubles with the sirens could be rife with risk. One altercation is all that is needed for the sirens and selkies to devolve into war."

"Your solution?" the sea witch asked.

Again, he was not willing to share information without the empress's permission. "Tell me, where would Jileana go if she were upset? Does she have a favorite place?"

"She does. There is a cove just beyond the cliff face, around to the left side. Just follow the beach and you will come to it."

"Thank you."

"Jaykun," she stayed him just as he was about to dive into the water.

"Yes?"

"Be careful with my daughter's feelings. She is open and loving and the most kindhearted person I have ever known, but she has never known the pain of unrequited love and I would spare her that."

"She knows I cannot feel love for her," he said uncomfortably. He didn't want to be having this conversation. He wanted to say it was none of her business, but it was. Jileana was her daughter and she was looking out for her.

"Cannot or will not?"

"What difference is there between the two?"

"One is out of your control; the other is within your power. If she thinks you are capable of love, she will want to convince you of it. She has grown up in a loving environment, however suffocating for her at times. She will want to share that love with you. She knows the rewards that come with love and she will want you to find them."

"Rewards?" He scoffed. He couldn't help himself. "Love brings no rewards. It is an illusory thing poets and bards made up to lure coin from a listener's pocket."

Ravi's laugh was soft and light. "Only a man who has loved with all of his heart could possibly be able to feel so much contempt for the emotion. You were betrayed, were you not?"

"I do not wish to discuss this with you," he bit out.

"Tell my daughter the truth of why you have closed yourself off. Make sure she understands. Only then will she be able to protect her heart from the hardness of yours."

Jaykun dived into the water.

CHAPTER
EIGHTEEN

Jaykun found the cove right where Jileana's mother had said he would. And sure enough, there she was, sitting in the sand where the inlet met the water, her legs in the gently lapping waves. The cove was very similar to the one where they had first met.

"I understand now why you despise the sirens so much," he said gently when she looked up and saw him approaching her.

"My mother told you," she said, a statement rather than a question.

"Yes, she did."

"It was a long time ago. Please don't mistake me . . . I would like for there to be peace between the selkies and the sirens, if for no other reason than to keep my father and other brothers safe."

"Your willingness to forgive past transgressions speaks very highly of you."

"Forgive maybe, but not forget. I will never forget that the sirens are not to be trusted and neither should you."

"Believe me," he said softly as he knelt down beside her. He took her chin in his hand and tipped her head back until she was looking directly into his eyes. He wanted her to believe the next words that came out of his mouth. "I will never trust a woman who seeks to manipulate me through love. In fact, it is the very core of everything I abhor."

She drew her bottom lip between her teeth. "Tell me, why do you hate the idea of love so much?"

He frowned. His instinct was to brush the topic away, to change the direction of the conversation. But then he remembered what her mother had asked of him, and he could see the wisdom in being completely honest and open with her. He had to make her see as clearly as he could why love between them was impossible.

"I have told you the tale of the journey my brothers and I went on that gained us our immortality, yes?"

"Yes."

"What I have told no one is what happened the day before I left. Not even my brothers know this."

"All right," she said carefully, already feeling in her soul that she was going to wish he had never experienced what he was about to relay.

"But first I must go back to when I was but a boy. I was only nine the first time I saw Casiria across the town green. She was the palest, prettiest thing I'd ever seen in my life. All delicate features and white-blond hair that trailed down her back. She had fair blue eyes as well, so light they seemed to jump out at you when she looked at you. I had never seen anything so beautiful in my entire life. I imagined she was a fairy queen come to live amongst mortals."

Jileana laughed and he grinned a bit bashfully. "I fell in love with her on the spot. I continued to love her with utter devotion into our adolescence. My brothers would tease me for being infatuated, but I didn't care. I knew she was perfect and I had to have her at any cost. My brothers didn't understand. They even cautioned me, claimed she wasn't as perfect as I thought she was, that she didn't deserve me or my devotion to her, that no woman did. I ignored them. They didn't believe in love. They didn't believe in devoting themselves to one woman and one woman only. They did not feel romantically inclined toward anything save their swords. I fancied myself embroiled in a love for all time."

"And Casiria? How did she feel?"

"She basked in my attentions. Blossomed beneath my love for her. She swore she loved me for who I was and that she would love me for all time. We were young and idealistic. I thought I could make it work. I would earn my living as my brother Dethan's second in command and come home to my loving wife whenever I could. But it did mean leaving her alone for long periods of time. Her loneliness grew over the years. She said she missed me and our love more than anything. She immersed herself in raising our sons and I thought she found satisfaction in that."

"You thought?"

"I found out differently when I last came home to her. My sons were left with a neighbor the night I was to set out with my brothers on our adventure to find the Fount of Immortality. My wife said this was so we may have our farewells in private. It was not the first time she had done this, and though I would miss them and wanted to see them, I would miss her and her bed quite sorely as well. You see, I did not believe in taking other women to my bed during those long months away from her. I loved her too truly for that. All other women paled in my eyes. And I believed she was just as faithful to me.

"So my wife arranged for a peaceful night for us together before I left her for my journey, and we made love. She was so beautiful . . . always so beautiful," he murmured, his mind clearly recalling that night. "I had told her never to worry, that if anything ever happened to me she would be taken care of. As my widow, my brothers would see she was settled with the bulk of my fortune and she would fall under their protection the rest of her days. My sons would be cared for and well raised in my absence." He frowned. "I had told her this to give her peace of mind and comfort, to help her know that although my life was a dangerous one, she would always be safe and comfortable." He rubbed at his neck wearily with a hand. "She waited until I was relaxed before she fed me wine laced with some sort of drug. I was soon barely able to move, and then she let a man into our home who took a dagger to my throat and came very close to killing me. They both attacked me. But even drugged as I was, I was too well seasoned a warrior, far better able to handle myself than they were. I killed the man right off, and in the scuffle, I thrust the dagger they had planned for me into Casiria. As she lay bleeding to death, I asked her why. With more venom than I thought possible, she told me she hated me. That she had fallen in true love with the man . . . I don't know who he was or even what his name was. She said she had never loved me. She had used me to get a comfortable life and a secure future. When she realized she could have my fortune and the man she had been having an affair with, they began to plot my death. But they depended too much on that drug. Still, they very nearly succeeded."

"And you never told your brothers?" she asked, completely horrified at the absolute betrayal. No wonder he had no faith in love any longer!

"I had intended to. I buried the bodies of my faithless wife and her lover and hired someone to care for my boys, then left on the journey as scheduled. Many times along the way I thought to tell my brothers of Casiria's betrayal, but I was too embarrassed and ashamed to share the degradation with them. Especially since they had often spoken against Casiria, had cited several times when they felt she was manipulating me to get her way. In hindsight, I could see they were right. She had used my devotion for her again and again to get what she wanted.

"So, you see, I do not believe in the love of a man and a woman. I believe in familial love, the bond between brothers and mothers and fathers, but bonds without bloodlines to connect them cannot be trusted."

"But that's so untrue!" she cried. "Just because one woman proved herself to be faithless does not mean all women are thus. It is unfair of you to judge us all by the actions of one inconstant woman."

"Perhaps," he conceded, "but it doesn't change how I feel. I will never love a woman again and I most certainly will never entrust one with my life or my heart."

"And yet you trusted me enough to follow me here. You trusted me enough to let me into your bed. Surely you are capable of more than you are giving yourself credit for."

Jaykun frowned at her logic. It was true. He had allowed her close in spite of his better judgment. But letting her into his bed was a far cry from letting her into his heart.

"I am telling you this story so that you understand why I will not let a woman get that close to me again. So that you might protect yourself from disappointment. I do not wish for you to expect more of me than I am able to give."

"I'm sorry, but that just isn't possible," she said with a stubborn frown. "I disagree with you. I think you are able to give a great deal. It is just a matter of what you *want* to give. And you do not want to give trust. The fact that you loved Casiria tells me you are more than capable of love. It is simply that you are too burdened by your pain to allow love back into your heart."

Jaykun pushed away from her, standing up in the

water and pacing away from her. "You aren't listening to me."

"I am. I'm just hearing something you don't want me to hear."

"I want you to keep your distance from me so you don't get hurt! You have too kind and open a heart, Jileana. It will only get you hurt if you entrust it to the wrong person."

"That implies there is a right person to entrust it to. Which is it? Trust no one or trust only certain some-ones? And why can't that certain someone be you? You have a kind heart as well. Would our hearts not be safe in each other's company?"

"Jileana, stop!" His hands clenched into fists, his body bunching tight with tensed muscles. "I cannot love you! Do you understand that? Giving your heart to me will be a waste of your time and a sure path to pain and heartache! I will never care for you the way you wish me to!"

"It sounds to me like you are caring about me a great deal. You are caring enough to try to protect me."

Jaykun cursed. "Is there nothing I can say that you will not take in a positive light? I am trying time and again to warn you away and you are taking it as some kind of great sign that I care for you!"

"Don't you?" she asked, her iridescent green eyes looking at him with open curiosity and more than a little hope.

Panic swept through Jaykun and his first reaction was to crush the source of his vulnerability. "I do not. You are a means to an end, Jileana. You brought me here to meet your empress, and outside of a little bed sport, that is all I needed you for. When I return home, I promise you, I will not give you or this place a second thought. I'm sorry if anything I said or did led you to believe otherwise. I tried to warn you."

His words stung her; there was no denying that. But she also saw them for what they were: a defensive gesture. He said he was trying to protect her, but what she saw was Jaykun trying to protect himself.

"So you did. But regardless of your warning or your intentions, I have come to care for you, Jaykun. Maybe that makes me a fool in your eyes, but I would rather love you in vain than not at all. The gods know you deserve to have someone love you. You deserve something good to offset all the pain you have suffered . . . still suffer. Thank you for sharing your story of Casiria with me. It means something to me that you trusted me with something you didn't even trust your own brothers with."

"I didn't tell you because I trusted you!"

"Didn't you?" She turned it around on him. "The biggest betrayal of your life and you chose to share it with me and no one else. If that isn't trust, then I don't know what is."

"I told you to warn you—gah!" He threw up his hands in frustration with her. Was there nothing he could say to deter her? She was so relentlessly loving and open, it utterly baffled him. Wasn't she afraid of being hurt? Did she have no sense of self-preservation whatsoever?

"You think you told me to warn me, but what you did was share a part of you that needed sharing. Desperately so. How can you possibly heal from something so damaging all on your own? You need someone to help share the burden of that kind of pain. I am happy to be that person."

"You don't understand," he said tightly. "I don't want to heal from this!"

"No, you don't. Because to heal from it would mean opening yourself up to possibilities again, and you are afraid of those possibilities."

"I fear nothing," he said, although there was no power to the declaration. Possibly because they both knew it was a lie.

"You fear me. Me and my heart."

"Stop," he whispered.

She came up close to him, leaned her body against his, and lifted her hand to run her fingers through his salt-riddled hair. The sun gleamed off it, adding light to the dark gold locks. He looked like a strong warrior god. A male version of Weysa. Full of conflict and searching for a resolution to that conflict. Only, for all the wars he fought outside himself, it was the inner turmoil that gave him the most trouble.

He said he didn't want to trust. He said he didn't want to love. But she saw both of those statements for the lies they were. He wanted very much to trust and love; he was simply afraid to do so. Afraid whomever he chose this time would be just as bad a choice as Casiria had been. No, it wasn't her he didn't trust . . . It was himself.

Jileana lifted up onto her toes and pressed a kiss against his stiff lips. He could have pushed her away, could have stormed off. But he did neither. That only served to reinforce her beliefs. He wanted more than he was admitting to. And she would be there to offer up whatever he was willing to take. Because even though it had been just a matter of days, she was aware of just how deeply she had come to care for him. To love him. He was a magnificent man, a creature unlike anything she'd ever known before. Oh, she knew men, knew their ways, but she had never met one so noble or so kind. So like her father and yet so much better than him at the same time. She couldn't have explained why she viewed him in a better light, only that she did. And she did not see him as faultless. He had a great many flaws. But she realized they made him who he was, made him the man she loved.

But she would not confront him with her deepest feelings. He wasn't ready yet. She had the whole of the next three weeks to win him to her and she would do so in small increments. She could not make him love her, but she suspected she would not be forcing his hand in the matter. He longed for someone to disprove his theories on love . . . He simply wasn't yet willing to acknowledge that.

"Enough, now," she said then. "I can see we are merely going to disagree over this. Let us put it aside. You have warned me away and I have heard you. You can be satisfied that you are no longer responsible for my feelings in this matter. There. Does that make you feel better?"

Honestly, it didn't. And not just because Jaykun knew she was merely placating him. Even if she wasn't, if she had been seriously put on her guard, she might now act differently with him. She might no longer be the open, warm, and delightful creature he had come to know. The thought saddened him profoundly. He did not like the idea of being the one who cast shadows over her personality, shading it from the bright sun she usually lived in. He would always give off a tremendous light when he burned, but he preferred to think of her basking in that light, not hiding from it, guarding herself from it, shielding herself from it.

Damn it! Why couldn't he make up his mind about this? No. No, his mind was made up. She had been warned and it was no longer his responsibility. She was a grown woman in charge of her own feelings.

But again, he found no comfort in the thought.

* * *

Both Jaykun and Jileana had a great deal on their minds, so the rest of the day passed in relative quiet. She showed him more of her world, and they pretended talk of emotions and trust had never transpired. After a while it became less uncomfortable and he once again found himself genuinely enjoying being in her company. He should have felt even freer now that he had made himself clear to her. Freer to act however he wished without fear of her reading too much into it.

But he did not. She was not to be trusted, he thought with bemusement. She had made her position quite clear and he needed to be on his guard against her.

But for now he relaxed and found himself enjoying her again. When she laughed, it was with commitment, with all of her heart and soul, and it made him smile every time. The sun would shine on her and highlight all her darkly beautiful features, making her seem brighter and happier still. Then all the innocence she had gained from the light of the sun would be silkily tarnished all of a sudden when she leaned her sultry curves up against him and slid along him like falling water. But she did not cool him off as falling water might; she scorched him instead, as if he had been put in a pot and set to boil. She made him hard both on purpose and when she wasn't meaning to. He couldn't help himself. She was a remarkable creature through and through, and as sexy as the day was long. And for him, a day was very long indeed.

They climbed up to her living quarters about an hour before dusk, intent on eating an early dinner. Dremu was there, eagerly tidying up the place and quick to obey their command to fetch food for them. Jileana couldn't help but notice the brightness of his features and how markedly happier he seemed to be. She wondered at the cause. Then again, escaping his former life seemed to be more than enough to make him happy.

"Dremu will return shortly," she said to Jaykun as she stood close to him, drinking in the warmth and strength of his body with the whole of hers. "What shall we do in the interim?"

The question was obviously leading and suggestive, and he couldn't help the laugh that bubbled out of him. She was audacious and wild, and he wouldn't have her any other way. He was relieved that their argument of earlier did not seem to be affecting her too negatively.

"There is nothing to be done in such a short amount of time," he said with a chuckle as her hand fell onto his chest and began to wend in a circuitous path down his torso. Eventually her fingernails were raking through the curling hairs of his pubis, then on up the length of his upthrusting cock.

"Surely there is something we can—"

"So! It is true what Silan tells me!" a male voice suddenly boomed into the cave.

With a gasp, Jileana spun around. She instinctively stepped between the owner of the voice and Jaykun. He might have been insulted had he not been so bemused.

The voice was owned by a large, lean male with a good two inches in height on Jaykun, though he was lighter by a few rocks. He had a craggy face, all sharp, stony features and hollow cheeks.

"Barban!"

CHAPTER
NINETEEN

A h, so this was Barban, Jaykun thought. The man
who Silan thought was worthy of being his sister's
mate. The man Jileana had described as being just shy
of cruel. But Jaykun could tell just by the look of him
that Barban wasn't just shy of anything. He was a man
who committed to things. And if he was committed to
being cruel, he no doubt would do a thorough job of it.

For a moment Jaykun felt vulnerable, being naked
and aroused in front of this man, who was clearly hostile, but he got over the feeling pretty damn quickly
when Barban reached out and grabbed Jileana by her
upper arm and yanked her forward, away from Jaykun.
Barban went nose-to-nose with her, giving her a sturdy
shake.

"What is wrong with you? Would you shame your
father's name and defile his house in such ways?"

"Barban, let me go!" she commanded him, squirming
in his iron grip. "I shame no one and defile nothing!
And even if I did, it would be no business of yours!"

"What a man's future mate is up to is very much his
business!"

"I have told you a hundred times, Barban, I am never
going to be yours no matter how badly you and my

brother wish it to be! I do not want you! I do not even
like you!"

"Quiet!" he hissed.

Then before Jaykun could react to stop it, Barban
backhanded Jileana with a powerful blow, sending her
sprawling on the floor of the cave, a brilliant slash of
scarlet appearing on her lip and teeth.

Jaykun lost all sense of caution the instant he saw it.
He forgot he was a stranger in a strange land with no
real concept of its customs and what was considered
appropriate—and what would be taken as a great offense. Attacking one of the empress's people could be
construed as an act of hostility, perhaps even an over-
ture to war. But he did not care. He saw Jileana bleed
and it made him see red. He attacked Barban with a
savage snarl of fury, punching the taller man so hard
Barban staggered back into the opposite cave wall.
Jaykun did not stop at a single punch. He fought Barban tooth and nail, drawing on decades of knowledge
as a warrior to help him gain command over the other
man—an uppercut, a body blow, a knee in his gut.

But Barban was no easy foe. Indeed he seemed ener-
gized by Jaykun's attack. Jaykun's first blow had split
his lip exactly the way Barban had split Jileana's and
Barban took a moment to tongue the wound before he
grinned and launched a full-on attack against Jaykun.
Oh yes, Jaykun realized. Here was a man who thrived
on violence. Jaykun recognized it because he had seen it
often enough in himself. The only difference was that
Jaykun had never been purposely cruel. Barban no
doubt reveled in his ability to bully others into submission. In Jaykun's experience, bullies tended to pick on
weaker targets. Evidently Barban saw him as a weaker
target.

Barban was in for a very rude awakening. He would
not find Jaykun all that easy to bully.

But far be it from Jaykun to underestimate Barban's strength and prowess. As they fought, Jaykun felt the power of the other man's blows down in his bones. But Jaykun answered him blow for blow, hitting him harder and harder until his knuckles were sore and his fists were burning. It took some time, but eventually he got Barban on the ground and was standing over him, gasping hard for breath.

"You will never lay hands on her again!" Jaykun hissed at him.

"And who will stop me? Surely not you!" Barban scoffed. "You won't be here long enough to make a difference. She is mine, little man. You will depart here shortly and leave her to me, and there will be nothing you can do to stop the inevitable. She may fight me all she likes, but I have her brother's blessing and her father will not intervene. I come from a powerful house and her father dares not anger my family! It would be the ruination of him and he knows it!"

"I will never be your mate, Barban!" Jileana said as she finally picked herself up from the floor. "I would rather die first!"

"Death is the only way you will escape me, Jileana," Barban said as he got to his feet as well. But he took a step back from Jaykun and his threatening stance. "Mark my words: I will have you and nothing you do short of killing yourself will stop me. So enjoy your little man pet if you must. When it leaves you—and it *will* leave you—we will settle this matter once and for all."

With that, Barban turned and walked out of the cave. The instant he was gone Jaykun turned his full attention on Jileana, drawing her up against his body, cradling her head in his hands and inspecting the damage done to her lip.

"I'm fine," she murmured. "It's nothing."

"Like hell it is! Jileana, why didn't you tell me how bad this situation is?"

"I did. I tried to. Why do you think I escaped to the Overworld? I was trying to get free. Testing to see . . . to see if I could survive there. Because Barban is right. There is only one way out of this alliance and that is through my death . . . or the next closest thing."

"Escape into the Overworld," he said with understanding.

"Yes."

"And yet you came back with me."

"I couldn't just leave without saying farewell to my mother and father. And besides, you wanted to meet with the empress."

"It was your suggestion," he reminded her.

"I was only trying to repay you for all of your kindness. Now I am afraid I have just made everything worse. I have exposed you to a siren. I have given you an enemy in one of the most powerful of selkie houses. I should never have brought you here. It was thoughtless of me. Despite so much being wrong here, there are equal amounts of beauty, and I wanted to share my world with you. Now you are stuck here for another three weeks and you have made a powerful enemy."

"I am not afraid of Barban," Jaykun said as he gently kissed her injury. "But you should be."

"I am. Believe me, I am," she whispered. "And he's right. I cannot depend on my brothers or my father for protection. His family is too old and too powerful."

"Well, I have no such restraints," Jaykun said. "So for the next three weeks you will be safe."

"Provided he only meets you one-on-one, you mean. Barban will not make that same mistake twice. He will have reinforcements next time."

"I don't care if he comes with twenty other selkies.

He will not lay hands on you again as long as I am here."

"Well, it doesn't sound like he is planning to return before you leave, but what could you do against twenty men? Even you are not that strong."

"Then we will take the matter up with the empress," he said. "Surely she can put a stop to this."

"I wouldn't be too sure about that. And besides, why would she want to get involved in the mating issues of her people?"

"Because it is the right thing to do. You need someone's protection and who better than the empress of all the selkies?"

"It will not be that simple," Jileana said with a sigh.

"Sure it will. Trust me. I will not leave you to this kind of danger. Tomorrow at midday meal, when we next see the empress, we will ask for her intervention."

"If you insist," she said with a little sigh.

"I do. I know you do not wish to leave your home. I won't have you chased away from it by a bully."

"Believe me, Barban is only part of the reason why I was drawn to the world of humans. The Overworld has fascinated me for as long as I can remember. I long to see as much of it as is possible. And I will do so one day."

Jileana didn't add that she now planned to see that world from a position at Jaykun's side. She could no longer envision a future without him in it. She was determined to find herself within his reach for some time to come. The difficulty was in trying to convince Jaykun of what an excellent idea it was. That would require him to acknowledge his feelings for her, and she wasn't sure he would be able to do that just yet. But watching him react to Barban, feeling the tender way he held her and touched her damaged lip, she believed more than ever that he cared deeply for her . . . whether he wanted to or not.

"You know," Jaykun said, "there's one thing in the Overworld I think you might appreciate more than anything else."

"What is that?"

"Doors and locks."

She laughed. "I seem to remember how nice they were. It took me a little while to get used to being shut away, not in the open, but I rather enjoyed the privacy your doors and locks provided. Also, the quaint practice of knocking before entering a room. I enjoyed that as well. It warned us when anyone wished to intrude on our time together."

"Yes, it did. Although, I think others got the idea rather quickly that intrusion would be most thoroughly frowned upon."

"I believe you are right," she said as she smoothed her hands up over where his were still cradling her face.

The touch seemed to change the intensity of his gaze a moment before it fell to her mouth. He frowned and leaned forward to gently kiss her bruised lip.

She saw the problem right away. He was afraid of causing her pain. But her lips didn't hurt half as much as being denied his favors would. She stood up on tiptoe, pushing her mouth onto his powerfully, sucking him into a deep and fervent kiss. He drew away at the first opportunity, his breath coming fast.

"Your mouth," he said.

"Does it seem as though I care about my mouth?" she demanded to know.

"Now that you mention it," he drawled with a grin, "not so much."

She grinned back. "Then I suggest you begin kissing me again before you make me very angry."

"The last thing I need is another selkie angry with me. I think Barban and your brother are quite enough."

"Well, I'm somehow certain you aren't going to stop there."

"How odd. I have that very same certainty," he said with a chuckle.

"M-my lady . . . m-my lord, excuse me, but I have returned with your food."

When Dremu spoke they looked at him with surprise. They had forgotten all about him. What was more, they had forgotten all about the time. They only had time for a quick meal before they would have to find Jaykun's place of solitude so he could burn. Thoroughly distracted from their passion, they sat down to eat the raw fish and boiled shellfish.

"Come and eat with us, Dremu, and tell us what you think of the Underworld," Jileana invited.

Dremu shook his head. "I couldn't possibly. I will have my own meal in a short while."

"Nonsense," Jileana said dismissively. "Why couldn't you? Just sit down and speak with us."

"Your pardon, my lady, but I am just a servant and my place is not at my masters' side but several steps behind them."

"That may have been true in the Overworld, but here things are very different. Here we eat with our servants quite often. It is infinitely more efficient that way, rather than serving separate meals. I have invited you and so you will join us. I will not listen to arguments otherwise."

Dremu hesitated again, looking at Jaykun.

Jaykun chuckled. "Don't look to me, boy. I have no influence on her. If she wants you, then she will have you. No sense in fighting her."

Dremu relented at last and sat down cross-legged beside Jileana. The moment he was seated he began to quickly devour whatever he could get his hands on. Thankfully there was a great deal of food on the trays he had brought.

"So answer her question, Dremu," Jaykun invited him. "What think you of the Underworld?"

"I've never seen such a place! Nor such people! The selkie are so much friendlier than I thought, but that could just be because I am unused to anyone being friendly at all. At first I was afraid, my heart likely to pound out of my chest and explode in the air, but now it's nothing at all. I'm learning my way quickly and even though most of them have never seen a man before, they treat me with friendly curiosity, not . . . not as though I am *trega* scum."

"I am very glad to hear that," Jileana said, beaming with pride for her people. Jaykun had to admit that, with the exception of Barban and Silan, he had been having a similarly welcoming experience. The selkie people were not unlike any of the other strange and wonderful cultures he had encountered on his journey to obtain new worshippers for Weysa. Granted, he wished he could encounter these races as something other than a conqueror, but he had a duty to perform.

"I imagine this must all be very exciting for you. I know it was for me when I was in the Overworld," Jileana said. "Would you prefer to stay here, Dremu, or do you wish to return to the Overworld?" Then she thought better of the question. "You know what? You have three weeks to decide the answer to that. But think on it carefully. If you decide to stay, then you will have a place here. I promise you that. If not with me, then with a friend of mine in need of a servant, who desires someone different and intriguing. Right off, I can think of three people who would love to have you."

"Th-thank you. That's very generous of you, my lady, b-but I wouldn't want to leave you."

If Dremu wanted to stay here, then he would not be with her, because she had every intention of following Jaykun on his journeys through the Overworld. She didn't believe Jaykun could do anything to stand in the way of Silan or Barban, so she had no choice but to leave if she wanted to escape their plans for her. She needed her freedom, and she could think of no better place to find it than at Jaykun's side. She also needed his love, but that was another matter entirely.

"Well, as I said, we have a great deal of time to figure all that out."

"Yes, my lady. But just so you know, no one's never treated me as kind as you and I'm not likely to forget it no time soon. Thank you, my lady."

Jileana blushed under the devoted tone in his words. Jaykun watched her interact with Dremu with admiration. It took a very special person to change someone else's life for the better, and he had no doubt that was exactly what she had done for the lad. He felt his chest filling with pride for her, even though he had no right to feel any such thing. She was not his to feel prideful about. He tried to reject the feeling, but he simply couldn't pull it off. He was just too overcome by her generosity of spirit and the very kindness of her nature. No amount of distancing himself from her could make him feel any differently toward her.

It was entirely disconcerting.

Jaykun finished his meal in silence, watching the exchanges between Jileana and Dremu with noisy thoughts and mixed emotions.

CHAPTER
TWENTY

The next day, when it was almost time for the midday meal, Jileana sighed and faced off with Jaykun. "What is it?" she asked him directly.

"What is what?" he asked in return.

"Why are you so quiet? I've had barely two words from you since the altercation with Barban. Is that what is troubling you?"

"That isn't troubling me in the slightest. I've hardly given Barban a second thought."

"Then why are you so silent? What is it that you are thinking or worrying about?"

"It's nothing," he lied. "I'm just concerned about my brothers."

Clever Jileana eyed him with suspicion, but she didn't listen to her instincts; she instead accepted his explanation at face value. "Oh. Well, I'm sure they are fine," she said, lacing her arm around his and pulling him toward the dining hall. "Don't you trust them?"

Of course he did. They would be just fine without him. But he couldn't tell her that he'd spent the past hours obsessing about her and his alarmingly expanding feelings for her. He didn't want her to get the wrong idea. She wouldn't be able to see his growing admiration for her as a simple, natural progression of their friendship. She would read far too much more into it. The feelings themselves were disturbing him, in spite of the fact that he kept telling himself that respect and appreciation for her were nothing for him to be afraid of. That he was completely in control of his emotions.

But the truth was, he didn't feel as though he were in control. He was growing closer to her and he tried to fight the ease he felt in her presence. He could not afford to relax his guard around her. Not even for a second. He absolutely would not allow himself to develop any fanciful feelings toward her. He had learned his lesson. He would never allow himself to forget it.

"I trust them," he responded to her. "That does not mean I cannot still worry about them. They are in a hostile environment. Attempts have been made on our lives already. Garreth is immortal like me and cannot be killed, but Dethan . . . he is a mortal man and can easily be harmed. I am merely worried for their safety."

"I am sure they will be fine. They are surrounded by your men and are very much on their guard after the three attempts that were made. They won't allow for another."

"Three? There were only two. The poisoned soup and the assassin in my bedchamber. What was the third?"

The third was Dremu's attempt on her life, but Jaykun didn't know about that, and if he ever found out, he would kill Dremu where he stood. She had no intention of ever telling him and she cursed her slip of the tongue.

"Right. Two. I'm sorry. I made a mistake."

Jaykun narrowed his eyes on her a moment, but eventually he nodded. "I'm sure you are right. They will be able to take care of themselves. I only wish I wasn't trapped here, unable to lend them any aid or even tell them where I am. They will be greatly worried when I do not return after only a few days. And no doubt highly peeved as well. They want to return home to their families and now I am delaying that trip."

"I'm sorry. That is my fault. I should have been clearer with you about the nature of your travel here."

"It's all right," he assured her soothingly. "I am glad to be here with you. I wouldn't trade this experience for anything. I am very cognizant of what a rare opportunity this is, how rare it is for you to welcome a man from the Overworld into your world. I am deeply honored."

"Do not feel so honored," she murmured as they came around the edge of the cave wall that housed the dining area. "I have done you no favors."

Jaykun stopped short when he saw Barban standing at the side of the room, talking to a shorter, more muscled man with streaks of iron-grey in his long black hair. But unlike the silky black of Jileana's hair, with all its deep richness, this black was as flat and lightless as deep, dark dirt. His eyes were small for his face, a dull brown, but everything in his bearing radiated that he was a man of confidence and power. A man used to getting his own way in things. A man very similar to Barban.

The empress entered the room and everyone moved to stand by their seats.

"No. Jaykun, Jileana, I wish for you to sit closest to me," she said, gesturing for them to move along the table to sit at her elbow on her right side. On her left sat Barban and the other man, indicating their position of power within the court. "Jaykun, may I introduce Horgon and his son Barban," the empress said, indicating the two men in turn.

Horgon. So this was the man who was next in line to the empress's throne. And that made Barban his heir and the next in line after him. No wonder they thought they had power over every other person in the selkie world. Because, with the exception of the empress, they did.

"I have met Barban already," Jaykun said, iced steel in his voice.

"Horgon has kindly graced the court with his presence. He has not eaten beside his empress for quite some time. You are very fortunate to be meeting him," the empress said. But it was clear from her tone that she was not impressed with Horgon's solicitude.

"I am my empress's servant," Horgon said, and it was clear by *his* tone that he was not at all impressed with his empress; nor did he take kindly to her power over him, which she had exercised in order to get him here.

"And my heir," the empress said. "Although if he had his way, I don't doubt he would maneuver himself onto my throne regardless of my being alive or dead."

The empress had taken the gloves off with that remark and Horgon's eyes narrowed on her. "I wouldn't think of—"

She shut him up with a sharp, dismissive cut of her hand. "Of course you would. Who wouldn't want the selkie throne? And it is no secret that you wish me dead so you might pick over the bones of my kingdom. But never fear. As long as I remain unwed and without heirs, your time will come."

"There is a solution to both of our perspectives," Horgon said with a tight smile. "If you agree to become my bride, we can join our two houses and—"

The empress cut him off again, this time with a snorting laugh. "I'd rather be chained to the ocean floor for the remainder of my life. For that is exactly what it would feel like."

Horgon bristled under the insult. But before he could say anything Jaykun jumped in.

"I believe Jileana shares your perspective. Barban has determined that Jileana is to be his—in spite of her many spoken desires otherwise. He thinks to force her hand just as Horgon tries to force yours."

The empress's brows shot up high. Then she narrowed her eyes on the seething Barban. "Is this true?"

Through his teeth, Barban said, "This is nothing you need to concern yourself with, Great Majesty. Jileana's brother and father and I will discuss the matter and it will be resolved to everyone's satisfaction."

"Everyone's satisfaction but mine," Jileana spat. "You will notice I was not named as a member of this consultation over my future."

"I had noticed that, yes," the empress said. Jalaya fell silent a moment. She seemed to be thinking, weighing whether championing Jileana was worth creating further friction between her house and Horgon's. Jaykun was filled with dread that she might turn her back on the situation, giving Barban all the power he needed over Jileana. "In the end, it is your choice, Jileana. No one can force you to do otherwise," she said, leveling a hard look at Barban.

"This is outrageous!" Barban exploded. "What gives you the right—"

"I am the empress!" Jalaya shouted, slamming a fist down onto the table. "Something you and your father conveniently forget every chance you get! If I say it is her choice, then it is her choice. If I say she must marry you, then she must marry you. I am the empress, and I am the first and last word on these matters!"

"There are those who believe you should not be empress at all," Horgon snapped, shooting to his feet. "The sirens are attacking our borders and you do nothing about it. The sea monsters make excursions into our waters and again you do nothing about it. The grots are causing trouble and you do nothing about it! The selkies do not feel safe. They would rather turn to me for help than continue to watch you flounder about helplessly like a fish out of water. You are in over your head, Jalaya! The people know this. It is only a matter of time before they depose you and put me in your place. Enjoy your power while you can, Jalaya. Your days as empress are numbered."

With that, Horgon and Barban exited the cave, leaving a table full of stunned courtiers behind. Then, all at once, the courtiers began to talk, calling reassurances down the length of the table to Jalaya, telling her they would never think any such thing about her. Jaykun wasn't at all sure he believed them.

Perhaps it was wrong to have stirred up so much trouble, but he had desperately wanted Jileana to feel safe. He had needed to have the empress in their corner. It was the only way she could be free.

"Majesty," he said quietly, "I am convinced more than ever that my solution to your problem is the only one."

That brought her attention sharply to him. They both knew what he meant. Killing Horgon was the only way to keep her throne safe. Only it wouldn't be just Horgon. It would have to be him and his son . . . because if she cut off the one's head, the other would quickly grow up in its place and she would end up right back where she was now.

But sometimes killing was necessary. Still, the empress had made her feelings on the matter clear, so another solution would need to be found. The empress needed to surround herself with loyal, powerful families, solidifying her position and supporting her right to be on her throne. From what he had seen, she was a just and strong ruler; she merely was in need of support from a council or some other group of dependable advisors. Right now she was an island, out there all on her own.

"If you support your empress," he said loudly over

the continued reassurances, "then you will help advise her in your areas of trouble. Majesty, I recommend a council made up of the finest families that support you. Members of this council will act as your advisors, bring the concerns of the people to your ears, and reduce the threats made both internally and externally. They should buffer you, protect you. Help you."

"A council?" The empress bit her lip, the first outward sign of vulnerability he had seen from her. "There has never been such a body before."

"Maybe it is high time there was. Whenever I take over a city government, I always install a single leader and a council to advise that leader. This way the leader's word is final, but he or she must also reasonably listen to the wishes, demands, and advice of others as a way of keeping grounded and in touch with the needs of the people."

"I would like very much to be in touch with the needs of my people. I thought I was. I didn't even realize that the issue of the sea monsters was worrying them so much. How is it Horgon knows this but I do not?"

"All the more reason to support the idea," Jaykun said. "Also, the beauty of a council is that the council members also share the responsibility when things go wrong. You do not have to shoulder all the blame yourself. Not unless you outright ignore their sound advice on a matter."

"I will gladly serve on such a council," one male spoke up from along the table.

"And I!"

"I would as well!"

"You have people eager to serve, but make your choices wisely. Make them varied and well rounded. You do not want people who will always say yes to you or who will always say no to you. That would be counterproductive."

"I am beginning to think of some individuals already. Jaykun, I am speechless with how to thank you for all the help you have given since you arrived. You have been here but a few days and yet your advice has done more for me than . . . well, I cannot say. I have prayed to Diathus day and night for solutions to my troubles and she has sent me you. She will be most pleased you have helped her favored children. Now I will help you in return.

"Do you recall telling me of your brother? The one who is buried deep in the ground?"

"Yes," Jaykun said, a strange sort of anxiety bleeding into him the moment she spoke the words. Somehow . . . somehow he knew what she was about to say would be instrumental in his search.

"I am certain I know where he is. I did not mention it before because it was merely a legend amongst my people, but the legend sounded so similar to your story. The legend tells of four brothers who angered the gods for whatever reason and they were buried deep beneath the ocean floor . . . where we chain our prisoners. It is considered cursed ground because of that. But I believe the legend has it wrong, that it isn't four brothers, but one. Yours."

Jaykun could hardly believe what he was hearing. So close! All this time! He must have swum past the chains at least twice in the past hours. He had ignored the area because of the serious faces of the guards patrolling the prisoners and the eerie look of the people chained to the bedrock of the ocean floor.

But as exciting as it was to know where Maxum was, it was just as devastating. The foundation of the entire area of the chains was solid stone. There was no telling where to begin; there was no telling how to begin. Even if they could free Maxum, the god Sabo might merely thrust him back into the ground somewhere else where they would never find him. Sabo, who had devised Maxum's punishment, was a cruel and unforgiving god. It would take another god to free Maxum. Nothing short of another god could do it.

"Thank you," he said quietly as he got to his feet. "Thank you."

"No. Thank *you*," Jalaya said, grabbing for his hand and squeezing it hard until his dazed eyes met hers. "What you have given me is priceless. The gods will reward you one day."

"The gods have forsaken me," he said numbly. He gently removed his hand from hers. "But I thank you for the thought." Jaykun turned and walked out, leaving everyone to stare after him.

"Aren't you going to go after him?" Jalaya asked Jileana.

"Not just now," she said quietly. "He needs some time to come to terms with this knowledge."

"I did not tell him previously because I knew how impossible it would be to retrieve his brother. I wasn't sure which would be worse: searching endlessly elsewhere or knowing that he is here but just out of reach. I decided it wasn't my knowledge to give or withhold. Eventually someone else around here who is old enough would've remembered the legend and told him. I didn't have the right to make the choice for him, in any event."

"I'm sure he is glad you have told him. And maybe there is a solution. It will just take some time to come to it."

"Maybe. Jileana, I must thank you for bringing him here. I don't know if I've done that yet, but I must. His advice to me has been invaluable and he gave it freely without expecting anything more in return. We had already negotiated the building of Weysa's temples, so he had nothing more to earn."

"I am glad I brought him. But I must thank you, for

the situation with Barban. Tradition is for the father to approve or disapprove of the mate of his daughters; you could have upheld that tradition."

"That tradition is dust and bones, where it should be. None of the fathers I know force their daughters to marry someone they do not wish to. Not even in the high houses, where marriages are advantageous. Certainly there is gentle coercion, but nothing more."

"It is standard practice now to let each daughter choose for herself and then have that choice approved by the father or parent. It seems my father was being forced away from that practice. After all, he dare not say no to the second-most powerful man amongst our people."

"Horgon is going to have to get used to hearing no. He will be hearing it a lot soon. His son as well. If they give you any further trouble, simply come to me and I will handle the issue more forcefully."

"Thank you, Your Majesty."

"Now I am hungry. Let's eat something."

The courtiers agreed and the food began to be served. The entire meal was spent with courtiers jockeying for positions on the blossoming council. The empress heard each of them thoughtfully in their turn.

Jileana, however, barely heard any of the exchanges. Her mind had walked out of the room along with Jaykun.

CHAPTER
TWENTY-ONE

~~~

It was nearly a week before Jaykun allowed Jileana to speak of Maxum without shutting her down immediately. That week had been spent helping the empress construct her new council and negotiate the finer details of the siren hunting parties. Jalaya had demanded Jaykun be by her side for all of this, and he had willingly complied and worked diligently on her behalf in both matters. They first had to decide how big the council should be. Then they had to decide who should be on it. Jalaya knew her people far better than Jaykun did of course, but she was able to give him brief pictures of each applicant's worse and better points.

The members of the court jockeyed for the open positions for all they were worth. Jileana had never seen so much kowtowing and foot kissing in her life. Courtiers sent Jalaya lavish gifts or poetic verses or whatever they could think of to sway her attention their way. But Jalaya ignored most of it and focused on what would serve her best and who.

Jaykun did not distance himself from Jileana entirely. They still spoke of other things. They still made love—although there was a taste of feverishness to his lovemaking that had not been there before. It was something almost desperate at times. As though somehow, in the warmth of her body, he could find the solution he was looking for.

She felt as though she let him down every time the solution did not come.

But finally, when she happened upon him sitting at the edge of the chains, staring out at the solid bedrock and the people bolted to it, he had something to say to her about Maxum.

"I suppose we could just chip away at it for the next thousand years," he said, his tone wry and full of pain.

"We could. Perhaps we could give the task to the prisoners . . . give them something to do. It might break up the monotony of their imprisonment."

"I have already thought of that. The truth is, there is nothing to be done to find him if Sabo doesn't want him found. But perhaps . . . now that we know where he is, perhaps I can beg Weysa to help us retrieve him. For I know only a god can offer me a solution to this. I do not care if he has to suffer the same fate I do night after night, as long as he is free the rest of the time. Perhaps I can convince Weysa that he would make another fine soldier in her army, that he can help us fight for her cause."

"You have the ear of a goddess. It seems the wisest course of action," she said.

"I have that ear only when it pleases her. I cannot make demands of her. She will not take kindly to it."

"Then ask. Beg. Supplicate. Do whatever you need to do."

He nodded. "If only there was a temple here."

"Jalaya has begun work on the ones she has promised to you. But they will not be complete until after you have left. Do you need a temple to contact her?"

"I don't know. I don't know how it works. I have never called for her before. Perhaps my brothers would know, but . . ." He trailed off. They both knew why he couldn't contact his brothers. She had cut him off from them.

"I'm so sorry. I never meant to cause you any pain or inconvenience."

He turned and looked at her with surprise on his features. "Do you think I blame you for something? Hold you responsible?" He then thought about it a second. "I do blame you. If not for you, I would never have heard this story. I would never have come here and found my brother. I would have sailed away to the next city on my list and been completely ignorant. Yes, I blame you for all of that."

He jerked her into his arms, up against the hard length of his body, and sealed his mouth over hers. Kissing him beneath the water like this always flooded her senses with the taste of the salt water first, then overwhelmed her with the taste of him. His kisses were bold and warm and so very much a reflection of what Jaykun was, it made her dizzy with sensation and excitation. He had not kissed her with such unfettered zeal in many days. Before, there had always been the shadow of his brother hovering over them.

But he had shared his pain with her and that had somehow lightened the weight of it. He couldn't explain it and neither could she. But he kissed her now on the edge of the chains as though someone were going to come along any minute and chain him down amongst the other prisoners.

Eventually she drew back, her fingers stroking along the side of his face, toying lightly with his hair. "It will be all right," she assured him. "Somehow, some way, you will get your brother back. I believe that with all of my heart."

"How do you believe it? How can you believe something about me that I don't believe myself?"

"I believe you have been punished enough for your sins, that something somewhere has to give way. One day it will all work out. I don't know how long it will take for it to come about, but it will happen."

"I wish I could believe the way you do. I wish I could have that kind of hope. But hope was something that was burned out of me a long time ago."

"I don't believe that for a second. If you had lost all hope, you wouldn't have bothered looking for Maxum in the first place. You would have merely abandoned him to his fate and carried on with yours. But you've had hope that you would find him and now that hope has been rewarded. You must continue to have hope. You must try."

He realized she was right. If he hadn't had hope, he would have given up long ago. By all rights, he should have given up. He should have lost any ability to see a future at all—for himself and for his brothers. But when he was rescued from that star and given a life again . . . perhaps that was when hope had been reborn in him. If he could be rescued from hell, then anything might be possible.

Including freeing his brother from his.

"From now on I will be dedicated to finding a way to free Maxum. I will win a thousand cities for Weysa if that is what it will take to convince her to free him. I will do whatever she asks of me in return. Surely she must grant me this one thing. I have always been loyal to her, even when I was not cursed. That has to count for something."

"I'm sure it does. Pray to her. See if that does not call her to you. Otherwise, it is only a short while before you can return to the Overworld, where you will find a temple that can bring you closer to her. She has to hear your call then. She just has to."

Jaykun reached to trace a warm pattern over her

cheek and nose and lips. "Ever the optimist. You have such a light heart; you believe anything is possible. I wish I could see the world like you do. All the good in it, all the joy in it."

"You can, you know," she said with a smile. "You simply have to open yourself up to it."

"I have. Since meeting you, I have. I look at the world through your eyes and it seems so much brighter, so much more special. Thank you for giving me that."

"You're welcome," she said. "Now come. Jalaya is expecting us. We need to make the final choices for the council."

"Of course," he said, turning to swim beside her.

Sometime later all but one of the council seats had been filled.

"So . . . whom do we choose for the last seat?" Jalaya asked.

"I don't think you'll enjoy my suggestion," Jaykun mused.

"Whom do you have in mind?"

"Horgon," he said.

"Horgon!" the empress exclaimed. "Never!"

"You said yourself he is from one of the most influential families of the selkies."

"But didn't you say not to choose someone who will always say no? Who will always oppose me? You are the one who wanted him eliminated!"

"And you are not willing to do that, so the best course of action is to keep him as close to you as possible. Give him a voice. Perhaps if he believes he is being heard . . . Plus, it will look good to your people, to see you trying to make the effort to pull all the most influential families along together. He may be a hindrance more than a help, but at least you will have your eyes on him. It might even mollify him to some extent. Although, it is clear nothing will keep him from wanting to be emperor and deposing you."

"The thought of eliminating him has grown more and more appealing over this past week," Jalaya said. Then she sighed. "But I am not as cutthroat as he would be."

"I know," Jaykun said with kind understanding. "And that is what will make you an infinitely better monarch than he would be. Better even than I would be. You are willing to find solutions to your problems—difficult solutions—rather than take the easy way out."

"So . . . Horgon on the council," she said uneasily.

"Remember, it is your council. You can just as easily remove him from it as you can place him on it."

"This is true," she said. "Very well. I will send messengers right away to inform all the members of their chosen status and we will convene a council meeting right away. And, Jaykun," she said, looking directly into his eyes, "it would mean a great deal to me if you were there for our first few sessions. Just to help me run things smoothly, and for your advice. I find I am quite lost without you."

"Nonsense. You have been ruling alone for decades. You know what it means to be ruler and you have earned your place at the head of your people a thousand times over."

"Except lately . . . lately things have been escalating out of my control. I am not too proud to admit that. You have helped me to find ways to bring order back to my life. I cannot tell you what a valuable gift that is to me and I have no idea how I will ever repay you for it. I can start by telling you this: If there is some way my people and I can help you to retrieve your brother, then we will do it. You need only ask it of us."

"Only a god can help to retrieve him, and now that I

know where he is, I hope my goddess will smile kindly on me and help me to bring him home."

"Then let me extend an invitation to you. You are welcome here, Jaykun, from now until the end of your days. You may visit here"—she cast a sidelong look at Jileana—"or even live here if you so wish. Perhaps one day when your goddess allows you to retire from her service."

"Perhaps," he said with a small smile.

Jileana knew what the empress did not. There would never come a time when he would not be in service to his goddess—and he didn't mind that. From what Jileana had learned this past week, he actually enjoyed working in service to Weysa. He did not need a curse to be reined in by her. Jileana could only hope that one day Weysa would see this and be benevolent enough to release him from his burden. He did not deserve to suffer any longer. He had paid for his hubris a thousand times over.

"I will be glad to sit in with you and your council for as long as I am here and as long as you will have me, Jalaya."

"Thank you. Now off, the two of you," she said, shooing them away with her hands. "There are many more things of greater pleasure than staying cooped up in this castle with your empress."

"Majesty," Jaykun said with a grin and a bow. Then he winked. "But not many."

He took Jileana's hand in his and they swam out of the castle together.

A short while later they surfaced before the cliff face and waited for their eyes to adjust to the bright, high sunlight. It was midafternoon, several hours before dusk threatened them. It was Jileana's favorite time of day. She and Jaykun would almost unfailingly climb to the very top of the cliff and make love for hours. They were rarely disturbed there; apparently the younger selkies used the spot for the same purpose, only they waited until after dark. There was something more daring about doing it in the daylight when anyone might happen upon them and easily be able to see them. Not that it mattered greatly. Selkies were not a shy people and happening upon any in the throes of passion was not an uncommon thing. She and Jaykun had stumbled upon more than one couple in their travels around the selkie kingdom, both above and below the waters.

Jaykun led the swim to the cliff face and dragged himself out of the water the moment he had a solid hold on the fossilized coral. When they reached the top of the cliff, he dusted off his hands and looked out toward where the distant horizon would have been, had it not been obscured by the ever-raging storms that protected the selkie lands. For a moment he was angry with Jileana for bringing him here, for exposing the way to travel to her home to someone who could easily exploit it. But he dismissed the emotion. No army could come through the portals. Between their location beneath the water and the fact that they were heavily guarded, there was no chance of an invasion having any kind of success. Besides, he suspected he had barely touched the surface of what Jileana's mother and the other sea witches were capable of. It would be hard to fight spells as well as the selkies *and* fight for breath beneath the water.

No, the selkies were well protected from the Overworld. Sirens, sea monsters, and internal politics were what threatened them most.

"You have become invaluable to the empress," Jileana said quietly. "She finds you to be indispensable." She came up behind him and threaded her arms around his waist until her chest was flush against his back and her forearms were crossed over his chest. Her right hand settled over the thundering beat of his heart. She liked the feel of it, especially after a rigorous climb or after they made love. It was like being connected to what made him alive and vital. She couldn't get close enough to that part of him. She needed to know he was there with her—for however long she had left. Because even though she planned to go with him when he returned to the Overworld, she couldn't escape the sensation that she was living on borrowed time with him. It was probably because she suspected there would come a time when he would try to violently push her away from him. Better to push her away than to face his growing feelings for her. And she knew his feelings for her were indeed growing. He never said anything, but she sensed his comfort with her, sensed how much fuller his life was since she had arrived in it. He was coming alive before her very eyes. As troubled as he was by his brother's plight, he was equal parts freer and lighter in his interactions with her. It made her heart happy to see it.

"So, what shall we do now?" she asked, amusement in her tone. They both knew what they liked to do in that spot at that time of day.

"Let's do something different," he said suddenly, turning about in her arms so he could see her face. It allowed him to view the immediate pout and disappointment in her features.

"Like what?" she asked, clearly trying to be polite but unable to hide her true feelings.

Jaykun threw back his head and laughed at her.

"What's so funny?"

"You could never lie to me," he said with a chuckle. "Not about your feelings, in any event. You are far too open. Your emotions can be read as plainly as a book."

"Not always," she said with another pout.

"Always," he assured her. "And I like it. I like knowing that what you are feeling is honest and clear. I like . . . I like being able to trust that."

Suddenly her entire face lit up. It was the first time he had volunteered any kind of statement that laid a measure of trust at her feet. It was by far a better gift than anything else he could have possibly given her. She wanted to ask him if he truly meant it, she wanted to take delight in the victory and draw attention to it, but she knew it would be better to let it slip by unremarked than to risk him becoming defensive and possibly withdrawing the sentiment. So she simply basked in its meaning.

"What would you like to do?"

"I'd like to go inland," he said.

Jileana's blood went instantly cold. "No," she said flatly.

"No?" He lifted a brow and a smile toyed at his lips. "I wasn't asking for permission, merely a companion on the journey."

"No! You can't go inland! What if you ran into a siren? One song and you would be lost forever! No! You cannot go!"

"So it is an entire song? Is that what it takes to fall in love with a siren?"

"Yes. The siren sings her special song, the one only she sings. She sings it, and by the time she reaches the end of it you are hers forever."

"And if the song is interrupted?"

"Then the spell is broken before it sets in. But a siren is rarely interrupted!"

"I could easily fight a siren the moment she begins to sing and cease her song."

"The moment she begins to sing, you will be enraptured. You won't want to fight her." She shook her head. "No. I will not let you go."

"You are very bossy," he teased, not taking any great offense.

"This isn't a joke, Jaykun! We are talking about your free will! It would belong to the siren for as long as she is alive and breathing in this world, and sirens are just as long lived as you are or I am."

"You seem quite distressed by this," he observed, taking great amusement in her concern.

"Because I love you! It would kill me to lose you!"

All amusement fled from his features. "I never asked for you to love me! In fact, I specifically said otherwise!" he snapped at her.

"Well, I'm sorry, but some of us cannot help the power of our feelings like you can! Or rather, some of us cannot deny our feelings like you can!" She threw all caution out the window as she said those words and she knew it. But it was better to risk everything than to have nothing.

"To deny a feeling means one must have that feeling in the first place, and I assure you, I do not feel love for you! Not in that way!"

"But in another way?" she asked, hope unfurling in her chest. He may not have realized it, but she had found a way into his heart.

"That is not what I meant! How is it you can twist my words into knots just to suit your own purposes? Don't you get it? I do not and will not ever love you!"

He regretted the words and their harshness, regretted the pain that lanced throughout her features. It colored her beauty in unattractive and pale ways. She was devastated and it was clear. It hurt him to see it, but she had to know the truth. She had to be made to realize what a futile and stupid thing it was to love a man like him. A cursed man. A cold man. A man who did not deserve the love of such a woman, if indeed there was any such thing as love. But as he looked at her, he believed that if anyone could truly feel love, it would be Jileana. If any love could be believed, it would be hers.

No, he caught himself in the thought. No! There was no such thing as love! It was an illusion! A lie people told themselves in order to make life feel worth living. A lie he refused to live ever again.

"You're wasting your time on me," he said hoarsely. "You're hurting yourself for no reason."

"For me to be hurting, it would mean my feelings are true!" she countered.

"You only think they are!"

"I know they are! I feel them! You don't get to tell me how I feel! You can withhold your own emotions all you like, but you do not get to tell me how I feel!"

"I am not withholding emotions!"

"So you say!" she snapped at him.

"Why won't you believe me? Damn you, Jileana. Why do you have to ruin this by creating problems?"

"Ruin what? What do we have that is going to be ruined? You say you have no emotions, so what is being ruined just because I say 'I love you'?"

"Our companionship. The fondness we feel for each other. The fun we have when we're not trying to look too deeply into things!"

"That's funny," she said with a dry laugh, "because I've known I loved you for the better part of a week and it hasn't seemed to hamper us much at all."

That took him aback and he stepped away from her. "The better part of a week? That's impossible. All of this is impossible. Love at first sight is a lie. You cannot love after only a week!"

"Oh, so it is possible to love someone, only not so quickly? Tell me, how long should it take before I know I love you?"

"That isn't what I meant!"

"It's what you said!"

"Stop it! Stop putting words in my mouth."

"They are your words. I am merely trying to understand them!" she cried.

"I don't love you!"

"You don't want to love me! There is a difference!"

"I assure you, there is not!"

"Fine. I recognize that loving a man who is completely closed off from his emotions is my responsibility," she said with sudden weariness. "It is as you said: I knew what I was getting into from the beginning. You made that clear from the start. I am not asking you to love me in return, only to leave me free to feel what I wish to feel."

"You are setting yourself up for pain," he said earnestly. "Please don't do this to yourself."

"If there is no such thing as love, then there is no such thing as a broken heart . . . so you have nothing to be concerned over."

"Just because I don't believe in the trueness of love doesn't mean one cannot deceive oneself into believing it. I should know. I took part in the same deception, and believe me, it hurt when I woke to the truth of the matter."

"You were hurt because you loved a woman who was faithless and undeserving . . . but you did love her. You did love her or she would not have been able to hurt you so much. You are capable of love whether you want to admit it or not, and I am willing to wait until you figure it out for yourself."

"You will be waiting a long, long time," he said quietly. "You will be waiting in vain."

"It is my time and my heart, and I will do with my heart what I will."

Jaykun didn't think he could bear it, bear her waiting

painfully for him to feel something he never would. It would kill her free spirit a little bit every day.

"Jileana," he said hoarsely as he pulled her up against his body, reveling in the sweet feel of her for a moment before saying, "in another two weeks I am going to leave you and this place, and I will never look back." He swallowed. "Even if I did love you, I am not free to do so. My goddess makes too many demands of me." He cupped her cheek in his hand and ran a thumb under one eye that was wet with an unshed tear. "It wouldn't be fair to you. None of this is fair to you. But I do know that this is your home and that when these next two weeks end I will leave you here and continue on my journey . . . alone."

"Not alone," she said hoarsely. "You have your brothers. You let them follow you. Why should I be any different?"

"Because they are my kin . . . my blood . . . and they have obligations to their gods, just as I do, that happen to coincide. A war camp is no place for a woman."

"You have female mems and other women for other reasons," she said, her tone making it clear they both knew what those other reasons were. "I am a sea witch, like my mother. Not as powerful as she is, I grant you, but I can still use magic. I could be of use to you. I could—"

"Female mems and whores are not my concern! They are meant for war. The mems heal for me. And the whores keep the men in good spirits. None of those women can hold a candle to you. You are beautiful and generous, and your heart is so clean and free and untouched by the soils of this world. I would not see that end!" He took a deep, steadying breath. "In two weeks we will part ways, Jileana. I do not want to spend that time fighting with you."

She wanted to argue more. She wanted desperately to grab him and throttle him, and she knew he could see it in her eyes. He knew the full measure of her pain, because once he'd had his love rejected. And yet it did not keep him from pushing her away; that was how deeply his pain and mistrust went.

But she knew that, for all of his protestation against the emotion, he loved her. She knew that even though he was a man who could slaughter other men by the hundreds and never flinch in the face of war, he was afraid to acknowledge the emotion.

Very well, she thought with a lift of her chin and determination steeling her spine. She had two weeks to change his mind. Two weeks to make him admit what he felt for her. And if she hadn't succeeded by that time . . . well, she didn't know what she would do. She would take that step when it came time to take that step.

"Yes," she said so softly she could barely hear herself. "Let us enjoy these next two weeks as best we can."

"There we go. That's better," he said with a smile as he stroked her face with his fingers. "Let's enjoy what time we have left together. Come. Let's go to the sea anemone bed and watch their colors. We can swim with the schools of fishes, explore a little. You like to do that."

"Yes. I do," she agreed. It had always put a smile on her face and he knew it. He was trying very hard to please her, when all he had to do to please her was one thing.

And that one thing was something he was most unwilling to do.

Her time was short and she had to make the most of it. No matter what she was feeling inside, she couldn't let it choke the remainder of her time with him. If she failed to make him realize that he loved her, these could very well be the last days she would ever have with him.

It was a thought she couldn't bear to hold in her head, so she pushed it aside and steeled herself with determination. She would win this.

She would.

CHAPTER TWENTY-TWO

Two weeks flew by so fast it was unbelievable. Jileana had never known time to move so swiftly. Now the moon was almost full and that meant the gateway would be open for the next week.

Jaykun was ready to depart that same day. He was preparing his trunk for his return. He looked down at it and smiled. The entire time he had been there he hadn't touched a single stitch of the clothing he had brought. After so many weeks, he wondered how he would be able to bear the confinement of clothes, never mind armor. He had never been so free as he had been these past weeks, in more respects than one. He couldn't remember the last time he had had so few demands on his time. Oh sure, he had been busy overseeing Jalaya's council meetings, had danced hard to keep Horgon in his place as he contemptuously took a seat at the table and did exactly what they'd expected of him: hindered more than helped. It was clear that power was his goal, not the true will and needs of the selkie people. If he gave a damn about them, he would have stopped balking and started helping. In the end, Jaykun believed Jalaya would have no choice but to eliminate Horgon's influence and threat, and he believed the empress was realizing that for herself.

But this was no longer any of his concern, he reminded himself. He was heading back ... Well, he could hardly call it home. He didn't have a home. He frowned. It was strange, but this place had begun to feel like home to him.

A dangerous thought. An unwelcome one. Home was merely an illusion of feelings. A sense of comfort meant to soothe one's soul whenever one was away. It was a place of belonging, and he most certainly did not belong here amongst the selkies. He was a man. Simply a man. A cursed man, an immortal man, but a man just the same.

He closed the trunk and looked around the cave one last time. Jileana was not here yet. She had said she needed to do something before they went. He had unpacked her dresses from his trunk for her, although he didn't really know what use she would have for them here. He felt a painful sensation in his gut as he came closer to realizing that he was mere minutes away from leaving her and never seeing her again.

The past weeks had been a whirlwind of unforgettable moments and lovemaking, and dozens of new and wondrous experiences in the world of the selkies. He did not deny that all of it had been made memorable and special just by Jileana's presence.

He had grown very attached to her. He wouldn't deny that. He would miss her when she was gone from his life. He did not examine too closely just how much he might miss her.

Then, as if his thoughts had conjured her, Jileana appeared at the mouth of the cave. He looked away from her, unable to figure out what to say to her now that the moment of his departure was at hand. He knew what she felt for him—what she believed she felt for him—and he knew that it would cause her pain to let him go.

This distressed him because he wouldn't wish any kind of pain on her and he didn't know how to avoid it. Perhaps he should've distanced himself from her beforehand, but he hadn't been able to do anything of the kind. He hadn't wanted to color their time together with sad thoughts of the moment when he would eventually leave her.

It had been wholly selfish of him. But he hadn't been able to be a better man. Now he would turn his back on her, swim through that portal, and never see her again . . . all the while knowing how much pain she would suffer in his absence.

"These go too," she said, making him realize she had come closer as he had wrestled with his thoughts. She picked up the dresses he had set aside and put them inside the trunk. He looked at her and raised an inquisitive brow. "I will need something to wear," she explained.

He tensed from head to toe. "Jileana," he said with warning in his tone, even as a part of him leapt with joy at the idea of her coming with him. A surprisingly large part of him.

"Just for the week," she said quickly. "Until the portal closes. Then I will return home."

He hesitated. He had intended to make a clean break from her, and that was exactly what he should do. Right here and right now.

But the idea of having another week of Jileana was too delightful to resist. His whole body relaxed as if a great weight had been removed from it and he gave her a measured smile. "Very well. But I think you might be making this harder on yourself in the long run. I do not wish to increase your pain."

"My pain will not be increased by another week with you. It will be relieved by it," she said softly as she moved into his arms. She reached to kiss his mouth, but he avoided her for a moment.

"Are you sure?" he asked. "I would not wish to cause you hurt."

"Then do not leave me," she said simply with a shrug of a single shoulder. "That is the only way you will avoid causing me pain. But," she said quickly when he opened his mouth to speak, "since you will not do that, I will gladly postpone my pain until a week from now. All right?"

He had little choice but to hesitantly nod his assent. So she packed the dresses and gave them a satisfied pat.

"Now come with me. The empress wishes to say farewell before you leave."

"I had every intention of saying goodbye to her of course."

"I know you did. Come."

"What about the trunk? Is Dremu coming with us?"

As if the mention of his name had conjured him, Dremu appeared in the mouth of the cave. For the first time in weeks, he was wearing the clothes he had arrived in, having gone native himself sometime after the first week. But the sight of his clothing told Jaykun that Dremu was indeed going with them.

"Only for the week," he explained. "I'm coming with my mistress and will return with her. I like it here, I do. I'm as different here as I was in the Overworld, but they don't seem to care none. They treat me with kindness and respect and fascination. I'm sure the novelty will wear off one day, that maybe one day I'll want to go back through the portal, back to the Overworld, but I can tell that day is a long time away. And, well, there's this girl . . ." He flushed. "I ain't never had a woman before, but she wants to be my woman. Her name's Luzi."

Jileana beamed at him. "Oh, Dremu! I'm so happy to

hear that! And I know Luzi. She's a very nice girl. I hope you'll be very happy together."

Dremu blushed. "Seems like we might be," he said bashfully.

Jileana gave him an enthusiastic hug, which only made him blush a deeper red. "Dremu, can you take the trunk and meet us at the portal?"

"Yes, my lady."

"Good," she said with a smile. "Come, let's say good-bye to the empress." She grabbed Jaykun's hand and led him to the ledge of the cave's exit. Then, without a second thought, she dived off. Jaykun had since grown used to her diving from such great heights, and he had grown used to taking those dives himself. So he followed her down, cutting cleanly into the water with hardly a splash to be had.

They arrived at the underwater palace minutes later, Jileana's father meeting them at the front gate.

"There's something of an uproar in council chambers," he warned them. "Horgon and his usual nonsense."

"I trust Jalaya can handle him," Jaykun said.

"Indeed she's gotten quite adept at it," Creasus agreed. "But it may mean she won't be able to say a proper farewell."

"That's all right. We'll take what we can get."

Jileana's father looked at his daughter with something like sadness in his eyes. "Take care, my daughter," he said, kissing her forehead for a long moment.

"I will, Father. And I will return," she promised.

"Good. Your mother would miss you," he said. But it was clear he too would truly miss her if she did not return as promised.

They entered the council chambers a short while later to hear Horgon's voice booming throughout the open water of the room.

"You are a disgrace to your crown! I swear to you, I will rip it from your head as soon as I am able!" he hurled at Jalaya. She was sitting at the head of the table and Horgon at the foot. Horgon was standing, shouting at her the length of the table away.

Jalaya stood up slowly, outrage simmering in her eyes. "Enough! I have had enough of your insults! I am your queen! You will not treat me thus!"

"And who will stop me?" he demanded of her, his son stepping in to stand at his elbow, a show of force against her.

"I will! Guards! Take Horgon to the chains!" she said, a terrible tone in her voice warning them all she had been pushed too far.

"For what?" Horgon demanded to know, although he didn't seem so cocky as the guards closed in on him.

"Treason," Jaykun said. "Anyone who disrespects or threatens the empress is a traitor and should be punished because of it."

Jalaya turned grateful eyes onto Jaykun, but the expression was fleeting as suddenly Horgon drew the blade attached to his side, his son doing the same, and they faced off with the guards advancing on them. Jaykun swam forward in a flash, leaving Jileana behind and insinuating himself into the fight, grabbing up a sword that had been taken from one of the guards. Jaykun dodged a deadly swing by Horgon, and in a flash of movement that proved how well used to moving in water he had become these past weeks, he was holding Horgon by his hair from a position behind him and had the blade against his throat.

"Stop!" he commanded Barban, who was still fighting the guards. "Stop or I end this contention with your father once and for all!"

Barban had no choice but to stop. The guards disarmed him and seized him by his arms.

"Take him to the chains as your empress commanded you," Jaykun said to the guards he handed Horgon over to. "Chain him well." He turned to the empress. "And what of the son?"

"He made no threats to me. He can go as long as he promises not to raise arms against me."

"I do so promise," Barban said through his teeth. It was clear he had no intention of keeping that promise, but that was a matter Jalaya was going to have to handle when it presented itself. She knew the repercussions slapping Horgon in chains might have, and an uprising was one of them. The families that supported Horgon might easily come to his aid, fight to depose her of her crown, and start a civil war amongst the selkie people. It would be the worst possible outcome. But the fact was, Jalaya could not let Horgon's threats and insults slide a moment longer. His behavior was just as damaging to her crown as a war might be. People watching her sit idly by as a man disrespected her would lose all faith in her ability to control those around her. If she could not rule a single man, then how would she be able to rule them all?

The guards dragged Horgon off and Barban stood seething in a corner of the room before turning to the empress. "You may come to regret taking the advice of this . . . this Overworld creature over the advice of my father!"

"Is that a threat?" Jaykun asked mildly. "Because that too would be treason."

Barban blanched. No one liked to be threatened with the chains. And if Barban ended up in chains as well, then all would most certainly be lost for his family. Jaykun knew it and so did Barban. It was clear by the contempt and rage simmering in his eyes.

"You see, Jaykun? You cannot possibly leave me," the

empress said with a tremulous smile. "Your council means far too much to me."

"I am sorry, Majesty, but my world has awaited me far too long already."

"Of course I know this," she said with a shake of her head, "but I do not have to like it. You are ready to go, then?"

"I am," he said.

"Then come with me for a while," she said, swimming to the nearest door, which led into the farther reaches of the castle.

Jaykun and Jileana obliged her and followed her out of the room, leaving Barban and the council behind. After several long minutes of swimming in silence, they came to Jalaya's private chambers and the three of them swam inside, with guards left posted at the door. Jalaya settled into a pacing swim that crossed and recrossed the room.

"Jaykun, how do I begin to tell you how valuable you have been to me?" she said.

"You do not need to," he said.

"Oh, but I do," she argued in earnest. "This council has changed everything. It will mean an entirely new era of peaceful coexistence for my people. The people will be well represented and the highest influential families are now working with me rather than against me. This has been a priceless gift."

"You have done all the work, Jalaya. If not for your strong leadership, a council would make no difference. A good ruler knows when to listen and when to rule; you know how to do both and that is why, contrary to Horgon's claims, you very much deserve your crown."

"And for the first time in a long time I feel that is the truth. I owe you for that." She came up to Jaykun and took his hands in hers. "Promise me you will return one day, that you will come visit. There are other portals that lead to us. All you need do is look for a place where large amounts of seals are congregating. Odds are that is a portal."

"I will remember that," he said with a smile.

"See that you do." She leaned in and kissed his mouth. It was a friendly gesture, an affectionate one. He realized then how much he had grown to value his friendship with the empress. She was a strong and intelligent woman with a great heart and an unbelievable amount of courage. It was hard not to like her. She had grown close to him, sharing much of herself with him these past few weeks. He believed he was the closest thing to a true friend she had experienced in a long while and he felt badly to be abandoning her. But like his relationship with Jileana, he had no choice but to end it. He would never forget it, but it must end.

"Farewell, my friend," she said to him, giving his hands a tight squeeze.

"Farewell," he returned to her. Then he kissed her cheek one last time and he and Jileana swam away from her.

Jaykun and Jileana headed toward the portal. About halfway there, Silan swam up to them, interrupting their progress.

"So you are going with him?" Silan demanded of his sister. "Just like that? With no thought to your own safety? With no thought to your father and mother and those who worry about you?"

"I can take care of myself," Jileana said defiantly with a lift of her chin.

"It's the Overworld! If they knew what you were, they would destroy you! Hurt you! Is it wrong of me to love you enough to not want that to happen?"

"No," she said softly, coming up to him and settling a hand on his face. "And I love you too. But this is my life to lead however I see fit and you have to stop trying to lead it for me."

He frowned deeply, but he took up her hand and laid a kiss in the palm of it. "Be careful, Sister. And come home as soon as you are able."

"I will," she said, reaching to hug him to her tightly.

After that, Silan left them and they continued to the portal. They found Dremu swimming at the surface above them and they surfaced next to him.

"Ready?" Jileana asked him. Dremu nodded, and with a deep breath, he followed them as they dived down toward the portal. As they rounded the shelf of coral that led to it, they stumbled right into a cadre of selkie males.

Unarmed and off guard, Jaykun was swarmed by them until they had him seized and helpless. Though he struggled and fought with everything he had, he was sorely outnumbered. More selkie males seized Jileana. Then the sea of selkies parted and exposed Barban, who approached them. Poor Dremu had been captured as well, but unlike Jaykun, he had never been given the gift of being able to breathe underwater. He had not wanted it or needed it before this. So he quickly began to look like he was in distress.

"Barban! Please! He will drown!" Jileana cried.

"Then he should not be here amongst creatures who live and breathe in the waters."

Barban jerked his head and the selkie holding Dremu dragged him through the portal and swam him up to the surface. Jileana nearly melted with relief. But that did not change her situation with Jaykun and she didn't know what Barban's endgame was.

"All the trouble in this world began when you arrived," Barban sneered at Jaykun. "Well, I am going to put a permanent end to your influence over the sickly empress."

"If she were so sickly, you would not be so scared," Jaykun shot at him.

Barban came up to Jaykun and punched him hard across the face, the blow snapping his head back.

"What are you going to do?" Jaykun demanded of him. "I am already leaving. What more could you ask for?"

"To make certain of it," Barban said. "And to make certain you do not take my wife with you."

"I will never be your wife!" Jileana spat at him. "The empress has said it is my choice!"

"Well, that is only one of the things that will change once Jalaya is deposed and my father is raised up in her place." He turned to his men. "Take him through the portal."

Jaykun struggled the entire way as they swam him through the portal and into the much colder water on its other side. Jaykun fought to free himself as he watched Barban swim up to Jileana and touch a possessive caress down her face and around her throat until her neck was encircled by his hand. He whispered something to her that Jaykun could not hear, but the revulsion that crossed her features told him everything he needed to know about the remark. He redoubled his efforts to free himself as Barban turned to his men and said, "Tear it down."

That was when he realized what they were about to do. Helplessly he watched as the men on the other side of the portal began to smash at the coral around the portal. They were going to destroy it with Jaykun on one side and Jileana on the other. With Jileana under the power of that selfish, evil bastard. Jaykun fought to free himself and fought valiantly. He cracked his head into the head of the nearest man, then bit the man on his left. He was making headway, but not fast enough.

In an explosive fall of coral and rock, the portal between his world and Jileana's was destroyed.

The minute the portal was demolished the selkies who had held him let him go. He swam to the surface, gasping for breath—not because he needed it but because he felt as if he were drowning suddenly. As if the spell Jileana's mother had cast had suddenly worn off. But he knew that wasn't it. The spell was intact. So why then did he feel as if he were suffocating?

He swam for the beach, then dragged himself out of the water and onto the sand beside where Dremu lay gasping and shaking with fear. The selkie males had turned into seals and disappeared amongst the seal population sitting along the jetty.

Jaykun pulled himself to his feet and the world spun around him. His heart hurt in his chest and panic infused his every cell. Jileana was in trouble! She was under the power of that bastard Barban! And now . . . now he had no way to get to her. By the time he found another portal, it would be far too late.

What could he do?

He began to run toward the city of Kriza.

CHAPTER
TWENTY-THREE

Garreth and Dethan were sitting before the fire with drinks in their hands when Jaykun exploded into the common area of the castle. Shocked, the brothers lurched to their feet.

"Jaykun! Where in the eight hells have you been?" Dethan ejected harshly.

"I have no time to explain!" Jaykun said, pushing past his brothers.

"You will explain!" Dethan demanded as he grabbed his brother's arm and stopped his progress. "Do you know what we have had to deal with in your absence?"

"It could not be helped!" Jaykun said. "I am sorry I was gone so long, I truly am, but there was nothing I could do about it! I was trapped where I was until tonight."

"Trapped! You mean you were held prisoner?"

"No! Look, I do not have time to explain!"

"You will make time!" Dethan thundered.

Jaykun could see his brothers would not be satisfied, and yet he could not bear to waste a single moment of time. He rapidly explained what had happened. Everything he could fit into the shortest amount of time possible, including what had just happened to separate him from Jileana.

"So, what will you do now?" Garreth asked as they followed their brother into his rooms. Jaykun was still naked. Before he could do what he was thinking of doing, he needed to put on some clothes.

He dressed quickly as he answered his brother's question. "I intend to take a ship into the maelstrom and find the selkie island."

"But you can't! You just told us that it's impossible to reach the island through the storms," Dethan said.

"I will find a way through!"

"Why?" Garreth demanded of him. "You were going to leave it all behind anyway. It is no longer your concern. What did you think was going to happen when you left? That everything would remain the way you left it and there would be no more troubles? They have to sort these things out for themselves. There is nothing you can do about it!"

"I will not leave Jileana in the hands of that bastard Barban!"

"Let her brother and father manage the problem. It is not up to you. You'll destroy a perfectly good ship in a folly that won't do you any good," Dethan said.

Jaykun pulled on his boots in tight silence, refusing to argue with his brothers any longer. They couldn't understand. He couldn't make them understand. He did not know how. He simply couldn't leave her like that. He couldn't turn his back on her and leave her like that. Panic and pain swamped him, threatened to overwhelm him. He couldn't bear the idea of what Barban might do to her. He had to hurry. He had to go!

He flew out of his room, his brothers hot on his heels.

"Tonkin!" he bellowed through the hall as he headed for the room the page had been staying in when Jaykun had left three weeks ago. Tonkin appeared in his doorway just as Jaykun reached it. "Tonkin! I need a ship ready to leave within a few minutes and a captain brave enough to pilot her into the storms. Do you think you can find me one?"

"I know I can, Sor Jaykun."

"Then do it! I'll meet you at the docks."

"Yes, sor. Right away." Tonkin didn't even bother to dress. He hurried away in just his breeches and bare feet.

"You'll risk the lives of others in a foolish attempt to reach the selkie island?" Dethan demanded.

"I won't risk anything," Jaykun said as he turned and headed out of the castle. "And yet I'd risk everything for her."

"Why?" Garreth asked.

"Because . . ." Jaykun came to a stop as he weighed the answer to that question.

Why? Why was he so determined to go back to the place he was just about to leave anyway? His brothers were right. What had he thought was going to happen after he left Jileana behind? That she would be safe without him no matter what?

Good gods, what had he been thinking? What had he been thinking, wanting to let her go where he could not protect her? Wanting to let her go at all.

He'd been an idiot. A fool. A fool afraid of his own feelings. Afraid to admit that . . .

"I love her," he said softly.

That made Dethan and Garreth look at each other with worry.

"You love her?" Garreth echoed.

"Yes. I love her. More than words can say. Damn, I was a fool to think otherwise! Just because Casiria . . ."

"Casiria?" Dethan said.

"Casiria betrayed me. Because she did, I could not trust myself to feel anything for anyone other than the two of you. I thought . . . I thought love was an illusion . . . even though I could see the strength of it in the two of you—with your wives—I thought it was safer to deny it even existed rather than trust myself to get it right this time."

"I thought you loved Casiria," Garreth said with confusion.

"I did. I loved her up until she betrayed me . . . and even beyond. I think that was what hurt so much. She betrayed me and yet I knew I still loved her. Faithless as she was. Damn her to the eight hells. And to think I almost let her ruin my one true chance at something real, something ten thousand times more powerful and special than anything I ever had with her."

"So because you love Jileana you are willing to go on this fool's quest?" Dethan said.

"Would you do anything less for your wives?" Jaykun demanded of them.

The brother's exchanged a look.

"No," they said in unison.

"What do you need from us," Dethan wanted to know.

"Dethan, you can do nothing. I will not risk your life. Garreth, I don't know that there's much you can do."

"If you can go, I can go," Garreth said.

Jaykun nodded. Garreth's immortality and sword hand might come in handy if they made it to the selkie island.

They were at the dock minutes later. Tonkin waved them over to a ship; the captain greeting them was one of their own men. Probably wisest since the Krizan people were superstitious about the selkies in general. Getting a Krizan captain to sail into the storms would've been difficult.

Jaykun impatiently paced the deck as he waited for the captain to launch the vessel. Luckily, the tide was with them and there was a strong wind up. They were at sea quickly, but their progress was still too slow for Jaykun to tolerate. He was left with nothing but his thoughts and his regrets. He didn't know how he was going to manage the future, how a relationship with Jileana could possibly work given that they were from different worlds and he had a mission he could not be swayed from, but he didn't care. He would figure it out after he knew she was safe. After he knew Jalaya was secure on her throne, despite whatever it was Barban had planned. And he knew Barban had planned something. He and Jalaya had chosen the council well, picked representatives from an equal number of houses in Jalaya's corner and in Horgon's corner in order to help sway loyalties toward Jalaya. But the council was young yet and there was no telling if he and Jalaya had changed anyone's allegiance. It seemed that civil war was imminent. The selkie people were about to be torn apart and Jileana was going to be caught in the middle of it.

Jaykun was standing at the bow of the ship as they approached, staring hard into the storms, trying to make out the island he knew was just beyond. When the first rains lashed the boat, they came violently, the winds whipping at the sails and the ocean churning beneath the ship.

"We'll never make it!" Garreth shouted at him through the storm.

Garreth was right. There was no way they would make it. Not above the water.

He grabbed his brother's arms and brought him to the edge of the ship.

"Jump!" he instructed.

"Are you out of your mind!?" Garreth asked.

"Jump! You cannot drown!"

"I *can* drown! Over and over again, I can drown. I just cannot die from it!"

He had a point, but there was no other way.

"Please," Jaykun begged him. "For me will you do this?"

"Ah damn," Garreth said as he shook his head. He stripped off his boots, made certain Dethan's sword was secured to his waist, then grabbed the rail of the boat and leapt down into the water. Jaykun shouted to the captain to turn the ship around and head back to port, then he was hitting the water after Garreth.

He grabbed hold of his brother and dragged him down beneath the churning waves and the raging storms. They swam down and down until they were well below the violence above them. Then they swam beneath the storms, heading toward the selkie island. Garreth struggled to breathe, drawing water into his lungs and choking on it. He drowned violently, but then, after a while, he grew used to the water in his lungs and was able to swim in his brother's wake.

They swam like that for a good half an hour until suddenly the water grew warmer, grew clearer, and Jaykun knew they were close. When he finally could see the honeycombs of coral, he thought he would scream with relief. But there was no time for joy. They had to make good use of their time, and Jaykun started by swimming into the cave that housed Jileana's sea witch mother. He surfaced cautiously, not knowing what he would find. He swam into the cave and lifted himself quietly out of the water. He came around the lit bend and saw Jileana's mother.

"Ravi!" he hissed.

Ravi turned with a start. "What is it?" she asked, instantly knowing something was wrong.

"You don't know? Jileana's been taken captive by Barban and his soldiers."

"I heard nothing of this! Are you certain?"

"Yes! Please, I need you to help my brother to breathe

beneath the water, and then I need your magic to help rescue Jileana."

"Of course."

Jaykun fetched Garreth from the water. His brother threw up a violent lungful of water once he was in the open air, but Ravi cast her magic quickly and it soothed him almost instantly. Now Garreth could breathe underwater and speak as well. They could better coordinate with each other.

Then the three of them went toward the empress's castle. They knew that if anything was happening, the coral castle would be at the center of the action.

At least this time Jaykun was armed. The sword would not be as graceful underwater as the shell swords the selkies used, but it would get the job done.

As they approached the castle, Jaykun tried to determine if the guards at the gate were friend or foe. He figured there was only one way to find out. Fully clothed as he was, he would stand out as an enemy, so they agreed to send Ravi forward. She went and took the measure of the guards as she came up close to them.

"I am looking for the captain of the empress's guard," she said.

The guards looked at each other, then lunged for her. Prepared, she sent a percussive wave of sound at them, setting their ears ringing, their eardrums popping under the pressure. They screamed and writhed helplessly under the pain, and Jaykun and Garreth came up and dispatched them completely.

"We're going to have to work our way into the castle one group of guards at a time. We can only pray they haven't killed Jalaya yet."

"We can only pray," Ravi agreed.

They entered the castle like that, killing any guards who attacked them, knowing that the guards were loyal to the wrong side. At the center of all of this would be

Barban and Horgon. Once they eliminated them, the threat to Jalaya's throne would end. The beast would fall apart without its head.

Suspecting where they would be, Jaykun led the way to the edge of the throne room. And sure enough, there Barban sat, one leg thrown indolently over the arm of the throne, picking at his nails with a short shell dagger. He was clearly waiting for something. Sitting on the floor beside him, bound and tethered to the ground were Jalaya . . . and Jileana. The two women fought their bonds helplessly.

"It seems only fitting that you be chained at my feet just as you have chained my father. But don't worry. Once they have freed my father and he takes his place here, you will no longer have to worry about being bound. We will gladly take that worry away. But as for you, my reluctant wife, you shall have no such reprieve. Once the courtiers are called and they realize they have a new emperor, you will be mine to do with as I please."

"I wonder that you bother with your father at all," Jileana said, "when you could be emperor yourself!"

Barban sat up straight as the thought played in his mind a moment. Then he chuckled. "Perhaps. One day soon. But the people are far more likely to follow my father than me at this time."

"They haven't become too firmly entrenched," Jaykun whispered to his brother. "I count only six guards in the room with him and no courtiers. I am willing to bet that no one even knows of this coup and so the true reaction is not yet felt. Barban knows that. That is why he has no choice but to kill Jalaya as soon as possible."

"It's a wonder he hasn't done so already," Garreth said.

"He's enjoying his victory over her," Ravi said. "And he wants his father to have the honor of killing her. If it were Horgon here, she would be dead already."

"We have to get in there, but we have to protect Jalaya at all costs," Jaykun said.

"Even at the cost of Jileana's life?" Garreth said. "Because he will grab one of them the moment he knows something is going wrong. The odds of him grabbing Jileana are just as high as him grabbing for the empress."

"He will go for the empress," Jaykun said assuredly. "He will want to kill her and solidify his position the instant he can. So your job, Garreth, is to get to her before he can do that. I will take care of the other guards. Cut Jalaya's tether and get her away from him as soon as you can. Let Ravi worry about Jileana."

The fact was, *he* was worrying about Jileana. Almost to the point of paralysis. But he had to move. He had to do something or all would be lost. He refused to see that happen. He refused to see this race plunged into an era of darkness.

Garreth swam away from him and around to the door closest to the throne. The minute he was in place, Ravi and Jaykun entered the room.

Ravi released her percussive blast at the guards in the room, knocking them back as Barban lunged to his feet.

"Kill them!" he screamed to his useless guards once he had recovered from the blast.

Jaykun plunged his sword into the chest of the first guard while out of the corner of his eye he kept watch on Barban, Jileana, and Jalaya. But he need not have worried about the empress. As promised, Garreth was there, cutting through the chain tether with his god-made sword as if it were butter and jerking her to his chest and the safe shelter of his body. He cut her hands free in the next instant. Then he hurried her out of the room.

Barban saw her escaping and flew into a rage. He grabbed Jileana as Jaykun's sword flashed in and out of the second and then the third guards' chests. He held the short shell dagger to Jileana's throat and screamed, "Stop or I'll cut her from ear to ear!"

Jaykun had to ignore him and continue fighting, hoping with all of his heart that Ravi would be able to rescue her daughter.

"Let my daughter go or I will turn you into a guppy," she said ominously, holding out her hands as if she could shoot fire from them. For all Jaykun knew, she could.

"You are not that powerful, *witch*," Barban hissed.

"Are you willing to take that chance, *guppy*?"

Barban hesitated, tensed. A small cloud of blood appeared in the water where the knife was pressed against Jileana's throat.

Then, seeing Jaykun cut through his fifth guard, Barban tightened his hold on Jileana. Now that the empress was gone, she was the only point of power he had left. As Jaykun dispatched his final foe, he turned to approach Barban with menace.

Facing Jaykun's and Ravi's powerful visages, not knowing what Ravi could truly do to him, Barban hesitated.

"I'll tell you one last time," Ravi threatened. She held up her hands menacingly. "Let my child go!"

"It's over, Barban," Jaykun said. "Let her go."

For the first time since Jaykun had known him, Barban finally did something smart. He dropped the knife and backed away from Jileana. Ravi immediately went to her daughter and released her from her bonds as Jaykun went to stand over by Barban. There was no sense in killing him. The room was already full of floating, lifeless bodies.

Holding his sword on Barban, Jaykun automatically reached out his arm to Jileana. She threw herself against him and he turned his head to catch her kiss, all the while keeping one eye on his captive. When they finally broke apart, Garreth was there with the empress.

"There are other guards of his in the castle, but not many," Jileana said. "They got here only an hour or so before you did. They have not had enough time to get firmly entrenched."

"I suspect they sent most of their resources to the chains to retrieve Horgon. Am I right?" Jaykun asked Barban. Barban didn't answer, but the slight widening of his eyes told the truth for him.

"There might be a large force of them," Jileana said to him. "The empress's guards are housed at the chains, but if Barban's guards manage to beat them and free Horgon, Jalaya will not be safe."

"Then Garreth and I must go and help defeat Barban's forces. I will not have this race embroiled in a civil war if it can be helped. We will put down this uprising and kill it quickly. Only then will Jalaya be safe. And this time, Majesty, you must execute the criminals who threaten you. Putting them in the chains will only give others a focal point if they decide to split into factions against you once again."

"I know it," Jalaya said grimly. "I wanted to avoid it, but I know it cannot be passed over this time. Barban, you and your father will pay for your betrayal with your lives."

"But—but my father had nothing to do with this! This was all my idea!" Barban sputtered.

"I highly doubt that. It is much more likely that your father set this in place in case he was ever taken prisoner," Jalaya said. "You were merely executing standing orders."

Barban paled and it told Jalaya that she was right. Garreth and Ravi found some rope and tied up their prisoner.

"Make it tight," Jalaya warned. "He has to be swimming in order to turn into a seal, but be careful just the same."

Jileana touched a hand to Jaykun's chest, feeling the odd sensation of fabric on his skin for the first time in weeks. Her smile trembled. "You came back for me."

Jaykun caught her eyes with his, pinning her to the spot. "I will always come back for you," he said.

She burst into tears and he tucked her head close under his chin, soothing her with soft sounds.

"Shh," he said. "It's all right. I will never let anything hurt you again."

"I won't leave you," she said with wobbling lips. "I can't. Y-you'll just . . . I'll just follow you as long as you let me. You don't have to give me anything; I won't be in the way. I-I just can't leave you. Don't make me leave you!"

"Jileana, I won't make you leave me. I love you too much to let you go."

"Wh-what did you just say?" she asked tremulously. "Did you just say . . ."

"That I love you? Yes. Yes, I did. And I'm sorry I didn't tell you sooner. I'm sorry I lied to us both about what I was feeling. You were right. I was just too afraid. But when I saw that portal come crashing down and I knew you were in danger . . . I realized . . . I realized I had lost my heart to you quite some time ago."

"Oh, please. You're making me sick," Barban sneered.

Jileana ignored him and squealed with delight. She wrapped herself around Jaykun and kissed him so deeply it was a wonder their tongues were still attached to their own mouths at the end of the kiss.

"Now Garreth and I have to go to the chains. I need to know what's happened. Jalaya won't be safe until it's over."

"Be safe, my love," Jileana whispered before giving him one last kiss for luck and sending him on his way,

promising to watch over Jalaya with her mother somewhere away from the castle until all the resistance was
soundly put down.

It actually took a lot less effort than Jaykun had antici-
pated. With Barban captured, Horgon still chained,
and the bulk of the empress's guard quartered just outside the area of the chains, the coup was over long before it really began. It boiled down to the council in the
end. Horgon had lost a lot of support because of that
council. By giving the most powerful people a place to
air their grievances and voice their concerns, Jalaya
had taken away their reasons for potentially standing
against her and answering Horgon's call to arms to that
degree of traitorousness.

Jaykun did not give Jalaya the opportunity to waver
and change her mind about executing Horgon. He did it
for her with one smooth swing of his brother's powerful
sword. He did not, however, have the opportunity to do
the same with Barban. Which he supposed was for the
best. This way Barban could be executed publicly as a
warning to anyone else who thought to become traitors
to the empress. In the end, it was a lot of bloodshed for
no reason. It was a shameful waste of life. But it could
have been much worse. Much worse.

To Jaykun's relief, when he got back to Jileana it was
to discover that Barban had not had the opportunity
to harm her too much. He had roughed her up a bit,
threatened her a lot, but he had been too focused on his
endgame to worry too much about his "future wife." If
Jaykun hadn't made it back to Serenity so quickly,
things might have gone very differently.

Later that day they were all in Jalaya's private rooms:
Jileana, Garreth, Jaykun, Ravi, Creasus, Silan, and Ja-

laya herself. The empress was sitting as she eyed the gathering before her.

"Jaykun," she said, holding out her hand to him.

He obediently stepped forward, dropped to a knee before her, and kissed the hand he held. "Majesty," he said.

"Jaykun, we will never forget what you have done for us this day. You have saved the selkie people from a lot of pain and strife. I thank the gods every day for sending you to me."

"I am glad to be of service to you, my lady empress."

She smiled and opened her mouth to continue, but a sudden eruption of bubbles appeared beside her seat, near where Jaykun knelt, and she leapt up in alarm. Not knowing what the disturbance was, Jaykun put himself between the bubbles and the empress and drew his sword.

Suddenly the bubbles dissipated and in their place was a beautiful woman, with hair as green as grass and eyes as blue as the turquoise ocean waters around her.

Jalaya gasped and dropped to her knees. "Diathus!"

It was indeed Diathus, goddess of the land and oceans. Warning bells went off in Jaykun's head. Diathus was a goddess of the faction warring against his goddess Weysa. Her being there could only mean trouble for him and his brother.

"Relax, warrior," Diathus said as if she could read his mind. "I am not here to harm you. Rather, to thank you."

"Thank me?" he asked warily.

"Yes. The selkies are my most beloved children. You have saved them from themselves. For this I am compelled to give you thanks. You have the gratitude of a goddess. The question is, what will you do with it?"

"What do you mean?"

"I mean I will grant you a boon, human man. Ask any favor of me and you shall have it."

Jaykun could hardly believe his ears. Here was a mighty god thanking him for his services? Willing to grant him anything he desired?

"Here is the dilemma," the goddess said with a chuckle. "Do you wish to be freed from your curse, or do you wish to have your brother returned to you? Which do you ask for?"

"How can you free me from my curse?" he demanded of her. "It can only be released by the god who set it upon me and that is Lothas."

"And Lothas is my husband. He will do whatever I ask of him."

Her husband. He had forgotten that part. "And what of Sabo? He has cursed my brother. What will keep him from casting Maxum back into the earth somewhere else?"

"That is not my concern; it is yours. But if I free your brother, he will suffer as you suffer. Every night from dusk till juquil's hour the earth will swallow him whole again. Suffocating him. Crushing him. Just as it is doing even now."

The dilemma was no dilemma at all. Not to Jaykun.

"Free my brother," he said quickly. "I will bear my curse for as long as he does if it means he will have some hours of life once again, some reprieve."

"Hmm. A selfless choice. You impress me. And I am not easily impressed." Suddenly the room dissolved around them and Diathus, Jaykun, and Jalaya found themselves at the edge of the chains. The earth began to rumble and bubbles rose up from a spot not too far from where they stood. Rock and soil spewed upward into the water, clouding the water with silt and making it impossible to see. But in the next instant, the rock and soil cleared away and the water was as clean as ever.

Jaykun knew it was the hand of the goddess that had made it so.

And there, floating naked and unconscious, was his brother Maxum. Jaykun swam to him and grabbed him up close. He could feel in the limpness of his body that every last one of his bones was broken, pulverized by the pressure of the earth.

But that didn't matter because he knew that Maxum had also drunk from the Fount of Immortality, which meant he would heal as rapidly and completely as Jaykun and Garreth did.

"Thank you," he whispered fiercely to the goddess. "Thank you with all of my heart."

"If you really wish to thank me, you can stop fighting in Weysa's name," Diathus said.

"This I cannot do. I have made a vow to—"

"Yes, yes," she said, waving the matter off. "I suppose it cannot be helped. What I need is a warrior of my own to fight in my name. Perhaps your brother would do this?"

"And pit one brother against the other?" he asked. "For that is surely what would end up happening one day. Didn't we just avoid a battle that would pit brother against brother? Selkie against selkie?"

"This is true. But I have not freed him so he could fight in Weysa's name. She is my enemy, after all." She thought on it a moment. "If you can vow to me that your brother will not fight in the name of any of the gods that oppose my faction, I will get Lothas to release you from your curse."

Jaykun couldn't believe the offer. It would be like getting everything he wanted all at once. His brother and freedom from his curse . . . and Jileana. What more could he ask for?

"I cannot make a vow for my brother," he said at last, knowing it was true. Maxum had always been his own

man. He had always done whatever he wished to do. He
had sold his sword to whatever cause struck his fancy.
Jaykun could not take that right away from him.

Then he felt the slight squeeze of a hand around his
arm. He looked down and met the pain-filled eyes of his
brother. Maxum could not speak under the water, not
having the benefit of Ravi's magic, but the nod of his
head was unmistakable.

It was as good as his word.

"We do so swear. Maxum will not fight in the name
of any god." He had said "any god" on purpose. He
did not want Maxum beholden to any of the gods. If
Maxum must suffer Sabo's curse, he would do so on his
own terms.

"Very well. As long as he holds to this promise, you
are free of your curse. I will speak to Lothas straight
away and it will be done. Congratulations. Your burning days are finished."

Then the goddess turned to Jalaya. "You are the
rightful queen of your people. Never doubt that. Never
forget it. I cannot protect you at all times—the war gar-
ners much of my attention—but if you need me, pray to
me. I will try to answer you if I can."

"Thank you, my beauteous goddess," Jalaya said,
humbly kneeling before Diathus.

"Enough of that. You are an empress. Stand and be
recognized as one. Farewell, beloved child."

With that, Diathus disappeared in a rush of bubbles.

CHAPTER
TWENTY-FOUR

Jileana snuggled into Jaykun's side, holding him as tightly as she could, as if she were afraid he might disappear . . . or burst into flames at any moment. But dusk had come and gone, and as promised, Jaykun remained free of his curse.

"I am afraid it might all be a dream," she said for the third time that night since they had settled back in her cave.

"So am I," Jaykun said. "I'm afraid Sabo will discover Maxum is free and take him away again. With any luck this war between the gods will take up too much of his attention for him to care about what happens to one man."

"But you said he cared enough to taunt your brother Garreth when he was in pain."

"I know." Jaykun gnawed at his lip a little. "I guess it's best to hope for the best. Perhaps Weysa will protect him. He may not have to fight for a god, but he can pray to one. He was always devoted to her. As a gold-sword, he thrived on conflict, solving it with his blade. But that was many, many decades ago. He has been suffering in the ground ever since."

"Has he said much to you?"

"Not much, but I will not push him. He has been through a great deal. If he is anything like me, it will take some time for him to adjust to a torment-free existence."

"Not free," Jileana noted. "Just less of it."

"Aye, this is true." He turned his head and pressed a kiss to her forehead. "And how are you doing? Are you certain Barban didn't hurt you?"

"He didn't have time to hurt me. He was focused on taking over the castle and freeing his father from the chains. I think he was supposed to kill the empress, rather than keep her captive, but he disobeyed his father's orders just for the opportunity to lord it over her."

"Well, it is a very good thing he did. And a good thing I came as quickly as I could. If the battle at the chains had gone badly . . . I don't know what would have happened. Nothing good—I know that much."

"Nothing good," she agreed. "But I still can't believe you tried to sail into those storms. I warned you they were impassable."

"I knew they were. I was hoping to get far enough in that we could swim the rest of the way. And it worked."

"It worked, but your brother had to suffer drowning."

"He survived it."

"I'm sure it is a memory he cannot put aside too quickly."

"But he need not worry about drowning any longer now that your mother has gifted him with the ability to breathe and speak beneath the waves."

"This is true." Jileana rose up on her elbows and kissed his mouth slowly and searchingly.

"What was that for?" he asked when she lifted away.

"Do I need a reason?"

"No. But it felt as though there was one."

"There was indeed. It suddenly occurred to me how

much I loved hearing you say you love me and I thought if I kissed you well enough perhaps you would say it again."

"Mmm, perhaps I would. But all you need do is ask me and I will gladly let you know how I feel."

"But asking is not the same as a spontaneous utterance."

"Ah. So you prefer that it be my idea."

"Something like that," she said with a prim lift of her chin.

He chuckled at her. "Very well, then. I shall make it my duty to spontaneously utter how very much I love you, how deeply you have entrenched yourself in my heart, and how I cannot face the idea of a future without you. I will tell you I was a coward and a fool for treating you the way I did, and I know how lucky I am that you have forgiven me for it."

"There is nothing to forgive," she said softly, kissing his mouth again until heat was bleeding all throughout his body. "You were in pain. I understood that. But I'll have you know I had no intention of going back home after the week of the full moon closed the portal."

"I see."

"That is why my father and brother were saying goodbye to me like that. They knew I wasn't going to come back for quite some time."

"They knew more than I did. Then again, I saw only what I wanted to see, what felt safest for me. For all that I am a man who takes great risks, I was afraid to risk it all on love. I confess I am still afraid. I fear all this good fortune. I feel as though somewhere, somehow another scimitar will fall and someone in my family will be in its path."

"You cannot live your life in such ways. You cannot refuse to celebrate just to dread what might or might not come next. If your experiences have taught you anything, have they not taught you to live and thrive in every moment? That there is no knowing what will come next?"

"That is exactly my fear: fear of what will come next."

"You cannot let it paralyze you. That is no way to live a life."

He took a deep breath and drew her tighter to himself, until their breaths mingled and her mouth was just brushing his.

"Then again, all is not perfect for us," he said softly. "My brothers and I have to get back to my brother Dethan."

"There are other portals. There is one that empties onto a beach only half a league away from Kriza."

"Ah. Well, this is fortunate. I have a schedule to keep and my brothers deserve time with their wives over the winter. Besides, Dethan must be worried and he should be told of Maxum as soon as is possible. He will be beside himself with joy."

"Never mind being beside himself with it," she said with an impish wrinkling of her nose.

"Hush," he scolded her with a click of his tongue before he kissed her deeply and put his tongue to better use. Their tongues tangled and rubbed sensuously against each other, the warm honey of her mouth something he devoured with great relish and passion. He rolled her beneath him and settled himself between her warm thighs as she raised them to bracket his lean hips. He broke from the kisses for a moment to look down into her face, staring hard into her eyes, almost as if he were searching for something. He was. An answer.

"What have I ever done in my cursed existence to deserve something as beautiful and charming as you?"

"Whatever it was, I am glad you did it," she whispered.

"As am I." He grew more serious. "Do not hurt me, Jileana. If you ever grow tired of me or feel you need to leave me for whatever reason, promise me you will tell me rather than let me live in ignorance."

"That will not happen."

"Promise me," he insisted, giving her a little shake in his desperation.

She reached up and took his face in her hands, making certain he was meeting her eyes. "I make you this promise. I will always tell you exactly how much I love you. Whether it is a little or a lot. But know this: As long as there is a little love for you in my heart, I will never do anything to hurt you. And since I will always love you, that makes this a forever promise. I am yours and you are mine. The only one who can ever break that bond will be you," she vowed.

He fretted a little more. "But if you—"

"I promise. I will not hurt you," she said softly.

This finally put his mind to rest, and with a smile, he kissed her again. He wanted to trust her, knew that she had never done a single untrustworthy thing in all the time he had known her, and so in the end, it was easy to trust her. The love he felt for her melted away all of his past pain, and what was left in its place was only love and passion.

He kissed her again and then again and again. He filled himself with the flavor of her, with the temperateness of her mouth. He devoured her eagerly and was just as eagerly devoured *by* her. He grew incredibly hard in the lee of her hips, his sex pressed firm and hot against hers. They were naked already; to be so felt more natural to him now than not. That would have to change of course once they were back in the Overworld, but here he would enjoy the freedom and the benefits that went with it.

He broke from her mouth and began to travel down

the length of her torso, trailing kisses down her breast-bone and into the soft spaces between her lower ribs. He traveled down over her belly and then drifted his lips over the soft mound that protected her sex. With a long lick, he parted the folds beyond and took the warm, syrupy taste of her onto his tongue. Like syrup, she was sweet and decadent, and he just couldn't get enough of her. His tongue danced across her again and again, and he listened to the increasing crescendo of her moans with the greatest of pleasure. Her fingers burrowed into his hair, grasping and clutching at him as her spine undulated like a sinuous snake. She cried out sharply and he knew to increase the intensity of his strokes. Even as he did this, he thrust two fingers deep inside her and waited for her to explode. She did so instantly, her inner walls clamping down on his fingers, her whole body pulsating with spending desire. Unable to bear being outside her body a minute longer, with his love for her swelling in his heart, he rose up and thrust himself deeply into her. He made love to her almost frantically until she came again, this time screaming out his name, the delight of it echoing into the room long after he had reached orgasm himself.

Panting for breath, he settled his weight onto her, shivering at the little pulses that still shimmered through her and around where they were still connected. He kissed her again and again, fearing he would never get enough of her, fearing the power of his own emotions.

But no. He would not be afraid. Fear wasted time and twisted minds. He had faced his fears before and was a better warrior for it. He would face these and be a better man for it. In the end, he knew there was little cause for fear. Jileana was so wholly different from Casiria. From her coloring to her selflessness to the capacity of her heart. So different. She was what he had deserved in the first place; she was worthy of the love he felt.

"I will love you as long and as hard as I can. This will be a very long time, since neither of us will age."

"I am aware of this," she said with a laugh. "And I am all the happier for it."

He smiled. "Good. Now let's get some sleep. It has been quite some time since I have fallen asleep before juquil's hour. I think I should like the indulgence."

"I do not blame you. But . . . do you plan to sleep while still inside me?"

He laughed and then reluctantly separated their bodies so they could lie side by side, snuggled up close together. "Perhaps another time," he whispered into her ear.

She smiled. "Perhaps."

At dusk, long before he had the chance to heal from his initial damage, the ground beneath the ocean shook and trembled and then parted to swallow Maxum whole. The earth and stone crushed him; the soil suffocated him.

But he soothed himself with the knowledge that come juquil's hour he would be spit back out into the open world, rescued by his brother's selflessness.

Provided a god did not come and smite him once again for his own entertainment. Maxum was angry. Blindingly angry. His temper had been simmering for a long time, growing more caustic with every year he had been suffocated and crushed beneath the rocks and stone and dirt, Sabo's forgotten plaything.

He would have his revenge against the god one day. He didn't know how, he didn't know when, but one day the god of pain and suffering would know pain and suffering for himself. Maxum would not rest until he had.

No . . . he would not rest at all.

Read on for an exciting sneak peek
of the next book in

The IMMORTAL BROTHERS series

BOUND IN DARKNESS

BY JACQUELYN FRANK

PROLOGUE

Maxum clawed himself up out of the soil, spitting dirt, coughing it from his lungs with a roar of fury and frustration. He would think he would be used to it by now, used to the pain that came from the sheer weight of the rock and soil that pressed against him from all sides. Suffocated him from all directions. Filled every orifice, every crack, every crevice of his body as it fought to get inside of him—crushing him didn't seem to be enough to satisfy it.

He finally pulled himself fully free of the dirt and laid on the ground, panting and coughing. He spit. Spit again. It was a lost cause. Dirt caught between his teeth, stuck to his tongue.

And so it would be. It would always be. He was cursed. Cursed to be swallowed by soil and stone every night from dusk to juquil's hour.

He supposed he should be grateful. Until several full turnings ago he had been trapped permanently in the ground, held deep in the soil of the bottom of the ocean, with no reprieve. He had since been rescued from his permanent fate and been given this one instead, thanks to his brother Jaykun, who had won the grace of a god, just as easily as the four brothers, Dethan, Jaykun, Garreth, and Maxum, had won the fury of the gods with a single act of hubris over two centuries ago.

He and his brothers had climbed the highest mountain in the world that day, finding there a fountain of immortality blessed and protected by the gods—and they had dared to drink from its waters without permission from the gods. The backlash for their gall had been instantaneous and severe. Each brother had been sent to suffer, each in his own way, each at the hands of a different god, as payment for that hubris. Dethan had been cast into the eight hells by Weysa, the goddess of conflict and war. Garreth had been chained to that very same mountain, within sight of the fountain that had been the cause of his curse, doomed to freeze time and again thanks to the bitter ironic nature of the goddess Hella. Then the god Grimu had taken Jaykun and chained him to a star, dooming him to burn endlessly again and again. None of the brothers had been given quarter, none a reprieve . . . until Weysa had fetched Dethan out of hell and set him on a path that had resulted in all three of his brothers being released from their curses. But while his brothers were now completely free of their curses, Maxum enjoyed no such reprieve. In order to be freed from his curse the god who had given it to him must lift it. But the god in question was Sabo, the god of pain and suffering, who thrived on the agony of others. It was safe to say he would never have cause to free Maxum from his curse.

And so he had lived through four winters now with his "reprieve" hours, each day living free of the curse until dusk settled over him and the ground opened to swallow him whole all over again. He didn't know which was worse. Having been trapped with no reprieve from the crushing soil or to be given a taste of freedom and release only to have it snatched away each night by a devouring maw of dark, suffocating loam.

After a few minutes Maxum righted himself, feeling the pain of every bone that had been broken by the pressure of all that rock and soil pressing in on him. Cracked ribs, snapped thighbones, crushed arms. The agony of it was brutal.

But he was immortal and so he would heal from all of those injuries until he was as good as new . . . or as close to it as he could be. His head hurt, his ears ringing from what was no doubt a cracked skull. He couldn't get up and walk yet, so he dragged himself across the ground toward his campsite not too far away. Once there he rolled onto his bedroll and lay panting for breath, each one of those breaths torture thanks to his damaged ribs.

It had to stop. One way or another, he would put an end to this. The easiest solution required a god-made weapon removing Maxum's head from his shoulders. But then he would very likely be sent to the eight hells upon his death and that would only mean trading one torment for another—one far more permanent.

The other solution was much more impossible on the surface of it. Convince Sabo to free him from his curse. The idea of the god doing that was laughable. His brothers might have been lucky enough to get their curses lifted by their various gods, but there was no hope for it in Maxum's case. They all knew it. It was apparent in every pitying look his brothers had cast him. That was one of the reasons why he had left their company. That and the fact that his brothers had proven to be enviably happy and in love with their wives and it had just about made him sick to watch them.

But he didn't begrudge them their happiness or their curse-free existences. He was glad they were free. Glad they had found happiness. He was an uncle several times over now as his brothers wallowed in their joy and made babies with their wives. The most recent had been Jaykun and Jileana's son, newborn when last he had seen them. He would be two now and no doubt getting into all manner of troubles.

Part of him had wanted to stay, to enjoy what time with his family he could muster. But just as adamant was his need to do something about his situation. The plan had come to him shortly after Jaykun's son had been born. Sabo would never willingly release him from this curse, so that left him only one option.

Maxum had to kill the god.

He didn't even know if such a thing was possible, but he saw no alternative. Sabo's death was the only way he could end his own suffering. He had heard tales . . . tales of magical items that could be very powerful, possibly powerful enough to kill a god.

So he had left his brothers to go on a quest. Several quests really. He wasn't going to face a god with nothing but a single talisman that may or may not do the trick. He was going to hedge his bets and gather as many such talismans as he could. He was going to face down Sabo and he was going to do it fully prepared with anything and everything he could think of. Including, perhaps, the help of some of the gods.

For the gods were at war. There were two factions, each with six gods. Well, seven to five if you take into consideration that Kitari, the queen of the gods, was being held captive by Xaxis's faction, Xaxis being the god of the eight hells. His faction also included Grimu the god of the eight heavens; Diathus the goddess of the lands and oceans; Jikaro the god of anger and deception; and, lo and behold, Sabo, the god of pain and suffering.

The faction that warred against Xaxis's faction was Weysa's, the goddess of conflict. On her side was Hella, the goddess of fate and fortune, her husband, Mordu, the god of hope, love, and dreams. Meru, the goddess of hearth, home, and harvest, Famun, the god of peace and tranquility, and Lothas, the god of day and night.

With the help of Weysa's faction and his gathered talismans he had high hopes that it would indeed be possible to kill a god.

Now all he had to do was gather his talismans.

And win over an entire faction of gods.

Impossible?

Well, that remained to be seen.

CHAPTER
ONE

Maxum slammed the hand of the large, stinking man who had challenged him down on the table. The rowdy gathering of men cheered and jeered, some thumping Maxum hard on the back in congratulations for winning the arm wrestle. Someone slapped a mug of ale into his winning hand and the reveling men began to sing a victory song in his honor.

Maxum moved away from the boisterous group and found a reasonably quiet corner of the inn, preparing to slowly enjoy the ale in his hand. He wasn't as drunk as the other men in the room, but he was going to catch up with them. They had been celebrating since sunset but Maxum had only joined them an hour ago—two hours past juquil's hour when he had finally clawed his way out of the ground. Once he had healed enough to walk he had come to the inn to join his men.

They were a motley crew; five in all including himself. Each with their own special talents and each necessary for him to obtain his next talisman.

He reached into the pocket of his pants and fondled the amulet they had retrieved just that afternoon—along with enough treasure to keep the men satisfied for quite some time.

This talisman was said to have great power; it made the wearer invulnerable to attack. He had not tested that yet so he didn't know if it was the truth. But a talisman like that would come in quite handy in a war with a god. For, as much as he was immortal, he was not invulnerable. He could be hurt and hurt badly. And there was that little bit about a god-made weapon taking off his head and ending it all right then and there. If there was one thing he could count on, it was that a god would have a god-made weapon in his hands.

He didn't take the amulet out, he didn't put it on. He would test it tomorrow, and he didn't want to flash it in front of the other patrons in the bar. He didn't want to invite a thief to take it from him. To try anyway. A thief was more likely to lose his hand than succeed.

Maxum took a swig of his drink and looked around the room. There were two women there. One was the barmaid and she was being kept quite occupied by the graspy hands of his men. There was Kyno, the big lumbering orc halfbreed with his shining bald head and large meaty hands that swung a spiked club like nobody's business. There was Dru, a slightly shy, slim figured, fiery-haired spirit mage who barely had twenty-five full turnings under his belt. There was Kilon, a slightly rotund archer whose arrows always hit their mark. And last but not least there was Doisy, a cleric, far more handsome than a religious man should be and with about just as much charm as could be fit into one person. He did not grab for the barmaid, instead preferring to tempt her with smiles and charm and wait for her to come to him. Smiles that were gaining him the fastest refills when it came to the ale in his cup.

What Maxum found interesting, however, was that his men weren't paying any attention to the other woman in the room at all. True, she was clearly a patron and should go about unaccosted, but though she was wearing men's leggings and a shirt and vest to hide her womanly curves, Maxum could see them all the same. She was a shapely thing, her close-fitting breeches leaving little mystery to the slender shape of her thighs and the cozy roundness of her ass. The vest hid her breasts for the most part so he couldn't get a good feel for their size, but he suspected they were enough to fill a man's hands.

She was toying with a bowl of the hot stew the inn-keeper was serving for dinner, nibbling at a piece of the questionable meat within it. She noticed Maxum's re-gard of her and she returned it in kind, looking him up and down. He let her look and smiled at the interest he saw flickering in her eyes. And she had pretty eyes. A beautiful jade green to complement her silvery blond hair which she had plaited into two braids on either side of her head, covering her ears. He was disappointed by the style. He expected it was quite pretty when let loose. It would be straight, he surmised, like a silver-gold waterfall, reaching somewhere around her breasts. Those mysteriously hidden breasts.

She sat back a little, picking up her mug and taking a thoughtful sip. Then she stood up, skirted the boister-ous goings-on in the center of the room, and came to stand before Maxum.

She was nearly a strap shorter than he was, slightly built—almost like a boy if not for those hips and . . . damn it, he wanted to see those breasts! But she had the face of a fairy, all fine bones and delicate points, right down to her small upturned nose with its gentle tip. She looked too genteel to be caught out in this kind of crowd in those kinds of clothes. She should be in a dress—with a corset that pushed up and showed off those breasts . . . wherever they were.

"A quiet corner," he said with a nod to the other side of the table. "Come and sit."

She regarded him for just a moment longer, but not because she was debating the wisdom of sitting with him. She had pretty much made up her mind to do that before she'd even gotten out of her seat. Still he didn't know exactly what was going on behind those jade eyes. It was one of the reasons he was glad she had come over.

"I didn't take you for the quiet corner type," she said as she slid into her seat and put her mug down on the table.

"I prefer quiet corners. My men have other ideas."

"You're celebrating?"

"Is it that obvious?" he said with a grin he knew was charming. His brothers had always said the gods had gifted him with charm, good looks, and a good singing voice—all great ways to woo the ladies. And they were right. He'd caught more than his fair share with that smile.

She smiled back and relaxed in her chair. "A little bit. They're throwing coin around like they could make it for themselves. They should be careful. It might attract the wrong element."

Maxum chuckled richly. "We *are* the wrong element," he said.

She laughed. It was a light, pretty sound but not a delicate little titter like the highborn ladies used. It was a laugh. A good, feminine laugh that made you smile to hear it. Maxum liked her more the more he discovered about her.

"What's your name?"

"Airianne," she said. "But you can call me Airi."

"A light, breezy sort of name," he noted.

She grimaced. "Oh, now you're being unoriginal. I may have to rethink this whole situation."

"Ah. Well, forgive me. I'll try to be more unique from here on out."

Maxum found that ironic actually. He was as unique as they came. It was simply a matter of not wanting everyone to know about what set him apart from everyone else on the Black Continent.

She made a show of thinking about it, but then she shrugged. "I'll give you another chance if you tell me your name."

"Wouldn't that ruin the mystery of it all?"

"I rather doubt there would be much mystery if I have to call you 'You there!' the entire length of our short acquaintance."

"Our acquaintance will be short?" he asked with an arched brow.

"Oh yes. If all it is based on is the mystery of your name then it will have to be short indeed. The moment I learn it, all would be over."

"Hey, Maxum! Come roll at dice!" Doisy shouted at him from across the room.

Airi laughed. "There, you see? No more mystery, nothing to compel me to stay."

"I'm sure I have other mysteries about me," he coaxed her with a lopsided grin.

"Do you? Do you think I would find them interesting?"

"I know you would. I promise I won't tell you a thing about me. You can discover the answer to all your questions on your own, thereby entertaining yourself for quite a long while."

"But I already know so much about you," she said.

"Such as?"

"I know your name." She winked at him. "And I know you do not like to be called Max."

"How do you know that?"

"Your man is so drunk he would have called you by the most familiar name he uses to address you. Since he called you Maxum and not Max I can assume he has been trained very, very well not to do it . . . so well he remembers even when in his cups."

"What else do you know?" he asked, leaning back and relaxing as he let his eyes roam over her again and again.

"Let's see . . . you are a mercenary."

"How can you be so sure?" he asked, surprise tightening him up.

"You are well outfitted. You have spent a good amount of coin on your armor and that sword you carry. That blade was not made in any ordinary forge, I'll bet my life on it."

She was right. The sword was his brother's. A god-made weapon and a gift from Weysa. Dethan had gifted him with it when he had told them he was leaving to "seek out his own life." He hadn't told them his plans or his ultimate goal. But having a god-made weapon would be crucial when fighting a god. It was a fair bet that no ordinary weapon could inflict injury otherwise.

"But being well outfitted does not a mercenary make," he pointed out.

"Ah . . . but here your friends give you away. A mage, an orc, an archer, and a religious man make for a pretty well-rounded group of skills. All quite marketable if someone is looking for a hired hand to help with this little or that problem." She tilted her head thoughtfully. "But you do not make all of your coin by being a sellsword, and I think selling your sword is just a means to an end. You have different goals in mind."

"Now you can't possibly know that from sitting across the room," he said, shifting uncomfortably in his chair. Her insights were uncanny. A little too uncanny. He was beginning to suspect she was some kind of mage like Dru. A spirit mage could tell a lot about a person if the right powers were used.

"I know that from speaking with you. You are clearly an intelligent man. You don't throw yourself into revelry with abandon like your men do, you keep yourself separate from their behavior. That tells me a great deal about what kind of man you are."

"It is an off night. Tomorrow I will get just as drunk as they are."

"I think not. No sense trying to mislead me," she said

with a smile. "Just because I can see you doesn't mean you must try to hide."

"But how do you know I have other goals in mind?"

"As I said, you are an intelligent man. An intelligent man knows he cannot sell his sword forever. Eventually he will get old and his body will not work quite the way it should. What will you do then? An intelligent man would have some other plan, something to take him into his golden years with relative ease."

Maxum smiled. "I do have other goals, but not for the reasons you surmise. So you see, there are still many mysteries about me to keep you interested."

"Perhaps," she said, pausing to take a sip of her ale. "What about me? Can you not divine anything about me?"

Maxum narrowed his eyes on her thoughtfully. "You do not like to wear dresses."

She burst out in a laugh. "How do you know that? How do you know these are not just my traveling clothes?"

"They are too well-worn to be used just for traveling. You've even mended your breeches at the knee, telling me this is likely your only set of clothing. Or perhaps one of two sets."

"Very good," she said, seeming impressed. "But that does not mean I don't like to wear dresses."

"If I were a woman used to running about in the freedom of breeches and cotton, I would not want to stuff myself into the confines of a dress and corset where certain behaviors would then be expected of me. Like this, you have all the freedom in the world. Why would you want to give that up?"

"Well, it so happens you are right, but I still say it's a lucky guess."

"No more or less lucky than your guesses."

"What else?" she asked.

"Hmm . . . I'll bet you're a scrapper. You avoid fighting where possible, because you are clearly intelligent, but get you in the mix and you'll hold your own in spite of your size."

"Oh ho! Now we're insulting?"

"Not at all. You're just being sensitive. I was merely stating an observation. It was a compliment actually . . . that I can see you holding your own in a fight even against a larger opponent."

"And what makes you think this?"

"You've got two daggers on you, one on each thigh. That tells me you're proficient with them left- and right-handed . . . a marketable skill if ever there was one. They are short daggers so that means you're used to fighting up close and personal. You travel alone, which means you're pretty confident you can take care of yourself. You're too clever to mislead yourself on that count so . . . that makes you a scrapper."

"Very good." She gave him a light round of applause. He nodded his head in gracious acceptance.

"There's one other thing," he said.

"And that is?"

"You're seriously thinking about having sex with me."

She laughed, a bright short burst of sound. "Am I, now? What makes you say that?"

"You got up and came over to me."

"I could just be looking for a diverting conversation. How does sex come into the picture? If I wanted sex I could choose any of your men."

"As I said, you came over to me instead of joining my men. That shows you have taste and are discerning. You didn't want to be alone tonight, so you thought I might provide you with a little companionable distraction."

"Distraction equals sex?"

He ran his eyes down over her, letting her see his appetite, which had grown considerably in the time they had been talking.

"It does in my book. And you haven't thrown your drink in my face and stormed off. That's also telling."

She smiled, stood up, and crossed over to him. She sat in his lap and wound her arms around his neck. "And does the idea have any appeal to you at all?"

"What do your deductive powers tell you?"

"That it does indeed have merit. A great deal of merit," she said, shifting her bottom a little on top of a steadily growing erection. He hadn't planned on getting friendly with anyone tonight, didn't really engage in it at all these days, his goals consuming his time and energies. But for some reason she appealed to him a great deal and now that he had started thinking about having sex with her, he found he couldn't stop thinking of it. The idea of running his hands all over that fair, delicate skin—all the while knowing she was just as tough as she was soft—that was more than alluring to him.

His gaze dropped to the pretty bow of her lips; her top lip was sculpted perfectly and her bottom lip plump and inviting. She was close enough that he could smell the cleanness of her. She must have had a bath recently. He could say the same. Every night after he dragged himself out of the dirt the first thing he did was find somewhere to wash the grime off him, to wash away any traces of his curse. It was a small little rebellion. An empty one. But he wanted nothing to remind him of what would come again all too soon.

She saw where his attention had gone and she licked her lips, wetting them invitingly. She opened her mouth to say "Kiss me," but he was already there. He pulled her forward onto his mouth, but savored the moment just before he really engaged her. It was a tease, a breathless pause before he covered her mouth in earnest. The taste of her spread over him like a balm. He engaged her tongue almost instantly, wanting her flavor. Her mouth was everything plush and decadent, sweet and heady . . . like strong drink, warming and dizzying. For just those few seconds he no longer felt like a cursed man.

It was a gift she gave without realizing it, and he was humbly grateful for it.

His hand went to the back of her head and he found himself frustrated by the two tight braids her hair was bound into. Her hair should be free and flowing, easier to bury his hands into, easier to feel the silkiness of it. And from what he could feel, he knew it would be very smooth and soft indeed.

One kiss ended and another began. Then another. His breath came hard as her hands dove into his hair. He was keeping it long these days, so she got a good handful of his loose curls and didn't let go.

She finally broke from his mouth, but only long enough to throw her leg over him, straddling his lap and tucking the seat of her bottom tightly to his erection. He was confined by the suddenly tight material of his pants—and the fact they were in a crowded room, but that didn't keep him from sliding his free hand up over her ribs beneath her vest and then . . . oh, there it was. The elusive breast.

She wore a simple linen shirt, but he could tell she had bound herself up with a snug wrapping beneath it, in an effort to look less like a woman no doubt. Still he could feel her just the same. He was pleasantly surprised to find she was quite well endowed for such a slight figured woman. He would have thought she'd run more to being built like a boy. But it was perhaps her mode of dress that had misled him. That and the damnable vest that had hid the true wealth of her feminine features.

With breasts like these it wasn't any wonder.

Her hands grew busy, drifting out of his hair and down his neck. She was running her hands in broad strokes over his chest a moment later and he growled from the fiery sensations the caresses sent through him. Their kisses grew more and more intense the lower her hands traveled, until she caressed his hips, pausing . . . teasing him. She lifted her mouth from his and said in a throaty, purring voice, "I have a room upstairs. Normally I would camp out in the open, but I decided to splurge tonight. I'm glad I did."

"I'm glad you did too," he said, his voice rough with passion and need.

"It's at the top of the stairs. I'll meet you there in a minute. I have to . . . take care of something." She blushed a little and he realized she needed to relieve herself. He chuckled.

"All right."

He patted her bottom and she dismounted his lap and headed for the front door of the inn. She shot him a shy little teasing smile and then slipped outside.

Maxum sat back a minute, grinning to himself. His fortunes really seemed to be changing for the better these days. First he had acquired the talisman—no mean feat that—then he had found something sweet to savor for the night. Yes, indeed, things were looking up for him. If the trend continued, he might actually one day succeed in what he was attempting to do.

It wasn't as though there weren't a precedent. There had once been other gods, but the current reigning gods had usurped their positions, killing off their competition. If a god could do it, then by the gods, so could he.

Feeling happy and magnanimous he got to his feet and said, "Boys! Next round's on me!"

He tossed a gold coin to the barmaid, who caught it expertly. Her eyes went wide when he said, "Keep the rest for yourself, honey." It was no wonder. She was doubtless more used to seeing copper and silver than gold. It was possible she had never seen a gold coin in her life.

"Have a good time," Kyno said. Clearly, despite their revelry, his men had been attentive enough to see what he'd been doing and they had figured out where he was going to be spending his night.

"Sleep fair, Maxum!" Dru said.

"Oy, there's not much sleeping going to be happening there, what?" Doisy said with a loud belch.

Maxum made his way up to the room at the top of the stairs with a grin on his face. He entered and found the standard for most inns. A bed just big enough to sleep two—although not two of Maxum's size, that's to be certain. It would barely suit one with its short mattress that would no doubt leave his feet dangling off at the ankles. Maxum didn't waste any time stripping off his shirt. He debated whether or not to rid himself of his pants as well, but she hadn't struck him as too much of the shy sort so he went for it and shucked them off. He was folding them when he fished into his pocket for the talisman. He wanted to make sure it was safely secured.

That was when he realized it was no longer in his pocket. He immediately searched the floor, thinking it had fallen out. Coming up empty he quickly pulled his pants back on and hurried, bare-chested, back out into the inn.

"Oy, that was quick!" Kyno belted out, making the other men laugh uproariously. Maxum ignored them and went to search the seat he had been sitting in . . . and that's when it hit him.

"Fuck me!" he cried out as he bolted for the door. He ran into the stable where he'd seen a fine stallion of dappled coloring tied up earlier. Something told him it was hers and sure enough it was missing.

He ran out into the darkness, but there was no hope for it.

The little thief had made off with his hard-earned talisman.